'Elegantly written tale of runaway daughter of Zurich banking family. Her link with jewelled sculpture leads to betrayal, terror, kidnapping and murder.'

Daily Telegraph

'Hilary Norman has developed quite a following and *Fascination* is sure to please her fans.'

Chicago Tribune

'Hilary Norman is an honest-to-goodness story-teller. Her integrity is rare.'

Jewish Chronicle

'Norman writes with an uninhibited warmth and immediacy sure to please not only readers of her three previous books but those who discover her first in *Fascination*.'

Tulsa World

'A great story teller . . . her writing is both elegant and colourful.'

Sunday Independent, Plymouth

'A winner all the way.'

Atlanta Journal

'An engrossing novel about the effect that a priceless treasure can have on three generations of one family.'

Glasgow Evening Times

'A grand yarn, touchingly told.'

She

Also by the same author,
and available from Coronet:

In Love and Friendship
Chateau Ella
Shattered Stars

About the Author

Hilary Norman was born and educated in London. After working as an actress she had careers in the fashion and broadcasting industries. She travelled extensively throughout Europe and lived for a time in the United States before writing *In Love and Friendship*, which has been translated into nine languages. She now lives in London. Her new novel, *Spellbound*, will be published in Autumn 1993.

HILARY NORMAN

FASCINATION

CORONET BOOKS
Hodder and Stoughton

First published in Great Britain in 1992 by Hodder and Stoughton

Coronet edition 1993

Printed and bound in Great Britain for Hodder and Stoughton Paperbacks, a division of Hodder and Stoughton Ltd, Mill Road, Dunton Green, Sevenoaks, Kent TN13 2YA. (Editorial Office: 47 Bedford Square, London WC1B 3DP) by Cox and Wyman Ltd, Reading, Berks. Photoset by Rowland Phototypesetting Ltd, Bury St Edmunds, Suffolk.

British Library CIP

Norman, Hilary
Fascination.
I. Title
823 [F]

ISBN 0-340-58088-7

For my brother, Neal

Acknowledgments

A great many people and organizations gave me kind and valuable assistance and support while I was researching and writing this novel, but I would especially like to thank the following (in alphabetical order):

Estelle and David Amsellem; Howard Barmad; Dawn Bates; Police Officer Frank Bogucki, Community Affairs Officer, 17th Precinct, NYPD; Clare Bristow; Carolyn Caughey; Sara Fisher; Sharon Freedman; Shelagh Harris; John Hawkins; Angela Heard; Peter Horwitz; Sabine Ibach and Sebastian Ritscher; Murray Klein and Zabar's; Mary Kling; Elaine Koster; Audrey LaFehr; Dot McCleary of the Burlington Bookshop, New York City; Barbara Müller of the Verkehrsbüro, Davos Platz; National Stroke Association (USA); Mrs H. Norman; Anna Powell; Anne Restall of TWA; Helen Rose; Anne and Nicholas Shulman; Ruth Sylvester of Barclays Bank; Dr Jonathan Tarlow; Michael Thomas.

New York City

December 18th, 1968

1

Outside the apartment, on West Seventy-fourth Street, it was cold and wet, half-sleeting, half-raining. Near by, on Amsterdam Avenue and another block west on Broadway, men and women who, generally, on a miserable night like this one, might have been glad to be home, were still purposefully going about the business of pre-Christmas merrymaking. Shopping bags crammed with parcels, they hurried into bars, emerged flushed from restaurants, huddled under umbrellas, slipped on shiny sidewalks, ran for buses, hailed cabs and, often missing them, went on walking.

Inside Maddy's apartment, snug and warm, the fairy-lit Christmas tree in one corner of the sitting room, Bing Crosby singing from the television set in the other, Gideon Tyler looked down at the small box on the dining table. It was made of glossy white cardboard, tied with blue satin ribbon. He knew that it was evidence and that he ought not to handle it, but he opened it anyway.

It took several moments before he understood what lay inside the box, beside the note. It looked, at first sight, like a piece of brown fabric, like brown suede. But then he touched it, and knew.

Dusty, the dachshund bitch Gideon had given to Maddy and her son at Thanksgiving, had disappeared the previous week whilst on a walk in Central Park with six-year-old Valentin and Jennifer Malkevitch, his sitter. One minute Dusty had been with them, sniffing in the undergrowth, the next she had vanished.

Gideon realized now that what lay in the box was a section of the dog's ear. The brown, silken piece that flapped joyously when the dachshund ran. It was cold to the touch, and the base of the box was damp and stained a little pink. Gideon thought that the ear had probably been packed in ice, maybe even snow.

Jennifer Malkevitch's body was slumped over the kitchen sink, the blood from the wound at the back of her head still leaking slowly onto the stainless steel. Maddy's kettle, lid off and half filled, was clutched in her right hand. She had been a tall girl and long-waisted, and so she flopped forward in death, folded bizarrely in the middle, her bare toes brushing the linoleum floor.

Gideon knew that he had no choice but to call the police, but he needed some time to think, to work out his next move before they arrived and turned him, for a few hours at least, into a suspect. The girl was beyond help – haste would make no difference to her.

Valentin was another matter.

He'd known that the child was not in the apartment even before he had put his key into the lock. He had pushed the buzzer first – his own, identifying buzz that always brought Valentin running unless he was sound asleep. It was after ten o'clock, a time when most six-year-olds ought to have been sleeping for hours, but Maddy's boy was nocturnal, like his mother, seldom dropping off before eleven and none the worse for it each morning.

Gideon had gone into the second bedroom – Valentin's room – straight away, already afraid. Finding it empty, his stomach had clenched with dread. The kitchen door had been closed; opening it, he'd smelled blood, smelled death, seen Jennifer. But there had been no sign of the child.

Only of the dachshund's ear, in the little box. And the note, typewritten on plain white paper and addressed to Maddy:

The boy's life, for Eternité.

Madeleine was singing, at Lila's on Second Avenue, her short golden hair glinting like a halo in the spotlights, when Gideon walked in; singing her heart out because that was the only way she knew how to sing, knowing that later, when she was finished, she could go home to the modest apartment she'd fought to turn into a happy, peaceful home for Valentin. She could have had so much more. Millions of dollars, whatever she wanted. But Madeleine had wanted her independence, and her pride.

And a slender, six-year-old boy, with shiny dark hair, and wide, navy blue, loving eyes, and a disposition to match.

She was part-way through singing 'Yesterday' when she saw Gideon. The expression on his face, a grimness she had never seen before, almost stopped her in mid-bar, but she forced herself to finish, spoke quietly to her backing trio, and came directly to him.

"Is it Valentin?"

He drew her gently outside, into the cold, bracing air, and in the light from a street lamp, he showed her the note.

"He's been taken, Maddy," Gideon said, the words choking in his throat. He looked at her, at the lovely face, at the turquoise eyes ripping wide with terror, and he could hardly bear to go on. "And there's worse."

She never spoke on the drive back to the apartment, never wept. She listened to what Gideon had to tell her, but she had no words, was beyond tears. She had known so much anguish, through the years, but now, at last, she had believed herself and Valentin safe.

First the dog. Now her child.

Madeleine knew what lay behind it. The note said it all. *Eternité*. A prize no more than fourteen inches high, created out of purest love. She had not set eyes on it for more than thirteen years, and at this moment, she would gladly have had it blown into ten thousand worthless fragments if that meant having Valentin home again.

It wasn't worth all the pain it had caused.

Nothing was.

Part One

MAGDALEN:
SWITZERLAND

2

On the night that she left home, two months after her sixteenth birthday, there were three objectives burning fiercely in Maggy Gabriel's mind: getting away from her family; tracing *Eternité*, her grandfather's creation; and finding her father.

Her earliest, happy memories were of sitting on Alexander's, her father's, knee, clasped gently against his chest while he read her stories. Only they were not the fairy tales told to most small children by their parents, but detective stories, thrillers by Dashiell Hammett, George Harmon Coxe and Raymond Chandler.

"More, Papi, more," Maggy would urge, if Alexander closed one of the novels and tried to return it to the shelves of his first edition library before she had had her fill.

"You have to go to bed, *Schätzli*. Mami will be angry with me if you can't sleep again."

"I will sleep, Papi."

It was not that she really followed or understood the stories, which Alexander carefully abridged as he went along to protect her tender ears from the harsher, more sordid narratives and dialogue, but nevertheless she thrilled to their innate drama, and to her father's excited voice, and she would not have given up the closeness of those late afternoons in the library for anything.

They lived in a large, handsome house on Aurora Strasse on the gently sloping Zürichberg, one of the most tranquil and select of Zurich's suburban residential areas. The villa, built in 1865, during the *grosse Zürcher Bauperiode*, by Maggy's great-grandparents, Leopold and Elspeth Gründli, had every possible tasteful comfort, but Maggy had always felt stifled by its sober grandeur. She liked its immaculate back garden well enough, but she loved the nearby forests infinitely more. As often as possible, returning from school down in the city, she deliberately missed her stop on the Dolderbahn – the little red cable train that shuttled up and down the mountain, day and evening – and continued up to the green and leafy terminus. There, she tramped about for a while in the leaves, and sat on fallen logs, watching the birds and squirrels and rabbits, breathing in the fresh, wonderfully free air, and often singing at the top of her voice. It was the freedom that Maggy cherished above all, for she never felt quite free at home.

She loved to sing, would have liked to sing from morning till night, for she knew that her voice, though low and a little husky, was tuneful, and the act of opening her mouth and releasing melodies from within herself, made her feel happy and alive. But singing at home was forbidden, and even in the choir at school she had been ordered to sing *sotto voce*, lest her very personal voice stood out from the rest.

Although her great-grandparents had died in the nineteen-twenties, and although their daughter, Hildegard, had married Amadeus Gabriel in 1914, the Gründli Bank of Zurich had continued to finance and rule the family's life; and even years after their son, Alexander Gabriel, had married a neighbour, Emilie Huber, the house on Aurora Strasse was still known to local people, tradesmen, visitors and servants as the Gründli Haus.

Until Maggy was seven years old, however, and her brother, Rudi, was four, Maggy knew no real unhappiness, only a vague awareness of a lack of fulfilment in her life. If she had not been a little girl, if she had been allowed to roam around the parts of Zurich she loved most – the narrow back streets of the old town, where she could fantasize about the people who must have wandered there in the ancient, pagan days, or the piously religious years they learned about at school; or the banks of the lake, where she could feed the swans and gaze, on a clear day, up towards the high mountains – Maggy would probably have been almost perfectly happy. But when her grandmother or her mother took her into town, it was to be held tightly by the hand and marched along the Bahnhofstrasse, while Hildegard or Emilie made their purchases at Grieder or Sturzenegger or Jelmoli. Maggy hated shopping, particularly if they were buying clothes for herself, for then she would have to stand still in hot, stuffy changing rooms while grown-ups, who understood nothing about the sort of comfortable clothes she wanted to wear, brought her dresses with starched white collars and, worst of all, elegant, dreadful suits.

"You look almost like a little lady in that," Emilie would tell her daughter, but there would still be a reproach in her voice, for it was one of her constant complaints that Maggy was always untidy.

"It scratches," Maggy would point out, her voice hushed, aware that a more vociferous complaint would be frowned upon as being ill-mannered.

"We'll take it, thank you," Emilie would invariably say to the saleslady, and Maggy would grow pink with frustration, but give in, silently vowing never to wear the disliked garment.

It was her hair that caused the most frequent laments by Hildegard, her grandmother, and Emilie. Maggy was a free-spirited, effervescent child by nature, and her wildly curling golden hair seemed to spring from her personality, quite untameable unless it was dragged off her face into plaits, which managed to work themselves loose no matter how tightly they were wound each morning. Usually, it was Maggy herself who loosened them, or even untied them and brushed her hair back into its natural, wild halo of gold, and then she would be punished as if for some cardinal sin.

"Since you choose to appear as a little savage, Magdalen," Hildegard would say (she was only ever called by her given name when she was being berated), "you cannot expect to eat at a table with decent people." And Maggy would be ordered up to her room, where Frau Kümmerly, the housekeeper, would bring her bread, a lump of cheese and a glass of water, and that would be all she had until her father tiptoed in, some time later, with the chocolate he regularly bought for her from Confiserie Sprüngli.

Rudi, her brother, was of little use to Maggy; he was too young, and much too well-behaved and complaisant for her to have much patience with. The hours she spent with Alexander, her beloved *papi*, made up for the rest. But the best times – the *very* best times – were when Alexander took her up into the mountains to visit Amadeus, her grandfather.

Amadeus Gabriel, like his father a jeweller by occupation, but an accomplished skier and dedicated mountain man by inclination, had travelled from Bern, his home-town, to Zurich in 1913, when he was twenty-two years old, and had become infatuated with the pretty, flirtatious daughter of the Gründlis, a prominent, highly-esteemed banking family. Hildegard had fallen in love with the flaxen-haired, broad-shouldered man, and after a whirlwind courtship (by circumspect Gründli standards), they had become betrothed, and had married within the year.

Having no special fondness for the jewellery craft that had been passed on to him, automatically, by his father, Amadeus, an easy-going man, had raised no objections when his parents-in-law had invited him into the bank.

The Gründli Bank was by no means one of the largest private banking houses in the town, but it was substantial and venerable. Leopold Gründli, in his late sixties, still ruled over the board with a firm hand; if he wished a space to be made for his son-in-law, there was no one who would presume to stand in his way.

The investment bank had been founded in 1821 by Leopold's father, and there were branches in Frankfurt and New York, but the heart of the business lay in the house on Pelikan-Strasse just off the Bahnhofstrasse, into which the *Hauptfiliale* had moved in 1872. Hildegard was a true heiress; the property itself was worth a small fortune, and a wealth of great art hung in the house – Rembrandts, Van Dycks and Gainsboroughs, most of which were displayed in the *Grosse Halle*, the large central room in which all the employees of the bank gathered daily before disappearing into their respective offices, most of them vastly less impressive than the *Halle*.

Amadeus came in as a salaried apprentice, to watch, listen, learn and then, it was hoped and expected, to identify the area to which he was most attracted and in which he was most likely to excel. No such area came to light. The world of finance, which, the young man observed, caused so many people's eyes to glitter with excitement, bored him immensely. Worse, his young wife had quickly ceased to be flirtatious, and had clearly fallen out of love with Amadeus. Her lips, which had seemed to him so soft and tender and kissable, now seemed clamped tightly in a stiff, straight line, and the blue eyes which had sparkled and smiled, now stared at him in daily, flinty accusation.

Amadeus tried to put Hildegard's changed attitude down to the fact that she was pregnant, imagining that perhaps she blamed her morning sickness and thickening waistline on him. The entire pregnancy was difficult, the birth of their son, Alexander, was agonizing and prolonged, and Hildegard's doctors declared that it would be dangerous for her to have any more children. Amadeus, delighted with Alexander, hoped that his wife, relieved of any further physical distress, might return to her former self; but the girl he had met and fallen in love with had vanished forever. They lived together in the Gründli Haus, tolerating each other, never exactly in the depths of misery, but never in joy.

In February of 1922, when Alexander was seven years old, Amadeus took his regular winter holiday in Davos. He always went alone, for Hildegard was a staunch city woman and detested snow sports. Amadeus stayed at the Flüela Hotel in Davos Dorf, rose early each morning, wrapped sealskins around his skis for the long, strenuous climb up the Parsenn, and then skied back down with utmost joy, usually returning at dusk. But one afternoon, coming back down early after a fall that had soaked him through, he stacked his skis in the rack outside Café Weber, and went inside for a warming *Glühwein*.

And saw Irina for the first time.

She sat at a corner window table, wearing a cherry red pullover, a dark sable coat draped loosely about her shoulders. She had removed her fur hat and her hair, pinned up in a soft French pleat, was a rich, dark brown. Her eyes were large, dark and lustrous, her cheeks were flushed. On her lap, accepting small pieces of strudel anointed with whipped cream, sat a glossy, long-haired dachshund.

Amadeus glanced around, and saw with a swift nudge of pleasure that all the other tables were occupied. He waited for another moment, composing himself, and then he walked towards the corner.

"*Pardon, gnädige Frau*," he said, and bowed. "Would you permit me to share your table?"

She nodded, and gave a slight smile. "By all means."

Amadeus sat opposite her. The dachshund growled, baring its teeth. After the waitress had brought him his mulled wine and a slice of chocolate cake, Amadeus placed a few crumbs on a paper napkin and offered them to the animal. It accepted them greedily, licking up every morsel – and then growled again.

The woman laughed. It was bell-like laughter, warm, gay and enchanting. Amadeus knew that he had never truly been in love before.

Her full name was Countess Irina Valentinovna Malinskaya, and she was from St Petersburg. She had fled Russia and the Red Terror in 1918 with her sister Sofia, and her pretty dachshund bitch, Anushka, after the shooting of their father in a street riot – their mother had died in childbirth many years before. The young women had travelled first to Finland, staying for a while in Terioki, then they had moved to Stockholm and from there to Paris, before coming to Switzerland so that Sofia, who had been diagnosed as suffering from tuberculosis, could be treated at one of the famous Davos sanatoria.

"How is your sister now?" Amadeus asked tentatively.

"She died, four months ago."

"A tragedy," he said softly, and was surprised to feel his eyes prick with tears.

"Yes."

They had been sitting in Café Weber for almost two hours, during which Amadeus's clothes had dried out, and he had ordered a plate of *Bündnerfleisch*, the air-dried beef that was a speciality of the Graubünden canton, more for Anushka than for himself, hoping to gain the dachshund's approval and to prevent her from growing restless. He did not want Irina Malinskaya to leave; he feared he might never see her again.

"Are you living in Davos now?" he asked her.

"I am," Irina answered. "I shall stay here always."

"It's a charming place."

"Is it?" she said.

They spoke in French, the language of the Russian aristocracy and one of the three languages of Switzerland, and Amadeus wondered at her candour and ease with a stranger. It was as if she had sensed, instantly, that she could trust Amadeus Gabriel, yet that it did not especially matter if she was mistaken.

"I have kept the room at the sanatorium that I took in the last months of Sofia's life, when I needed to be close to her. It is more like an hotel than a hospital."

"But surely now –" Amadeus stopped.

"Afterwards," Irina went on, "I planned to return to Paris." She looked wistful for the first time. "I adored Paris."

"Then why did you stay?"

Her shrug was slight, refined but eloquent, and its significance, without words, froze Amadeus's heart with horror and sorrow, for her and for himself, for he understood that although he had only just found Irina, she was already lost to him.

They overwhelmed one another: Irina, infected but still vigorous, starved of normal, healthy human conversation, Amadeus, starved of love and warmth and passion. It began there in the café and swept on out into the Promenade, she wrapped in her sable, he in his admiration, fascination and adoration. Anushka tried valiantly to maintain decorum between her mistress and the flaxen-haired foreigner; when Amadeus attempted to fondle her ears, the dachshund bit his gloved finger and refused to let go until he backed away to a respectful distance. They laughed again, and their breath steamed in the icy air. But it was breath that Irina was short of, and she began to cough, and Amadeus was abruptly desperate with fear. He would not give in, would not allow her to surrender. Perhaps her sister had been weak, but Irina was strong. He could not, *would* not lose her.

They met almost every day, usually when Irina took the walks that were a recommended part of her cure. Amadeus began to learn about tuberculosis and its treatments; her sanatorium was not an overtly unpleasant place to be, better by far, Irina told him, than many equivalent establishments in other countries. Food was plentiful and of a fair quality, but meals were served at rigid times, and were dull and unimaginative. Her care, thus far, was comprised mainly of rest, frequent and lengthy measurings of her temperature and gentle walks, if she felt fit enough and if the weather permitted.

"Surely you shouldn't walk in this weather?" Amadeus asked her one afternoon as they strolled around the ice-rink in Davos Platz in the snow.

"Not according to Professor Ludwig," Irina answered with a glint in her eyes, "but I know my body and my mind far better than any doctor can, and I know that if I don't come out, I shall wither away."

"But what do they *do* for you there?" he wanted to know. "It seems to me they do nothing at all – how do they expect to cure you?"

"I'm thankful." Irina grimaced. "There are many so-called cures, many terrible treatments. Once, they injected Sofia with the blood of poor little rabbits which had, in turn, been injected with tuberculosis from humans and cows. Now we hear of a vaccine made from turtles." She smiled. "It all seems so wild somehow, a clutching at straws." She paused, and her face grew very sombre. "When Sofia grew worse, they collapsed one of her lungs so that it might rest and recover. They punctured her again and again with great needles, torturing her. All in vain."

The mere thought of Irina suffering in this way appalled Amadeus beyond words. He comforted himself with the fact that although she was undeniably ill, often ran a fever in the late afternoon and at night, and sometimes grew very pale, Irina appeared, for the most part, to feel quite well. Sofia must have been far worse, even at this stage; that she had died meant nothing. Many people recovered.

It was when he visited her in the sanatorium itself that Amadeus grew most depressed. As Irina had said, it was not a fearsome place at all, and the directors and staff were kind and pleasant to the patients and their visitors, yet a dreadful atmosphere pervaded the institution. He had visited numerous hospitals in the past, and there were inevitably wards in which one witnessed acute suffering and tragedy, but in ordinary hospitals the majority of patients were there in order to be treated, and to recover. Here, in spite of the air of commendable bravado displayed by most of Irina's fellow sufferers, were a great many hopeless men and women. Even if they professed to feeling better, Amadeus sensed that they never believed it themselves. They seemed to have become obsessed with their sickness, with the constant taking of their temperatures, with the ugly little sputum flasks many of them carried at all times and with the latest rumours of who had died the previous night, and who had asked to see the priest.

When Amadeus returned to the Flüela after a visit, he was so intensely disturbed that he needed several glasses of schnapps before he could get any rest at all. Even Irina was a different woman within those walls, subdued by the unnatural atmosphere, lulled almost into acquiescence, her vivid life-spark diminished.

He made up his mind. Irina must quit the sanatorium before it destroyed her as it had her sister. He would care for her outside, in the real world. He would do everything that the doctors advised for her, but he could do far more for her than they ever could, for he could love her back to health.

"What about your family?"

"They will be hurt, Hildegard will hate me. I have never

wished to cause her pain, but it will be her pride that is wounded, not her heart. She stopped loving me a long time ago."

"But Alexander, your little boy." Her voice was gentle, like soft rain.

He had no answer, had not found one in all the similar conversations he and Irina had had since he had declared his intentions to her. She had felt her emotions buffeted as if by a hurricane, one moment almost ecstatic with joy and gratitude, the next distraught with guilt and shame. She had shared the same soaring happiness and excitement that Amadeus had experienced at their first meeting, and after that, although he had told her that he was married with a son, it had been impossible for her to reject his friendship. But they had both known from the beginning that it was infinitely more than friendship that Amadeus offered, and that Irina longed for.

The guilt weighed heavily upon her, tempered only slightly by the silent burning resentment at the unfairness of her fate. Irina's childhood had been carefree, her youth marred for a few years by her mother's untimely death, but in most respects filled with gaiety and love. Everyone had adored the two Malinskaya girls, who had been beautiful, fun-loving, sweet and, on occasions, bold. But with the rising power of the Bolsheviks had come fear, and the shock of their father's murder, followed by the terrors of their flight from St Petersburg, had only just begun to recede a little when Sofia had fallen ill. Now she had found this man – this wonderful, extraordinary man who loved her – and decency decreed that she must try to send him away, back to his wife and child.

Decency lost, or perhaps she did not try hard enough, but Amadeus Gabriel was, in any case, far too much in love to pay any heed. He was obsessed by Irina, and by his need to be with her, to help her, to *save* her.

* * *

He abandoned his family, and once the deed was done, after he had made the stomach-churning journey down to Zurich and had faced Hildegard and her appalled parents, after he had attempted, impossibly, to explain to young Alexander that he still loved him and always would, Amadeus took his most personal belongings and left the Gründli Haus for ever. His only profound regret was for his son, but by the time he had reached Landquart to change trains, he had already determined that somehow, once the ashes of their marriage were settled, he would prevail on Hildegard to allow him to see the boy regularly. For now, he focused his mind and heart on the moment when he would see Irina again.

He set about making a life for them in Davos. Never in his thirty-one years had Amadeus felt such energy, such a sense of purpose. With the financial help of his father in Bern, he took over a small jeweller's shop in the Dorf, returning to his original craft with renewed vigour so that he might begin to pay off the money he had borrowed from a local bank to buy the house in which he and Irina would live.

It was a small, run-down timber farmhouse in the Dischma valley on the lower slopes of the Schwarzhorn. Built into the incline, it had stabling and grain storage space at the rear, tiny leaded-glass windows and a carved, painted frieze below its gable roof.

"Well?" he asked anxiously, the first time he brought Irina to see it.

She stared, saying nothing.

"You don't like it."

"No," she said.

Disappointment filled his throat, so that for a moment he could not speak. He cursed himself – he was a fool not to have shown it to her before committing himself. In Russia, Irina had been accustomed to splendour and luxury, to a home in the city and a superb *dacha* in the countryside. Just because he had not cared about leaving the comforts of the Gründli Haus did not mean that Irina – a countess, after all – would take to modest rural living.

"Forgive me," he said, desolately.

"For what?"

"For my folly. I had such plans for this house – I saw it, and straight away I began to dream – I had visions of –"

"Had?"

"I don't know if I can sell it," Amadeus went on, knowing that it would be almost impossible to sell, but knowing, too, that he would do anything and everything to make her happy.

"Why would you think of selling it?" Irina asked softly.

"You said you don't like it."

"That's right." Irina stepped between Amadeus and the house, looking up into his face, fastening her dark eyes on his. "'Like' is far too trivial a word." She paused. "I love this house."

He frowned. "You're saying that to please me."

Irina smiled. "It's true that I might do that if it were necessary. But it isn't. I think it's a wonderful house –"

"Not yet," he interrupted, gloom evaporating and eagerness flowing back in full strength. "But it will be, I swear it. Just a few months, and it will be quite comfortable for you."

"I don't want to wait a few months."

"Weeks then – I'll work more quickly."

"Why can't we move in straight away?"

"Because it's cold and damp, and there's no bathroom – you cannot live without a bathroom, and even if you could I wouldn't let you. And besides, there's no bed."

Irina laughed, the same, bell-like laugh that had entranced Amadeus in Café Weber in the middle of February – was that really less than three months before? he wondered. It seemed to him that he had known her for ever.

"I'm making a bed for you," he said. "For us."

"Truly?" Irina's flush heightened, and for once the colour gave him pleasure, for so often he feared it as one of the symptoms of her illness.

"I'm carving it myself, but we'll buy the mattress together – it must be exactly right for you, the most comfortable bed you've ever slept in."

"Or loved in," she added.

Amadeus worked day and night, eking out a modest living at the shop between eight in the morning and four in the afternoon, and then locking the door, no matter how busy he was, so that he could adjourn to the house and continue with his task of making it first habitable, and then as snug and easeful for Irina as he could manage. It was August before he arrived, in a horse-drawn carriage, to collect her from the sanatorium for the last time, and then he brought her again to the little house and carried her over the threshold and up the stairs, and laid her down on the beautiful, big bed that he had carved with his own hands.

"Aren't you afraid?" she asked him, quietly.

"Of what?"

"Of the *tuberculose*." Her eyes were suddenly wary, anxious.

Amadeus sat down on the edge of the bed and took both her hands in his own. "For myself?"

Irina nodded, wordless.

"The only thing I fear in this life," Amadeus said, his deep voice vibrating with emotion, "is losing you."

Her eyes filled with tears, but still she said nothing, only opened her arms to him. He came into them, lay down beside her. They had never made love, until then. They had both dreamed of it, felt their bodies throb with yearning, but his marriage, and propriety, and her life in the sanatorium had stood between them. Till today, Irina had been a patient first, a prisoner of her disease. Suddenly, she was, again, a normal human being, a woman.

Her body was so pale it appeared almost translucent. She was twenty-five years old, at the peak of her physical beauty, slender, silken and fragrant. Amadeus had feared making love to her, had been anxious that in his passion he might hurt her, for he was a strong man and he was conscious, every second, of her fragility. Yet as they began to kiss and to embrace, and then to touch and to caress, he witnessed a magical change in her, saw her skin begin to glow pale rose, felt her nipples grow erect under his fingers, felt wondrous strength and appetite and eagerness flow into her.

"*Je t'adore*," she said to him, as he entered her for the first time, yearning to thrust, forcing himself to be gentle, and it was as if her heart had flown into her voice, and Amadeus felt as if he might explode with love for her. And Irina opened herself to him, and began to move with him, wanting to help him, to release him from his fears, wanting his fierceness, his lust, wanting him to forget the past and the future, everything except the present, this moment, this glory.

Amadeus had, before taking Irina away from the sanatorium, consulted at length with Professor Ludwig and the other doctors and nurses as to the best way for him to care for her. They had fought him at first, but the force of his determination, and their patient's, had worn them down, and at last they had reached a compromise, whereby Amadeus should bring Irina to see them once each month and, in the meantime, should maintain a temperature chart and a note of any other developments in her condition.

"No," Irina said. "I shan't go back there."

"Only for a check, once a month, my darling."

"No." Her face was obstinately set.

"I promised them that I would look after you."

"You are looking after me, wonderfully well." She looked at his anxious face, and relented a little. "Very well, let them come here once a month if they must. Let them come and tap my chest and back, and listen to the noises in my lungs, and I will cough for them, and then they can go away again and leave us alone."

"What if they don't agree."

"It's that, or nothing."

He had been constructing a strategically placed sun terrace for her, where she could take her essential rests in almost any weather, warmed by the sun, shielded from the wind, braced by the glorious alpine air. Irina watched him as he worked, and the sight and sound of him, bare-chested and often singing or whistling, sawing, hammering and carving, pausing sometimes to scan her face to check that she felt well, or coming to her to plant a kiss on her mouth, did her much more good than all the months she had spent in the sanatorium. The terrace completed, Irina took her rests on a *chaise longue*, Anushka on her lap, while Amadeus sat beside her, reading or looking around at the wild beauty surrounding them, or simply watching her. Professor Ludwig came, as promised, every four weeks, and appeared quite satisfied, but he never spoke of real progress, nor did he ever say the words that Amadeus most longed to hear: that she was cured.

The end of summer dealt a blow, for Amadeus, in his haste to find their home, had not been aware that the position of the house in the Dischmatal, with the Jakobshorn mountain before it and the Schwarzhorn behind, meant that for most of the winter the sun, when it shone, would be blotted out. Life in the Alps, Amadeus began to understand, was hard and sometimes unremittingly bleak out of season. Without holidaying visitors,

Davos Dorf and Davos Platz lost their cheerfulness, inhabited only by stoical, toughened mountain folk and by the patients and staff of the clinics; their house, Amadeus began to fear, a good walk from the little road that wound its way up from the Dorf, might be cut off when the snows came. He did not care for himself, but Irina, who needed sunshine and security. . . He became distressed, angry with himself for his folly. He had wanted to give her the best, but the house was damp and cold and the sun terrace was useless. He had failed her.

Irina never complained, but in November she caught a bad cold and for the first time since they had met, Amadeus was faced with the irrefutable proof that she was as gravely ill as her doctors had insisted. Till now, it had hardly seemed quite real; so long as she behaved with a degree of common sense, and so long as Amadeus cared for her properly, they could keep it at bay, almost forgetting its existence. But now he saw that it was a tiny devil that had simply slept within her, deceiving them with its temporary inertia.

Irina's fever soared, her skin was ashen, her cheeks unnatural points of colour, her eyes were moist yet dull and darkly shadowed; she perspired and shivered, she had no appetite, she suffered bouts of pain; she coughed harshly, rackingly, often hiding her handkerchief from Amadeus, so that he knew, with growing terror, that she had coughed up blood. Professor Ludwig recommended taking her back into the sanatorium, and Amadeus, more heart-sick than ever, was forced to agree, but Irina would not go.

"It's for the best, my love," he tried to assure her. "Just for a little while."

"It would not be a little while," she said, and the rasp in her throat pained him. "They would never let me go again."

"I would make them."

"You could not, and once they began their monstrous tests and their treatments, I would not have the strength to fight them." Her eyes implored him. "This will pass, *mon amour*, if I stay here."

She remained adamant, and the gentle physician came up every second day to examine her while Amadeus, beside himself with fear, paced outside in the rain, certain after each consultation that he would hear her death sentence pronounced. He blamed himself, cursed himself for endangering her, and sought silent pacts with God, or Lucifer, or whoever might hear him and be willing to trade his life for Irina's.

By Christmas, she had recovered, the disease retreating once again to slumber deep within her. Irina was thinner, but swiftly regained much of her strength and all of her spirit. They skated together, arms linked, laughing like the other carefree couples on the rink; they ate pastries at Café Schneider in Davos Platz, shared romantic candle-lit dinners at the Flüela restaurant, ate fondues in the Jenatschstube, and then they came home and made love. They even skied together on the lowest snow-covered mountain slopes, and Amadeus was more thankful than he had ever been, though he watched her like a hawk every second he could, painfully aware now that this heightened, acutely joyful period of their life together was borrowed and, therefore, intensely fragile.

Having escaped unscathed the bleakest months, as spring came, and then summer, they took long walks together, with Anushka scampering at their heels, and Irina seemed stronger and more vibrant than ever. The darkness had receded from her life, and she no longer hankered after the old St Petersburg days. She adored the mountains, their savage beauty tamed by summer, loved the many varieties of alpine flowers that sprang in exquisite bunches of colour from even the rockiest slopes, liked to lie on her back in the grass on hot days, waving away the rug that Amadeus would try to place under her, wanting to feel the blades of grass brushing her arms, tickling her feet.

It was on one of these walks that she found the spot, not too far from their house, which was to become, in her eyes and heart, the perfect, visible expression of the glorious beauty that Amadeus had brought into her life. It was a waterfall – simply a small waterfall, of which there were so many in the mountains. But it seemed to Irina so especially entrancing in its natural, unceasing turbulence, so filled with colour and light and life, never allowing itself to be dominated by the massive, dwarfing rock face.

"Look into it, *mon amour*," she told Amadeus. "See how the flowers toss their colours back into the cascade!"

"I see it." Amadeus put his arms about her, and Irina clung to him, still staring into the splashing water.

"It's so hot everywhere today, so stuffy," she said, "but not here – it cools everything around it. It's so lovely, so strong – I envy it its immortality."

Even when winter came again, the waterfall still compelled her, drew her like a magnet with its power. Even now, when much of the tumbling spray hung, suspended in sparkling, frozen needles, Irina fancied she still saw eternal life, unvanquished, surviving deep within its core. And when, in the first weeks of 1924, she fell suddenly ill again and grew too weak to venture out, the waterfall, so symbolic to her of the strength she yearned for, still remained vital to her.

"Bring me the binoculars," she whispered to Amadeus, hoarsely, for her throat was painfully sore, and Professor Ludwig had been unable to ease it for her. "I want to watch for a while."

"You should sleep, my love," Amadeus said, but he brought the glasses anyway, having already moved her *chaise longue* to the end of the terrace from where she could just see the frozen cascade, even though she could no longer stand close to it and stare, mesmerized, as she had done before.

Amadeus knew that she was dying, that this time there would be no remission, that no amount of prayers or secret pacts with God would make any difference to the disease which seemed, suddenly, to be devouring Irina. He had never felt more helpless, more hopeless, and her courage in the face of the fate of which she was utterly certain, only enhanced his agony.

"What can I do for you?" he asked her countless times each day.

"Stay with me," she replied every time.

"Always."

Just once, her pale, pinched but still lovely face grew fearful, as though a terrible thought had just struck her, destroying her peace.

"*Qu'est-ce que tu as, mon amour*?" he asked. "What's wrong?"

"Don't send me back." Her voice rasped anxiously. "I don't want to die in the sanatorium."

"What makes you say that? I would never send you back there, my love – this is your home, here with me and Anushka."

Irina struggled to sit up a little. "When I left, when you took me away, they told me that I should return before the end. They said that they could make it more comfortable for me –" Her eyes filled with tears. "Perhaps they could help me to sleep more, to feel a little less –"

"Then perhaps –"

"*Non! Jamais*." She grasped weakly at his hands. "I don't want to miss one moment with you, not even one instant."

Amadeus felt his own cheeks wet with silent weeping. "Thank you," he whispered, hardly able to speak.

"Why should you thank me?"

"For showing me how to live – to love."

"We showed each other." Irina drew his hands to her lips and brushed them with her kiss. "If you had not found me, had not brought me out of there, I might have had a few months longer, but I would already have been dead for years." Her mouth trembled. "I thought my life was over after Sofia, after they told me that I had it, too. I didn't realize that the best part was still ahead of me."

The dachshund, on the quilt at the foot of the bed, began to whine, and Amadeus picked her up and placed her closer to her mistress, so that Irina could stroke her a little. "Poor Anushka," he said.

"She will have you," Irina said, then added softly: "And you? How will you be? Afterwards."

He did not answer.

"I know," she said, and her poor voice was full of pity for him. "I know how it would be for me, if you left me first." She paused, her breathing more laborious than it had been even the previous day. "But it would help me – to hear you say that you will live."

Amadeus nodded. "I will live."

Irina shook her head. "Not that way – not a living death. Promise me you will try – you will seek it out –"

"What, my love?"

"Life," she said.

On the tenth day of April, Irina, rallying a little, asked Amadeus to help her downstairs and out onto the terrace. It was a beautiful day, the sunlight having broken through the winter gloom, and a breath of early spring had penetrated the timber house.

"Won't it be too much for you?" he asked, cautiously.

"It's what I need," she said.

"I'll make a bargain. If you drink a little soup, then I will take you down to the terrace." Irina had hardly taken any nourishment for several days. "Shall I heat the soup?"

She smiled. "If you insist."

He fed her *Kürbissuppe*, a light vegetable marrow soup, with a spoon, and she managed half of the bowl, and then she lay back against her pillows to rest, she said, for just a few minutes. When she awoke, it was already late afternoon, and Amadeus imagined that she would give up the idea of going down until the next day, but she was insistent.

"I want to look at my waterfall," she said, and there was an urgency in her hoarse voice that he felt unable to ignore.

He wrapped her up in a thick blanket, and picked her up in his arms, and his heart wrenched in anguish at the lightness of her, for she weighed hardly more than a small child. And he carried her down the narrow stairs, and out onto the sun terrace, and he laid her carefully down on the *chaise longue*, and placed Anushka on her lap.

"I'll bring the glasses," he said.

"Not yet. Hold my hand a little while."

He sat beside her, holding her frail white hand, sometimes stroking her cheek and murmuring to her, small endearments, hushed little expressions of love and tenderness.

"Now," she said, "the glasses, please."

She was too weak to hold them by herself, so Amadeus raised the binoculars to her eyes, and helped to tilt her face in the right direction so that she could see what she wanted.

And Irina gazed up at the distant waterfall, made more glorious than ever by the sunset. And then she pushed the glasses away from her face, and looked back at Amadeus, and her beautiful, dark eyes brimmed with tears.

And she spoke to him for the last time.

"*A l'éternité.*"

Till eternity.

3

Amadeus was bereft and alone. His only companion was poor Anushka, grown prematurely white-faced and pining for Irina almost as palpably as her new master. Amadeus had not seen his son, Alexander, for over six months; his brief visits to Zurich over the last two years had been rendered almost intolerable by the frigid presence, during the single hour he was allowed with his son, of Elspeth Gründli, his mother-in-law, and Amadeus had all but given up. After Irina's death he became a semi-recluse, working automatically at his bench in the rear of his shop and employing a local girl to deal with the customers, for he had no interest in seeing anyone.

He left Davos, once, to go to Bern for his mother's funeral, and three months later he went again, to his father's. And when, just before Christmas that same year, he heard from Hildegard that both Elspeth and Leopold had been killed in a motoring accident, Amadeus steeled himself to travel down to Zurich for yet another funeral. Alexander, now almost ten and in physical appearance, at least, a slight, slim version of his father, with the same white-blond hair and vivid blue eyes, was understandably aloof; but to Amadeus's surprise and gratitude, Hildegard seemed almost compassionate. Now that her rival was dead, she was ready to divorce him, and while she wished never to set eyes on Amadeus again, she would permit him to have lunch with Alexander once a month, if he wished. A boy, she said, should know his father, even if the father did not deserve to know his son.

On an April afternoon the following spring, a lawyer from Zurich came to the Dischmatal to see Amadeus with regard to the last will and testament of Countess Irina Valentinovna Malinskaya.

"My firm owes you an apology for the delay in contacting you, Herr Gabriel," the white-haired lawyer said courteously, "but this was caused by the need both to authenticate the will and to ascertain that, as the lady declared, she left no surviving relatives."

Amadeus had grown pale, and he trembled slightly.

"Perhaps we should be seated, Herr Gabriel," the other man said, observing his shock. They were still standing just inside the front door, Amadeus being unaccustomed to visitors and having lost, for the time being, the art of simple good manners.

Amadeus nodded. "Please." He indicated the armchair closest to the window, and took the lawyer's hat and coat. "Would you like some tea? Or something stronger – a glass of schnapps, perhaps?" He had been taken completely by surprise. It had never entered his head that Irina might have left him anything at all; possessions had played such a negligible part in their life together.

The lawyer accepted a schnapps, as much for Gabriel's sake as his own. "I shall, with your permission, read the will to you, sir, and then, if it is convenient, we shall need to adjourn to the sanatorium where the Countess was a patient."

"What for?" Amadeus asked sharply, for the mere mention stabbed at his heart.

"Countess Malinskaya and her sister deposited a strongbox in the safekeeping of the Director of the sanatorium, Herr Jäggi. It is necessary for me to accompany you when you collect the box, and to be present for the signing of essential papers."

Amadeus swallowed his schnapps; it burned a little, and gave him strength. "Do you know what is in this box?"

The lawyer permitted himself the smallest of smiles. "I am led, by the will, to believe that the strongbox contains the Malinskaya gems."

Gems. Such a hopelessly inadequate description of the jewels that lay inside the steel box that Irina and Sofia had left with Herr Jäggi on their arrival in 1920. Rubies, emeralds, diamonds and sapphires – a staggering collection by any standards for their clearly remarkable quality as well as their size and quantity. Amadeus could not believe the evidence of his eyes. Irina had never mentioned any jewels; naturally, he had realized that she must have had some means to pay for her expensive suite at the sanatorium, but he had never thought it his place to enquire as to her means, and she had never volunteered any information.

A brief letter of explanation had been folded into an envelope and placed with the jewels in the strongbox. The stones were part of their late mother's collection, and all that the Malinskaya sisters had managed to smuggle out of Russia when they had made their escape. They had wrapped each gem in dark brown, fine spun silk, and had concealed them in their long, thick hair which had been intricately braided and pinned decorously high on their heads. Irina explained that she had sold a few stones in their early days in Paris and Switzerland, but an extremely valuable collection remained.

"I was directed to wait until after you had opened the strongbox, to pass you another letter," the lawyer told Amadeus, after they had called at his bank in the Dorf to arrange a safe-deposit box, before returning to the little timber house. "It was sent to us in Zurich, together with the Countess's will, early in 1923."

Irina had written the letter soon after recovering from the first acute bout of illness through which Amadeus had nursed her. It was simply written, in her modest, calm fashion, but her love sprang from the page. Amadeus had already given her the greatest joy she had ever known, the greatest gift any man could bestow on a woman, and Irina wanted him to have all the Malinskaya jewels except one: a remarkable, rich velvety green Colombian emerald.

This gem, I hope, can one day be given to my very dear friend, Konstantin Ivanovich Zeleyev, from St Petersburg. You know, my dearest, that I have spoken of him often. We must never forget that it was he who arranged safe passage for Sofia and myself, and I owe him a great debt of gratitude.

Irina had always prayed that Zeleyev – a goldsmith and enameller taught by his father who had, from his own workshop, worked exclusively for Peter Carl Fabergé – had safely left Russia. She had left a trail of forwarding addresses on her journey through Finland, Sweden and France, never giving up hope that some day he would appear in Davos, and make her happiness complete.

The immediate shock of Irina's will and her astounding bequest having diminished a little, Amadeus began to examine the jewels more closely. He was a jeweller, by no means unskilled, but he had never experienced the slightest excitement, let alone passion, for his craft. Then again, although he had seen plenty of fine jewellery on both his wife and his mother-in-law and their contemporaries, he had never had in his hands gems such as he now laid out before him. That he now *owned*.

Though his father, too, had been a 'bread-and-butter' jeweller, he had impressed on his son the need to learn at least a little about truly fine stones, just in case excellence were, one day, to come his way. Amadeus had never seen a Kashmir sapphire, nor a Mogok ruby, yet here they were, he felt almost certain, in all their cornflower-blue and pigeon's-blood-red glory. Here, too, were exquisite diamonds, some rose-cut, burning with blue-white fire, and a truly remarkable yellow diamond, fifteen carat and totally flawless. . .

Amadeus knew, already, what he would do with the jewels. He was, of course, perfectly aware that if he sold only a small number of them, he would be a wealthy man, but he had no interest in riches. He would never leave the house he had shared with Irina, would never go back to live in the city, nor have any yearning to travel. His parents had left him adequately provided for, his own shop ticked over comfortably and, in any case, the years of prosperity he had experienced with the Gründlis had brought him no happiness.

He did not know how to begin. His limited expertise at his craft had not prepared him for the task he now wished to undertake. Yet nothing would stop him. He was going to create a memorial to Irina, and he intended to use the Malinskaya jewels to recreate her beloved waterfall – her '*Eternité*' – in a sculpture.

It was Konstantin Zeleyev, arriving at the house in the Dischmatal nearly two years after Irina's death, in February of 1926, who transformed Amadeus's dream into a genuine ambition.

He was striking in appearance, stockier and shorter than Gabriel, but strong and vigorous, with red hair, green eyes and a neat fiery moustache over a wide, sensuous mouth. When he learned that Irina and Sofia were both dead, Zeleyev broke down and wept unashamedly and Amadeus, witnessing the thirty-five-year-old man's inconsolable grief, felt more touched by the stranger than he had by anyone since Irina.

"I never met Sofia, but it seems we both loved Irina," he said, gently, as the Russian wiped his eyes after the first storm had passed.

"I adored her." Zeleyev's eyes were distant and sorrowful. "There will never be another woman like her. Her sister was an enchanting girl, but Irina Valentinovna was –" He paused. "– joy," he finished.

"Will you stay here a while?" Amadeus offered. "It is what she would have wished, and I should be glad of your company."

"Thank you."

They had almost nothing in common, yet they were friends from the first. Amadeus gave Zeleyev the Colombian emerald, and a handsome ruby, and then shared with him his hopes for the sculpture.

Konstantin brought Gabriel back to life. He went with him to see Irina's waterfall, and right away he understood the other man's vision, made sense of the rough sketches Amadeus had shown him. It was still mid-winter, the bleakest time of all, but Zeleyev stared into the heart of the waterfall and, as the sun broke through the clouds and penetrated the cascade, he saw, as Amadeus saw and as Irina had seen, diamonds and sapphires dancing in the half-frozen water.

"Is it possible?" Amadeus asked, later, when they drank hot coffee back at the house.

"Possible, yes – but also very difficult."

"Tell me."

Zeleyev smiled. "You, my friend, are a jeweller in a small town where there are purveyors of *haute joaillerie*. You sell engagement rings, you repair necklaces, you engrave wedding rings and sometimes you make a pair of earrings to a client's specifications."

"My skills are limited, yes."

"You have, however, a beautiful imagination, and a determination to achieve what you set your mind to." Zeleyev paused. "I am a goldsmith, and I am also an enameller of considerable talent." Again, he smiled. "I see nothing to be gained by false modesty, *mon ami*. Had it not been for the Bolsheviks, I might perhaps have risen to the heights of Michael Evamplevich Perchin – you know of him, of course."

Amadeus shook his head.

"Only the man responsible for some of the most exquisite of the Master's objects. You have not heard of him?" He shook his head in disbelief, then went on. "I mean to say that together, we have at our fingertips some of the abilities necessary to create such a piece as you dream of, but even so, I fear that we shall often be stumbling in the dark before we accomplish a satisfactory end."

"You say 'we'." Amadeus hesitated. "Do I understand that you would be prepared to help me?"

"You could never do it without me," Zeleyev said bluntly.

"But your own home – your life." The Russian had told Amadeus that he had lived for a time in London, working for the house of Wartski, before he had moved on to Geneva; yet now it seemed that he contemplated abandoning a sensible, structured existence for the seduction of a fantasy that was not even his own.

"I am an artist," Zeleyev said. "Your vision is wondrous, but mine is miraculous. I have looked at your sketches, and at the waterfall itself, and in my mind, I have already created things you could never even dream of – a textured white-gold mountain with *cloisonné*, rubies and emeralds springing in tufts from the rock face to represent the colours of summer, and with a filigree cascade, networked with *plique-à-jour* enamelling through which the light can shine, tumbling as rose-cut diamonds and sapphires into a void halted by rock crystal and diamond icicles."

Amadeus was speechless. He stared at the other man, saw the narrow green eyes sparkling with exhilaration, and he knew that the months, perhaps even years to come that had stretched ahead like the most barren desert, would now be filled with purpose.

"It will be very hard, my friend," Zeleyev said again, "but I think we shall do it, *n'est-ce pas?*"

"For Irina," Amadeus said, and he thought, for an instant, that he felt her presence in the room, beside him, and for the first time in two years, he felt comforted.

It would take years. First, to select the most suitable of Irina's gems, and to sell others in order to buy the materials and equipment they required; to utilize Amadeus's small workshop in the Dorf, disrupting its daily routines as little as possible, and to set up an entire new workshop and sculpture studio at the house; to build a kiln for the firing of the original clay model from which the solid gold mountain face would be cast, and to build a forge for the fierce heat essential for the melting of gold and, later, for the enamelling processes.

In the early days, while Amadeus refined the designs, Zeleyev came and went, travelling to Zurich and Geneva, to Paris and Amsterdam, purchasing materials with care and then returning to the Dischmatal, sometimes bringing with him a few personal belongings from his apartment in Geneva. Mostly, he brought books – his two favourite novels, *Anna Karenina* and *Les Misérables,* which he confessed to Amadeus that he had already re-read more times than he could remember, finding endless fascination in the romance, lyricism and, above all, tragedy of both books; but he also brought with him clothing of great elegance and comfort, a suit of raw silk, pullovers of cashmere, shirts of purest cotton and made to measure, and fragments of his past, smuggled out of Russia at some peril: a handsome silver samovar and two relics of the glorious Fabergé days, a cigar box in red guilloche enamel and a curved dagger with a nephrite and gilt handle.

Amadeus was intrigued by him, by the complexities, idiosyncrasies and contradictions of his nature. Zeleyev was fastidious in his personal habits, and highly self-indulgent. Twice a day he bathed, luxuriating in steaming hot water lightly scented with a bergamot oil he bought periodically in Geneva, and twice a day he shaved lengthily with a cut-throat razor, and trimmed his neat red-gold moustache with small, sharp scissors. Every morning, whatever the weather, he exercised on the sun terrace with almost military precision and discipline, before admiring his physique in the cheval glass into which no one had peered since Irina, for Amadeus no longer had the remotest interest in his own appearance. He kept his possessions in place, his bedroom scrupulously tidy and clean, and if his handmade leather boots suffered the tiniest scuff, he fell to and polished them for a half-hour at a time until they gleamed again.

Much of this changed, however, when Zeleyev was working. When the sculpture, or his plans for it, came to the forefront of his brain, he appeared to depart the real world and to enter another, as far removed from the modest mountain house as St Petersburg was removed from Davos Dorf. With the precious materials and with the tools of his craft, the fastidiousness remained, but if anything was amiss or if an instrument was not to hand, or if Amadeus, his apprentice in the workshop, failed to grasp immediately what he demanded of him, Zeleyev flew into a monumental rage and flung things, often at Amadeus himself.

"I can't understand you," Amadeus protested, driven into rare anger. "You pamper your body and your face as if you were a beautiful woman, you weep genuine tears when you read those books as if you were a young girl – and then your roar at me and rampage around my house like a wounded bear!"

"I am difficult," Zeleyev admitted, calm again.

"You are impossible."

"I am a genius."

Drink transformed him even more dramatically than work. Zeleyev did not drink on a daily basis, sometimes not even for a month at a time, but when he did begin, it was invariably vodka that he drank, and equally invariably he drank to excess. Though it took some time for him to become intoxicated, half-way through a spree, he became intensely sexually aroused. At those times, Zeleyev would storm out of the house and head for the village, driving Gabriel's old Opel if it was in working order, or catching a Post Bus if one happened along, or otherwise marching all the long way down, even if it was icy, his craving for a woman too desperate to give up.

More often than not, he failed to find satisfaction, since the female inhabitants of Davos were more likely to turn their backs or, if sufficiently provoked, to give him a hearty slap, than to acquiesce. And so Zeleyev would retreat into a *Stübli* and continue to drink until he was falling-down drunk, and Amadeus would be summoned to remove him.

"You'll have to do your drinking on your visits to the city," he told the Russian, after the police had cautioned him on one occasion. "There are no prostitutes in Davos, my friend, and no decent woman would look at you twice in this condition."

"An uncivilized place," Zeleyev grumbled.

"If you don't like it, why don't you leave?"

"I shall – tomorrow."

But the next day, once recovered from the worst of his hangover, he would wander into the workshop, and the sculpture would take over again, for the longer he stayed, the more involved he became in the dream he now shared with Gabriel, the more unthinkable it became for him to leave. Konstantin Zeleyev was a man whose considerable ambitions had been brutally trampled underfoot; now he saw a means to achieve true greatness and recognition, perhaps even immortality. *Eternité*, he was determined, would not only be his finest work, but also one of the most unique, highly valued and exquisite sculptures ever created.

It took six months before both men were sufficiently satisfied with their original clay model for them to risk making even the first of their experimental moulds with which to cast working models in cheap metal. They achieved near perfection right away, then accidentally cracked the mould. Zeleyev went into a frenzy, and Amadeus only narrowly prevented him from smashing the clay model.

"You're crazy!" He held the fired clay high over his head for safety. "You spend months fussing over the minutest detail, and then you would hurl it at the wall like an empty vodka glass."

"Because I work with a clumsy oaf!" Zeleyev bellowed, panting with rage and frustration. "There is no *point* going on, since you will always destroy my perfection with your ugly, ham-handed fingers!"

"You cracked the mould!"

"Because I had to take it from you before you made another mark on it – because you are a village jeweller with as much artistry in your touch as a blacksmith!"

"And you have the self-control of a small child. I only put up with you for Irina's sake!"

Zeleyev's face, already flushed with anger, grew quite scarlet. "You are not fit to speak her name! Irina Valentinovna must have grown weak in her mind as well as her body to have allowed you to take control of her life – to have allowed you near her!"

Amadeus punched him hard on the jaw, then stepped back in horror. He had never struck another human being since he'd been six years old and taunted into fury by a kindergarten bully.

"Forgive me," he said.

The Russian sat down slowly on his workbench stool, gingerly touching his chin. "Impressive," he murmured, working his jaw gently to make sure it was not fractured.

"Unforgivable." Amadeus was trembling. "I call you uncontrolled, then I behave like an animal."

"I deserved it."

"No."

Zeleyev was smiling now, though still ruefully cradling his face. "Absolutely. You were entirely in the right, *mon ami*. And thank God you protected the model." Amadeus still held it in the crook of his left arm, had kept a grip even when he'd punched Zeleyev with his right fist. "It's safe to put it down now."

Amadeus returned it to the workbench. "Shall we make another mould right away?"

"You're not too tired?"

"I never felt fresher."

"Fighting agrees with you, my friend."

Three months later, the solid white-gold miniature mountain had been completed, and they were ready to discuss the next stage. Again, Amadeus took the role of pupil as Zeleyev explained to him the technique known as *samorodok*, by which a rough, ridged surface could be fused onto the existing rock face. Though Zeleyev had seen it done in Russia, he had never attempted it himself, but he knew that the effect was so suitable for their sculpture that they must try it, for nothing else would satisfy him. Tension mounted to nightmare levels as the experiment neared completion, for the gold they used would have to be heated to a temperature of perfect precision if they were to achieve the desired finish, and not a molten ruin.

Ecstatic with the results, the two men decided on a period of rest; Zeleyev needed the stimulus of the city to revitalize himself, and Amadeus was keenly aware that he had not visited Alexander for months. They parted in high spirits, the Russian looking forward eagerly to his holiday in Paris, and agreed to begin work again in the early spring. At the end of May, however, Amadeus was impatiently waiting for Zeleyev to return, and by mid-June he was still alone in the timber house with only the presence of the other man's beloved Fabergé artefacts allowing him to hope that he would, eventually, come back.

He came in August, offering neither apologies nor explanations. He looked more weary than refreshed, and it was clear to Amadeus that he had spent the last week, at least, on some kind of bacchanalian binge.

"I thought you were dead."

"As you see, I am not."

"There was no word from you – I expected you back in March."

"Are you now my wife?"

Amadeus bit back his retort, for he was gladder than he was willing to admit to have Zeleyev back again on any terms. The house, which at first he had been content to have to himself, had seemed after a time quite unbearably lonely, for he had grown accustomed to the Russian, with all his maddening eccentricities. And besides, though he had considered continuing with the sculpture alone, he had been painfully aware that without Zeleyev's skills and courage, he would be lost.

They went back to work, Amadeus beginning on the intricate white-gold filigree that would form the base structure of the cascade itself, while Zeleyev experimented with various methods of enamelling, intent that no single element of the sculpture must be permitted to outshine or detract from the rest. *Eternité*, when completed, was to be a miraculous abstract representation of a work of nature; the beholder was to gaze on the whole with pleasure, only observing secondarily the exquisite placing of the Malinskaya jewels, or the areas where *champlevé* enamelling had been used instead of *cloisonné*.

Zeleyev was to disappear twice more before their work was finished, on both occasions with the same unpredictability and lack of consideration, and in January of 1929, while Amadeus and he were skiing, Zeleyev fell badly and broke his left wrist. Both men plunged into gloom, only slightly alleviated when a letter arrived from Zurich stating that Hildegard had decided to permit Alexander, now fourteen, to visit Amadeus in his own home. The news threw Amadeus into a state of partial dismay and partial panic.

"I hardly know him," he tried to explain to Zeleyev. "My own son, and he's little more than an acquaintance I lunch with every now and again. We both pick at our food for a while, hardly knowing what to talk about, and just when I find some way to crack the ice a little, it's time to take him back to that damned house."

"This will be better," the Russian told him. "You'll be on your own territory, and he'll see you as you really are, a mountain man in his natural habitat."

"I don't even know if the boy wants to come."

"Of course he does. From what you've told me of your former wife, *mon ami*, she would never have agreed to let your son come here if he had not begged her."

"Why would he do that?" Amadeus said morosely. "It's not as if he was a baby when I left him and his mother. He was old enough to understand betrayal, and I know he hated me for it."

"Perhaps he hopes to understand more now that he is

older. Maybe he has grown to realize that you are not the black-hearted traitor he once thought you were."

Amadeus still looked anxious. "Will you stay?" He was afraid that with his arm encased in plaster of Paris, Zeleyev would escape to one of his beloved cities for an open-ended visit. "With you here, perhaps Alexander won't feel so pressured."

"He might disapprove of me. I'm sure his mother would."

"Alone with me, he'll be bored in no time – I'm a dull man."

"Irina Valentinovna would never have loved a dull man," Zeleyev said generously. "If your son had known her, he would have understood you right away."

"But he did not."

Alexander's city-stiffness took a few days to melt away. The snow helped, for the boy had been keen to learn to ski for years, and Amadeus was delighted to be asked to teach him. He was not brave, found it hard to keep his nerve when his skis scraped over an icy patch, and generally sat down deliberately rather than chance a hard fall; but the bracing air and the happy laughter of the other youngsters on the easy slopes invigorated Alexander as nothing in any of the cities or beach-resorts Hildegard had taken him to, ever had.

Zeleyev, as Amadeus had predicted, also helped to ease the atmosphere between father and son, as did poor Anushka, now more than twelve years old, and growing frailer with each week. The dachshund, who had seldom taken to strangers without considerable encouragement and effort, trusted the youngster almost immediately, allowing Alexander to pick her up and carry her around, taking titbits straight from his fingers and, at night, selecting his bed as the one she most wished to sleep on.

"Your son has a kind nature," Zeleyev told Amadeus

when they were alone. "He's so gentle with Anushka – he didn't even make a fuss when she messed in his room." Only the fact that the dachshund had been precious to Irina had prevented the fastidious Russian from tossing the old dog out into the snow when she had done the same in his bedroom.

"There has never been a dog in the Gründli Haus," Amadeus explained. "And having no younger brothers or sisters, Alexander has never had anyone to look after."

"I like him."

"He finds you exciting, Konstantin. And you treat him as an equal, something else I'm sure he has never experienced at home." Amadeus shook his head. "I sound bitter, I know, and of course I have no right to be. I abandoned them for Irina, and Hildegard had to bring up our son the way she thought best."

"She has not done so badly," Zeleyev commented.

"And she has allowed him to come to Davos, for which I will always be grateful." He hesitated. "But there's a softness in Alexander that troubles me a little, yet I'm not sure why that should be. I'd far sooner my son had a tender heart than a hard one, but –"

"But one needs a little toughness in life to survive."

"Exactly."

Zeleyev smiled. "You can't expect to guide the boy, or have much influence on him in a three-week visit, *mon ami*. Consider yourself fortunate if he allows you to become his friend."

Two days before Alexander was due to return to Zurich, Anushka died in her sleep. She had been showing signs of a growing weakness in her back, and Amadeus had feared that she might become paralysed, a fate which befell many dachshunds, and so whilst he felt deeply saddened by the loss, the greatest part of his sorrow was in the slipping away of another memory of Irina.

Alexander was distraught. "She was on my bed – I didn't even notice that she was ill."

"She was sleeping," Amadeus consoled him. "There was nothing you could have done for her. It's the best thing."

"How can it be best?" the boy flashed, tears in his eyes. "Anushka is dead."

"She was old, Alexei," Zeleyev tried. "More than eighty in human years."

They buried her near the timber house, under a silver fir tree that she had often slept beneath in the summer. Alexander insisted on digging the small grave by himself, no easy task in the frozen ground, and when Amadeus laid the dog to rest, his own eyes moist with the recollection of the sad, lonely years he had shared with Anushka and the companionship she had given him, Alexander wept again. When it was over, and they all went back inside, he still looked pale and unhappy.

"We should all have a drink," Zeleyev said.

Amadeus found a bottle of apricot schnapps and poured a little into a glass for Alexander. "It will make you feel better."

"Mother doesn't allow me to drink alcohol."

"You never had a drink?" Zeleyev looked astounded.

"A drop of wine on New Year's Eve. I like that."

Amadeus looked at the vodka bottle in the corner of the cupboard, thought better of launching Zeleyev on one of his sprees while Alexander was present, and poured brandy for both of them. "Let's drink a toast to her," he said, raising his glass. "Anushka."

"Anushka," the other two echoed, and they all drank, Alexander coughing a little as the harsh schnapps caught at his throat.

"Careful," Amadeus advised. "Sip it slowly."

The boy drank some more, and gazed into the glass. "It's warming," he said, and sniffed at it. "Good." He had another sip, then raised the glass again. "Anushka," he repeated, and suddenly, without warning, gulped down the rest.

"Alexander!" Amadeus laughed. "Not that way."

"Feel better?" Zeleyev enquired.

Alexander considered, and licked his lips. "A little."

"Have some more." The Russian rose to fetch the bottle.

"He'll get drunk," Amadeus cautioned. "Or sick."

"I won't." Alexander's cheeks were less pale, but his blue eyes were still anxious. "Please, Konstantin," he said, "just a little more."

"You should try vodka." Zeleyev smiled.

"No." Amadeus's voice was firm.

With their supper that evening, the two men drank beer, and Alexander drank only water, but later, in the early hours, having woken to see a light downstairs, Amadeus came down to find his son sitting on the floor with a glass of brandy in his hand.

"In God's name, what are you doing?"

"What does it look like?" The boy's voice was a little slurred.

Amadeus took the glass from him. "How much have you had?" he asked sharply.

"A little."

"But why?"

"I couldn't sleep."

"This isn't the way." Amadeus was upset. "You should have come in to see me. This is bad for you."

"You said it was good for me." Alexander sounded sullen.

"One drink after the burial. Even the second was a mistake. And I never told you that you could drink *Branntwein*."

"It burned even more than the schnapps at first, but I like it."

"It can make you ill. You're far too young."

"Why should you care?" For the first time since his arrival, Alexander showed an open sign of resentment.

"Of course I care."

"Since when?"

Amadeus had no answer. "Go to bed."

"Let me finish my drink first." The alcohol in his bloodstream made him insolent.

"Do as your father tells you, Alexei."

Amadeus and Alexander turned around to see Zeleyev standing at the foot of the staircase. Even with the sling supporting his left arm, he managed to look elegant and immaculate in his silk dressing gown. "Go to bed," he said quite softly, and the boy, suddenly shame-faced, clambered to his feet and made his way, a little unsteadily, up the stairs.

"Don't take it to heart," Zeleyev said to Amadeus. "He'll have a head full of hammering in the morning, and he'll probably be sick. He won't do it again in a hurry."

Though hung over and ill next morning, Alexander's good manners had returned, and he took great pains to apologize both to his father and to Zeleyev with sincerity, and when, the next day, they all stood on the platform at Davos Dorf station and he thanked them for his stay, he spoke with unmistakably genuine warmth.

"I'm sorry about Anushka," he said, and held out his hand to his father. Amadeus hesitated only for an instant, then followed his instincts and embraced his son, filled with gratitude when the boy hugged him back.

"Please thank your mother again for letting you come," Amadeus said, his voice husky. "I shall write to her myself, of course."

"Would you write to me too?" Alexander asked.

"If you want me to."

"I do, very much." Alexander turned to Zeleyev.

"Thank you, too, Konstantin. I'm sorry about your wrist – I hope it feels better soon."

"Another few weeks, and I'm sure it will be back to normal." Zeleyev, too, hugged him, and his green eyes twinkled. "Your father believes that I was a bad influence upon you the other night."

"You were," Amadeus said.

"I didn't mean to upset you, Papi."

"It's already forgotten."

The train chugged into the station, stopped briefly to allow passengers off and on and then, without much ado, pulled out again. They all waved, Zeleyev pulling out a large white handkerchief and flapping it in farewell. The train disappeared from view, and he turned to look at Amadeus, expecting to see sadness on his face, but instead there was an expression of actual joy, for although Zeleyev had not noticed it, Alexander had just called his father *papi* for the first time in seven years.

Eternité was completed a little over two years later, in the spring of 1931. It had taken them five years, and they had worked more slowly towards the end, partly because the intricacy of the work demanded great care, but partly, too, because they both realized that once the sculpture was finished, they would have no reason to stay together. In spite of the differences between them, and the battles that had continued, at intervals, to rage in the workshop and in the house, the two men had grown intensely fond of each other, and Amadeus knew that he was afraid to finish – afraid of the emptiness that would return afterwards.

It stood just over three hundred and fifty millimetres high, and Zeleyev suspected that if Fabergé himself had laid eyes on it, he might have rejected the sculpture because, by the Master's supreme standards, it was surely flawed. Yet Konstantin Ivanovich Zeleyev had never experienced such intense pride and satisfaction, for he knew, without a doubt, that *Eternité* was exactly as he had hoped and dreamed it would be: an exquisite work of art, wrought by hand out of priceless materials, created with love, skill and infinite patience.

"What now?" Zeleyev asked, the day after the final polishing had been carried out, after which they had both fallen asleep in their armchairs from utter exhaustion.

"I don't know." Amadeus felt hollow. "What will you do?"

Zeleyev shrugged. "Go away."

"To Geneva?"

"I think to Paris." The Russian paused. "Paris is what I need now." He waited another instant. "You could come, *mon ami*."

Amadeus smiled. "I don't think so."

"Will you stay here then?"

"There is nowhere else for me."

They had been strangers, alien to each other in almost every way, yoked together by their love for Irina, and by their common purpose. Now that their vision had been fulfilled, the discordances seemed, once again, amplified to the point of mutual discomfort. Yet neither wished to wound the other; the fondness would remain, long after they had parted.

"What shall you do with it?"

"With *Eternité*?" Amadeus shook his head. "Nothing."

Zeleyev leaned forward in his chair, his eyes glittering. "It is a great work, a unique piece."

"I believe so."

"Great works of art must be seen, my friend."

"If they are created for that purpose." Amadeus paused. "But all I wanted was to recreate Irina's waterfall in her memory, to use her gift in that creation, and thanks to you, we have achieved just that. I don't need anyone else to see it, except my son. I should love Alexander to see it, to understand what we have done."

Zeleyev was silent for a while. Then he asked: "Would you allow me to take it to Paris with me?"

"No." Again, Amadeus shook his head. "I want it to stay here. It belongs here. I'm sorry, Konstantin."

"Then we should at least take it to Geneva, or to Zurich if you prefer. I realize that the jewels and the gold are your property, *mon ami*, but you will admit, I'm sure, that the greatest part of its creation is mine. As a craftsman, as an artist, I naturally wish my work to be seen."

The tension in the room had grown quite palpable. Suddenly, there was a real barrier between them. Amadeus had thought that Zeleyev had understood his personal ideals. The final perfection of the sculpture, to him, had nothing to do with either its value or any possible recognition of their skills in fashioning it.

"I thought you realized, Konstantin, how I feel – have felt from the beginning – about *Eternité*." He tried again to explain. "I thought that you understood that I wanted it to be an intimate expression of my love for Irina. A private memorial."

The other man rose from his chair. "I did understand." A small coldness had crept into his voice. "But it has taken five years of my life, as well as yours, my friend. It has taken all of my creative strength – my soul, not only yours."

Amadeus stared at him. "What is it you want?"

"Very little." Zeleyev paused. "It is the finest work, by far, that I have ever produced and, I feel, the most beautiful. I also believe that it may, in its own way, be the most wondrous *objet de fantaisie* that has been created since the demise of the House of Fabergé." For a moment, he stroked his red moustache, and his eyes were hazy. "All I want is for someone – just one individual, if that is all you will permit, but an individual of expertise, of substance – to examine the sculpture, and to give his opinion."

"On what? Its worth?"

"Not in monetary terms, *mon ami*. In terms of excellence." Zeleyev's voice and eyes implored him. "That is all I ask. Is it too much?"

Amadeus did not reply for several moments. "No," he said. "On one condition."

"Which is?"

"Its anonymity." He looked intently at Zeleyev. "You may take *Eternité*, as you have said, to this single expert, and you may show it to him. But you may not mention either its connection with me, or with Irina. There can be no whisper about the Malinskaya gems."

A glint of irony sharpened the green eyes. "Am I permitted to mention my – interest – in its creation?"

"Of course." Amadeus paused again. "But if your expert gives you even a hint of the sculpture's value, I do not want to hear of it." He held out his hand. "Are we agreed?"

"Completely." Zeleyev's fingers grasped the other man's firmly. "And I thank you."

"You have nothing to thank me for, Konstantin."

The elegant wryness slipped back into the Russian's expression. "There would be many who would agree with you, my friend, but though it seems you would doubt me, I do understand you, Amadeus Gabriel."

Zeleyev left, one week later, for an undisclosed appointment at an undisclosed destination, the sculpture lovingly and carefully wrapped in his smallest leather suitcase.

"It will never leave my grip," he assured Amadeus. "And I shall return within one week, I swear it." He smiled. "Do you trust me?"

"Completely."

"Most would consider you a fool for that, *mon ami*."

"Nevertheless, I trust you." Amadeus regarded the Russian calmly. "Just as I trust you not to get drunk while this is in your possession, for I know that you care for it as much as I do."

Zeleyev came back six days later.

"Well?" Amadeus asked, gently.

"Do you want to know?"

"Only whether you are content, Konstantin Ivanovich." Amadeus watched his friend's face keenly, seeking either elation or disappointment, but he saw neither. "You should have been a gambler – you could play a fine hand of poker."

"It has been known."

"Are you content?" Amadeus asked again.

Zeleyev smiled. "Thank you, my friend."

He stayed in Davos for one month, partly because Alexander was due to visit them again in the middle of May. He had come twice more since the winter of 1929, and on both occasions, although his father and Zeleyev had been hard at work on the sculpture, they had not allowed him even a glimpse of their progress, nor had they explained to him what it was that they were in the process of creating.

Alexander was now sixteen, as tall as his father though much slighter, and with a pleasing face that owed more to Hildegard than Amadeus.

"It's finished, isn't it?" he said on the afternoon that he arrived.

"How did you know?" Amadeus asked.

"The atmosphere in the house – it's different. Quieter."

Amadeus looked at Zeleyev. "Shall we show him?"

"It's your choice."

"Papi?" Alexander turned to the other man. "Konstantin, don't you want me to see it?"

Zeleyev laughed. "I want the world to see it, Alexei."

"Well then?"

Amadeus's eyes were warm. "Come."

It stood, under a cover, on the central table in the workshop at the back of the house. When Amadeus unveiled it, his legs suddenly unsteady, his hands trembling, Alexander stared, hardly blinking. For a few long minutes, he stood motionless, then moved slowly around the table, seeing the sculpture from every angle, taking it all in.

No one spoke, but after a while, Zeleyev came silently to the table and showed Alexander three hinged jewels beneath which initials had been engraved: his own under a rose-cut sapphire on the *samorodok* rough gold rock ledge; Amadeus's beneath a Russian emerald on the far side of the filigree and enamelled waterfall, with its needle-sharp rock crystal icicles pointed with tiny rose-cut diamonds; and finally Irina Valentinovna Malinskaya's initials under the great, yellow diamond that gleamed, like the sun, at the summit of the cascade.

"Well?" Amadeus could bear it no longer.

Alexander still stared at the sculpture, could not tear his eyes away. "I can't take it in," he murmured. "I've never seen anything like it."

"I have told your father, it is unique," Zeleyev said quietly.

"It's – wonderful." Alexander paused. "The most beautiful thing I've ever seen." Tentatively, cautiously, he leaned closer to brush it with his fingers.

"You can touch it," Zeleyev said, and glanced up at Amadeus, whose face was taut with emotion. "It is called *Eternité*."

Alexander's right index finger hovered above the yellow diamond. "Is it for her?" He turned to look at his father. "Papi?"

Amadeus came closer. "I'll tell you."

* * *

They walked out, at sunset, to the waterfall, just the two of them, Zeleyev tactfully claiming to be in need of a rest.

"It's glorious." Alexander gazed at the sight. "I can understand why she loved it so much. Yet, in its way, yours is even lovelier."

"In its way."

"I never knew," Alexander said, "that you loved her so very much. You said so little to me, and Mami pretended that she didn't exist."

"You cannot blame her."

"No."

They were quiet for a while, and then Alexander said: "It must be very –" He stopped.

"Valuable?" Amadeus finished for him. "I expect it must be."

"You really don't care about that, do you, Papi?"

"Do you mind?"

"Why should I ?"

"Some sons might."Amadeus looked away, into the cascade. "Your mother might, though only on your behalf, not her own."

"Mother would not be interested," Alexander said, flushing a little.

"No," Amadeus agreed. "You're right, of course."

They began to walk again, following the grassy path back towards the house. A meadow of butterwort and lady's slipper glowed strangely in the rosy dusk, and a pair of red squirrels scampered ahead of them. The air was soft and quite warm.

"Konstantin would like it if *Eternité* were on display," Amadeus said.

"That's understandable."

"Do you think I am very unfair, wanting to keep it private?"

Alexander shook his head. "It only exists because of you."

"I would never have achieved it without him. I could dream of it, but it took Konstantin's genius to make it happen." Amadeus sighed. "Even so, I cannot do what he wants."

Alexander took his father's arm. "That is your right."

One week after Alexander had returned to Zurich, Zeleyev left Davos. On the last night, Amadeus gave him a cabochon ruby and two brilliant-cut diamonds, half of what remained of the Malinskaya collection.

"You are a fool," Zeleyev said.

"So you have frequently told me."

"You could have untold wealth, and now you give away what you have left."

"I have enough."

Zeleyev shrugged. "What of Alexander? Did you discuss this with him, any more than you discussed what you intended doing with the rest of the jewels?"

"Alexander's mother has more money than she could spend in ten lifetimes. He has nothing to fear in that direction."

"The desire for a birthright is not always measured in money, *mon ami*. These gems have nothing to do with him, of course, but our sculpture set your son's eyes alight."

Amadeus shook his head. "He understands my feelings for *Eternité*."

"That doesn't mean he shares them. He is as much Hildegard's child as yours, remember."

"What are you trying to say, Konstantin? That Alexander will want our pretty waterfall after I'm gone? That makes me happy."

"He may not be the only one," Zeleyev said softly. "Once you create something of priceless beauty, there will always be people who will be fascinated by it, who will want to possess it."

Amadeus glanced at him sharply. "Did you betray my

trust when you took *Eternité* away with you? You promised anonymity."

"And I kept my word."

"Then your predictions are meaningless to me. I don't care what happens to my possessions after I'm dead – not even to *Eternité*. I know what it signifies to me, and that's enough."

They fell silent for a time, and Amadeus looked around his living room, noting the empty spaces left by the personal belongings Zeleyev had already packed.

"Shall you be lonely, do you think?" Zeleyev asked, reading his thoughts.

"Of course." Amadeus was gentle again. "But I thought that my life was finished when Irina left me. And then her gift, and your generosity, brought me back to the living, and for that I will always be grateful."

"They have been wonderful years," Zeleyev said, and there were tears in his eyes. "Suspended from real time, from the harshness of the real world."

"You will come back."

Zeleyev nodded. "But it will never be the same again."

Before they left for the station next morning, the two men went to look at the sculpture again. They had dismantled their workshop, for it had served its purpose, and they had reinstated the original stables with their hayloft.

It was in that hayloft that they had decided to store their treasure, in a recess specially carved out of the wall and concealed behind a pile of bales. They had shown the hiding-place to Alexander before he went home, and now no one except Zeleyev, Amadeus and his son, would ever be aware of its existence.

Until Maggy.

4

She was born to Alexander and his wife, Emilie, on the seventh day of December, 1939, three months after the general mobilization of the Swiss army, and ten months after her parents' marriage had united their two neighbouring families on Aurora Strasse. The Hubers owned a large printing firm, and their house was substantial, but nevertheless inferior to the Gründli Haus, and the Hubers' wealth, also considerable but similarly trailing behind the Gründli fortune, was in any case too recently accumulated to be taken entirely seriously. Emilie had two brothers, both destined to control the Huber companies, so her destiny, from an early age, lay in making a fine marriage. Hildegard was well aware of the shortcomings of the match, but she was equally conscious that her son had failings that might stand in the way of his marrying into any of the great Zurich families.

Alexander drank too much. He was a charming young man, attractive with a winsome smile, and he had never been anything but a good son to her. But he had, over the last nine years, spent more time with his father, the Gründlis' *schwarzes Schaf* – their black sheep – than she liked, and she felt uneasy with the clear evidence that Alexander admired and respected Amadeus, a man who merited neither admiration nor respect. Amadeus, however, had at least always had a great strength of personality, despite his irresponsibility and selfishness. Alexander

Gabriel, his mother feared, was a much weaker man. And he drank far too much.

At first, after his marriage to Emilie and especially in the early years after Magdalen's birth, it seemed that stability at home – they were living, of course, in the Gründli Haus, for no other option had ever been considered, at least by Emilie, who got on famously with her mother-in-law – together with his job at the Gründli Bank, were having a steadying effect upon Alexander. The on-off nature of his military duties (between 1939 and the end of the war in Europe, Alexander was alternately mobilized and demobilized several times) prevented him from becoming too bored, and when he was safely at work in the bank, he made a considerable effort, for after all, even if marriage did demand a certain sobriety which did not sit comfortably with him, there was not much more he could ask of life. He liked his pretty, fair-haired wife, when she didn't nag him, and he adored their little daughter, Maggy, with her riotous golden curls and her wondrous eyes that were, in some lights, according to her grandfather, the colour of lapis lazuli, and in others, the colour of Persian turquoise.

"She is the light of my life," Alexander told Amadeus on one of their visits to the Dischmatal, when Magdalen was four.

"Not only yours." Amadeus watched his small granddaughter dismantling his bookshelf, turning occasionally to bestow beaming smiles on them.

They came as often as possible, under the circumstances, which meant that whilst Hildegard seldom said anything, Emilie was aware of her feelings and had, from the first, refused to come with her husband and daughter, pointedly staying in Zurich and complaining when they came home looking too fit and happy. Davos had developed considerably over the last decade as a winter resort; the opening of the Parsennbahn, a ski lift on the

Strela and a contraption called the Holzbügel-Skilift, which allowed skiers to grasp wood and iron bars attached to a steel rope and to be dragged up the mountain on their skis, had opened up the town to a much more relaxed kind of skiing than in the old days, when only the strongest enthusiasts, like Amadeus, had come regularly.

Maggy loved these weekends and holidays more and more with every passing year. They were special times, shared only with her father and Opi, for even when her brother, Rudolf – born in 1942, exactly three months to the day before her third birthday – was old enough to accompany them, Maggy and Alexander still travelled up alone.

Although Zurich itself was accidentally bombed a number of times, mostly because of the blackout, and though both Alexander and Maximilian, the butler, were meant, by order, to carry their rifles and forty-eight rounds of ammunition each wherever they went, life down in the city was still comfortable and impeccably ordered. Maggy slept between silk sheets, and apart from the black-out blinds her bedroom was beautifully decorated in pale pink, and when she grew too old to be bathed, a maid still helped her out of the bath and held her warmed, monogrammed Turkish towel for her. Family meals were served in the grand *Speisezimmer* on silver platters by Maximilian who, in peacetime, doubled as the chauffeur, driving Hildegard's Hispano-Suiza and Alexander's Mercedes-Benz, though now, because of shortages, private motor cars were not allowed on the road.

Maggy was taught – which did not mean that she learnt – to sew, to embroider and knit, and to be ladylike at all times. 'Ladylike' meant, apparently, carrying a clean, freshly-pressed handkerchief, but not using it unless absolutely essential, never voicing an opinion nor, indeed, speaking at all unless she was spoken to, never running in a public place, and certainly never singing, except in church.

Up on the mountain, her grandfather's timber house was heated by a wood-burning stove, and Maggy slept under a simple cotton and goosedown quilt and, when the snows came, under an extra rough blanket. She and her father and Amadeus ate delicious, simple food: beef stews, or fried sausages with *Böleschwäizi*, fried onions in a thin gravy, or raclette, made by dripping melted cheese onto steel dishes from a big fork over the open fire. And her grandfather allowed her to lick foam from the top of his beer glass, and he encouraged her to sing at the top of her voice, filling her lungs with pure air; and he let her run about freely, and he taught her to ski and to skate and to climb. And life up there was joyous, and seemed infinitely more vivid than it ever did below.

It all changed one night in 1947. All in one single night, in the space of a few hours, when everything Maggy loved was spoiled.

She was seven years old, and her brother, Rudi, was not yet five. The war in Europe had been over for two years. Alexander and Emilie Gabriel had been married for eight years, and they were not nearly as contented as they had expected to be. Emilie, at twenty-nine, was still a pretty, frothy woman. With men she could be soft and foolish, but with other women she took much less trouble. She respected and liked Hildegard, but with Maggy she tended towards impatience and often unreasonable severity. Rudi was male and consequently, in Emilie's narrow view, more worthwhile, but her own husband was a great disappointment to her. She and Alexander argued frequently over their children and most other things, not least the bank, which he, like his father before him, had found less fulfilling than he had hoped. But unlike Amadeus, who had found the strength to leave, Alexander Gabriel was a weak man, lacking courage, tenacity and conviction.

More and more, Alexander sought to escape from his disapproving wife and mother, first in the pages of the American hard-boiled fiction that he enjoyed and, whenever possible, in Davos, but gradually he took his comforts in the drinking places of Zurich and in the arms of prostitutes, infinitely more experienced and imaginative than Emilie. The bars he frequented became increasingly sordid, and before long he was experimenting with drugs. In the back rooms of the city, he smoked marijuana and fornicated and drank whisky and chewed cannabis; and then he went home, back to Aurora Strasse, and tried to be a son, a husband and a father again. He became increasingly less fit for work, his restlessness and growing need for narcotic, stimulant and hallucinogenic help, incapacitating him. Soon nothing held his attention for more than a few moments, not even his old detective stories, nor Rudi. Not even Maggy.

It was a Saturday evening in June when Maggy, peeping over the balustrade at the top of the circular staircase, watched Frau Kümmerly, their housekeeper, admitting a stranger to the house. He was a man with straight red hair and a neat moustache.

"*Herr Gabriel, bitte.*" The man gave a little bow and handed the housekeeper a visiting card.

"*Einen kleinen Moment, bitte.*" Frau Kümmerly disappeared towards the library. The stranger looked up, saw Maggy and smiled. His eyes were green, and the smile was warm and somehow pleased, as if he knew who she was, even though they had never met.

"Konstantin!" Alexander came hurrying into the entrance hall, both hands outstretched, and Maggy backed away, in case her mother emerged from her dressing room and caught her.

"Alexei, how are you?"

"The better for seeing you. When did you arrive? Have you seen my father?"

Maggy crept back to the staircase, curiosity prevailing, for she knew now who the man was. Her grandfather had spoken often of the Russian, his great friend. Konstantin Ivanovich Zeleyev. Even his name fascinated her, though she had always visualized him as dark, with black eyes and a fur hat.

"Not yet," he was replying to Alexander's question. "I will go up to Davos in a few days, but first, I hoped to take you to dinner. If you are, by chance, free." Again, he glanced up, perfectly aware that Maggy was still watching and listening, but she lifted her finger to her lips as if to hush him, and in a moment of perfect conspiracy, he averted his eyes and looked back at Alexander.

"It can be arranged," her father said. "I'll give you a drink, and have a word with Emilie."

"If you have plans, then –" Their voices were cut off as they went into the drawing room and closed the door. Maggy hovered, waiting. She would have liked to have gone in, wanted very much to be introduced to the Russian, and knew that her father would not mind, but that both her mother and grandmother certainly would, and whilst she didn't always mind getting into trouble, Papi had promised to take her to the zoo the next afternoon.

Reluctantly, she wandered slowly towards her bedroom. If she walked really slowly, then maybe she could attract her father's attention when he came upstairs to see her mother. But when Alexander did come up, he went straight into Emilie's dressing room and didn't even notice her. Maggy waited a few moments longer, heard her parents' voices raised a little, clearly in anger, and gave up.

Ten minutes later, her bedroom door opened.

"Papi!" Maggy bounced out of bed. It was such a farce,

insisting that she go to bed at half past six when everyone knew she could never sleep until ten o'clock, or sometimes even later, and yet she never felt tired next morning as they all threatened she would.

"Not asleep yet, *Schätzli*?" Alexander put out his arms and she ran into them and snuggled against his waist, the buckle of his belt cold against her cheek.

"Are you going out, Papi? With the Russian?"

He held her at arm's length. "Were you listening at the stairs again?"

"Yes, Papi." Her eyes twinkled up at him. There was no guile in her nature, and in any case, she could always be honest and open with him. "He's Opi's Russian, isn't he? The one who used to live with him."

"The very same."

"Can I come down and meet him?"

"Not tonight, no, *Schätzli*. You must go back to bed and behave yourself."

"Where are you going?"

"To dinner – I don't know where."

"Is Mami cross?"

Alexander smiled. "Just a little. Now do as you're told, Maggy."

She jumped back onto her bed, and her father drew the covers up over her, bent down and kissed her forehead. "Sweet dreams."

"Will you come and see me when you get home?"

"It'll be too late."

"Please, Papi. If I know you'll at least look in, then I promise I'll go to sleep, otherwise I'll make myself stay awake until you come."

"That's blackmail." He stroked her hair, gave her another kiss, and walked to the door. "I'll peep in when I come, but you'd better be fast asleep."

"I will."

* * *

They drove in the taxi that Zeleyev had asked to wait for him, down the steep roads towards the Römerhof, then heading west to cross the Quaibrücke into the heart of the city.

"I'm grateful to you, Alexei," Zeleyev said in the back of the car. "Was Emilie very angry with me for taking you away?"

"No more so than she usually is. We had no special plans – only to eat together at home. My mother is there, so she won't be alone."

"Where to?" the driver asked.

"The Baur au Lac?" Alexander asked Zeleyev. "I thought we could start at the Grill Room and then go on – make a night of it. I've found one or two places that might interest you since we last met."

Zeleyev smiled. "You're not a dull man, Alexei, are you? Not always the wisest, either, but seldom dull."

Alexander's tone was ironic. "My life, for the most part, is terminally dull, Konstantin. God knows I have to make up for it somehow."

In the Gründli Haus, Hildegard did her evening rounds before retiring for the night. She looked in first at Rudi, ensured that the small boy was sleeping sweetly as he always did, planted a gentle kiss on his golden head and shut the door softly before moving on past his nanny's room towards Maggy's bedroom.

The child was, for once, actually asleep, lying on her back, her long curling hair fanned out around her face, one arm clutching her pillow, the bedclothes rumpled and kicked away. Hildegard felt her heart clench at the sight of her granddaughter in repose, felt a pang of regret at the knowledge that Maggy thought of her as a sombre, rigid grandmother. It was her own fault, she realized, but she could not help being a stickler for rules and good behaviour. If only Magdalen were as good as her little brother, it would make life so much easier for her and for Emilie, who did not, alas, have a natural talent for parenthood. Mothers were supposed, ideally, not to overlook failings in their children, but to love their sons and daughters in spite of those failings. Besides, Maggy might not be a perfectly behaved little girl, but she had a spontaneous warmth and generosity, and an undeniable courage that would, in the long term, prove far more important.

The warmth, Hildegard supposed, Maggy had inherited from Amadeus; she remembered that genuine amiability, that kind-heartedness in the young man she had fallen in love with so many, many years ago. She would never forgive him for what he had done to her, but she was an honest enough woman to recognize that she had, in part, driven him away. Maggy's courage, she thought, must also stem from her grandfather, for though Emilie had a strong, tenacious streak, Hildegard doubted if she had ever possessed the bold free-spiritedness that this little girl had. And it certainly, regrettably, had not been planted in her by her father.

Alexander, she sighed to herself, shutting Maggy's door, was always running away, from situations, from responsibilities, from life. He'd done it again this evening, going off with that man, putting a friend of his father's before his own wife. Heaven only knew what condition he would be in when he came home – if he came home before morning.

"You should go home," Zeleyev told Alexander.

"Why?"

"Your wife will be waiting for you."

"Emilie?" Alexander made a disparaging face. "She'll be in bed by now. We all have to retire early in our house, you know. My mother and my wife, they make rules."

His eyes were bloodshot and his speech was slurred. They had moved from the elegance of the Baur au Lac to the relaxed atmosphere of the Zeughauskeller, a huge beer hall on the Bahnhofstrasse where Alexander had so far drunk six tankards of Hurlimann beer and Zeleyev had made short work of half a bottle of vodka.

"At least you have a woman in your bed. Emilie is pretty enough, isn't she?" Zeleyev had never met the younger Frau Gabriel, but he had gathered that she was more than charming.

Alexander shrugged. "She's a beautiful woman, on the surface – but she's so damnably disapproving."

"Is she a sexy woman?" The pupils in Zeleyev's green eyes had grown large, and he had an erection. He knew that excessive alcohol rendered many men impotent, but as always, in his case, the vodka had reinforced his own libido.

"Once upon a time she wasn't bad." Alexander lifted his tankard to his lips and a trickle of beer ran down his chin. "Nowadays, I have to find my pleasures elsewhere."

"In this town? Always so straight-laced, so refined?" Zeleyev's eyes sparkled mockingly.

"You know as well as I – better, probably. Papi has told me of your exploits –" He paused. "Of your hungers."

The Russian laughed. "Your father used to have quite a time of it when I went on the rampage. His words, not mine, Alexei. So far as I'm concerned, it's merely a question of relaxation."

Alexander leaned forward, and his face seemed abruptly quite vulpine. "And do you want to relax tonight, Konstantin?"

"Even more than I want to piss." Pointedly, Zeleyev rose from the bench seat and glanced around. "Can you arrange something?"

"Consider it arranged."

At half past eleven in the Gründli Haus, Emilie put her copy of that month's *Die Elegante Welt* onto her bedside table, looked at the clock on the mantelpiece over the fireplace and, with a sigh, turned out her light.

Two doors away, Hildegard sat at a table in the sitting room of her suite, playing patience. She did not need to check the clock to know the time, for in spite of herself, she had been counting the minutes for the last hour, perfectly aware that her son had not yet come home. She felt annoyed with him, as she often did, and upset for Emilie and the children, but more than that tonight, for reasons she could not explain, she felt uncommonly anxious.

In the nursery, on the far side of the landing, Rudi Gabriel slept the peaceful sleep of the innocent and untroubled. He was only four years old, and those few people who mattered to him most, his mother, his nanny and his grandmother, were all home with him. He was surrounded by love and kindness, warmth and security.

In the pink bedroom, his sister was dreaming. She was skiing, with her father, on a wonderful snow-covered mountain. The snow was thick and crisp and soft, and she was skiing in her father's tracks, as competently as any adult, swinging round her turns, her movements so assured and confident that she did not need to concentrate at all; it was like flying, only better, and the frosty powder thrown up by her skis swirled around her in a silver cloud –

"Don't lose me, Papi," she called out, suddenly uneasy as his figure became obscured by the snow mist.

"Never, *Schätzli*," he shouted back over his shoulder, and Maggy felt all his love, and all the perfect knowledge of his care for her, and the small fear disappeared again as she continued to fly, with her father, down the mountain.

Zeleyev and Alexander were in a sordid little room in a run-down house in a tiny dark alley off Niederdorf-Strasse, a long, narrow cobbled street running parallel with the Limmat river, littered with bars, Bohemian cafés and characters. Alexander was smoking the last of a marijuana cigarette; his chest felt a little tight, and he was aware that his muscles were less co-ordinated than usual, but the euphoria the drug had momentarily lent him was exquisite. If only, he thought, it would last.

The Russian had a fresh bottle of vodka, not yet opened. He did not need it yet, and he did not need the drugs young Gabriel appeared, quite desperately, to require in order to maintain his own level of intoxication. He had what he needed, there in the glass bottle, and there, before him, on the bed. She was about twenty-five and in good shape, brown-haired, hazel-eyed with large breasts and clear, clean skin. There was only one woman for them both, but sharing was something he had always enjoyed, when the circumstances were right.

"Ready, Alexei?"

"Not yet." Alexander took two pills out of an envelope. "Vodka," he said, and held out his hand.

"What are they?" Zeleyev thought young Gabriel looked as if he might pass out. Mixing drink was bad enough; Alexander had drunk whisky before dinner, then red wine, then all those beers and the dope on top of it all. Now he swilled the pills down with vodka straight from the bottle.

"What's he taking?" The woman spoke for the first time since they'd entered the room, her voice uneasy. "I don't want anything rough."

"Don't worry," Zeleyev said, his eyes on Alexander. He didn't mind waiting for the younger man. His own erection was rock steady; his cock never failed him. He would drink a little more, and watch as Alexei got undressed. He had not seen his naked body since the boy's first visit to Davos, long ago, when Zeleyev had walked into the bathroom when he was standing up in the tub, washing himself. The Russian had thought him beautiful then, and now the anticipation pumped fresh, greedy blood through his veins. He seldom did it with boys, but soon they would get the girl started, and have a little fun together, and then he would spread those round, female thighs and he would fuck and fuck until his brain exploded –

Time passed. Alexander's face was changing, the drunken lethargy melting away in the face of the latest, forceful charge. Amphetamines, Zeleyev thought. Gabriel dropped his tie on the floor and began unbuttoning his shirt with suddenly impatient fingers.

"I'll want extra," the woman said.

"Shut up," Alexander said quietly, and Zeleyev felt an extra surge of powerful excitement at the idea of all that uncontrollable sexuality being unleashed in the other man.

Alexander's trousers and shorts joined the shirt and tie on the dingy carpet. His body was pale, though not as white as Zeleyev's, and his penis was smaller, but thrusting energetically upwards. Zeleyev looked away from him to the girl. Her nipples were large and dark beige and erect, and he saw that in spite of herself, she too was genuinely excited.

There was a force at work in the sordid room, a growing, frenetic agitation, a mutual raising of body temperature. A wildness of the mind.

They were all three ready.

The scream woke Maggy. Her mother's scream, hysterical and shocked, swiftly cut off by voices. Maggy sat up in bed in the dark, her heart beating furiously, her ears alert for more.

She climbed out of bed and ran to the door to listen. The voices were continuing, male and female, one instant shrill, the next muffled, impossible to understand or to identify. She opened the door and stepped, bare-footed, into the corridor.

"Magdalen, what are you doing?" Her grandmother,

wearing a peach-coloured dressing gown, her white hair in a net, swept down towards her, her arms extended as if to halt Maggy, to push her away.

"I heard a scream, Omi."

"It was nothing, child." Hildegard's face was quite pale.

"Was it Mami? What happened to her?"

"Your mother had a small shock, but everything is well again now, and you must go back to bed."

"Is Papi here?" Maggy tried to pass her grandmother, but Hildegard took her firmly by the arm.

"Back to bed – now." It was a command.

She tried to sleep again, but it was impossible. The voices went on for a long time, sometimes raised, mostly hushed. Her curiosity became unbearable and she crept back to the door, to find it had been locked, silently, from the other side. Her door was *never* locked. She was outraged, and she wanted to shout in protest, but some instinct kept her silent, and she retreated into bed again, huddled under her quilt, suddenly goose-pimpled and afraid.

Until the sound of a motor car sent her flying to the window to stare out into the night. Her grandmother's Hispano-Suiza stood in the circular driveway, its headlights switched on, lighting up the entrance to the house. A moment later, Maximilian, the chauffeur, emerged from the front door. A man walked beside him. Maggy strained her eyes, and saw that the second man was the Russian, Konstantin Zeleyev, who climbed into the back of the car, closing the door himself just before Maximilian drove him away.

Probably, Maggy decided, her father and the red-haired man had come home a little drunk. She had heard her mother complain several times that her father stayed out late and 'behaved badly' – she had heard her parents arguing often about that and other things. Maggy remembered characters in the books her father read to her, drinking whisky and beer; it seemed normal enough in the books, seemed to be something that men just did. Maggy didn't mind what Papi did, so long as he came home and still loved her. She wished he would come to her room now, as he had promised, and unlock the door and peep in to see if she was asleep. If he would just come in and give her a hug, one of his quick, comforting hugs, she would be able to go back to sleep, and in the morning everything would be normal.

He did not come. Maggy dozed, fitfully, for a while, waking every now and then to hear sounds of movement around the house. Footsteps, passing her bedroom, footsteps on the staircase, on the parquet floor of the entrance hall. More voices, whispering, then her grandmother's voice, briefly louder, as if she was talking on the telephone. She heard her mother again, quite clearly – and then she heard Papi too, and when she looked at her clock, she saw that it was almost five o'clock and fear gripped her again. *Why* had Papi not come in to see her as he'd promised? Mami said sometimes that he was unreliable, but Maggy knew that she could always depend on him. He was solid and real, he loved her more than anyone else in the world – more than Mami, more even than Rudi – and she adored him. But still, tonight he did not come.

She tried the door again and, finding it still locked, she began to knock on the oak panels. No one came. She grew angry and frustrated, hammered with her fists and began to weep with vexation. She could see, in the gap beneath her door, that the lights were all on in the house. She could hear them close by, walking around, busy, hurrying, ignoring her.

And then, just after dawn, the Hispano-Suiza returned, and Maggy flew back to the window. Maximilian stepped down, turned out the headlights but left the motor running. He came into the house and then, moments later, emerged again, this time with her father.

Maggy's eyes widened. Papi was leaning heavily against the chauffeur, who gripped his arm with one hand, and carried a large suitcase in the other. Maggy could not see her father's face, but then Emilie and Hildegard came out from beneath the *porte-cochère*, and the bright light from the entrance hall illuminated them quite clearly. They were both fully dressed, wearing dark, elegant suits. They reminded Maggy of the time when they had left the house for her grandfather's funeral – Emilie's father – for they had that same stiff, formal bearing, and her mother was holding a handkerchief up to her mouth.

Maggy could bear it no longer. Rattling at the handle, she pushed the double window open wide.

"Papi!" she called.

Alexander turned, and stared up at her. He looked ashen and ill, and even in the dawn light, Maggy saw that his blue eyes were swimming with tears. He did not speak.

"Papi, what's the matter?"

Maximilian drew him towards the car. Alexander looked back at his wife, said something Maggy could not hear, but the two women stood like statues, implacable, merciless. Maggy grew desperate. Her father was leaving, being taken away, and she had a sudden, agonizing premonition that she might never see him again.

"No!" she screamed through the open window, and scrambling wildly, she climbed up onto the broad stone sill. "Mami, what's *wrong*? I want to know what's happened!"

"Magdalen, get back down immediately!" her grandmother said sharply, though Emilie still stood by wordlessly.

"No, I won't – I want Papi! I want you to let me *out*!" She stood on the sill, holding onto the frame, the early morning breeze making her nightdress billow around her legs. "Papi, make them let me out!"

"Maggy, please –" Her father's voice was strange and weak. "Get down from there, it's dangerous."

"But Papi, I want to talk to you. I want –"

"*Schätzli*."

That was all he said, but she saw how fearful his expression was, and for him, just for him, Maggy obeyed and climbed back down off the sill, though the tears were streaming down her cheeks. And when she looked back out of the window, Alexander was just getting, unsteadily, into the back of the car, and Maximilian shut the door with a solid, final sound.

"Papi?" Maggy said once more, tremulously, as the chauffeur loaded the suitcase into the dark, cavernous boot, and got into the driver's seat, and slipped the car into gear. And drove away.

And Maggy stared down, uncomprehendingly, at her mother and her grandmother, but they seemed to have forgotten her, seemed not to hear her sobbing as they walked slowly back into the house and closed the heavy front door, shutting in the electric light and leaving her with the pale, bleak dawn.

It was another hour before the key turned in the lock, and Frau Kümmerly came into Maggy's bedroom.

"*Müüseli*," she said kindly, seeing the child's tear-streaked face, and drew her to her bosom.

"What happened, Frau Kümmerly?" Maggy tried to draw back a little, but the housekeeper's embrace was hearty. "Where has my father gone? Why did they lock me in?"

"There, there, child," Frau Kümmerly soothed, stroking her hair. "All will be well."

"But what will be well?"

The housekeeper released her. "Now let's get you washed and dressed for church. You'll feel much better after a good breakfast –"

"I don't *want* breakfast!" Exasperated, Maggy pushed her away and ran past her, out of the room. The house was silent now, all the other doors on the first floor were closed. Maggy ran straight to her father's study and threw open the door. It looked as it always did; there were Papi's papers and a Chandler thriller on his walnut desk, nothing offering any clue. Maggy ran out, passed Hildegard's door, and stopped outside her parents' suite. She heard the sound of weeping and, without knocking, she turned the handle.

Emilie Gabriel sat in a chintz-covered armchair. She had removed the dark suit she had worn for her husband's departure, and now wore an eau-de-Nil satin negligée.

"Maggy," she said and, with a rare display of warmth, held out her arms to her daughter. Maggy ran into them, instinctively seeking comfort, but the evidence of her mother's distress made her more afraid than ever. Emilie's eyes were red, and the white lace handkerchief clutched in her right hand was wet with spilled tears.

"Mami, what's the matter?" Maggy looked down and saw that the silver framed photograph taken of her parents on their wedding day lay smashed on the carpet near the armchair. "Where did Papi go?"

The moment of intimacy was over, and Emilie dropped her arms from around Maggy's shoulders in a gesture of helplessness. "He's gone, and that's all there is to it."

The finality in her mother's voice sharpened Maggy's fear. "But where has he gone? And why did you scream, Mami? I heard you, and I heard voices – and I saw that man –"

"What man?"

"The man with red hair." Maggy forced herself to concentrate on pronouncing the name she had memorized because she had thought it such a wonderful name. "Konstantin Ivanovich Zeleyev. Opi's friend."

"How do you know him?" Emilie's tone was suddenly colder.

"I don't, but Opi told me about him. He's from Russia, and I saw him when he came this evening." Maggy flushed just a little, since she knew she was confessing to having spied from the top of the stairs, but that was of no importance now. "And I saw him go away with Maximilian in the night." She paused. "Why did you scream, Mami?"

Emilie dabbed at her red eyes with the handkerchief. "Go and get dressed, Maggy."

Maggy stared at her in disbelief. "But I want to know –"

"You 'want'. A young lady does not 'want', Magdalen," Emilie said stiffly, all the warmth gone now. "I wish to be alone. I've had a very terrible night, and I'm exhausted."

"But Papi –"

"Not another word about your father. Go and get dressed. Frau Kümmerly will take you and Rudi to church this morning."

"But Papi looked ill, and –"

"Not *now*, Magdalen," Emilie almost shouted at her, and burst suddenly into sobbing, the ferocity of which alarmed Maggy so much that she backed away in confusion.

"I'm sorry, Mami," she said, and then with a pang of unexpected pity for her mother, she ran forward again, wanting to comfort her. "Please don't cry. I only –"

"Leave me alone." Emilie's voice came out harshly at her, and her face was abruptly contorted by what seemed to her daughter to be uncompromising dislike. "Get *out*!"

Maggy ran.

The explanation, as presented later to Maggy by her mother and grandmother, was vague, unsatisfactory and even more distressing. It was just before lunch, and Rudi was in the nursery with his nanny, for the grown-ups had decided that there was no need for the four-year-old to be unnecessarily upset. He was much too young to understand and would, in any case, accustom himself in due course to whatever they felt was in his best interests.

"Your father," Emilie told Maggy, "has, through his intemperance, caused a terrible accident."

"What does intemperance mean?" Maggy asked.

"It means that your father is a drunkard." Emilie was calmer now; though the soreness of her eyes still betrayed her, her manner was almost glacial. "Do you understand what a drunkard is?"

"I'm sure she does," Hildegard interceded quickly. She, too, was almost as composed as always, but her face was paler than usual and her broad-fingered, capable hands trembled a little.

"You have witnessed his over-indulgences often enough," Emilie went on, her tone resigned. "Regrettably, your father never showed any genuine consideration for you or for Rudi, any more than he did for his wife or even your grandmother." Emilie's eyes met her daughter's directly. "So there is no point in shielding you from the truth now, Maggy, is there?"

"No, Mami." Maggy waited anxiously.

"The truth is that he has brought disgrace and scandal upon our family, and he has left home for ever."

"No!"

"I'm afraid that is the truth, however unpalatable."

"But he wouldn't!" Maggy's face was chalk white. "He can't have gone – Papi would never leave me!"

"He would, and he has, my dear," Emilie said. "And now you must forget him."

"Never!" Hot tears sprang to Maggy's eyes.

Hildegard stepped in again. "Of course you can't completely forget your father," she said more gently. "But your mother has only given you the facts because we both feel you are a big, brave girl, and we would not wish to lie to you." She paused. "It has been a terrible shock to us all, believe me. Your father is my only son, Maggy – I love him just as you do."

"He's not worthy of love." Emilie's fragile calm was deserting her, and her voice shook with the bitterness of her emotions.

"But I still don't know what *happened*," Maggy cried out. "What accident did he cause? And where has he gone?" She implored them both. "Where did Maximilian take him? I know he didn't want to go – I saw it in his eyes –"

"Where your father has gone is not for you to know," Emilie said sharply, needing to end the matter. Her head was pounding, she felt quite ill. "Alexander Gabriel is a wicked, sinful man –"

"No!" Maggy's voice was shrill with despair. She appealed to her grandmother. "Tell her, Omi – tell her Papi isn't wicked. *She's* wicked to say such things!"

Emilie's right hand itched to slap her daughter's cheek, but she held herself in check. Hildegard stood very straight, swaying slightly but saying nothing.

"You are never to mention your father again in my presence," Emilie said, turning to leave the room. She could not eat lunch – she wondered if she would ever feel able to eat again. "Never, do you hear me?"

"I don't care what you say!" Maggy was crying unconstrainedly now. "I don't *care* what you say Papi did – I don't believe you!"

"Magdalen," Hildegard rebuked her. "Don't speak to your mother so disrespectfully."

"But she's telling lies about Papi – and she made him go away!"

"Our lives will be much improved by his absence," Emilie said, and the icy calm returned.

* * *

Maggy tried in vain to discover the truth, but the servants had been well rehearsed, and neither her brother's nanny nor Frau Kümmerly nor Maximilian would tell her any more than she had already been told. The chauffeur was sympathetic, but he had been in Gründli employ for decades, and his loyalty was absolute.

It was the first anguish of Maggy's life, but there was not a single thing she could do about it. She despised them all, resented bitterly the fact that she was only seven, just a child, to be told nothing but lies and to have no power to demand the truth. She had never thought her father a saintly man. He had been exciting and full of fun and warmth, always laughing with her, cuddling her, loving her. Maggy would never believe, even for an instant, that he could be a wicked man as her mother claimed. But there was no one else in the world who cared what had happened to Papi except perhaps Opi, and Maggy knew without being told that she would not be permitted to visit Amadeus any more. Rudi questioned their father's disappearance, but he had always been Emilie's favourite, her little darling, and at his age, he seemed to care more for what was present in his life, rather than for what was missing.

As Maggy had guessed, with Alexander's departure came an end to her visits to Davos. She felt that she had lost the only two people she had ever truly loved, and the enormity of this injustice and cruelty made her determined to be a constant trial to Emilie. Whereas before, her mischief had stemmed from her natural exuberance, now her stubbornness and disobedience came out of her unhappiness and resentment, and an emotion she had never previously experienced.

Maggy hated her mother.

5

On a warm September morning in 1950, three years after Alexander had left Zurich, Emilie Gabriel, having obtained a divorce on the grounds of desertion, married a wealthy arms dealer named Stefan Julius. At forty-four, Julius was twelve years Emilie's senior, and it was his second marriage, too. They were a perfect match. He was a grey-haired, grey-eyed, distinguished looking man, who suited the Gründlis – for that was how Hildegard and Emilie still thought of themselves – far better than either Amadeus or Alexander ever had. Julius brought even greater prosperity to the Gründli Haus; where previously there had been graciousness and comfort, soon there was luxury and opulence.

Julius had no children by his previous marriage, and so Maggy and Rudi had been the only bridesmaid and page at the wedding in St Peter's Kirche, but though her brother had wholeheartedly enjoyed himself, Maggy had been an unwilling attendant to her mother. She disliked her grey, calculating new stepfather intensely, and Julius disliked her equally in return. He had usurped her Papi's rightful place at the head of the family, and to her great chagrin, as the months passed, it became clear that he had usurped it thoroughly and with masterly control.

"I hate him," she told Rudi.

"Do you?" Her brother, now eight, seemed genuinely surprised. "I like him."

"That's because he brings you presents," she said scornfully.

"And he makes Mami laugh."

This, Maggy was forced to admit, was true. Emilie had, thanks to her new husband, recaptured the frothy, feminine aspects of her personality that she had lost early on in her disappointing marriage to Alexander. She felt fulfilled, secure and infinitely happier, all of which made her a much more pleasant person to live with. Hildegard was glad for her, satisfied with the alliance and gratified that whilst Stefan was bound to make changes, he understood and appreciated the old Gründli values and possessions, and was unlikely to question her place as the matriarch of the house and family. Rudi loved anyone who was kind to him; there was no malice in the boy, and no artifice. Only Maggy continued to be a thorn in her mother's flesh, a discordant stirring through her contented new life.

"Can't you make an effort to be a little nicer to your stepfather?" Emilie asked her daughter, after they had been married for six months. "As it is, you're barely polite to him. He only puts up with it for my sake, and I don't see why he should."

"He doesn't like me," Maggy said mutinously.

"Why should he when you're always so difficult?" Emilie paused, fighting to keep her temper, to remain as patient as possible. "What do you expect of him, Maggy? Of us. What do you want, child?"

"I want to see my father." They had all told her that she would forget Papi, but Maggy had known that she would never forget, and that she would, one day, see him again in spite of them.

"That's impossible," Emilie said wearily.

"Why is it?"

"You know very well why."

"That isn't true." Maggy's turquoise eyes glared defiantly at Emilie. She had not forgiven her mother any more than she had forgotten her father, and the more time went on, the stronger her will became.

"Oh, Maggy," Emilie sighed, "can't you surrender just a little? What's past cannot be changed, no matter how passionately you feel."

Maggy waited a moment. "Then let me at least see my grandfather."

Her mother shook her head. "You never give up, do you? You really are the most exasperating girl."

"If you let me visit Opi, I promise I'll try to behave."

With another child, that might have been dismissed as cunning, but Emilie knew that her eleven-year-old daughter was too honest, too straightforward for that. Maggy was entirely founded on emotions, but extraordinarily determined. Her proposal was logical, the making of a compromise. If they allowed her to see Amadeus, then she would, Emilie truly believed, make at least some degree of effort.

"I'll speak to your stepfather," Emilie said. "But I can't promise you anything."

Her poor relationship with Stefan proved, thereafter, to have one redeeming feature so far as Maggy was concerned. Julius found her such an irksome child that he was only too pleased to have her out of the house as much as possible, and as a consequence, her trips to Davos were reinstated, and the atmosphere in the Gründli Haus relaxed a little.

Amadeus was not quite sixty, but with his white hair and mountain-weathered skin, he looked, to Maggy, a very old man. He had travelled down as far as Landquart to meet the Zurich train, and all the joy he had felt in his heart had been abundantly evident in his face. His blue eyes glinted with emotion, and his big, strong arms wrapped her close, and Maggy had not known such a feeling of warmth and safety for years.

It was in the timber house, on the second evening of the first visit, that Amadeus left Maggy for a moment, sitting on the sun terrace, while he went to answer a knock on the front door. When he returned, he was not alone.

"*Schätzli.*"

The voice brought Maggy jumping to her feet. Her eyes opened wide as saucers and her cheeks flamed with joy. "Papi!"

They both stood very still, staring, and then, after just an instant, Maggy flung herself at Alexander, sobbing with happiness, while Amadeus watched from the doorway, saying nothing.

"Papi, I knew it, I *knew* if I came up here, I would see you! I knew everything would be all right! Oh, Papi, I missed you so *much*!" Weeping all the while, Maggy clung to her father, the words tumbling out of her. "Where have you been? Where did you go? Why did they make you go away? They did make you go, didn't they?"

Alexander held her tightly, feeling her, seeing her, smelling her sweetness, experiencing again the fervour of his daughter's love. No one he had ever known loved with such energy and fierceness and honesty as his Maggy, and the bitter knowledge of what he had thrown away was too great to bear.

All through that evening, she pounded him with torrents of questions about the night he had left home, but Alexander evaded every question and told her nothing, except that he had loved her then, and would always love her with all his heart. And while Amadeus sat and smoked the meerschaum pipe he had lately taken to, watching them thoughtfully, Alexander and Maggy huddled close, and the father told the daughter his old, remembered detective stories, yearning to rekindle lost, happier days, but his voice and manner were changed. He was changed in many ways, Maggy realized; he was so much more sombre and wistful than he had been before, and his eyes were unhappy.

"Why are you so sad, Papi?" she asked him softly.

Alexander smiled. "I'm not – not now, while I have you."

"That's good," she said, and gave him the tenderest of kisses. But he looked altogether different, if she observed him closely – thinner, wearier, with shadows beneath his eyes and hands that often trembled. And she understood, as he continued to evade her questions, that he would not answer her – perhaps not for as long as she was still a child – and she still felt frustrated, but not angry. She could not be angry with her father, she loved him too much for that, and in any case, it didn't matter now, for they were together again.

It was short-lived joy. Though Maggy was staying with Amadeus for six days, Alexander left after only two nights.

"But why must you go, Papi, *why*?" She was weeping again, but now it was with sheerest misery.

"I have no choice, *Schätzli*."

"But I don't understand!" Her grandfather had tried to explain a little to her, had told her that the family believed Alexander to be out of Switzerland, and that there might be trouble for him if they learned he was here. And she had sworn that she would never tell anyone, no matter what, but still her father was going, was leaving her again.

"Don't be unhappy, Maggy," he begged her, his face more drawn than ever. "I can't bear to see you hurt."

"Then stay here!"

"I can't."

"Just one more day, and I promise I won't make a fuss when you go." Her eyes beseeched him. "No one need ever know you –"

"It's impossible, *Schätzli*," he stopped her. "But your grandfather will let me know when you next come to visit, and then I swear to you I'll come to see you again."

"But where will you be, Papi? Where are you going to?" Maggy knew by now that he would not tell her, but she had to ask, needed to do everything in her power to stop him from walking back out into that void, that terribly black, empty, mysterious space in which he hid from their family, for reasons that she might never understand.

But she was still only eleven, and she had no power. Being a child was hateful, a waste of time, of life. When she grew up, she vowed she would seize control of her own destiny.

"When I grow up," she told Alexander just before he left, "I won't have to wait until they say I can come to Davos, and I won't wait for you to come to see me, either – I'll come and live with you, wherever you are – and if you don't tell me where you are, I'll find you anyway!"

Her father bent down and tilted her chin up so that he could look straight into her wonderful eyes. "When you grow up, my little Maggy, you will be a beautiful woman, and many, many men will fall in love with you, and you won't have time for your foolish, wicked old Papi."

"You're *not* wicked, and I'll always have time for you!"

Alexander swallowed down his own tears. "There is no one like you, *Schätzli*, in the whole world." He kissed the top of her golden head. "God bless you and keep you safe."

And they were both lost, in their weeping and in their mutual sorrow, and they held each other tightly, until Amadeus came quietly to tap his son gently on the shoulder, and to tell him that it was time to go.

Maggy went to Davos, after that, during almost every school vacation, and on two occasions, Rudi was allowed to go with her. And they had good times together, for Amadeus was overjoyed to have his grandson there, too, and Rudi was still such a good-natured boy. But he had none of his sister's boldness or audacity; he was tractable and docile, and almost always did as he was told. When Maggy and their grandfather wanted to go skiing, Rudi naturally agreed to go, but when Amadeus planted him beside his sister on the chairlift on the Strela, he grew as white as the snow surrounding them, and trembled visibly all the way. Maggy felt genuine pity for him at the time, and put a protective arm about his shoulders, but afterwards she complained to Amadeus.

"I wish he hadn't come – he's such a weakling."

"That's unkind, Maggy." Amadeus frowned at her through his white eyebrows, grown a little bushier with age. "And unlike you."

"But he doesn't really like it here." Maggy paused. "And besides, when Rudi's here, Papi doesn't come."

Amadeus patted her arm. "I know, *Herzli*, it's hard."

"But why can't he come if Rudi's here? Doesn't Papi trust him?"

Her grandfather hesitated before replying. In truth, Alexander did not have the same faith in his son as in his daughter. Rudi's loyalties, if they were put to the test, would undoubtedly lie firmly with Emilie and Stefan, which was perfectly understandable since the boy hardly remembered his father. Yet it seemed quite wrong to suggest to Maggy that her little brother was in any respect untrustworthy.

"Rudi hasn't seen your father since he was four," he said at last, aware as always that it was vital to speak truthfully to Maggy. "It's not his fault that he doesn't feel about your papa as you do. He's a very open boy, much as you were at his age –"

"I was never like Rudi," Maggy said with mild disgust.

"You were always open and honest, and so is your brother. So much so that the first thing he would do when you got home after seeing your father would be to tell your mother and stepfather. Even if we were to tell him not to say anything, he might easily forget."

Whenever Maggy went alone, however, to the Dischmatal, Alexander did appear within days of her arrival. He never said where he had come from, and he always vanished again just as mysteriously as that first time. And so far as Maggy was concerned, she only felt really alive when she was with Amadeus and Alexander. Down below, in Zurich, she merely existed, and waited.

Though Emilie Julius believed her former husband to be safely out of the country, and had no idea that her daughter saw him periodically in Davos, she was unhappy that Maggy was coming increasingly under the influence of the first of the Gabriel black sheep. Stefan, however, still encouraged the visits and Emilie, happily wed for the first time, intended to do nothing whatever to jeopardize her marriage. If only, she sighed privately, Maggy could be more like her darling Rudi, who was so easy-going, and was perfectly content to stay at home, and who adored his stepfather. . .

Maggy's visit to Davos in the early winter of 1953 proved especially memorable. On the first morning, Alexander arrived at the house carrying, in his arms, a small, wire-haired dachshund bitch.

"Papi, she's beautiful," Maggy breathed, as her father handed the little dog to her. "How old is she?"

"Just six months."

Amadeus was enchanted by her. "Does she have a name?"

"She's called Hexi, apparently, because she has the knack of bewitching people into doing exactly what she wants." Alexander paused. "I've never forgotten Anushka, Papi, and when I saw this little one for sale, I couldn't resist her. I thought she'd be company for you."

"Where did you find her?" Maggy asked quickly, hoping for a chance to catch her father out.

Alexander smiled. "On my travels, *Schätzli*," he said.

Hexi was an instant charmer, stronger, bolder, more extroverted and much more amiable than Anushka had ever been. She was an accomplished thief, snatching slices of ham from the supper table and slippers from beneath their beds with great facility, but when they began to scold her, she fixed her little brown eyes on their faces, and in moments they were smiling.

They were sitting over their lunch two days later, when they heard a knock at the front door. Without a word, Alexander stood up and hurried up the stairs, while Amadeus swiftly cleared away his son's dishes, glass and place setting.

"Opi?" Maggy was unnerved. "What should I do?" she whispered.

"Just be normal – we're alone, you and I, you understand?"

She nodded, and her grandfather went calmly to open the door.

"And about time – I thought you'd died."

Amadeus let out a bellow of laughter and embraced the man standing on the threshold. "Konstantin Ivanovich! I can't believe it!"

"Large as life, *mon ami*."

Maggy stared as the man removed his fur hat. She recognized him easily, for he had scarcely altered. His hair was still red, and his moustache was still fiery and perfectly trimmed. The Russian. The man who'd gone out with her father on that fateful night more than six years ago.

"And who is this charming young lady?" Zeleyev asked, in French, coming into the room in a rush of cold air.

Amadeus closed the front door, shutting out the snow that had just begun to fall. "This is my granddaughter, Magdalen."

Maggy stood up, looking into the friendly, remembered green eyes.

"Can it be?" Zeleyev clapped his cheek. "The girl on the staircase? But she was just a child, and you are truly a young lady." He paused. "How old are you, if it isn't indiscreet to ask?"

"I'm fourteen, Monsieur," Maggy replied with dignity.

"Konstantin!" Alexander came running down the stairs. "*Quelle bonne surprise!*"

"For me too," Zeleyev said, and they, too, hugged warmly. "How have you been, Alexei?" He held him at arm's length and scanned the younger man's face. "Not so good, eh?"

Alexander drew away. "It's not easy." For a moment he flushed darkly, but then he went to Maggy and put his arm around her. "You've been introduced to my daughter?"

"To Magdalena Alexandrovna," Zeleyev said solemnly. "Indeed I have, and it's a very great pleasure."

"Why did you call me that?" Maggy asked.

"It's the way you would be addressed in Russia," he answered. "It is called a patronymic, but the second name simply means that you are the daughter of Alexander. Do you like it?"

"Very much." She paused. "But it's a little long for everyday, isn't it? Most people call me Maggy."

"Then I shall ring the changes, according to my mood," Zeleyev said, "for Maggy is pretty, but not quite suitable enough for a young lady as lovely and intelligent as you."

"Don't try to charm my granddaughter, you old reprobate," Amadeus said, and chuckled.

Zeleyev laughed, too, but Alexander turned away and Maggy, sensing his disquiet, went to him and slipped her hand into his. In spite of the fact that Papi was clearly glad to see the Russian, she sensed that his presence nevertheless disturbed him, and she understood why. That night. He disturbed her, too, in a way, and yet she felt excited, for at last she saw a way to discover what had led up to her father's unexplained exile.

She waited three days, having learned enough about the secretive ways of adults to realize that an approach either too direct, or too swift, might just fasten the lid even more tightly on the six-year-old mystery. They got along wonderfully well, she and Zeleyev. Many friends of her mother and stepfather had complimented her on her golden hair, or on the colour of her eyes, and she realized that flattery was often not terribly sincere; but the Russian had a way of looking at her that made her aware that he meant what he said, that he found her special, that he liked her as an individual. And though Maggy had never met anybody like him before, with his oddly fastidious ways and his sudden eruptions of humour or temper or other emotion, she knew with certainty that she liked him too.

Her opportunity arose one afternoon when they went, together, down into Davos Platz. Zeleyev wanted to buy a new comb, for his had broken the previous night, and he would not rest until he had found a replacement. Any comb would not, of course, do for him; it was vital that it be a particular English make, and if he could not find it here, then he would not hesitate to go all the way to Zurich. Amadeus and Alexander had gone out for a day's skiing, but since Maggy was feeling unusually out of sorts, she had stayed indoors in the morning, before deciding to go out with Zeleyev.

Thankfully, they found the Kent comb he wanted in the second *Drogerie* they tried and, with plenty of time to spare before the evening, found a table in Café Schneider. Zeleyev brought a selection of chocolate-topped *Mohrenköpfe* and sugar-dusted doughnuts from the counter at the front of the shop, and for several moments they sat in companionable silence, the Russian eating two cakes with relish while Maggy nibbled at a doughnut and sipped her hot tea.

Zeleyev spoke first. "When will it begin?"

"When will what begin?"

"The inquisition." Zeleyev smiled at her. "I've been waiting for days. You have been very patient." He saw her flush. "Don't be embarrassed, *ma chère*. It's simply that I observed the glint of determination in your eyes when you first decided to tackle me."

Maggy looked at him. "You mean about Papi."

"Of course."

"It's only that –" She stopped, and bit her lip.

"Go on."

"It's just that I love him so much, and I can't bear not knowing – not being able to help him."

"You help by loving him," Zeleyev said.

"But that's not enough." Maggy kept her voice low, though the table beside them was unoccupied. "He should be able to come home."

"Your parents are divorced, Maggy."

"Then he should at least be able to live in Zurich. I don't even know where my own father lives." She took a deep breath. "And he's so afraid. You should have seen him when you knocked at the door when you arrived. His face went quite white, and he ran upstairs as if –"

"As if?"

"Almost as if he were going to be arrested or something." She paused. "And I'm sure he's done nothing to be ashamed of. He wouldn't. He *couldn't*."

Zeleyev leaned closer. "No one is going to arrest your papa. So long as he's careful, everything will be all right."

"But why does he have to be careful? I don't understand. I need to know what happened that night. You went out with him – you must know."

"There's nothing I can tell you, Maggy," Zeleyev said

gently. "Your father is the only person who can –"

"But he won't!" she interrupted, forgetting for a moment to speak quietly. "And how can I help him if I don't understand? My mother said that Papi caused an accident, that he was a drunkard, that he had brought shame and scandal to our family. But I knew she was lying, that it couldn't be true." She remembered every word that Emilie had said, and the burning, aching misery that every single syllable had caused her.

"Are you sure you're being fair to your mother, Maggy?"

"She said such awful things about him. Even if there was some kind of accident, even if Papi was drinking –" She paused, waiting for Zeleyev to speak, but he said nothing at all. "My father is a good man," she persisted. "A kind man. Look at the way he brought Hexi for Opi because he knew he must be lonely."

"That was a kindness."

"I think it may be a terrible injustice, like what happened to Captain Dreyfus." Maggy had listened attentively at school when they had learned about the Dreyfus case, had held fast to the fact of the captain's eventual exoneration, dreaming about a time when her family would have to beg her father's forgiveness.

"I sympathize with you," Zeleyev said, "more than you can possibly realize, but –"

"Then please just tell me. You were with him. And you were in our house in the middle of that night. I saw you – I saw Maximilian driving you away."

"You must understand that this is your father's private affair. I don't have the right to tell you anything. When he considers that it's time for you to know, I don't doubt he will tell you himself."

"But he still thinks I'm too young."

"Maybe he does. Maybe you just have to be patient, *ma chère*, and think about what matters most."

"What is that?"

"That you are together, right now – you and your Papi and grandfather, up here in this wonderful place."

"And you."

He smiled. "Yes indeed." He reached for her hand and gently squeezed it. "You must learn, in life, to live for the moment, Magdalena Alexandrovna. You still have your father, in spite of the others, and you are proud of each other. No one can take that away from you."

Maggy did not speak. She felt suddenly very drained, as if all her energy had been spent in her appeal, and now, since she still found herself in the same state of elongated suspense that she had been in for years, she had no more strength to fight. Tiredly, she excused herself from the table, and went down the stairs to the cloakroom, but by the time she returned, the lethargy had been replaced by a mixture of agitation, excitement and fear.

Zeleyev stood politely, but she did not sit down.

"Shall we go?" he asked.

"Please." Her face was very pale, with two spots of colour bright on her cheeks. "But –" She stopped.

"What is it, *ma petite*?" Zeleyev frowned. "Are you ill?"

"No," she said. "At least, I don't think so."

Without another word, Zeleyev paid their waitress, took Maggy's arm and guided her out into the street. The fresh, cold air revived her, but her agitation remained.

"Shall we take a sleigh?" He enjoyed the jangling sounds and horse smells of the *Pferdeschlitten*, which reminded him of the troikas at home in the old days.

Maggy looked around furtively. "I need to –"

"What is it you need? Is there something you want to buy?"

"Yes," she nodded. "At the *Apotheke*."

"By all means." He still held her arm, and turned her about in the direction of the nearest chemist, but Maggy stiffened and did not move. He looked down into her face. "Something is wrong, *n'est-ce pas*? Are you sure you're not ill? Do you feel sick?"

She shook her head, and her cheeks became suffused with hot colour. "I'm not ill, but –" She stared at the white, snowy ground, suddenly agonized with embarrassment. "I'm afraid to walk far," she said haltingly.

"But why?"

Maggy's desperation magnified. She would not have told him for the world under normal circumstances, but there *was* no one else, and so, since it must be better to humiliate herself before one man than before a whole townful of strangers, she stood on tiptoe and whispered in his ear:

"I'm bleeding."

For just a fleeting instant, Zeleyev looked confused, and then he understood. Comprehending her embarrassment he, too, bent his head and spoke in a hushed voice. "Is it your first, Maggy?"

She nodded, her face still aflame. She knew so little about this, except that most of her contemporaries at school had already begun, and that they all seemed to know everything because their mothers had prepared them. Emilie had never said a word, and now suddenly, in the middle of the street –

"Come, *ma petite*." Zeleyev was taking control, hailing a passing sleigh. "You climb up and cover yourself with the rug." He helped her, and addressed the driver. "Please wait a few moments – I have something I need to purchase."

Within a matter of minutes, he was already hurrying towards the waiting sleigh, a paper bag in one gloved hand, and he got up beside her. "All right?" She nodded gratefully. "Then let's go home."

By the time they got back to the timber house, Maggy could feel the warmth trickling down her thighs. She almost always wore trousers up here, but just today she'd put on a wool tartan skirt and the matching hat her mother had bought her in Zurich a week or two earlier. After she'd seen the blood that had seeped right through her panties and thick wool tights, she had been terrified that she might stain the snow in the street, and then she would certainly have died of shame.

Zeleyev was magnificent. Quickly he went upstairs and ran a warm bath for her, putting in a little of his own favourite bergamot oil – something he would not ordinarily have shared with anyone. And then he gave her the bag from the *Apotheke* and quietly, gently but clearly, told her what to do with the contents.

"And after that, you simply change it whenever you need to," he finished. "Now go on and have your bath, *ma chère*, and when you're finished, we will have a little celebration before the others return."

Maggy was calmer now, but still awkward. "What will we celebrate?"

Tenderly, Zeleyev patted her golden hair. "Your womanhood," he said. "I am honoured to have been part of it."

Maggy felt an intense closeness to the Russian after that day. He had been so kind and helpful, and so wonderfully matter-of-fact, explaining to her the miracles of her ovaries and womb in such a way that he sounded almost envious of her creative potential. He had comforted her, had lent her his fluffy towelling bathrobe, and had held her close, soothing away the tribulations of her day. And afterwards, he had not once referred to the episode again, and for that Maggy was almost more grateful than for anything. Konstantin Ivanovich Zeleyev was certainly a man to be trusted with any secret; he had proved that beyond doubt by refusing to betray Alexander's confidence even to her.

Two days on into their holiday, yet another remarkable event occurred. It was a beautiful, sunny morning, and they had all breakfasted together at a table on the sun terrace, when Amadeus stood up.

"I think the time has come, Alexander," he said, "to show your daughter *Eternité*." He paused. "Do you both agree?"

"How could I not?" said Alexander.

"Konstantin?"

Zeleyev's smile was a little wry. "You know, even after all these years, *mon ami*, that if it were my decision I would show it to the world. But as it is, there is no one I would rather have see our treasure than Maggy."

"Treasure?" Maggy looked up at her grandfather curiously.

"Buried treasure," Alexander said, and laughed.

They put on their boots and walked around the house to the back, and into the old stables. Amadeus's hens, brought inside for the winter, pecked around in their enclosure, cackling as Amadeus approached the hayloft.

"Here?" Maggy said.

"Just wait, *Schätzli*," Alexander said, as her grandfather and Zeleyev used pitchforks to pull down the bales at the front. "Let me go up, Papi."

Alexander climbed the ladder, removing the last bale and the loose straw that filled up the spare space in the hiding place, and then he reached in and withdrew the sculpture.

"Here it is," he said softly, and passed it carefully down to Amadeus.

Just as her father had done, more than twenty years earlier, Maggy gasped with wonder, and her eyes grew immense.

"Well?" Zeleyev's voice nudged her.

"It's the waterfall, isn't it? The one just across the valley," she breathed, staring at it, longing to touch it, yet afraid she might damage it. "The one that sparkles even in the dark."

"That's right," Amadeus said, touched beyond words that she had looked beyond the gold and the jewels to see what they represented. "We called it *Eternité*."

"Where did it come from?" she asked.

"We made it," Amadeus replied.

She looked up in disbelief. "You?"

"Konstantin and I. More he than I, in truth."

"Really?" Her eyes darted to Zeleyev for confirmation. "When did you make it?"

"We began in 1926," Zeleyev said, his voice a little dreamy with memory. "And it was finished five years later. I lived here in those days, with your grandfather and Anushka."

"Irina's dachshund," Maggy said. "The one you helped to bury, Papi." Her father and Amadeus had often spoken of those old days to her, though always with cautious moderation, remembering Maggy's mother and, of course, Hildegard. It had been a fine line to tread, especially for Amadeus, who had wished to be honest and open with his granddaughter, but who had been aware that a young child might blurt out stories told to her, and might then risk offending the family she lived with or, worse still, risk having her visits to the mountains banned again.

Now, however, Maggy was fourteen, and mature for her years, with the kind of common sense and self-reliance rare in a child still living in the confines of family. Even now, at eleven, Rudi lagged light years behind his sister, not in intellect but in practical, everyday qualities such as courage, ambition and energy. Neither Amadeus nor Alexander would have considered it safe to show *Eternité* to Rudi, but as Amadeus impressed on Maggy that no one else must ever learn of the existence of the sculpture – for they were bound to see only its monetary value, not its true worth – he knew, just by looking into his granddaughter's wide, exquisite eyes, that he could trust Maggy with his life.

"Tell me more about Irina," she begged him, once she had heard the tale of the Malinskaya gems. "Tell me how you loved her."

"I loved Irina," Amadeus began slowly, "with every particle of my soul." He smiled wistfully. "In truth, I think I worshipped her, which in many cases may not be a wise way to love, but Irina gave back even more than I could give to her, and made me believe that I, too, was worshipped."

Though he had frequently spoken of Irina, he had seldom talked openly of the intensity of their love affair. Now, with Zeleyev and Alexander at his side, and Maggy at his feet, he began to talk frankly, and once he had begun, it was as if he had unlocked his half-frozen heart, and all the love, all the adoration and pain and grief, poured out of him, like the shimmering cascade of Irina's waterfall.

Maggy had never heard a more romantic, more tragic, more glorious tale, had never seen anything lovelier and more touching than the sculpture the two men had created in Irina's honour.

"Perhaps," she ventured, once, "if you had explained it all to Omi, she might have understood better." It had always wounded her to hear Amadeus described as the *schwarzes Schaf*.

It was Alexander who answered her. "If my mother had realized what they were doing with the jewels, or that for five years, two men had virtually cut themselves off from the rest of the world, putting their life and soul and earning capacity into producing a work of art, simply for love – I think she might have tried to have my father committed to an asylum, Maggy."

"Maybe she and Emilie still would," Zeleyev interjected quietly.

"I will never tell them," Maggy said stoutly. "Never."

"We know that, *Schätzli*," Alexander said. "Or Opi would not have taken you into his confidence."

Maggy turned her attention to Zeleyev. "Tell me more about the old days in Russia, when you and she were friends – and about Fabergé and the Imperial Easter eggs –"

Transfixed, she listened for hours, Hexi snuggling on her lap, with the three men she had grown to regard as her only true family, and she became increasingly fascinated by Irina Valentinovna, and by the glow that still, after thirty years, came over Amadeus and Zeleyev when they spoke of her. And Zeleyev told endless stories of the St Petersburg of his youth – and then, when these were almost exhausted, he spoke of the years that had followed, the years he had spent in Paris, and Geneva, and the months he had stayed in London and Berlin and Amsterdam, all the great cities of Europe in which craftsmen and dealers and collectors traded in precious metals and jewels, and *objets de fantaisie*. . .

"Paris is the greatest of them all," he told his audience. "As Hugo says, 'Paris is the ceiling of the human race'. In Paris one can feel oneself in love even if one is quite alone."

"Is that where you live now?" Maggy asked him.

"Alas, no," Zeleyev said with regret. "I must live where the very best work is, and at present that is in Geneva, though there is nothing – and I fear there never will be anything – that I can do to equal what we achieved here, in this little house."

As always, when Maggy was in her grandfather's home, she was encouraged to sing in precisely the manner that was absolutely discouraged in the Gründli Haus, and Zeleyev taught her a favourite song of his, 'La Vie en rose' and, loving it instantly, Maggy memorized it swiftly, for her aptitude for learning music and lyrics was vastly superior to her aptitude for learning at school where, more often than not, she was bored. And even though she was still so young, her rich, gently husky voice captivated the three men and caused the pale, red-gold hairs on Zeleyev's arms to rise.

"See what you have done." He showed her, making her giggle. "That is the sign of a great performer, Maggy. Ah, you may laugh and be embarrassed, *ma chère*, but my instincts are sound."

"Do you think I really could become a singer?" she asked, suddenly shy.

"You are a singer already," Zeleyev said confidently. "But with training of the right kind, and with hard work, you could bring audiences to their feet." He paused and looked at Amadeus. "You know, *mon ami*, she reminds me sometimes, in spirit, of our Irina Valentinovna – you never knew her when she was young and still blooming with health. They share the same freeness of soul."

Alexander embraced his daughter, saying nothing, and Maggy pressed against him, savouring his closeness, even as she felt the strange, sad trembling in his body, painfully aware that within days, perhaps even hours, they would be apart again.

"Paris," Zeleyev went on, dreamily. "You must go there, Maggy, some day, just as she did. It's a city that makes even ugly things shine. They understand beauty there, and talent – they invented *joie de vivre*. If you go to Paris, Magdalena Alexandrovna, I think that you will dazzle."

She believed him.

6

In the two years that followed, Maggy made numerous visits to the Dischmatal, and they were almost always happy, precious times, and Alexander kept faith with his father and daughter. But Maggy never learned the truth of what had happened on the night he had left Zurich, and as time passed, she ceased to care as intensely, for she still had her father, and their private, secret life together, and that, after all, was all that really mattered.

In the winter of 1955, however, when Maggy was just sixteen, the snows fell heavily and relentlessly above Davos, and the road that led up to the old timber house became blocked. In Zurich, Maggy, Rudi, Hildegard and Stefan had all caught influenza, and though Maggy was already quite recovered, Emilie would not consider allowing her to visit her grandfather until the weather calmed, and the whole family was well again.

Maggy felt like a caged creature, trapped in the Gründli Haus, smothered by a prevailing odour of *Kamillentee* and eucalyptus oil. She fretted over her grandfather, who had seemed quite ill himself when she had last seen him, and she fretted over the missed opportunity of spending time with her father. She had hoped to be with them for Christmas this year, had hoped to escape the formal festivities at home, but since her mother and Frau Kümmerly were depending on her to help with looking after Rudi and her grandmother, so that Emilie could devote herself more fully to her husband, it would be a miracle if she got up to Davos before the new year.

Amadeus was aware that this was his last winter. He was only sixty-four years old, but in the past few months he had begun to feel like an old, old man. He knew the cause of his sickness, of his weakness – had known it for a long time. He looked into the mirror in the bathroom he had first installed for Irina, and he saw the dullness of his eyes, and the unnatural flush on his cheeks, and he had seen it all before, more than thirty years ago.

Maggy had asked him months ago, hearing him coughing and spitting in the night, if he had consulted a doctor. Her expression had been so sweet, so concerned, and he had told her yes, of course, and that there was nothing for her to worry about. But he had lied to her, for he had needed no confirming diagnosis, and he had no intention of seeking any of the antibiotic drug treatments that had not been available in Irina's time. Life had been good to him on the whole; he had been much luckier than he had deserved to be. But the zenith of Amadeus Gabriel's existence – the greatest joy, the deepest sorrow, the only time when he had felt a true awareness of his heart and soul and identity – had been encapsulated in just two years. Two brief, eternal years.

He was ready to die. Yet still he hung on, waiting, hoping to hear news of Maggy's next visit, so that he could send word to Alexander, for he wanted to take his leave of them properly, gently, lovingly.

But the snows continued to fall. And down in Zurich, in the sombre old house on Aurora Strasse, the *Grippe*, having relaxed its hold on Hildegard, Stefan and Rudi, now concentrated itself on Emilie and Frau Kümmerly, making it more impossible than ever for Maggy to leave.

The news of Amadeus's death reached Zurich in the first

week of February, but though the roads were by now completely passable, and though the inhabitants of the Gründli Haus were all now fully recovered, Stefan and Emilie forbade Maggy to attend the funeral.

"Of course I must go!" Maggy was stunned.

"I'm afraid not," Emilie said, not unkindly. "It would not be proper."

"How can it not be proper? He was my grandfather!"

Maggy was beside herself with outrage, grief and fear. She had felt immediate anguish at her loss when she had first been handed the letter from Frau Kranzler, who had managed the Gabriel shop in Davos for over fifteen years; but her sorrow had been almost engulfed by the shocking realization that her one sure link with her father had died along with Amadeus.

"If it hadn't been for you, I would have been with him when he needed me," she flung at her mother and stepfather now.

"You were needed here," Julius pointed out. "Your mother needed you."

"She's never needed me."

"That's certainly not true." Emilie spoke with dignity, while Stefan grew red with the anger his stepdaughter invariably provoked in him. "You have often enough made it clear that you preferred that man's company to that of your family. You cannot simply turn the truth around to suit yourself."

"But Opi was family too!" Maggy protested. "And you let him die all alone."

"We didn't know that he was dying," Emilie said stiffly. "And besides, he chose his way a long time ago."

Maggy fought to calm herself, conscious that anger would not win this battle. "But you let me visit him so often – you even let Rudi go sometimes. Why not now, of all times?" she appealed more gently. "It's completely correct that I should be there. I don't understand."

"Haven't you considered your grandmother?" Julius asked.

"She doesn't mind."

"She most certainly does."

"Why?" Maggy's confusion was genuine. "Why now, after so long – when he's gone?"

It was her mother who replied. "Because he is to be buried beside her." Her voice was harsh. "Beside his mistress."

"Beside Irina? Of course," Maggy said.

"Don't speak her name in this house," her stepfather snapped.

"Why should you care?"

"Because I care for your mother, and for your grandmother, and for what your family stood for before it was sullied by Gabriel and his son."

For once, the grey man, as Maggy had always thought of him, addressed her with something approaching true feeling. Julius had never feigned any care for her, and his frequent anger with her usually manifested itself in short bursts of irritation, followed by cool disregard. Yet now Maggy heard pride in his voice, and saw it in his grey eyes, and she understood, with a pang of surprise, that he did love her mother and that, more importantly perhaps, he respected her. And she realized that any more discussion or argument would be futile, for Stefan had no such respect for her, and never would have, and neither he nor Emilie would agree to allow her to attend the funeral. For whilst it had been vaguely acceptable for Maggy to have had some contact with the old black sheep during his life, good Gründli–Julius taste had prevailed, and the decision had been made. That enough was enough.

Amadeus was laid to rest three days later, while Maggy, watched over zealously, at school by her teachers and at home by the family or by Maximilian and Frau Kümmerly, mourned silently and kept her grievances and fears strictly to herself. She had no intention of surrendering, of being denied her farewell. She was sixteen now, no longer a child with no alternative but to have her life ruled by others. They would drop their guard after the funeral, and then she would seize her chance. She would go to Davos, would visit her grandfather's grave, would see the house again. And somehow, she would be there when her father came, for she realized that he, too, could not have been there for the funeral. It was possible that Alexander did not even know that Amadeus had died; if he did know, he would come, as Maggy would, when it was over, when it was safe.

She slipped away from school at midday six days after the funeral, took a tram to the Hauptbahnhof, caught the first train to Landquart, changed to the alpine railway and arrived in the Dorf as the first skiers were returning from the slopes. She had visited the little *Friedhof* with Amadeus in the past, when he had shown her Irina's grave next to her sister's, and now she retraced their old steps through the walled cemetery, seeking them all. Dusk was already settling over the mountains, casting an eerie, mauvish tinge over the snowy, silent place, but Maggy knew that she could not risk waiting till morning, for Stefan and Emilie might already have learned that she had left school without permission.

Their headstones were separated by just a few feet, and Maggy saw that someone had cleared the piled snow from the top of Irina's memorial stone when Amadeus's had been erected, for now the covering on each was quite level and lower than on those close by, adding to the impression of unity, and Maggy fancied that the lovers lay close enough to stretch out their arms, beneath the good Swiss earth, and to link hands.

She looked at the simple engraving on her grandfather's stone.

RUHE IN FRIEDEN

"I'll come again," she said softly, "with flowers."

But for now, she had too little time, and so she hurried back down into the Dorf, and went to the shop in the Promenade, looking for Frau Kranzler, who had always been pleasant to her, and kind to Amadeus. The door was bolted, the windows shuttered, and a small, black-bordered notice informed customers of the demise of the proprietor.

She found Frau Kranzler at her home on Tschuggenstrasse, her salt-and-pepper hair hidden beneath a headscarf, her usually smart appearance made dull and ordinary by an ugly, floral pinafore. She was pink-faced from putting her house in order, her employer's death having given her an earlier-than-normal opportunity to commence her spring-cleaning. She embraced Maggy, invited her inside and made tea.

"Herr Gabriel died in his sleep," Frau Kranzler told her. "I found him, after I had not heard from him for more than a day. Your grandfather did not always come to the shop, as you know. I told him to have a telephone installed, but he never wanted it. I visited him most days, when he was unwell, or he gave the postman messages for me."

"Did he suffer much?"

"Not so very much," Frau Kranzler said gently. "The doctor told me that his heart just stopped." She paused. "He spoke of you constantly."

Maggy's face felt stiff. "They wouldn't let me come."

"I know. The influenza." Frau Kranzler paused again. "He understood."

Maggy finished her tea as quickly as she could. She wanted, more than anything, to ask about her father, but so far as she was aware, the manageress had not known about Alexander's visits. Maggy supposed that Frau Kranzler probably disapproved of her family for staying away from the sick, old man, and it was possible that if Maggy had confided in her, she might have been sympathetic, but it was too great a risk to take.

"Where's Hexi?" she asked. "I thought you might have her."

"The Meiers took her. It seems Herr Gabriel made the arrangement some months ago." The Meiers were a farming family living a little further down the valley.

"Is the house locked up, like the shop?" Maggy asked.

"*Ja ja.*" Frau Kranzler nodded. "Herr Walther, the lawyer, has the keys. He has his office on Obere Strasse, in the Platz." She rose from her chair. "Would you like me to telephone him for you?"

"No," Maggy said quickly. "Thank you, but it's late. I'd rather wait till morning."

"Of course. Where will you be staying tonight?"

"At the Belvedere," Maggy lied, and then asked, casually: "Did anyone come to see my grandfather in the last few weeks, Frau Kranzler?" Her heart beat faster.

"Not since November." Frau Kranzler pursed her lips. "I believe his foreign friend came for one week then. Monsieur Zeleyev."

"No one since then?" Maggy's mouth was dry, in spite of the tea.

"Who else could there be?" The woman was gentle again. "He had only you." She paused. "And his memories."

Maggy left in the taxi that Frau Kranzler insisted on calling to take her to the Belvedere Hotel, but as soon as they were out of sight, Maggy told the driver to take her up Dischmastrasse instead. She knew there would be no point in approaching the lawyer for the keys, for he would certainly have called Zurich for permission before handing them over. In any case, she wanted to be alone there for a while, private.

She paid the driver, and walked the last few hundred yards, enjoying the tug of the deep snow on her boots. The night sky was crystal clear, sprinkled with stars; a new crescent moon soared high over the Jakobshorn, the air was pure, icy and silent. Maggy looked straight ahead and saw the house. Always so welcoming, now it looked like a dead shell, its windows black, its chimney smokeless.

She broke a side window, knocked away the shards of glass and climbed over the sill into the living room. Even in the pitch darkness, the house was full of Amadeus. The old, familiar smells: his pipe, wood smoke, a tinge of his favourite schnapps, his soap in the bathroom. The electricity supply had been cut off, so Maggy found a candle in the sideboard and lit it. She roamed around, looking, touching, remembering. For a little while she stood out on the terrace that Amadeus had built for Irina more than thirty years before, and then she came back inside and sat down in the chair that Alexander had generally used during his visits, and Maggy closed her eyes and prayed for an instant miracle, prayed that her father would come, right now, as he had always come when she had been there, as if her grandfather, the wizard, had lifted a wand and summoned him. But the wizard was gone, and Maggy knew that there would be no miracle, that the time for magic had gone with Amadeus, leaving her alone.

His possessions were all around her, such as they were, for Opi had never been a man to whom material things had been important. The cheap Hodler print on one wall, the pipe rack carved by a local craftsman, and the photographs: one of Irina wrapped in her sable coat, another of her, arms linked with Amadeus on the Parsenn, looking like any settled, contented married couple, one of Alexander, holding a two-year-old Maggy, and one of Zeleyev, beautifully turned out in a silk smoking jacket.

Maggy climbed the wooden stairs, went into her old room and lay on her bed for a few minutes, burying her face in the soft quilt, inhaling the whiff of security and happiness she had always felt up here in this house, and then she took the candle and went back downstairs, and outside, and she walked around to the stables at the back.

It was the first time that she had thought about *Eternité*.

Carefully, she dripped wax onto some floorboards, and stuck the candle firmly down, before turning to the hay-loft. It looked as it had always done. Grasping a pitchfork, she climbed the ladder and speared several of the old, mouldering bales, until she came to the cache itself. Trembling with the physical effort as well as the sudden anticipation, she pulled away the straw padding, and peered into the hiding place.

The sculpture was not there. In its place, weighted down by a large stone, was a folded piece of paper. Maggy climbed back down and took it to the candle light, crouching on the ground to look at it. It was a note, written in her father's hand, and very brief.

I will let Zeleyev know where to reach me. Tell no one. God bless you, my darling Schätzli. Trust me.

Maggy read it three times, then burned the precious scrap of paper in the candle's flame, her heart pounding. As quickly as she could manage, moving mechanically, she climbed the ladder again, packing the straw back into place and heaving each bale back up again with the pitch-fork, and then she came down, picked up the candle and scraped away the solidified wax at its base. The hayloft looked as if no one had touched it. Maggy went back round to the front of the house and let herself inside. And then she went upstairs again, this time to her grandfather's bedroom, and she lay down on his bed, felt his closeness and warmth wrapping itself about her for the last time. And wept herself to sleep.

The lawyer, Herr Walther, woke her just after eight in the morning, after a troubled night in which he had been roused from his bed by a call from Stefan Julius, commanded to find Maggy as rapidly as possible and to escort her back to Zurich himself.

"You told Frau Kranzler that you were staying at the Belvedere," he said mildly, somewhat impressed, in spite of himself, by this lovely, tousled young girl who had been bold enough to break into this house, all by herself in the dead of night.

"I'm sorry for your inconvenience," she said, docilely.

"I'll have to arrange for the window to be boarded up."

"Would you like me to do it?" Maggy offered.

"I think I had better get you back home," Walther said. "Are you ready?" He glanced at his wristwatch. "If you're hungry, we might take a bite of breakfast first, perhaps at Café Weber?"

"You're very kind." Maggy hesitated. "What I would like, if you don't mind, is to see my grandfather's dog before I leave. Frau Kranzler said that she's at the Meier farmhouse."

Seeing no harm in it, the lawyer drove her, with quiet courtesy, to the farm and waited for her in the car.

Maggy found Frau Meier and Hexi in the kitchen, the door wide open and the dachshund tied to a table leg. Seeing Maggy, the animal went into an ecstasy of joyous, high-pitched barking and frantic tail wagging, and the plump, grey-haired woman rose quickly to her feet, wiping her floury hands on her apron.

"*Grüezi mitenand, Fröili Gabriel*," she said, having to raise her voice above Hexi's persistent yapping. They had seen one another once or twice over the years. "Frau Kranzler told me you might come."

They shook hands, and Maggy turned her attention to the dachshund, quivering from head to tail with excitement, and still barking unceasingly. "It's very kind of you to have taken her in," Maggy said, untying the cord attached to Hexi's collar.

"It was the least we could do." Frau Meier looked at Maggy dubiously. "Don't let her loose, whatever you do."

"Why not?" Maggy picked the dog up. "Has she been any trouble?"

"Trouble is not the word, Fröili." Frau Meier's round cheeks were rosy and her dark eyes bright with wry amusement. "The creature's impossible, always barking or whining, night and day, nipping at the cows and terrifying the chickens. It's a great relief you've come for her – I don't know how much longer Herr Meier could have stood it."

Maggy hesitated only briefly. There had never been an animal of any kind in the Gründli Haus, and she knew perfectly well that Opi's dog would be less welcome than most, but the prospect of poor Hexi spending her life tied up –

The lawyer, waiting patiently outside, looked surprised.

"Do you mind, Herr Walther?" Maggy smiled at him. "I'll hold her on my lap."

Looking into her turquoise eyes, Herr Walther found that, despite the leather seats in his three-month-old car, he didn't mind at all, though he wondered if Stefan Julius would be as accommodating. "Are you taking her home with you then, Fräulein?"

Maggy climbed into the car, Hexi snuggled close to her chest. "I'm taking her to Zurich," she said, and realized, with a stabbing of sorrow, that she could not call the house on Aurora Strasse home. Home was the old timber house in the Dischmatal, which she knew she had just left behind for ever.

* * *

It was the dachshund who inadvertently triggered the final explosion in the Gründli Haus. Neither Hildegard nor Emilie wanted a dog in their lovingly preserved house, but it was Stefan who was the most vehement. If he had ever wanted a dog at all, he said darkly, it would have been a real dog, not a spoiled, sausage-shaped creature with bandy legs. Hexi did nothing to further her cause. On her first night, she urinated on the creamy Aubusson carpet in Emilie's dressing room. On her first morning, she vomited in Hildegard's bathroom, and on that same afternoon, she nipped Rudi on his ankle.

"Why did she do that?" Rudi asked, his astonishment more acute than his physical discomfort. Maggy's brother was utterly unaccustomed to being treated harshly or unkindly by anyone, except perhaps by Maggy herself, who had never lost her prejudice against him for his lack of support for Alexander and his unswerving loyalty to Stefan.

The storm erupted a little over an hour later, soon after Emilie and Stefan, returning from a business luncheon at the Dolder Grand, heard from Frau Kümmerly about the latest incident. Maggy was out in the back garden, attempting to persuade Hexi to use the flower beds in preference to either the perfect lawns or the pristine carpets inside.

"Magdalen!"

She heard her stepfather's voice, and knew right away that Rudi had been telling tales. Anger and irritation began to simmer in her, and she called Hexi to her side – in vain, for the dachshund was bent upon exploring the barren, cut-back rose bushes.

"Get that damned animal away from there and come to the library immediately!"

They were all there, waiting for her, her grandmother, too, and her brother, looking wretched but sitting still and obedient just the same. Her line of accusers, Maggy thought, and the anger bubbled higher.

"Where is the little beast?" Julius asked her.

"In my bedroom."

"Is the door locked?"

"She's only twenty centimetres high," Maggy said defiantly. "She can't reach door handles."

"You see?" Julius turned to his wife. "All I get from her is cheek and more cheek, and you ask me to put up with it."

"Maggy," Emilie began. "You must understand –"

"Of course she understands!" Julius snapped. "She's not a fool, she understood perfectly well that she was forbidden to go to Davos, and she knew very well the reasons we forbade her, but still she went. She's always been an impossible child –"

"I'm not a child." Maggy could not help herself.

"Then that makes it worse, for you've proved that you're deceitful, too, that you cannot be trusted."

"Stefan, don't upset yourself," Emilie tried to intervene.

"There's no real harm done," Hildegard pointed out reasonably.

She had been disturbed, it was true, by her granddaughter's defection at such a sensitive moment, but then again, had it not been for Stefan's perhaps overly adamant support for Hildegard before the funeral, she might have talked it through with Maggy and relented. Now she feared the matter had grown out of all proportion, and she sensed a dangerous turbulence in the normally becalmed atmosphere of the house.

"No *harm*?" Julius seldom shouted, but he was no longer prepared to leave the discipline of his stepdaughter to her mother. "The girl lied, deceived and, may I remind you, broke the law. If Peter Walther had not taken care of things, the police might have been called in."

"But they weren't," Emilie said.

"And then she brings us that *ridiculous* creature with no more self-control than its master had – and if all these things were not enough, the little beast attacks Rudi for no reason!"

"It was nothing." Rudi spoke for the first time.

"It bit you."

"Just a nip," the boy said. "Truly, Father, it was just a tiny nip."

Maggy turned on him. "If it was so tiny, why did you tell them?"

"I didn't."

"Then how did they know?" she accused. "From Hexi?"

Emilie defended her son. "Frau Kümmerly told us, as it happens, not that it makes any difference."

"And why did he have to go crying to her?" Maggy said in disgust. "He's fourteen now – he still acts like a baby."

"How dare you criticize your brother!" Julius thundered. "Just because he understands simple courtesy, basic decent behaviour –"

"So do I," Maggy countered.

"Good. Then you'll understand that there's nothing more to be said about the animal."

"What do you mean?"

Julius ignored her. "Emilie, if you find the number of a veterinary surgeon, I will telephone right away – Maximilian can take it to him."

Emilie looked at the clock. "It's too late today."

"For what?" Maggy's voice was strained.

"Very well then," Julius said. "First thing tomorrow morning."

"For *what*?" There was a tight, painful knot in Maggy's stomach.

"An injection." Julius spoke coolly now. "I believe that is what is done. Quite painless, I'm sure."

"You want to kill Hexi?" Maggy had known immediately what her stepfather had intended, but she had been unwilling to believe it. "For one small mistake?"

"Father, please –" Rudi had grown pale. "I expect I frightened the little thing – I don't think she meant to hurt me."

Hildegard, too, looked uncomfortable. "It seems rather harsh, Stefan," she said gently. "Perhaps Maggy could try to find an alternative home for the dog."

"Where? In the country?" Julius was sarcastic. "She behaved so well with those other people that they had to keep her tied up day and night – Magdalen herself told us as much." He paused. "No, I've made my decision, and there's an end to it."

"You can't," Maggy said flatly.

"He does have a point." Emilie was reluctant, but since her husband seldom made unpleasant demands on her, she felt obliged to be supportive. "You must see, Maggy, that –"

"I see nothing except his cruelty."

Emilie bit her lip.

"You have a choice," Julius said abruptly to his stepdaughter.

"Yes?"

"I could shoot the creature." Like every other adult Swiss male in the country, Julius kept his army rifle in his home at all times. "Would you prefer that, Magdalen?"

Maggy stared at him.

"Father," Rudi began, then stopped.

"Well?" Julius waited.

All Maggy's pulses were racing, and she felt sick. She realized that she had held herself in check for years. Saved by her visits to Davos from an otherwise repressed and asphyxiating existence, she had elected, on the whole, to suffer in silence. Warned by Amadeus at the end of every holiday not to let a word about Alexander slip out, she had regularly returned to Zurich concealing her emotions beneath a veil of reticence.

Now, she snapped.

"You are a loathsome man," she told Julius, her voice trembling. "I knew it from the first moment I ever saw you, but I was just a little girl, without rights."

"You've always had rights," Hildegard said, distressed.

"Have I? Did I have any rights when you sent Papi away without even letting me *talk* to him?" She swung around to face her mother. "Did you think I would ever forget that night when you locked me in?"

"It was for your own protection," Emilie said.

"I don't believe you. And I never forgave you, and I never will."

"That's quite enough," Julius broke in.

Maggy could not stop. "It would have been enough, but you all acted as if Papi was a criminal, so that he couldn't even come to Switzerland – couldn't even see me. But he did." Her colour was high, and her eyes sparkled with rage. "He saw me often – every single time I went to Davos!"

"Not when I was there." Rudi was wide-eyed.

"Of course not. Papi didn't come when you did, because he knew that you weren't to be trusted." At the back of her mind, behind the fire of her anger, Maggy realized that she was being overly hard on her brother, that none of it had been his fault, but still she could not stop herself.

"I told you," Hildegard whispered, white faced. "I said that Amadeus would help Alexander, no matter what he had done."

"He didn't do *anything*," Maggy flung at her grandmother. "Nothing to compare with what you did to him – to me!" She took a deep breath. "But we fooled you all. We had wonderful times together, in spite of you, and you never guessed anything."

All Maggy's hatred and recriminations burst from her

with undiluted passion, together with the declaration of her abiding, unquenchable love for her grandfather and father. Utterly abandoned, she told them everything, for she knew that it was all over anyway, that she was risking nothing because she could never go back again. The family listened in appalled, riveted silence as she described idyllic days and nights with Amadeus and Alexander, as she told them about Konstantin Zeleyev and his fascinating, bewitching tales of Irina and St Petersburg and Paris – and of a sculpture made of solid gold and diamonds and sapphires and rubies, a sculpture more beautiful and precious than anything they had ever seen –

"Tell us," Stefan Julius said at last, interrupting her impassioned torrent of words for the first time, and his voice was steely calm. "Tell us more about this sculpture."

Too late, Maggy realized her mistake. Hexi's fate temporarily forgotten, even her revelation about Alexander set aside, her stepfather began to interrogate her, his controlled hostility awesome.

"Herr Walther made no mention of a sculpture when he spoke of the old man's possessions. He said nothing about gold or jewels. He said there was nothing of any value except the house itself."

Silently, Maggy flayed herself for her stupidity.

"She's making it up," Emilie said, uncertainly.

"I don't think so," Julius said, his eyes not leaving his stepdaughter's face. "She may have embellished a little, but there's some substance to this."

Still Maggy said nothing. She thought of the note her father had left for her, and swore a silent vow never to say another word that might betray him, no matter what might happen to her.

"All those wonderful times." Emilie's eyes had grown cold. "How wonderful could it be to sit in a shabby old house with an adulterer and a savage?"

Maggy stared at her mother with hatred, longing to lash out again.

"You really believe that your father is a good, decent man, don't you?" Emilie asked, clearly, icily. "And why not, since no one wanted you to know the truth, not the whole truth."

"Emilie," Hildegard warned.

"We didn't want you any more hurt than you had to be," Emilie went on. "You thought that I didn't care about you, that I was being wicked and vindictive. And all these years I've swallowed the truth, however impossible you were, however badly you tried to punish me."

"Emilie," Hildegard tried again, but Julius overruled her.

"Let her go on," he said calmly. "The girl is old enough to know."

"But Rudi?" Hildegard was distressed.

For a moment, Emilie wavered, looking at her son, who sat still and straight-backed, but then she shook her head. "I can't keep it from him any longer," she said. "Rudi's never harboured any unrealistic fantasies about Alexander – he hardly remembers him, do you, darling?" She smiled, a brief, wry smile. "And he may have the Gabriel name, but not the nature. Not like Maggy."

Maggy had been standing since she had entered the library. Now her legs felt suddenly weak, and she sat down on the nearest chair.

"What new lies do you want to tell me, Mother?"

"No lies," Emilie said. "The plain, ugly truth."

Alexander Gabriel, Emilie told her daughter and son, was a weak and pathetic man who had, for years, resorted not only to alcohol, but also to drugs, to help him escape from the realities of life. Until that night in June nine years ago, he had managed to retain a modicum of self-control, but that night was different. That night, an old acquaintance had come into the city; the man of whom Maggy had spoken as if he were a hero in a fairy tale, Zeleyev, the Russian.

"I didn't know that he was a friend of your grandfather. He was just a stranger – I didn't even see him until he brought your father back in the middle of the night." Emilie looked directly at Maggy. "You describe him as the most elegant man you've ever seen. When I saw him, he was a stinking, disgusting drunk."

"Go on, Mother." Maggy's voice quivered only slightly. She felt numb, protected by a strange, heavy cocoon of unreality.

"It was the Russian who told me what had happened. Your father was hardly conscious at that time – I remember it took an ocean of black coffee to revive him at all. I remember your grandmother and I pouring it into him. I remember him choking, vomiting over us." Her face soured at the memory.

Hildegard reached over and touched Emilie's arm. "I wish you would not do this," she said. "No good will come of it."

"It's doing me good," Emilie replied harshly.

"Go on, Mother," Maggy said again.

"The Russian told us that he had drunk too much vodka. He confessed that he drank infrequently, but that when he did, he behaved badly. He told us that my husband had drunk whisky, wine and beer, and that he had smoked a marijuana cigarette. He told me that they had picked up a whore in Niederdorf-Strasse, and that they had taken her to a room in a backstreet house."

"Mami, please," Rudi said quietly.

"I can't stop, Rudi, I'm sorry." Emilie continued, relentlessly. "The Russian said that Alexander had been too intoxicated and too disabled by the drug to make any use of the prostitute, and that against his advice, he had swallowed some pills. Benzedrine, he said, a type of amphetamine. I had not even heard of such things before that night, but the Russian explained that they wake one up, revive one, speed up one's metabolism." She focused on Maggy, the story slipping from her smoothly, evenly, without hysteria. "In your father's case, they drove him over the brink of madness, turned him into a wild animal."

"I don't believe you." Maggy was losing the protective numbness – the cocoon around her heart and mind was splintering. She clenched her fists tightly, bunched her toes inside her shoes.

"Believe me, Maggy, it's a truth no decent person could invent. He was my husband, remember, not only the father of my children. Your cherished Papi –" She waited a beat. "Who raped, battered and half-strangled that woman before his comrade dragged him off her."

"How can you tell such lies?" Maggy whispered.

Emilie had not quite finished. Zeleyev, to his credit, had retained enough presence of mind to get the prostitute, unseen, out of the house, and to leave her in an alley with a bundle of francs substantial enough, he hoped, to keep her silent when she came to. And then he had brought Alexander back, half-dragging him, half-carrying him, to the Gründli Haus.

"Your grandmother organized everything – I admit I was useless with shock."

"Who would not be?" Julius said.

"Hildegard knew that it was impossible for Alexander to stay here for even one more night. If the woman had called the police, or if she had been found, anything might have happened. Our marriage was obviously finished – I could not bear to have him in the same house, let alone near me. And then we had you children to consider."

"Do you understand now?" Julius asked Maggy quietly, but she did not, could not respond.

Hildegard took over the tale. "I woke my lawyer, insisted he come here right away to draw up the necessary papers. I told Maximilian to drive the Russian to the Hauptbahnhof, and to be prepared to take Alexander over the German frontier within a few hours." Her blue eyes were bright, and she was trembling. "You were only seven years old, Maggy. We locked your door to save you from discovering the truth. It was better for you that you should feel resentment towards us, rather than face up to what your father had done."

"How did you make him go?" Maggy's voice was stark now. Shock and horror, and still, above everything, disbelief, were making her swirl from one internal physical reaction to another, one minute rigid, the next weak and drained. "How did you make him leave me?"

"He had no choice," Emilie answered. "He couldn't stay here, and if he had been arrested, if he had been sent to prison, he knew he could not have borne it. He was pathetic," she said again. "We put him under a cold shower, helped him put on fresh clothes – we burned the ones he'd been wearing. He signed everything the lawyer put before him – I remember how his hand trembled as he wrote his name."

"What did you make him sign?"

"One document giving up all his rights to your grandmother's estate, another surrendering his rights to his father's –"

"Such as it was," said Hildegard.

"Perhaps more than we thought." Julius remembered the sculpture.

"He signed one paper confirming that he was deserting me, and that he would not contest our divorce, nor make any claims on me." Emilie, nearing the end, did not shrink away from it. "And the last."

"Yes?" Maggy's eyes burned.

"Your father swore that he would never see either you or your brother again, for the remainder of his life."

* * *

All Maggy's jagged, jumbled emotions converged sharply, agonizingly, into a single, violent response. If she thought she had experienced hatred in the past, she realized now that it had simply been the impotent passion of a child, trivial in comparison to the searing detestation she felt now.

Her mother was lying, that much was clear to her. Maggy would never believe the hideous story Emilie had just told – *never*. Something dreadful had taken place that night, but it could not have been as she had described it. Her mother – married to a man who had made his fortune selling weapons of destruction, many of them to the Germans before the war – had spoken of her father as a depraved monster. Maggy knew that Alexander Gabriel was a gentle man, a loving, caring father and son.

Now, very slowly, Maggy rose from her chair and looked at them all, her family gathered together. Her loathsome stepfather. Her grandmother, always so dignified, a woman capable of banishing her own son into an unjust exile. Rudi, her own brother, so shocked and chalky faced, yet not for one instant trying to defend their father or his sister. And she looked at Emilie, the worst of them, worn out now, sapped by the effort of her inventions, her cruelty.

Maggy knew now what real hate felt like.

7

Maggy left the Gründli Haus that night.

She took with her Hexi, poor condemned dachshund, one small Mädler leather suitcase and her passport, silently retrieved from the secretaire in her stepfather's study, and slipped out of the house shortly after four o'clock in the morning.

She felt no regret. Perhaps a trace of guilt, over Rudi, but nothing greater than that. She and her younger brother looked alike, but they had never had anything in common, had never been close, had seldom shared even the most insignificant of secrets. There was only one person alive who mattered now, and Maggy had made up her mind that she was going to find him.

She walked down to Römerhof and, following the route taken by the Number Eight tram, made her way past the Schauspielhaus and continued down Rämistrasse. At the Quaibrücke, Maggy hesitated; the route along the Limmatquai was more direct, but she was more likely to encounter late-night revellers, and she was anxious to avoid trouble at any cost. She crossed the bridge, gazed out over the dark lake to her left, the far bank threaded with lights, walked through Bürkli Platz and turned right into Bahnhofstrasse.

"This is one of the most elegant streets in the world," she told Hexi, who promptly squatted at the base of a linden tree and then, wagging her short tail, tugged on the lead, impatient to reach wherever they were going. "Mami and Omi spend half their lives here, shopping and drinking coffee and gossiping, but I never liked it."

Most people she knew loved the town; Zürichers were proud of it, and visitors declared it the most civilized and charming of cities. Maggy wondered, sometimes, whether she might have felt differently had she been born into another family, raised in a less stifling household. Her friends at school were very happy – and if she was honest, she, too, had been happy enough until Papi had left. . .

The Paradeplatz was hushed, the soft squishing of Maggy's rubber-soled boots and the scratching of Hexi's claws almost the only sounds in the five o'clock peace. They passed Franz Carl Weber, the big toy shop, then Goldschmidt, Omi's favourite shop, then the department stores, Jelmoli and Globus, set back behind the Pestalozzi garden, then the two hotels near the top of the street, the St Gotthard and the Schweizerhof, giving off light and warmth, but asleep. Everything was silent, almost ghostly, yet Maggy felt the strangeness calming, soothing her nerves, encouraging her to go on.

The Hauptbahnhof was quiet too, every small sound echoing in the great building. Maggy purchased a one-way ticket to Geneva, and then she locked herself, with Hexi, into a cubicle in the ladies' washroom, until the first train of the day was due to depart.

Worried that the dog might disgrace herself on the journey, and not wanting to draw attention to herself, Maggy sat with Hexi on the floor in the goods car, trying to think rationally, to plan ahead as far as possible. She was going to Geneva because when she had last seen Konstantin Zeleyev, he had said that he was working there. Papi's note had made it plain that the Russian was now the only man he would trust. Maggy had to find Zeleyev.

She had emptied her money-box – a big china pig that

Alexander had given her when she was four and into which he had almost daily, until he had left, slipped spare coins and notes, and which Maggy had continued to feed when she had remembered ever since then – and she had brought with her, too, her personal savings book for the account that had been opened for her on her twelfth birthday at the Schweizerische Bankverein. She realized that she might not be able to withdraw cash without parental permission, and she knew that the funds invested on her behalf at the Gründli Bank might be lost to her forever, but somehow she would manage. She was wearing two pieces of jewellery, the white-gold Patek Philippe watch that Hildegard had given her on her last birthday, and the little gold signet ring engraved with her initials that had been her father's last gift to her. She had left behind the other items of value: her pretty sapphire earrings, her gold charm bracelet and the eighteen-carat gold cross and necklace she had received at her confirmation, had all been given to her since her mother's marriage to Stefan Julius, and Maggy wanted no part of them. She would sooner die than sell her gold ring, but if she needed to raise money, she would sell the watch.

The journey was beautiful, culminating, just outside Lausanne, in a breathtaking view of Lac Léman, and arriving at the Gare de Cornavin, Maggy was almost overwhelmed with excitement. She knew that Geneva was smaller than Zurich, yet it felt bigger, more flamboyant and foreign. Wide-eyed but undaunted, she deposited her suitcase at the left-luggage counter, bought a bar of Lindt milk chocolate which she shared with Hexi, and walked out into the rue des Alpes, coming before long to the Quai du Mont-Blanc and the beautiful Lake Geneva.

The morning was bright and cold, an icy wind whipping off the lake as Maggy crossed the Rade de Genève, gazing at the moored pleasure boats and the famous Jet d'Eau to her left, shooting water high up into the sky. For over two hours, she wandered through the streets, along the lake, criss-crossed the Rhône from left to right bank, enjoying the sunshine, the sounds of French-speaking voices and staring, with pleasure, into shop windows. This was a city of watches, she observed, seeing watches by the hundred, all beautiful and expensive: Baume et Mercier, Blancpain, Rolex, Audemars Piguet, Vacheron Constantin. Geneva was certainly *not* the city in which to try to sell her Patek Philippe. She thought again how much she had always disliked shopping at home, for however magnificent the stores and their wares, however lovely the Bahnhofstrasse was when all its linden trees were in blossom, Maggy had invariably been towed along in her mother's or Omi's wake; whereas this afternoon, for the first time, she was free of them. Yet still she was aware that she could not risk staying here for long. Julius Industrie AG had large corporate offices here, in rue Rothschild, and her step-father came to Geneva once each week, usually on Mondays, but not always; today was Wednesday, but Maggy did not want to run any risks. Besides, she had come for one purpose only.

Zeleyev had spoken of a firm of goldsmiths named Perrault et Fils. Now, tightening her grip on Hexi's lead, Maggy stopped at a public telephone, flicked through the directory and found the address easily. Her optimism surged – before long, she would come face to face with the Russian again, and then she would find her father, too.

The house of Perrault et Fils, on the rue du Rhône, was old and impressive, its retail showroom on two floors, a hushed place with an atmosphere of reverence that reminded Maggy a little of the *Grosse Halle* in the family bank. A lady sat on a velvet chair in the far corner, being attended by a silver-haired gentleman in grey morning dress. She wore furs, and clutched a tiny dog to her bosom. Maggy, mindful of the plush, pale pink carpet, did the same with Hexi; the dachshund struggled for release, but Maggy held her more tightly as another elegantly attired salesman approached her.

"*Bonjour, Mademoiselle.*"

He spoke with the utmost courtesy, yet disapproval oozed from every pore of his face. Her clothes were to blame, Maggy realized immediately. Possessing a wardrobe crammed with superb, expensive clothes, chosen mostly by Emilie – the kind of clothes which would have been a passport to acceptance and respect in an establishment of the highest calibre – Maggy had fled her home wearing her favourite black ski pants, a vivid turquoise, baggy pullover and her old sheepskin jacket. Clothes to wear up on the Schwarzhorn, but not in this shrine of refinement, certainly not after a night spent in a ladies' washroom and a train journey in a goods car.

"I am looking for Monsieur Zeleyev," she said, and held her breath. Hexi squirmed in her arms, and whined.

The salesman was impassive. "Were you expecting to meet the gentleman here, Mademoiselle?"

"No, Monsieur. That is, I did hope to see him, but –"

"Monsieur is a client?" He inclined his head slightly. "I'm afraid I do not recall a client named –" He hesitated.

"Zeleyev," Maggy repeated. "He works here."

The disapproval returned. "No, Mademoiselle."

Maggy's heart sank. "Or rather, he did work here a little time ago."

"How long ago?" The front door opened, and a distinguished looking, elderly couple entered. The salesman bowed in their direction.

"Two or three years ago," Maggy answered, "but Monsieur Zeleyev would not have worked in this department, Monsieur. He is a craftsman." She read the ennui in his eyes, and tried harder. "Formerly, he worked for the House of Fabergé in St Petersburg."

"Indeed?" His mouth pulled wryly at the corners. "That would have been a very long time ago, *n'est-ce pas*? In any event, the gentleman does not work for Perrault et Fils now. I am sorry."

Maggy had come too far to give up so easily. "Perhaps you could check through your old records."

"There is no need for that."

"But there is," she insisted. In her arms, Hexi growled, a nasty little sound from the back of her throat. "It's imperative that I find Monsieur Zeleyev."

Disapproval turned to distaste. "Then I suggest that you leave me your name and address; if any trace of the gentleman can be found, then *la compagnie* will write to you."

"I can't do that – I mean I can't wait for a letter. It's too urgent."

"Then there is nothing more I can do, except to bid you good day." He moved smoothly towards the door and grasped the handle.

"Please, Monsieur –" Maggy appealed to him for the last time, but to no avail. The door opened.

"*Bonjour, Mademoiselle.*" Pointedly, the salesman did not bid her *au revoir*. The door closed behind her. Maggy gave Hexi one quick, reassuring squeeze, as if the dachshund, too, had been insulted, and put her down.

"Now what?" she asked, and getting no reply, answered her own question. "We go on."

Knowing that she could not afford to waste any more time, Maggy embarked on a rapid tour of as many goldsmiths, silversmiths and jewellers as she could find. There were numerous glamorous stores on the rue du Rhône, several more on Quai Général Guisan, Place du Molard and, on the opposite bank of the river, in the Place des Bergues.

It was a glittering, but intensely depressing experience; no one knew Zeleyev, no one had even heard his name. Maggy adjourned to the post office in rue du Mont-Blanc, and began to pore through the directories for the city and surrounding districts, but found no listings under his name – she went to a counter and exchanged francs for centimes, went into a booth and began telephoning every single *orfèvrerie* and jeweller she had not already called on in person. Hexi, growing hungry, restless and fretful, whined and scratched at the walls, then began to bark, making it impossible for Maggy to hear the voices at the other end of the line – but in any case, she had by then concluded that her mission, for the time being at least, was impossible. If Konstantin Zeleyev was still in Geneva, which Maggy had begun to doubt, she was not going to find him.

For the first time, she felt unnerved. It would soon be dark, and she had nowhere to stay. Surrounded by extravagant, handsome hotels, she realized that if she began paying for hotel rooms, her money would not last more than a few days. Yet if she gave in now, went back to Zurich, Maggy felt that she might be gobbled up, like a meagre oyster, into the greedy, callous world of the Gründlis and Juliuses. Her individuality, her hopes and aspirations, would be steamrollered into dust. And she might never see her father again.

She walked, more slowly now, towards a small park beside the lake, where Hexi, under cover of evening, relieved herself on the grass, scampered around for a few minutes and then, as if remembering her hunger and weariness, ran back to Maggy and scraped her little paws up and down her new mistress's legs until Maggy gave in and picked her up.

"And now?" She sat on a bench, Hexi on her knee. "Do you fancy a night here?" The dachshund burrowed her long nose into the pocket of Maggy's jacket, where the now eaten bar of chocolate had earlier rested. It seemed safe enough, Maggy mused, though if the police did question her, she would probably be back in Zurich before daybreak, and that would be the end for Hexi.

And then the answer struck her. Of course they had to go on, and suddenly there seemed only one place for her to go on to. The city of which Zeleyev had spoken so avidly, so poetically; the city in which Irina Valentinovna Malinskaya – the woman Maggy had never met, but with whom she had sometimes felt she had more in common than her own mother – had been so happy. The most likely place for Konstantin Zeleyev to have gone to if he had left Geneva. The city in which he had told Maggy she would dazzle.

"That's it," she murmured, and planted a kiss on Hexi's rough fur.

She had made her decision. She would go back towards the railway station and find a room for the night in a cheap *pension*, and in the morning, she would make one more effort to locate the Russian in this city. And then she and Hexi would get on another train, and leave Switzerland.

For Paris.

She caught the early afternoon train, and had another uncomfortable ride, for though this time she had tried sitting in a second-class compartment with Hexi, the *chef de train* had wanted to dispatch the restless dog alone to a goods car, and so Maggy had accompanied her.

She didn't mind the discomfort, for the world was flashing by just beyond the windows in the corridor outside the compartment. Maggy's passport had already been checked over twice, first by the officials on the Swiss side of the border, then by the French. The Alps were behind them, they had stopped for a while at Lyons, and now they were following the River Saône north through southern

Burgundy, passing through countryside that looked exceptionally pretty even in drab February, full of rolling hills, forests, vineyards and great herds of peaceful Charolais cattle.

Just after their stop at Dijon, the *chef de train* feeling remorseful at having banished the beautiful young girl to the goods car, appeared in the doorway carrying a small tray on which he had set a plate with Camembert cheese and pâté and a chunk of crusty bread, a glass of red wine and a linen napkin.

"*Pour vous, Mademoiselle, avec mes compliments.*" He set it down on a packing case, and smiled as the dachshund came instantly to life, wagging her tail and whimpering with hunger. "Perhaps your *p'tite amie* may care for the pâté," he said. "And for yourself, we have lately passed the lovely town of Beaune, and since it is almost a blasphemy to depart this region without tasting at least a sample, I have brought you a glass from an excellent vineyard."

"*Merci beaucoup, Monsieur.*"

Maggy was touched, and flattered. No sooner had she left home, than she was already being treated like an adult – it was a splendid feeling. She remembered that Zeleyev had given her that sense of individuality and of self-worth, but although she had enjoyed it, she had at the same time recognized it as a trick of the Russian's great charm. This time, with this stranger, this uniformed official, she had a sense that she had charmed *him*, that he truly saw her not as just a teenager, but as a young woman.

It was a little strange, she thought, having so few misgivings about leaving her native country. She loved Switzerland itself, its beauty and its magnificence – as she had reflected on leaving Zurich, she knew that she might have been wonderfully happy amongst its people if she had not been born into the Gründli family. But her life there was now in the past. She was moving forward, on and on, leaving wine country and gliding north-west through the Ile de France. Towards her new life.

The train pulled into the Gare de Lyon shortly after six, and Maggy, exhilarated but almost overwhelmed by the force of the evening crush, picked up her suitcase with her right hand, rescued Hexi from the platform with her left, and made her way through the bustling, noisy, impatient crush of humanity and out of the station into Boulevard Diderot. Maggy knew that she was dusty and dishevelled, that her thick, wild hair had long since escaped the satin ribbon with which she had tied it back early that morning. She knew that if she had been alone and vulnerable last night in Geneva, then she must logically be ten times more at risk in this *terra incognita*, this foreign city. Yet she had never felt more certain of herself, more convinced of the rightness of her actions.

Instinct made her turn left into the busy, two-way boulevard, and brought her to the Quai de la Râpée. There, on the far side of the street, flowed the Seine. The river of poetry and of the songs they had sung in her grandfather's house in happier days.

"It's an omen, Hexi," she told the dachshund who, sensing her excitement, promptly sneezed and squirmed. "Just a few more minutes – we have to cross this street."

Maggy crossed, first the street, then her first *pont de Paris*, for she had seen, on the far side of the river, stone steps leading down to the embankment. Her anticipation increased – it *was* a propitious omen – and new strength flowed into her long legs as she descended the steps and, at last, put Hexi down onto the path. It was very broad and pebbly, with patches of grass and trees, and the little dog, overjoyed to be let off the lead, scampered about, sniffing, squatting to pee, frequently turning back to Maggy and giving little, high-pitched barks of encouragement.

It was dark, and quite cold, yet Maggy still felt none of the anxiety she had felt at this hour in Geneva. She felt free and safe, for no one would look for her here. Even when she had exploded at them in the library – could it be only two evenings ago? – and spilled out the truth about her father, and their meetings, and about Zeleyev and his adventures and tales, she had only tossed in a mention of Paris as an illustration. If her family did search for her, they would look in the mountains, where they knew she had been happiest. The leather suitcase in her right hand felt suddenly lighter, her instincts, strong and natural, seemed to speak to her almost as distinctly as another human voice, encouraging her: *March on*, they told her. *It will be all right – go on, go forward*.

A thickish mist descended on Paris. The river bank, lit only by occasional gas lamps, became more deeply shadowed, darker and less welcoming. Weeping willows bowed gracefully over the wide path, and from time to time, couples walked by, moving quite briskly and huddling close, perhaps having come down to the river to seek romance, but finding it too chilly to linger. Hexi, growing tired again, and impatient for dinner and comfort, jumped up at Maggy's legs, demanding to be carried. Passing a cluster of moored barges, Maggy smelt delectable, mouth-watering aromas of cooking, stood still, for a moment, basking in a great puff of warm air that flowed out from an open door in one of the barges, heard laughter and raised voices. She walked on, her stomach beginning to gnaw on itself a little uncomfortably, for the energy that the early afternoon's bread and cheese had given her, had long since been expended. The dachshund fretted in her left arm, the suitcase grew heavier again.

"We need to make a decision," she said to Hexi, and an instant later, seeing steps a few yards away, leading to the streets away from the river, she climbed them, hoping to find some welcoming, benevolent sight to renew her optimism, but instead she felt disoriented and anxious, and scurried back down again to the embankment, the case banging against her legs, her feet cold and aching. Perhaps it was because the Seine was such a famous landmark; she felt that so long as she stayed close to the river, she could imagine herself less lost than in those foggy, damp streets.

Her confidence began to dwindle. This was February, one of the least pleasant months of the year almost anywhere. The Paris of which Zeleyev had spoken had been a city of springtime, a town of gay boulevards and street cafés, in which a girl could sit over a single cup of *café noir* or a bowl of soup for hours if she wished, watching the world of the Impressionists float by. . .

"I should have taken my time," Maggy told Hexi, "at the station. I ought to have changed some money into French francs – I should have bought a map and some food – I could have asked for advice." She grew angry with herself; she was always too impetuous, always too much in a rush to think things through properly, to consider the consequences of her actions.

A big, brightly illuminated boat, about one hundred feet long, sailed past, and Maggy saw, through steamed-up windows, men and women eating and drinking. They looked happy, warm, secure. The cobbles beneath Maggy's feet were large and time-flattened, difficult to walk on. The suitcase felt like lead, her shoulders ached – she put Hexi down on the ground, but the little dog whined and scrabbled fiercely at her legs to get up again.

"No," Maggy said, and Hexi barked sharply, rebuking her, but Maggy took no notice. A man was walking towards her, through the mist, shoulders hunched, a cap on his head. As he came close, she saw that his jacket was worn and that he had a large scar down one cheek; he smelt of old sweat and garlic and mouldering vegetables, as if he'd slept in a heap of rubbish, and his dark stare, scanning her up and down, made her nervous. Quickening her step, Maggy patted her side for Hexi to come, and the dachshund barked angrily, her ears flapping as she bounced on her short legs, warning the stranger off, and relieved, Maggy watched him walk away.

Just ahead of them, Maggy saw that the river split into two, divided by a small island – two islands, in fact, the lights from the buildings on them glowing like beacons through the mist. Maggy stopped and stared. A great and beautiful cathedral with towers and flying buttresses had loomed out of the fog, a lovely central spire piercing the clouds of mist. Her heart thumped suddenly with the pleasure of recognition. Notre-Dame de Paris. And the island she now faced was not simply an island, but the Ile de la Cité, the heart of Paris, floating on the Seine.

Her legs abruptly weak, Maggy sank down onto a wooden bench. She was so *cold*, her throat felt scratchy from the damp, foggy air, she had begun to shiver. Hexi whined and Maggy picked her up and placed her on her lap, unbuttoning her jacket and letting her snuggle close for warmth and comfort. It was time, Maggy knew, to make another decision. Perhaps she should retrace her steps, return to the Gare de Lyon and shelter there till morning, or maybe she should cross the ghostly bridge she now saw a little way ahead, linking the embankment on her side to the Ile de le Cité. Was Notre-Dame, although one of the great cathedrals of Europe, still fundamentally a church – a house in which she could seek sanctuary? Either way, she realized, they could not stay here, for it was too cold, too damp –

But when she attempted to rise from the bench, she felt suddenly ill; her head spun like a top, her legs refused to hold her up, and she was compelled to sit down again. For the first time since leaving home, she felt an intense desire to weep, and the tears began to well up in her eyes. But then, instead, she did what she had often done in the past when she had felt stirrings of despair – she began to sing, softly, to herself. The words of one of the songs of Paris that Zeleyev had taught her, came back easily to her as she tried to warm herself with a lyrical, mental image of what the Seine would be like in August – its waters gently cooling, lapping serenely against the banks, accompanying strolling lovers with its own benign music –

She sang quietly, huskily, fervently, as Hexi licked the bare, cold skin of her wrist where her pullover did not quite meet her gloves –

And then suddenly, she heard a second voice, masculine but sweet, joining with her own in harmony –

Unnerved, Maggy stopped singing. The voice was disembodied, coming out of the fog. Her heart pumped a warning, she gripped Hexi tightly to herself, heard the little dog growl.

And then she saw him, walking slowly towards her, wraithlike at first in the mist, then gradually taking shape and form. A man wearing a trench coat, collar upturned, and a trilby hat, his hands thrust into the pockets of the raincoat. He was still singing, his breath steaming as he completed the song for Maggy, and came to a halt in front of the bench.

"*Bonsoir, Mademoiselle.*" He smiled, and courteously removed his hat. Hexi stopped growling.

Maggy looked up and saw a face of perhaps thirty years, with soft, hazel eyes and dark, slightly receding hair. "*Bonsoir, Monsieur.*"

"I hope I didn't alarm you," he said, gently. "I heard your voice, and I was intrigued to know who was singing that summery song, so wistfully, on a cold February night."

He looked respectable, and kind. She put out her hand. "Magdalen Gabriel," she said.

"Noah Levi," he responded, and smiled at the dachshund. "And your pretty friend?"

"Her name is Hexi."

"Ah," he said. "A little witch."

"You speak German, Monsieur?"

"I was born in Berlin." He paused. "Would you mind if I sat down?" Maggy shook her head, and he sat, leaving plenty of space between them. He regarded the suitcase. "Just arrived, or on your way?"

"Arrived."

"Nowhere to stay?"

"Not yet."

He was gentle and easy, a man who, with few words and without the slightest pressure, invited trust and candour. Within ten minutes of sitting on the bench beside Maggy, he had completely understood her predicament, and had a simple solution to offer.

"It's one thing," he told her, "for you to choose to sleep rough in a strange city, on a night like this – but it's quite another matter for you to inflict such an ordeal on a dachsie."

Dachshunds, he reminded Maggy, were most particular about their comforts; it was evident that Hexi had already found the warmest, safest place she could under the circumstances. He knew dachshunds well, for he had grown up with them in his family.

"Before I go on, I think perhaps it would be wise for me to give you my complete title, just in case you misunderstand my intentions."

"Your title?"

"I'm the Reverend Noah Levi –"

"A priest?" Maggy was surprised.

He shook his head. "*Un chantre*," he said. "A cantor."

Maggy smiled. "You sing in a synagogue."

"*Exactement.*" Levi paused. "I have a large *appartement* in the Opéra district, with two empty bedrooms. It would be my pleasure to offer you and Hexi bed and board until you find something more suitable."

"I can't," Maggy said, startled.

"I understand," he continued evenly, "that a well-bred young lady from a fine Zurich family would instinctively refuse such a dubious invitation from a strange man, but –"

"On the contrary," Maggy interrupted him.

"Really?"

"My instincts tell me to accept," Maggy said, and felt herself redden. "But I'm always following my instincts, and I promised myself that in future I would try not to be so impulsive."

"I see." Reverend Levi thought for a moment. "But in this instance, Magdalen, what is your alternative? Not to stay here, surely – you'll catch your death of cold."

Maggy bit her lip. "I thought, perhaps, the church."

He followed her eyes. "Notre-Dame?" He smiled. "A little grand, don't you think? Though I suspect that your mother might prefer a priest or pastor to a cantor."

"I don't see why – we're not especially devout."

"Then you'll come?" He eyed Hexi, who was trembling. "If not for yourself, then for *la petite*."

Maggy stared at him. "You're so kind," she said softly.

"Just a fellow human being. One who understands."

And so it was that Maggy and Hexi spent their first night in Paris drinking chicken noodle soup and eating chopped liver and *gefilte fish* in the comfortable apartment, at 32 *bis* Boulevard Haussmann, of the Jewish cantor of a synagogue Libérale.

Noah Levi had, as he had told Maggy, been born in Berlin in 1925, and had spent the first thirteen years of his life in grace and comfort, living with his musical parents, two sisters and two dachshunds, until the Nazis had wiped out the whole Levi family, except for young Noah, who had been hidden until the end of the war by a Belgian Protestant butcher. Noah had learned that a Jew could exist quite well on a diet of pork scraps, if he had no choice, and he had learned much about the art of survival. This lovely young girl, with her unruly golden curls and remarkable eyes, and her strange, mezzo-soprano voice, had her whole life ahead of her – and Noah Levi had simply not been capable of leaving her at risk on the streets.

"We shall go back, if you like," he said, as they ate, "during daylight, and you will see the fishermen, and the commercial barges unloading their goods from all over France. And then there are the *clochards* – the most exclusive and snobbish tramps on earth. In weather like this, they often take over the barges of absent owners to sleep and even cook in."

"I think I passed them tonight." Maggy remembered the wonderful aromas that had made her so hungry.

"But tonight you felt vulnerable, and a little nervous," Levi pointed out. "In a day or two, you will feel quite different, with a home to go back to when you wish. You will feel like *une Parisienne*."

Maggy watched the *chantre* as he sang his strange, sonorous grace after dinner, and as he put clean sheets on the bed in the room that was to be hers, and as he clipped Hexi's lead onto her collar, so that they could all go out for a last walk. She saw him smile, a sincere, indulgent smile, when the confused little dog spread a large, wet puddle on the parquet floor of his entrance hall. And Maggy had not felt so much at ease, nor so welcome, since the last time her grandfather had greeted her up in the Dischmatal the previous September.

And she knew, again, that she had been right to leave

Zurich, that she had been right to come to Paris, and that she would make a life for herself here. And that she would find Konstantin Zeleyev and, through him, her father.

The Reverend Noah Levi was another good omen.

Part Two

MADELEINE:

PARIS

8

Maggy came out of her bedroom on her first morning in Paris to find the Reverend Noah Levi seated on the tiny, narrow balcony outside his *petit salon*, a large, bowl-shaped cup of milky coffee on a white painted wrought-iron table to his right, and Hexi on his knee, eating a generously buttered croissant.

"*Bonjour, Maggy.*"

"*Bonjour, Monsieur.*" She stood, uncertain for a moment. The dachshund wagged her tail to acknowledge her appearance, but did not otherwise move.

"Didn't we agree that you would call me Noah?" Her host indicated a second chair on the other side of the table. "Please – be at home. Pour your coffee and eat a little breakfast."

Maggy squeezed her way out, and sat down. It was a chilly morning, and she was glad that she had dressed before emerging, putting on one of the two other pullovers she had packed. But despite the temperature, the sun was shining, and although the throng of people on the broad pavement below the balcony were mostly making their way to work, Maggy felt that there was an air of verve and energy emanating from them that swirled up and enveloped her, beckoning her to hurry down and join them.

"*Voici Paris.*" Noah smiled. "You like it already."

"It's wonderful." Maggy picked up her cup with both hands. "I slept so well, and the moment I woke up, I knew where I was and I felt so *happy* – and I can't believe my luck in meeting you."

"*C'était le bon Dieu*," Noah said. "The good Lord sending me on an evening walk that normally I would not contemplate until March, at least."

He was the calmest person Maggy had ever met, apparently prepared to accept whatever cards the *bon Dieu* dealt him, though not necessarily without a battle. Unlike many adults, he did not fuss. When Maggy informed him that she intended to sell her watch, in order that she might pay for her keep – if Noah was still willing to let her stay – until such time as she found a job and a place of her own, Levi did not argue.

"I told you last night that you and Hexi may stay as long as you like or need to." He paused. "The only suggestion I would make is that instead of selling your watch, I could take you to the *mont-de-piété*."

"What's that?"

"It is where French people go to pawn their valuables. In some places, you would go to a simple pawnbroker, and then say that you had left the watch '*chez ta tante*', but here in Paris it is wiser to go to the Crédit Municipal. They will advance you immediately a part of its value, and then later, if you wish them to sell it for you, you know you can trust them."

Levi having finished his croissant, Hexi jumped off his lap and up onto Maggy's.

"You're shameless."

"They all are." Noah brushed the crumbs from his tie. "I have just one demand to make of you, Maggy. You must inform your family that you are safe."

"All right."

"And you must give them your address."

"No." She shook her head. "I can't do that."

Levi tilted his head to one side, and eyed her steadily.

"You're only sixteen, Maggy. They will be anxious about you."

"I'll write to them."

"And the address?"

"If you insist on telling them where I am," she said stubbornly, "I'll have to leave. I won't stay here, waiting for them to come and fetch me back." She paused. "And they won't come because they care – they think they own me, they think they can rule my life."

"They can, by law."

"I shan't let them, not any more."

They arrived at a compromise of sorts. Maggy would write her letter immediately, would mail it from the main post office in rue du Louvre, and she would then spend two weeks trying to find both Konstantin Zeleyev and a job. Noah Levi would ask *une dame respectable* from his congregation to move temporarily into his second spare room, so that Maggy was properly chaperoned; and at the end of the fortnight, if Maggy had found neither the Russian, nor a job and suitable lodgings, Noah would personally contact the Juliuses. If, on the other hand, Maggy insisted on moving out, and if Noah felt that she had made a prudent, rational decision, he would abide by her wishes and say nothing. Noah considered himself a fair judge of character. This girl was young, but courageous and utterly determined. She was also, he felt certain, absolutely honest. He trusted her.

For the remainder of that first day, Noah did not let Maggy out of his sight. He showed her around the Opéra district, bought her a small, maroon-coloured book containing street maps and bus and Métro routes, and then, having returned Hexi to the apartment, he accompanied her to the Crédit Municipal on rue des Francs-Bourgeois, where Maggy parted with her Patek Philippe watch in exchange for a substantial wad of French francs, which Noah tucked inside his wallet for safekeeping. Being in one of his favourite sections of the city, the Marais district, he showed Maggy the Place des Vosges, the oldest square in Paris.

"I come here," he told her, "when I want to leave the hurly-burly behind for a little while. It's so solid and *distingué*, and yet so tranquil and pretty."

They lunched at Coconnas, looking out onto the square, sitting splendidly on Louis XIII chairs, surrounded mostly by businessmen. Maggy, glancing at the prices on the menu, and aware that Noah had deliberately selected an expensive restaurant, felt embarrassed.

"I would have been happy with a sandwich," she whispered to him.

"You can have sandwiches – or rather *baguettes* – any day of the week," Noah smiled. "But not with me, on the first day of your new life in this city of restaurants."

Luncheon over, they visited Noah's synagogue in a quaint, narrow alley off rue Montmartre. Noah explained to her that they were now in the *deuxième arrondissement*, and that Paris was divided into twenty of these districts, and that each of them possessed its own character and style.

"You cannot expect to learn this city swiftly," he told her. "You will lose yourself frequently, I expect, in the beginning, but being lost in Paris can be one of the great pleasures, and it's always fleeting, for all you have to do is to ask, and you will be on course again directly."

The synagogue seemed, at first glance, drab and uninspiring, yet as Noah showed her around, pointing, with quiet pride, to the Holy Ark, in which rested the Torah scrolls, Maggy sensed in the hall a simple and somehow natural air of community, of belonging. She had never, knowingly, met a Jew before; Noah Levi seemed, to her, more Christian than anyone she had ever known.

They hardly stopped all afternoon. From the synagogue, Noah whisked Maggy down into the Métro and up to Montmartre to see Sacré-Coeur, the magnificent view from *la Butte* and the Place du Tertre, the pretty cobbled square surrounded by cafés and restaurants and, even in this month, busy with local artists trying to sell their work to the tourists.

At six o'clock, true to Levi's word, the *dame respectable* arrived at the apartment. Madame Wolfe, grey-haired, stern yet comforting at the same time, regarded Maggy with undisguised suspicion and Hexi, who had just puddled the Persian rug in the sitting room, with condemnation.

"How long will they be staying?" she asked Noah, confidentially, though Maggy was with them in the room. "No more than a few days, I trust."

"Two weeks, at least," Noah answered contentedly, for he could not recall when he had last enjoyed a day more. "Longer, perhaps."

"And her family approve of this?" Already Madame was weakening, for though she found the Reverend an impulsive young man, he was also, in her eyes, incapable of wrong.

"How could they fail to?"

If Maggy had liked him before, now she adored him.

Madame Wolfe shared their evening meal, supervised Maggy's washing up, and witnessed her chaste departure into her bedroom. In the morning, she ate breakfast with Maggy and the Reverend, before Noah left for the day to attend to his duties, leaving Madame Wolfe free to go to her own home until nightfall. Maggy, watching the front door closing behind her and hearing the sound of her stacked heels disappearing down the stone staircase, looked down at Hexi and gave a small whoop of pleasure. They were wonderful, kind people, but in their own way they were as stifling as her family.

"Another few hours," she said aloud, "and I think I might have *died* from protectiveness."

She brushed her hair until it sparked with electricity, clipped on Hexi's lead, and went out, armed with her map. Noah, discussing her quest, had suggested that she follow up her visit to Perrault et Fils with a letter, but he had told her that the most elite jewellers in Paris were clustered around Place Vendôme, and that the majority of jewellery workrooms were located in rue du Temple in the Marais. But before she began her hunt for Zeleyev, before she had to consider the promise she had made to Noah to look for work, Maggy wanted just a few hours for herself.

"No mission," she told Hexi. "No escort. No safety net."

Coming out of the house on her own, everything she had seen the day before with Noah looked entirely different. The busy junction, with Galeries Lafayette to the right and a cluster of signposts, beckoned her, tempted her. There was no one to tell her which way to go – it was her choice.

Independence, she thought, with mounting excitement. *This is freedom, this is living in the real world.* She saw a flower stall on the corner, and made a mental note to buy armfuls on her way back, so that she could fill the apartment with her gratitude, but for now she crossed first the boulevard, then rue de la Chaussée d'Antin and turned left into rue Halévy, making for the Place de l'Opéra. Oh, it was grand and beautiful, with its handsome steps and columns and friezes – Maggy considered climbing the steps and looking inside, but that was not for today, not for her, that was for tourists, not for a novice Parisienne. This morning, she was a human arrow, pointed towards her own future; there would be other days in which to slow down, to stroll, to take her time and observe, at leisure, the details and the minutiae that made up the city, but not today, not this morning.

She walked with verve, with a wealth of energy and confidence, secure in the knowledge that she had, at least for a fortnight, a safe house and a friend, and the liberty she had longed for for so long. She had lost her beloved grandfather, yet somehow, on this lovely, sunny winter's morning, she felt that Amadeus was beside her; she sensed his approval, and it was almost as if he linked arms with her and pushed her on along the Avenue de l'Opéra towards rue de Rivoli and then on into the Jardin des Tuileries.

Here, suddenly, she wanted to sit down, not because she was weary, but just because she *wanted* to, and so she sat down, in the quiet, almost deserted gardens, on a bench near an empty, silent carousel, and unclipped Hexi's lead so that she could trot around, enjoy the freedom that she, too, deserved. It was strange, Maggy thought, that she felt so comfortable here, for they were such formal gardens, with more gravel than lawn; yet where she sat, on the edge of one of the little grassy squares planted with sculptures, she sensed an intimacy that was not obvious, but was there nevertheless. It was a chilly morning, and only a trickle of off-season visitors wandered along the central gravel avenue, but Maggy felt a curious warmth spreading through her, as if this place was special to her in some, as yet unknown, way.

Leaving the Tuileries again, Maggy paused for just a moment on the brink of the gigantic Place de la Concorde, debating whether to plunge into its majestic, breathtaking expanse, but deciding instead to lead Hexi away from the traffic into rue Royale. Maxim's was on her left – she remembered that Zeleyev had spoken with reverence of Maxim's – and she registered a jeweller's and Christofle, the goldsmiths, on the opposite side, but she was already focused upon a structure at the summit of the street resembling a neoclassical temple. Coming closer, she saw that, in spite of its unfriendly Corinthian colonnade, it was a church, set in the centre of an attractive square, and flanked on two sides by a pretty flower market.

Saint Mary Magdalen, she read. *La Madeleine*.

"My church," Maggy told the dachshund, who was showing signs of tiredness. She looked up and saw the street sign. *Place de la Madeleine*. "My square," she said, and smiled.

There were two food shops at one end of the square into and out of which impeccably dressed customers were flowing at a regular pace. Fauchon and Hédiard; both, Maggy thought, venturing closer, looked sublime. She stood for a while outside Fauchon's windows, and each time the doors opened, the wondrous aromas of *charcuterie*, fresh-baked bread, cheese and chocolate, wafted out in her direction, making her mouth water.

Hexi whined.

"We shouldn't."

It was, clearly, very expensive, and Maggy knew that in her altered circumstances, not knowing how long it would take her to find work, she ought to buy a ham *baguette* at a cheap café, and share it with the dog, but then again, this was a special day, and one without rules.

It was strange, almost perverse, to feel more spiritually uplifted by the sights, smells and tastes of food than by the glories of Sacré-Coeur or even the generosity of Noah Levi. Yet during the three-quarters of an hour in which Maggy loitered inside the two buildings that made up Fauchon, she had the curious sense that she was undergoing a kind of metamorphosis. No longer was she being propelled dynamically forward, made almost frantic by the fierce joy of liberty, fearful in case it was wrenched away from her again; suddenly she was being drawn, with a feeling of magnetized, luxurious tranquillity, back and forth down the heavenly aisles. Hexi, left tied up outside, was temporarily forgotten as Maggy's eyes widened and her mouth watered unbearably. There must, of course, be beautiful food shops in Zurich, she realized, but she had never visited them, had never needed to enter them, since Frau Kümmerly, driven by Maximilian, had bought all the provisions for the Gründli Haus.

Here was bliss. Maggy watched a gentleman sprinkling dried herbs over the floor, saw him stand back, satisfied, as the shoes of customers ground them underfoot, sending tiny, delicate eddies of scent swirling up into the already heavenly air. She saw magnificent, rare fruits and vegetables, wooden buckets of *pâté de foie gras*, healthy, plump sausages, truffles, preserved cocks' combs – here was sophistication. Here was Zeleyev's city, and perhaps, in time, her own.

Maggy bought a cooked sausage baked in a brioche and, reluctantly, left to retrieve her outraged, panic-stricken dachshund.

"I'm sorry, I'm sorry." She scooped Hexi up into her arms, and the dog's nose, alerted by the fragrance in her bag, pushed hungrily at her. Yet Maggy's mind was not on the animal, it was still consumed by her own continuing transformation. She had entered Fauchon a still displaced, still confused, runaway Swiss teenager; but as she had floated around the store, and now, as she re-emerged into the Place de la Madeleine, blending with the mid-morning shoppers, she felt swept up by the city, into the city. She was already altered, magically, intrinsically different. *Une Parisienne*.

And by the time she was back in the apartment on Boulevard Haussmann, finding vases for the flowers she had remembered to buy, tidying herself and shutting Hexi into her bedroom before setting out for the first of the *haute joaillerie* stores, she had already decided to change her name to match her new identity. She had never liked her name; Magdalen was so outmoded, so *holy*, whereas

Madeleine had a certain sound to it, a certain *élan* –
Madeleine Gabriel. . .
She loved it.

She found no trace of Konstantin Zeleyev in Place Vendôme, nor in any of the more commonplace jewellers and goldsmiths she called on in the *quartier des bijoutiers* over the next few days. None of the enamellers or craftsmen knew the Russian, and so far as she could ascertain, from all her checking of directories, and her determined enquiries in the area between the Gare Saint-Lazare and the Square des Batignolles, where she was told many Russian émigrés had lived in the old days, Zeleyev was living neither in Paris nor even in the suburbs.

Gritting her teeth against her intense disappointment, she moved on to her next priority: finding a job. It proved just as fruitless. A sixteen-year-old Swiss girl, without working papers or even a *carte d'identité*, unqualified, without previous experience and unwilling to give family details, was at a considerable disadvantage. Madeleine – for that was how she had already begun to think of herself – could, of course, have washed up in a restaurant or bar, waited on tables for a pittance or perhaps even have modelled for a sleazy photographer, but she knew that Noah would sooner carry her back to Zurich kicking and screaming than permit her to take such unsuitable work.

Her two weeks were almost over when, at half-past four in the afternoon of the last day of February, sitting over a *café crème* inside Café de Flore in Saint-Germain, and browsing through *Une Semaine de Paris*, Madeleine glanced up just in time to see a black-haired girl at the next table slump from her chair in a faint.

"All right," she soothed, as the girl came to and let Madeleine help her up. "You're all right." She signalled a waiter. "*Un cognac, s'il vous plaît, Monsieur.*"

"I'm sorry," the girl murmured weakly, and closed her eyes.

"No need," Madeleine said. The cognac arrived, and she tilted the glass gently against the girl's lips so that just a little trickled into her mouth. "Take it easy, there's no hurry."

"Three times," the girl said, and began to cry.

"Don't," Madeleine said, dismayed. "Maybe you need fresh air – shall I help you outside?"

The girl shook her head. "Not yet." She found a handkerchief in her handbag and dabbed her eyes. "I'm sorry," she said again.

"I can't see why you should be. You're unwell, that's all."

"Not unwell," the girl said, and the tears ran afresh. "Pregnant."

"Oh." Madeleine saw that her hands were ringless, and did not know what else to say.

"Go back to your coffee," the girl said. "I'm fine now."

"No, you're not." Madeleine paused. "What's your name?"

"Simone."

"Sip your cognac, Simone."

The girl obeyed. "And your name?"

"Madeleine Gabriel." She paused again. "Are you sure?"

"That I'm pregnant? Completely." Simone's eyes were black cherries, red rimmed, her skin was pale olive, her lower lip was full but chapped, as if she had chewed on it. "Three months," she said. "And when they find out, I'll be on the street for good."

"Who?"

"Monsieur and Madame Lussac, my employers. I am their *bonne à tout faire*, their housemaid, and I am not strong enough to hide the truth from them – I've already fainted three times."

"Perhaps they would help you?"

"No." Simone shook her head. "How could they? They are decent people, with young children. And in any case, there are things that maybe I shouldn't do any more, if I want to keep my baby."

"Of course you want to keep it."

Simone shrugged. "It would be easier to –" She stopped.

Madeleine looked at her. "Come on."

"I don't have to go yet – I want to sit."

"Not back to your work."

"Where then?"

"With me." Madeleine smiled. "Home."

Madeleine had already formulated what seemed, to her at least, to be a plan of simplicity and brilliance. Even if this girl's employers were more kind-hearted and broad-minded than Simone believed them to be, she would still have to leave before much longer because she would be unable to perform her heavier duties. That, of course, would leave a vacancy for which Madeleine was not as unqualified as she was for most jobs.

"I'm strong," she told Simone decisively. "I'm willing, and I'm desperate to find a job. And it's a living-in position – it's just too perfect!"

"But what about me?" Simone asked reasonably. "Where will I go?"

"You can stay here, with Noah." Madeleine had worked it all out. "He needs a maid, but it will be far lighter work than you're used to – he is the kindest, gentlest man in the world."

"But he doesn't know me. You don't know anything about me – you just picked me up off the floor in a café, a total stranger – you don't even know my second name."

"What is it?"

"Daïa."

"What kind of name is that?"

For the first time since they had met, Simone smiled. "My father is Algerian, my mother French."

"*Bon*," Madeleine said. "So now I know your name."

When Noah came home, Madeleine was ready for him. Telling Simone to stay in her bedroom, she confronted the *chantre* with the most tragic rendition of the girl's story, following it rapidly with her own plan.

"I can present myself to Madame Lussac at her *grand appartement* – they live on two floors at the Palais-Bourbon end of Boulevard Saint-Germain – as the perfect answer to her problem, almost before she even knows she has a problem. She won't even have the time and trouble of looking for a new maid because I can just start as Simone finishes." She stopped, for the first time, and looked at Noah's face for his reaction.

"May I speak now?" he asked mildly.

"Of course."

"How does this help Simone?"

Madeleine confided the second part of her scheme. "And please don't say that you don't need a maid, because you do. A gentleman of your standing should have a housekeeper. You have far more important, more spiritual things to think about than stupid domestic chores. Simone could do your shopping –"

"I like to shop."

"For some things, perhaps, but not for the boring things like soap powder and polish. Anyway, you don't much like cleaning, and I know you hate to iron shirts. Simone irons wonderfully."

"You've seen her work?"

"Not yet, but she told me, and I believe her – she has an honest face."

"May I perhaps see this face?" Noah enquired. "I presume she is the reason that Hexi is scratching at your bedroom door."

"I'll fetch her."

"If you please."

Simone was wretched with embarrassment, her eyes redder than before. "I'm so ashamed, Monsieur," she whispered.

"Where does your family live?"

"In Avignon, Monsieur."

"Wouldn't it be best for you to go home to them?"

"In time," Simone admitted, "I may have no choice, Monsieur, but I still hope that –" she blushed hotly "– that my boyfriend will marry me."

"You love him?"

"Very much."

"And he knows that you are having his child?" Noah asked gently.

Simone nodded. "He's afraid, I think. But he's not a bad boy – he may come back to me. But if I have to leave Paris now, there's no hope."

"I see."

"You do?" Madeleine said eagerly. "I knew you would."

"I see that Mademoiselle Daïa is in a sorry position."

"But it's not so sorry, not now at least." Madeleine's eyes were even brighter than usual. "It's such a wonderful solution – it helps us all."

"It's impossible," Noah said.

"It's not only possible," Madeleine argued, "it's very sensible, too. You said that if I could find a suitable, secure job and somewhere to live, you would approve, and Monsieur and Madame Lussac are very respectable."

"They are," Simone echoed.

"What is Monsieur Lussac's business?" Noah asked Simone.

"He deals in antique furniture, Monsieur. He has a gallery in Faubourg Saint-Honoré – the apartment is filled with beautiful things."

"It sounds wonderful," Madeleine said. "I can hardly wait to see it."

"I can't stop you applying for the position." Noah looked at her gravely. "But I think it would be best if Mademoiselle Daïa told Madame Lussac of her condition, before you jump to the conclusion that there is a vacancy."

"But it's too hard for Simone, and anyway, if she can come here –"

"No," Noah said, firmly.

Simone began to weep again, and Madeleine put an arm protectively around her shoulders. "It would only be for a limited time," she appealed to Noah. "With your help, Simone is bound to talk her boyfriend into marrying her – and if he doesn't, then she'll have to go back to Avignon anyway when she has the baby."

Noah regarded the two girls, one so impulsive, so irresistible, the other so sad, so pathetic and lost. "Even if I was willing," he said, "I have to consider my congregation. They would certainly disapprove, and Madame Wolfe cannot be expected to chaperone indefinitely."

Madeleine glanced at the clock on Noah's mantelpiece, and realizing that it was just a matter of minutes before *la dame respectable* was due to arrive for the evening, she remembered a Hebrew word that Madame Wolfe had used repeatedly over the past twelve days, mostly in reference to Noah. *Mitzvah*. It meant a good deed, particularly of the charitable kind.

She took her own handkerchief from her pocket, and handed it to Simone to wipe her nose. And then she looked directly, challengingly, into Noah's kind, hazel eyes. "You would be performing a wonderful *mitzvah*," she said solemnly, knowing that this was her trump card, that if this did not work, she had lost.

The smile broke over Noah's face like a welcome wave, defeating him just as Madeleine had. And he knew, with certainty, that she would convince the as yet unknown

Madame Lussac, and that she would probably be the most extraordinary *bonne à tout faire* that those good people had ever known.

And he knew that he would miss her.

9

"You have no experience, have you, Madeleine?"

"Not exactly, Madame, but I am young and strong."

"You can, of course, sew?"

"*Oui, Madame.*"

"And iron?"

"*Naturellement, Madame.*"

"Père Beaumarchais tells me that you come from a fine family, and that your home is filled with beautiful things. He seems to believe that this means you will have respect for our possessions."

"Oh, it does, Madame."

"Your hair is rather untidy, Madeleine. Monsieur Lussac and I would wish you to be neat and tidy at all times."

"Of course, Madame. It was rather windy outside." Madeleine paused, seeking to impress. "I can cook quite well, Madame."

"We have a wonderful cook, Madeleine. Though you will be required to serve at family mealtimes, and also at our more modest dinner parties. Shall you be able to manage that, do you think?"

"I shall enjoy it, Madame."

"Very well then."

Within forty-eight hours of meeting Simone Daïa, Madeleine was already ensconced in her new lodgings, a small, whitewashed garret room with a sloping ceiling, a skylight and a window hardly bigger than a man's handkerchief.

Her only furniture was a narrow bed, a little table and a single chair, upon which she sat on her first evening, struggling with her first task: altering Simone's two uniforms to fit her. Madeleine, who prided herself on her honesty, had lied shamelessly about her sewing skills. It was true enough that she had been taught, first by Hildegard, and then at school, but that kind of painstaking, dreary work had been anathema to Madeleine, and she had never troubled to pay the slightest attention.

"I'm paying for it now," she muttered to herself, as she pricked her finger for the fifth time, sucking the spot of blood away before she stained the white collar or cuffs of the black uniform; but she knew that it was vital that she appear with impeccable neatness tomorrow morning, for otherwise all Noah's efforts would have been in vain.

He had worked a minor miracle, calling on Père Beaumarchais, a local priest and a friend, for assistance. While the priest had gone to visit Monsieur and Madame Lussac in Boulevard Saint-Germain, explaining Simone's predicament and suggesting Madeleine as a fine and worthy replacement, Noah and Simone had gone to work on Madeleine, finding her something suitable to wear for her interview, battling with her wild hair so that she might pass muster.

The only insurmountable snag had been Hexi. There was simply no way on earth that Gabrielle Lussac would countenance an animal in her beautiful, immaculate home. Once again, Madeleine's lovely eyes had turned imploringly to Noah.

"You know, better than anyone, about dachshunds."

"I know how much trouble they are," he had grumbled.

"Simone will walk her – it will be good for the baby, force her to get plenty of fresh air. And I will visit every chance I get."

"You won't have much time, you know," Noah had gently warned her. "You came to Paris seeking freedom, but I'm afraid you have tossed it away after only two weeks."

"It was your deadline," she had reminded him. "And you were quite right. I'm prepared to work hard, and when it's very difficult, I'll try to remember that it's just a means to an end."

In less than one week, Madeleine knew that, as usual, she had acted rashly. Anyone less suited to being a housemaid would have been hard to find, but she was determined, nevertheless, to make it work, for she knew that she had no real alternative. Until she found something better – which was unlikely – or her father, or at least Zeleyev, she was blessed to have landed so firmly on her feet.

It was a splendid apartment, filled, as Simone had told her, with lovely, valuable things; beautiful, powder-soft rugs, perfectly hung curtains, fragile porcelain collections, magnificent, heavy pieces of furniture, the finest art, lovingly polished silver. Madeleine had grown up in a house of similar splendour, but she had been a child, a resentful child, who had regarded precious objects on the whole as obstacles to her pleasures. She realized, however, that to Gabrielle and Edouard Lussac, these possessions were truly important, for they had presumably gone through life collecting their prizes together. The task had now fallen to Madeleine to care for these belongings, and the new responsibility alarmed her.

She was always exhausted by the end of the day, had never worked so hard in all her sixteen years. Her employers were in no way unkind, but their standards were high. Their two daughters, Andrée, who was fourteen, and Hélène, two years her junior, were lively, well-behaved girls who were little trouble to Madeleine, since they were out at school or visiting friends for much of the time, and in any case, Madame Lussac, who had come to motherhood rather later than most, took great delight in caring for her children herself.

"Madeleine is hardly older than Andrée," Edouard Lussac commented to his wife. "I feel it is sometimes a struggle for her not to make overtures of friendship to both the girls."

Gabrielle Lussac nodded. "Everything seems quite a struggle for her, I would say. She is not accustomed to hard work."

"But she's eager enough, *n'est-ce pas, chérie*?"

"Certainly she tries hard." Madame Lussac smiled. "And occasionally she succeeds, but it does not come naturally."

It was Madeleine's duty to keep every centimetre of the handsome and spacious two-floor apartment spotlessly clean, to do all the washing and ironing, to assist the cook, Madame Blondeau – a majestically proportioned, steel-grey-haired, fifty-five-year-old woman of great strength – if she so decreed; to clean the family silver – an interminable and thankless task, Madeleine felt, for it seemed to her that no sooner had she finished than she had to begin all over again; and to serve every meal, from breakfast in bed to Madame Lussac, to dinner parties that her *patronne* might consider modest, but that to her new maid seemed lavish and wearyingly frequent.

She did, as her employers had recognized, try very hard, refusing to give in, and since she was young and strong, she knew that the work was within her physical capabilities. But the discipline and the fastidious nature of the job grated against her very nature. Madeleine wanted to run free, to roam the city and beyond – she wanted time to find Zeleyev and Alexander. She had chosen to abandon family life, but in so doing, Madeleine feared that she might have made it impossible for her father to find *her*. She found that as time went by, she missed Amadeus and his loving warmth increasingly, and missed her father even more, though they had spent so little time together in recent years. If she had just known where he was, she could perhaps have tried to accept their separation. But as it was, Alexander Gabriel might as well have been dead, as dead as her grandfather.

In July, Simone Daïa's boyfriend came to 32 *bis* Boulevard Haussmann to claim her and their unborn child, and Noah Levi had his home to himself again, except for Hexi, who was demanding, but made up, in a very small way, for the loneliness he had felt ever since Madeleine's departure. Simone was a good and grateful girl, and had tried her best to please him, but although Madeleine had only been with him for two weeks, that golden hair and those rare, turquoise eyes, together with her courage and – he could only call it *chutzpah* – had made a lasting imprint on his heart. Their friendship, he was certain, would endure, but Noah also sensed that the girl would not stay in Paris for ever, and not to see Madeleine again would be a considerable sadness. She had that effect upon people – she charmed everyone. Noah suspected that she always would.

The Lussacs, too, had apparently fallen under her spell, for otherwise they would undoubtedly have sacked her many times over. Try as she might, Madeleine never looked as a maid ought to look. Her hair, having an undeniable will of its own, refused to remain pinned up beneath the demure white cap she was required to wear – she was *incapable* of looking demure. Over a period of just a few months, Madeleine scorched the Lussacs' silk sheets with the iron, dented their Victorian silver tea service, smashed numerous pieces of Sèvres porcelain and a Meissen figurine and washed Hélène's red lambswool pullover together with Monsieur Lussac's favourite cream cardigan.

"It came out with pink streaks," she wailed to Noah,

on one of her afternoons off. "And he was so kind about it, even though I knew he must be angry."

"I expect he realized it was a mistake," Noah said, in his usual gentle way.

"Of course it was a mistake, but I make so *many*." Madeleine sagged against Noah's settee, fondling Hexi's ears for comfort. "I seem to be so clumsy – most of the time I'm all thumbs, but sometimes I'm an *elephant*!"

"You shouldn't take it so much to heart."

"How can I not? They are really good to me – she can be strict, but she's never unkind or even unreasonable. Madame Blondeau calls me names – she even slapped me once –"

"You're not serious." Noah sat forward, outraged.

"I didn't blame her. I dropped a jug on one of her perfect cheese soufflés just as it was ready to be served – she apologized afterwards for losing her temper, but I'm sure she hates me."

"Nonsense."

"But I'm not giving up." Madeleine stood up. "They've given me chance after chance, and I'm just going to have to try harder." There was a glint in her eyes. "I'll make a good housemaid even if it kills me."

The next afternoon, having beseeched Madame Lussac not to send her new satin and lace peignoir to Moisset in the Faubourg Saint-Honoré for monogramming, so that Madame could see how well her own needlework had progressed, Madeleine completed her laborious task only to discover that she had stitched through both layers of satin on the pocket, thereby effectively sealing the pocket shut. Three days later, having cleared the table after dinner, Madeleine set the appliquéd table-cloth ablaze with a candle she had believed extinguished. And on a free afternoon in November, after walking Hexi for more than an hour on the boulevard, she brought the dachshund through the front hall, Hexi immediately puddling on the Lussacs' soft green carpet.

And yet they did not fire Madeleine. Sometimes, she almost wished that they would.

Madeleine had been placing regular advertisements for several months in the classified sections of two trade journals of the jewellery, gold and silversmiths' world when, one afternoon in April of 1957, she was summoned to take a personal telephone call.

"*Allô?*"

"Magdalena Alexandrovna, is that you?"

"I don't believe it!" Her heart raced with excitement. "Where are you?"

"In Paris."

They met, for a late supper, at Brasserie Lipp, opposite Saint Germain-des-Prés. It was four years since they had last seen one another, but Zeleyev seemed, to Madeleine, hardly to have altered. His hair was just as red and perfectly combed, his moustache just as fiery and neat, his eyes just as green and dancing.

"Maggy, you look wonderful!" His embrace was fierce, his cheek smelt of his favourite, old familiar bergamot oil.

"So do you – but it's Madeleine now."

They sat down, facing each other. The *art nouveau* decorated restaurant was as busy as it always was, buzzing with conversation and the chink of beer glasses.

"Why did you change your name?"

"It seemed right. I changed my life, why not my identity?"

"Your identity did not need changing – but Madeleine suits you."

"Where have you been?" Madeleine could still hardly believe he was there; she felt an urge to reach out and touch him, just to persuade herself that he was real. "How did you find me?"

"I arrived in Paris two days ago," Zeleyev told her. "And yesterday, a colleague in rue du Temple showed me your *annonce* – I was so happy I almost flew to the telephone. I had written to you in Zurich several times, but never received a reply."

"Because I left, more than a year ago."

"After Amadeus," Zeleyev said, and nodded. "I wondered."

"But where were you? I've advertised for months, and I went to Geneva to look for you before I came here – no one had heard of you."

"How quickly they forget," Zeleyev said wryly.

"I remembered you'd said you were working for Perrault et Fils."

"You went there?"

"Only to the store – they were unhelpful."

"I have been in America," Zeleyev said. "In New York City. My talents became a little unfashionable in Europe – over there, I've been appreciated." He paused. "But I still like to travel, and I hate being away from Paris for too long."

"So here we both are." Madeleine paused, and felt all her muscles tautening with tension. "And my father?"

"I have little news, I'm afraid."

"But do you know where he is? He left me a note, saying that you would know how to reach him, that he would tell you." Her painful longing spilled into her voice. "Where is he?"

"I wish I could tell you, Maggy –" He smiled. "I can't just stop calling you that – do you mind?"

"Of course not."

They ordered dinner and two *chopes* of Alsatian beer, before Zeleyev was able to continue. "I have kept an accommodation address here in Paris for years – your father knows of it, but I have only heard from him once since Amadeus died."

"When?"

"Three months after. The letter was postmarked from Hamburg, but there was no address, and Alexander indicated that he would soon be on the move again. There's been nothing since."

"But what did he say in the letter?" Madeleine felt like a starving person – if she could not have the whole meal, she would settle for crumbs. "Do you have it with you?"

Zeleyev shook his head. "I never dreamed I would be seeing you, *ma chère*."

"No."

"I can remember what he said."

"Yes?"

"He wrote briefly, mostly about you, and then about *Eternité*."

"You know then?" Madeleine probed quietly.

"That he took it? Yes, he wrote that he was afraid that the Juliuses or Hildegard might have found it before you could get there, so he took it for safekeeping. He wrote that he loved you more than ever, and that not being able to see you was the greatest sorrow of his life. He said that *Eternité* was for you, and that one day he would be able to give it to you in person, and that until then, he swore to keep it secure, for his father's sake, and for you."

Their beer arrived, and Zeleyev drank thirstily, while Madeleine watched him, waiting to hear more. But there was no more.

"If he writes to you again, you'll be able to tell him where I am."

"Yes. If he gives me his address."

"Why wouldn't he?" She asked the question softly.

"He might not feel able to."

"Why not?" She paused. "Because of the woman? Because of what happened that night?"

Zeleyev's green eyes sharpened. "Who told you?"

"My mother. That's why I left, because of her lies."

"I see."

"Do you?"

Madeleine was overjoyed to be seeing Zeleyev again, to be renewing that most important lost link with her past, and she was relieved beyond words to know that her father had, at least one year before, been safe in Germany. But the anguish that she had pushed away the night she had left Zurich, the outrage against Emilie and, above all, the fear that some of what her mother had said about Alexander might have been true, had never ceased to burn silently deep inside her, waiting, longing to be laid to rest.

"Please, Konstantin, tell me the truth." She saw his pale cheeks flush. "I'm not a child any more." She waited. "You can't make it any worse by telling me what happened. Please."

"Right now?" he asked.

"I've waited ten years," she said, and her voice quivered. "No more."

His eyes narrowed with old, remembered distaste, then softened with pity for her. And then he told her. The same story as Emilie had told, though he told it differently, his voice gentle and stumbling occasionally as he tried to palliate her father's crime.

"We were both to blame," he said. "We were both drunk – I was monstrously drunk. But the drugs, the damned drugs took Alexander over – maddened him, stifled his decency."

"Go on," Madeleine said, her throat tight.

"Your father has paid for his sins – his weakness and his folly – a thousand times over since that night, Maggy. But I, too, have never stopped blaming myself for the part I played."

"You didn't beat the woman," Madeleine whispered miserably. "You didn't try to kill her."

"No, but nevertheless I was to blame." Zeleyev's face was suddenly lined with the pain of memory. "If I had not come to Zurich that day, if I had not needed, like some immature boy, to drink myself stupid, to buy a whore, to lead a married man astray for an evening, your father and mother might still be together – unhappy, but together – and you would still be living in the comfort you were born to."

"You think I care about that?"

"Not for a moment." He sounded bitter. "But I care."

They met as often as possible in the time that remained before he was due to leave Paris again, and sometimes their meetings were the greatest fun Madeleine had experienced since she had last seen him in Davos, but on other occasions they quarrelled heatedly, for Konstantin was deeply concerned, almost to the point of fury, that she was working as a housemaid and wasting her God-given talents.

"You should be taking voice lessons," he told her repeatedly. "Not scrubbing floors! That kind of humiliation has its place in novels, not in real life."

"But you adore your precious novels," Madeleine teased him, remembering that Zeleyev had told her that he never travelled without his two favourites, *Les Misérables* and *Anna Karenina*.

"I am happy to weep over and over again for Fantine and poor Anna," he retorted, "but I have no desire to shed tears over one of the very few people in the world that I love."

They embraced then, for Madeleine was deeply touched by his care, even though his anger amused her, the knowledge of which upset Konstantin even more. She introduced him to the Lussacs, hoping that meeting them would make him feel better, but he only said that he would be delighted if Gabrielle and Edouard Lussac were her friends, but as it was, they were her employers and as such, wrongly considered themselves her superiors. He met Noah Levi, too, and was gratified when Hexi greeted him with passionate wagging and whining, but Madeleine felt that he was aloof with Noah, which distressed her.

"I don't understand you," she said afterwards. "Noah practically saved my life when I first arrived in Paris. Without him, I can't imagine what might have happened to me."

"And I'm grateful to him, of course, for that," Zeleyev said. "But he's still not for you, Maggy."

"Madeleine," she corrected. "And I don't know what you mean by 'not for me'. He's not my boyfriend, for heaven's sake."

"Don't be vulgar."

"Don't you be stuffy, it's not like you."

Zeleyev came to meet her, one day, when she had a free afternoon, and his face was filled with excitement.

"What a morning I've had, Madeleine!"

"Where have you been?"

"*Les égouts*," he told her. "The sewers."

"Why on earth?"

"For Valjean, of course."

"For who?"

"The hero of *Les Misérables*, Jean Valjean." He raised his eyes towards heaven. "You still haven't read it? Obviously not."

"I'm sorry." She smiled.

"It was fantastic. I always wanted to do it – I can't imagine why I never did before, but now that I have, I am addicted!"

"To sewers?"

"To the underside of Paris."

They were sitting in Fouquet's on the Champs-Elysées, crowded as always with glittering types, as well as with the more mundane who liked to stare and listen and to hope that perhaps some of the glitter might rub off.

"So from now on, you will travel everywhere by Métro," Madeleine joked.

"Forget the Métro," Zeleyev scoffed. "I have a much more thrilling prospect in mind."

"Which is?"

"Just wait and see."

He paid the bill, and drew her outside into the street, where he hailed a passing taxi.

"Place Denfert-Rochereau," he told the driver.

"What is there?" Madeleine asked him, intrigued.

"The cemetery of Montparnasse is close by," Zeleyev said.

"We're going to a cemetery?"

"In a sense."

Getting out of the taxi, Madeleine saw a group of people standing outside a green-painted door. Tourists, holding cameras, wearing sunglasses, carrying maps and guide books.

"What is this place?"

"Look." Zeleyev pointed to the paving at their feet. There were three words carved into the concrete: ENTRÉE DES CATACOMBES.

"No," she said, and looked up at him. "Konstantin?"

"You're not afraid of the dark, are you?"

"Not especially, but I like the sun better."

"Then after one hour of darkness, the sun will seem even more wonderful."

The door was opened a few minutes later, and the waiting group were permitted to enter. Zeleyev walked ahead of Madeleine, paid their entrance fees and beckoned her, smiling, towards the steps.

"*Viens*," he said.

The steps were very narrow, spiralling endlessly, dizzyingly down and down into the earth until they reached the bottom and the tourists, who had climbed down with them, began to move away into the first of the tunnels, murmuring, their chuckles uncertain and nervous.

"Why are we doing this?" Madeleine asked Zeleyev.

"For pleasure."

She grimaced. "You are a man of strange tastes."

"Come," he said, and taking her hand, began to lead the way forward. They were moving through a series of tunnels, dark and damp and clammy, stale-smelling and desolate. Occasional, inadequate lamps lit their path, but the clayish ground was uneven, and Madeleine stumbled several times.

"My shoes will be ruined," she complained.

"I will clean them for you, *chérie*." Zeleyev kept hold of her hand. "It will be worth it, I promise you." He stopped and peered into her face. "Are you afraid, *ma petite*?"

"Of course not," she lied.

"Not even a little?"

"Sorry to disappoint you." Water dripped onto her hair. "Hurry up," she urged, wanting to get on, through and out.

They walked on, and Madeleine's eyes grew accustomed to the dark, but her feeling of anxiety intensified as they moved further into what was clearly a labyrinth of tunnels, their safe route marked off by barriers and chains to prevent them from choosing wrong turnings by mistake.

"If we were to leave this path," Zeleyev said, his voice echoing, "we would soon be lost."

Madeleine shivered, and held tighter to his hand. "How much further?"

"We'll soon be at the heart," he told her.

From a distance, ahead of them, they heard a small squeal of fright, followed soon after by another of laughter, and then, just a few minutes later, they arrived at an inner entrance painted black and white.

"Look, *ma chère*," Zeleyev said, and pointed up.

ARRÊTE! C'EST ICI L'EMPIRE DE LA MORT.

"What *is* this place?" Madeleine asked, appalled by the sign.

"The empire of death," he answered simply, and tugged her through the doorway. "The best part."

A moment later, Madeleine halted, abruptly, and jerked her hand out of his. She was staring, mesmerized, at the walls that now surrounded them. No longer made of clay, no longer dark and dismally barren. Now they were built out of bones. The long bones of human bodies, tibias and femurs. And of skulls. Predominantly skulls, hollow, gaping and ancient.

"Take me out of here," she said.

"It's not so far," Zeleyev said, and his eyes, their pupils huge and black, glittered with amusement. "It's fantastic, *n'est-ce pas*?"

"Now," Madeleine said, and her voice was suddenly harsh and insistent. "I don't want to look at this – I don't want to stay another *minute*. I want you to take me out right away, or I will never, ever speak to you again."

"Better now?" Zeleyev asked, when they were back up in the open air. "Would you like some tea? Or a cognac, perhaps?"

"I want to go home." In spite of her intense relief at being back in the real, sweet-smelling world, as sunny and safe as it had been less than an hour earlier, she still felt acutely angry with him.

"Was it really so terrible for you?" Zeleyev was concerned. "I never thought it would upset you so, *ma chère*."

"Didn't you?"

"Of course not." He looked hurt. "A little prickle of fear, maybe, as one might experience on a ride at the funfair, but no more."

"Those were the bones of human beings," Madeleine

rounded on him. "I would never have thought you so insensitive, Konstantin Ivanovich – and how could you bear the dirt?" She brushed at her arms furiously. "I feel quite filthy – how could you *enjoy* it, when you bathe twice a day – ?"

"At least."

"It isn't funny."

"Not if it caused you such discomfort," he said gently. "I thought it would intrigue you to see the real underside of Paris – I should not have inflicted it on you."

"No, you should not."

"I am truly sorry," he said humbly. "From my heart."

Madeleine said nothing.

"Will you forgive me?"

She looked into his face. "I felt trapped down there."

He took her hand again, thankful when she allowed him to. "Forgive me, Maggy, please." His distress was palpable.

"Of course I forgive you," she said, but she felt that she had seen an unfamiliar, unsettling aspect to her friend.

And later that night, she dreamed that she was being crushed alive by a falling mound of skulls, while skeletons danced around her, bones clattering like castanets in a macabre flamenco, and she woke with a start, her hands flailing in the air, and perspiration on her cheeks. Her heart pounding wildly, Madeleine wiped her face, and realized that she was crying.

"Don't be foolish," she told herself softly. "It was nothing."

But it was several more nights before she slept uninterruptedly through till morning, two weeks until she switched the light off before dawn, and a month until she felt able to use the Métro again.

On Zeleyev's last day in the city, he bought Madeleine a gift: a charming antique watch from Au Vieux Cadran in rue Bonaparte, to replace the Patek Philippe that had long since been sold at auction for her by the Crédit Municipal.

"This is to remind you," he told her, "that time is speeding by, and is not to be frittered away. This job of yours –"

"I thought you understood," Madeleine sighed.

"I do. At least, I can accept that sometimes in life one must compromise, but I want you to swear to me that you will remember that this is for you only a temporary measure, a means to an end, as you yourself said."

"I swear it, Konstantin."

"Each time I think of you, wearing a uniform, at the beck and call of employers, however pleasant they may be, I shudder." As if to underscore his words, Zeleyev shuddered theatrically.

Madeleine smiled. "I'll remember."

"You are not singing," he went on. "You should be singing, not cleaning."

"How can I?"

"Don't you want to sing any more?"

"Of course I do."

Madeleine tried not to think too much about that particular longing, for it was, after all, only one of many lacks in her life, and in any case, one had to have strength to sing, and she seemed to use up most of her reserves in the course of her daily work. She remembered it, though, the magical feeling of release, of soaring happiness, that had always accompanied the songs when she had gone up into the forests above Zurich, or when she had been at her grandfather's house.

"Never give up," Konstantin said. "Not the singing, nor anything else you desire of life."

After he had returned to New York, Madeleine experienced a terrible sense of anticlimax. She felt empty and flat, as if she had lost her sense of purpose. The longed-for contact with Zeleyev had been achieved, and since he had sworn to her, at their emotional, tearful parting, that he would telephone her as soon as he heard from Alexander again, she could sustain the hope that she would, one day, see her father again. But for now, there was nothing to be done but to carry on.

The worst of it was that at last, after so many years of uncertainty, she now knew the truth about that night, and in knowing, Madeleine had to accept that Emilie had not, after all, lied. It was like accepting defeat. And yet the essential differences between Madeleine, Hildegard and her mother seemed more strongly emphasized than ever, for Madeleine knew now that her love for her father was unconditional. He was a flawed man, he was not the gleaming hero of her childhood, but then again, she was no longer a child, and Alexander's weaknesses, and even his sins did not, she found, diminish her care for him at all.

She did regret the romance and adventure that had disappeared from her life. Madeleine had come to Paris to find her father and to make a new start, feeling like a heroine in a film, prepared to make sacrifices for what she knew was right. Now she was left with reality, and the knowledge that she had left behind a life of luxury, comfort and security for a job as a *bonne à tout faire*, with little more freedom than she had had before.

On her afternoons off, she took to wandering through the moneyed streets of the city, reminding herself of what she had given up without a backward glance. She gazed in at the windows of Hermès, remembering her grandmother's *glacé* kid gloves, sent back periodically to the Faubourg Saint-Honoré for cleaning; she looked through the *vitrines* of Louis Vuitton, and recognized her stepfather's dark brown, gold-lettered trunks, recalled him bragging that he had inherited them from his father, and that the Juliuses had their own registered locks and keys, noted down for posterity in Avenue Marceau. She passed by Balenciaga, Guy Laroche and Nina Ricci, and heard again Emilie's sighs of pleasure as she had admired photographs in her glossy magazines. She looked at marble baths and Turkish towelling robes and *grand luxe* hotels and gourmet restaurants, and then she returned to her tiny, inadequately heated room, and put on the black and white uniform that scratched her skin, and hurried downstairs to the kitchen to assist Madame Blondeau with the dinner preparations.

Madeleine was too honest to deny to herself that she did have some regrets, but she remembered Konstantin's admonition that this life must be only temporary, her means to an end.

And she knew that, in spite of everything, she had not been wrong to leave the Gründli Haus. And that she would never go back.

10

Edouard and Gabrielle Lussac continued to tolerate their unusual housemaid, never quite certain why they did so, knowing only that Madeleine brought a little extra sunlight into their home that they, as well as Andrée and Hélène, enjoyed, and knowing too that they would have been overcome by irrational guilt if they had asked her to leave.

Madeleine had, however, grown bored. She still adored Paris, but she had too little opportunity to enjoy what the city had to offer. She had Noah for her friend, loyal, gentle man that he was, and she was immensely happy when he became engaged to be married to a pretty, dark-haired girl from Lyons, named Estelle Gallant, who was deeply in love with her fiancé, and as fond as he was of Hexi. Madeleine liked her enormously for her humour, kindness and patience, but in a way, her friends' great happiness laid bare the emptiness of her own life that she had fought to ignore. She was lonely.

One day before her eighteenth birthday in December, giving way to one of her characteristic fits of impulse, Madeleine vented all her frustrations on her hair. She knew that it was beautiful hair, but it drove her *mad*. All her life it had caused her nothing but trouble. As a child, Hildegard and Emilie and her teachers had been forever reprimanding her for her untidiness, had twisted her detested plaits even more tightly, scraping every unruly strand of gold off her forehead and cheeks. Madame Lussac would never dream of laying a finger on her, but her mild looks of disapproval were eloquent enough.

Madeleine had had enough. She seized the scissors from her wicker sewing basket, marched into the bathroom, stood before the mirror and began to cut. Too small, too blunt – she ran back to her room to fetch the shears she used for cutting cloth. *Snip, snip* – that was too slow. She became bolder, lopping off the length at first, she could worry about styling and shaping after the thick mass had been pruned away –

Long before she had finished, Madeleine knew that she had made another grievous mistake, perhaps the most ghastly blunder *ever*. She had wanted to look chic as well as neat and tidy, but now, as she stared with appalled eyes into the glass, she saw that she resembled nothing so much as an upturned kitchen mop!

"Madeleine!"

She heard Madame Lussac's voice, summoning her, and realized that she was late. Panic-stricken, she brushed the hair up as well as she could, stuffing the severed gold into a paper bag, and then she hurried into her uniform, more than grateful, for once, for the white cap which she tugged down as far as it would reach and gripped firmly into place.

"Madeleine, where on earth have you been? I'm late for an appointment with the dentist and I want to give you a shopping list."

So rushed was her *patronne*, that she did not, mercifully, even glance at Madeleine, who took the list and scurried away, sending up a quick prayer of thanks. She would perform all her tasks in record time, and try to do *something* with her atrocious hair before the rest of the family came home. Plenty of time after that to weep at her disastrous appearance, for she knew already that she would have to live with her mistake for months.

*   *   *

Madame Lussac having given her an additional day off for her birthday, Madeleine was expected for lunch at Noah's apartment. It was a very cold day, giving her an excuse to pull a woollen hat down over her ears, but although she insisted on keeping the hat on while Noah and Estelle toasted her, when she attempted to sit down at the table still wearing it, Noah reached out, laughing, and plucked it from her head.

"*Dieu.*" The laughter died on his face. Hexi growled.

Madeleine's lower lip quivered, but she refused to give way. "You like it?" she enquired brightly. "It's the very latest."

"What happened?" Estelle asked.

"Did you set fire to it?" Noah stared at her. "Were you attacked?"

"Don't be ridiculous," Madeleine said huffily.

"But what happened?"

"I cut it."

"With what – an axe?"

"Noah, don't be horrid," Estelle scolded him.

"I'm sorry – it's just the shock. Your beautiful hair."

"I know." Madeleine stared at the soup plate that Estelle had set before her. "But can we please not discuss it any more."

Estelle stood up. "*Viens*," she said.

"Where?" Noah asked.

"Not you. Madeleine, come with me."

"Why?" Madeleine looked up at her.

"Repairs," Estelle said.

"Do you think you could do something with it?" Hope flared in Madeleine's eyes. "I tried and tried, but it just got more and more ragged."

"I wouldn't dare touch it." Estelle hurried from the room, and came back wearing her own coat and carrying Madeleine's. "But a fine hairdresser can perform miracles."

"Truly?" Madeleine looked dubious.

"Just go," Noah said emphatically. "Do whatever Estelle tells you to do. Take my word for it, she's almost always right." He paused. "In any case, nothing could make it any worse than it is now."

Madeleine rose, and Hexi growled again. "It seems I have no choice."

"None at all," Noah agreed.

"But what about lunch?" Madeleine asked Estelle, feeling guilty. "You've gone to so much trouble. Shouldn't we eat first?"

"We have to go immediately." Estelle held out Madeleine's coat. "At Charles of the Ritz, they are booked for weeks in advance, if not months. As it is, we shall have to beg. I'm only hoping that if someone there takes a glance at you, they may rise to the challenge."

Three hours passed. The two young women emerged from the *salon de beauté*, one unchanged, the other feeling entirely transformed.

"It isn't me," Madeleine whispered, still trembling as she clutched at Estelle's arm for support. "It can't be."

"I assure you it's very much you." Estelle cast an approving, admiring gaze over the younger girl. "I feel almost like a Pygmalion."

Madeleine turned back to stare at herself again in the reflection of the window. "It's wonderful, *n'est-ce pas*?"

"It's stupendous."

"Thank you." Madeleine spun around again, and her eyes were ablaze with gratitude. "I don't know *how* to thank you, Estelle. You saved me – I thought – I hoped that perhaps he might be able to make me look at least decent, but I look –"

"Beautiful."

"Truly?"

Estelle smiled. "Until now, your hair – which was

wonderful hair, a wild halo – but it overwhelmed your face, your body, even your personality." She scrutinized Madeleine carefully. "Suddenly I can see that you have lovely cheekbones and a perfect neck – and a sexy mouth –"

"Really?" Madeleine felt herself blushing.

"And what you need now is a new wardrobe."

"I can't afford any more clothes. This coat used up all my savings." Madeleine plunged her hands into the deep pockets of the hooded tweed coat she had leapt upon with uncharacteristic acquisitiveness on a stall in the *Marché aux Puces* the previous month. She had never worn second-hand clothes before, had found the notion unappealing, but this coat had beckoned her from two hundred yards. "Don't you like it?" she asked Estelle. "It has such a swing to it."

"I like it very much, but you can't wear a coat indoors, can you?" Estelle paused. "Let me buy you something new."

"Certainly not," Madeleine said definitely. "You've been much too generous already." Estelle had insisted upon paying the bill at Charles of the Ritz, saying that it was a birthday gift from her and Noah, and much as Madeleine had wanted to argue, she had known that it would have been almost impossible for her to find the money.

"Then buy yourself just one thing." Estelle was not giving up. "We have time – let's at least go and look in the rue de Sèvres."

Madeleine settled, in the end, for a lapis-coloured lambswool pullover that Estelle assured her set off her eyes, which looked more enormous and brilliant than ever now that her hair no longer overshadowed them; and then, after embracing Estelle fervently and lovingly, she had excused herself from returning with her to Boulevard Haussmann, for it was growing quite late, and she had a sudden forcible and undeniable need to be alone for a while. This truly was, she felt, the new Madeleine – Maggy, the child, had gone for good. It was a special, exhilarating feeling, and she wanted to share it with Paris, for the city had already given her so much: good friends to cherish, a decent, secure job and a roof over her head, and the gradual, gentle revelation of her true, developing self.

It had begun to snow, but Madeleine did not want to put up her hood, and she had tossed her woollen hat into a waste bin. Nothing was going to make her cover her glorious new hair. Large, wet flakes settled fleetingly on her head, dampened her cheeks and chilled her small, flat, newly revealed ears, but she did not care.

Suddenly hungry, and finding herself near the Place de la Madeleine, she went into Fauchon. She had not entered the store since her second morning in the city, but today was her eighteenth birthday, today was different. *She* was different. She bought two miniature quiches lorraines and a feathery *mille-feuille*, then walked over to Tanrade and bought two small boxes of marrons glacés, one for Estelle, the other for Madame Lussac, and then, armed with her purchases and the bag in which the saleslady had slipped her old, rejected pullover, she walked briskly to the Jardin des Tuileries.

Dusk was settling over the gardens, and Madeleine had only just brushed the soft snow off a bench so that she could sit down and eat her quiches, when she saw the man.

He was just a few yards away, almost close enough to touch. Tall and thin – very thin – angular yet graceful, he wore a black pullover and black trousers beneath an open, olive-green raincoat. Hatless, his hair was straight and brown, his eyes were, in the half-light at least, dark blue with thick black lashes. A cigarette, alight and sending a small stream of smoke up into the air, stuck out from the side of his mouth, casually, naturally, as if it were a part of him, an extension.

It had stopped snowing, and Madeleine was able to study him closely, though he did not appear to see her. His skin looked smooth and pale, as if it seldom saw sunlight, and his hands, ungloved, were slender and long-fingered. He was a beautiful man, she thought.

He was feeding birds, a small cluster of little city birds, with what looked like croissant crumbs, and Madeleine realized after a moment or two that he was speaking to them in a gentle, low voice. She continued to stare, holding her breath as a sparrow hopped onto his left boot, its tiny claws tap-tapping on the leather, and quite unconsciously, Madeleine refrained from eating, even from raising her quiche to her lips, loath to move in case she spoiled the moment.

The crumbs were finished, and most of the birds had carried off their spoils, but the man still spoke softly, addressing the bird on his boot, not moving either foot until, at last, the ash that had gathered at the tip of his cigarette broke away, falling to the snowy ground, and the spell was broken. The sparrow flew away, and the man turned to face Madeleine.

"Thank you for waiting," he said.

His smile, Madeleine thought, was warm and genuine. She guessed that he smiled often, for though his face was young, the laughter lines around his eyes and his straight mouth were quite pronounced.

"Would you like to sit down?" She felt no qualms about clearing a second space on her bench.

"*Merci.*" He sat. "They look delicious." He looked at the quiches.

"Will you have one? I can't eat both." Madeleine held one out, and he accepted it, easily.

They began to talk, a warm, bubbling sense of pleasure and excitement coursing through Madeleine's body, like central heating just turned on. This was all a part of today, her special day. His name, he told her, was Antoine Bonnard.

"Like the painter?" she said.

"*Exactement.*"

He had been born and raised in Normandy, but he had been living in Paris for seven years, where he now worked as the manager of a small restaurant in Saint-Germain.

"It's called Fleurette," he told her, and she saw pride in his eyes. "It was doing okay when I first came, but now it's doing better."

They were silent for a few minutes while they ate, and Madeleine noticed that his teeth were white and sharp, and that he smelled wonderfully of a light cologne, dusted over with the Gauloise cigarettes that he had smoked right until he had begun eating, and which he began smoking again immediately after he had finished.

"Do you like it here?" he asked her.

"The Tuileries?" She nodded. "Very much, though there are much lovelier gardens in Paris, don't you agree?"

"For me, the Luxembourg are the best," he said. "They are beautiful and joyful all the year round – I go there when my mood is dark and I need to cheer up so that I don't depress the customers."

"And here?"

"I come here when I feel especially content and, consequently, benevolent, and particularly in the winter months, for I always feel that the hungry birds in this *parc noble* are much less likely to be fed by the passers-by than in the Luxembourg."

They spoke for almost an hour, sharing the *mille-feuille*, he smoking another two cigarettes, and Madeleine told the stranger all there was to tell about her life in Paris, though she made little reference to Magdalen, or to any other aspect of her past. She told him, briefly, about her work as a housemaid, and he laughed when he heard about all the mistakes she continued to make, and she told him about the generosity of the Lussac family, and about her wonderful friends, Noah and Estelle, and about Hexi. And she told him about her ambition to become a singer, and about the impossibility of even trying to fulfil that ambition, since she had neither a place to practise, nor the money with which to pay for the lessons she badly needed.

And as Madeleine spoke and spoke, unburdening herself as if they had been friends for years, Antoine Bonnard listened attentively to every word, and licked the custard cream from the pastry off his fingers, and lit yet another cigarette, by which time it had grown quite dark, and the lamps marking out the paths to the exit gates were alight.

"Aren't you cold?" Madeleine asked him, suddenly aware that she was chilled to the bone.

"Icy."

"I should go." She did not want to go.

"Shall I walk with you?"

"Please."

They left the gardens together at the Place de la Concorde, and Madeleine thought how remarkable it was that they both lived and worked within just a few kilometres of each other on the Left Bank, and yet they had met on the Right, in that very place she had visited almost two years before on a wintry day, sensing at that time the mysterious importance of the Tuileries to her. They crossed the Pont de la Concorde, and Antoine Bonnard walked beside her, quite close, yet not touching, not even brushing, and Madeleine thought that he was courteous as well as beautiful, and that she could hardly wait to see him again.

They came to the Lussacs' apartment house, and it occurred to Madeleine to pretend that she lived further on down the boulevard, so that she could go on and on, with no farewell, but discipline stilled her feet and made her stop.

"I have to go inside."

"It's a fine house." Antoine Bonnard looked through the tall, wrought-iron gates beyond the small gravel courtyard at the impressive stone façade. "Not a bad place to work."

"No," she said. "But not like Fleurette."

"No." He paused. "It's a pity to have to work on your birthday."

"They gave me the day. This evening they are entertaining."

"And they need you."

"To spill soup on the guests," she laughed ruefully. "It wouldn't be the first time. I can't imagine why they put up with me."

"I think I can." He opened the gate for her. "I am late." Unexpectedly, he reached for her right hand, removed her glove and raised the hand to his lips, kissing it lightly. "*Joyeux anniversaire*," he said.

And then he turned, and began to walk away, slowly, down Boulevard Saint-Germain, tossing away one cigarette and instantly lighting its successor. And Madeleine, staring after him, watching as he grew smaller and more distant, her hand still tingling with the brush of his mouth, realized only then, with a terrible pang, that they had made no plans to meet again.

"I can't bear it," she said aloud, and it was all she could do not to rush down the street after him, to abandon the Lussacs – but then she remembered her pride, and that she was by now more than one hour later than she had promised Madame, and so on legs suddenly heavier, she went inside and up to her room, and she took off the lovely lapis pullover, and put on her uniform.

The white cap no longer had to conceal a tangle; now it

perched, quite irreproachably, atop Madeleine's gleaming new head. And when she went downstairs, and when Gabrielle Lussac saw her, she raised her eyebrows in surprise, and then smiled, yet Madeleine sensed that it was not altogether a smile of approval.

Monsieur Lussac's reaction was even more confusing. "What have you done, Madeleine?" He looked disappointed.

"Don't you like it, Monsieur?"

He regarded her thoughtfully, and she saw a glimmer of admiration in his eyes. "Very pretty," he admitted. And then, a little disturbingly, she felt, he looked quickly away.

Much later that night, after Madeleine had put away her black dress and washed her white apron, and was wearily rinsing through her thick, sensible black stockings, she glanced up at her reflection and saw, suddenly, what she guessed had taken her employers by surprise. The new hairstyle had done much more than emphasize her natural good looks. It had stripped away the artless innocence that her wild halo had bestowed on her, and it had stamped something brand-new and startling upon her. Sensuality. In her uniform, until tonight, Madeleine's appearance had elicited amusement and sympathy; she had appealed to Edouard and Gabrielle Lussac as a young girl from a fine background, thrown on harder times and struggling to keep a position to which she was unsuited. Now, Madeleine realized, she looked provocative. And that realization made her think again of Antoine Bonnard, and to wonder in exactly what light he had seen her.

Hanging up her stockings to dry, she remembered him so vividly that he might have been standing beside her now, so thin and strong, a kind of tensile strength . . . his navy blue eyes, his narrow lips, dragging on the cigarettes . . . his gentleness with the birds, the warmth of his smile . . . his kiss on the back of her hand . . .

"Antoine," she said aloud. The name sounded wonderful, felt beautiful as she repeated it, softly, over and over again, her lips forming a kiss with the second syllable. "Antoine."

It was only as she turned out the light and lay down in bed, that she understood what had happened to her that afternoon, in the snowy Tuileries.

"*Ich bin verliebt*," she murmured, and then, preferring the sound in French, having grown accustomed to the charm of her second language: "*Je suis amoureuse.*"

It was the same in any language. Madeleine was in love.

Christmas came, and went, and then the New Year celebrations. The *grand appartement* was aglow with festivity, parties, goodwill and *bonhomie*. The Lussacs, considerate as always, hired outside help so that Madeleine should not feel exploited, and after Andrée and Hélène had begged their parents to invite Madeleine to sit at the table with them on Christmas Eve, though Gabrielle Lussac had felt compelled to refuse so as to protect Madame Blondeau's sensibilities, Madeleine was asked, as a guest, to their Saint-Sylvestre party, since the cook had gone home to Marseilles for a week.

"What should I do?" Madeleine asked Noah and Estelle, who had also invited her to spend New Year's Eve with them. "I'd much rather be with you, but they were so kind to ask me – I don't want to offend them."

"Surely they wouldn't be upset," Noah said.

"They might," Estelle said. "I'm sure Madeleine is the first maid they've ever invited."

"And so they should," Noah said.

"Maybe so, *chéri,* but whereas with us, Madeleine knows that we would not dream of being offended if she refuses us, with Monsieur and Madame Lussac, she might be risking their friendship."

Madeleine, wearing a cut-down black velvet dress of

Estelle's, saw in the New Year in the company of antique and art dealers, a handful of aristocrats and a sprinkling of actresses and playboys, all mingling in a wondrously comfortable atmosphere of *vieille richesse*. She was ogled by an eighty-year-old count, flirted with by a three-times married racehorse breeder, and for one dangerous half-hour, Andrée's new boyfriend, a seventeen-year-old golden boy named Marc, buzzed around Madeleine with all the enthusiasm of a juvenile bee on its first foray into the honey pot. Madeleine shook them all off with good grace and tact, and steered a wide berth around Marc for the rest of the night, but though in many respects she had never enjoyed herself more, the one person she most longed to see was not there.

She could not eradicate Antoine Bonnard from her mind. The holidays over, she tried hard to plunge into work, but she found that she saw his face on every surface she polished, on every sheet and shirt and blouse that she ironed, and whenever she thought of him, which was almost all the time, she nearly burst with the need to sing at the top of her voice, and had to calm herself instead with a discreet humming under her breath.

She went to the Jardin des Tuileries three times, carrying bags of bread-crumbs, and each time she sat for a while, then strolled, and was rebuked for littering the gardens, for whether it was because the birds had no need of her crumbs, or whether it was simply because she was not Antoine, they did not approach her. Neither did she see him.

"Perhaps," she said to Hexi, on the third occasion, as she began to walk back to Boulevard Haussmann to return the dachshund to Noah's care, "I'm too young for pride. Perhaps I should just find his restaurant – his Fleurette. Perhaps I should go to him."

Hexi, always extravagantly keen to go out on her walks, was by now impatient to go back home to warmth, dinner and her own armchair. She lunged forward, half choking herself on her collar, and coughed disgustedly in reply.

"Noah says that I don't really know anything about him, that I shouldn't speak to strange men in parks, but if that were true, we'd never have met Noah or Estelle, would we?"

Halting before crossing the rue de Rivoli, the dachshund decided it was time to be carried, and scrabbled demandingly at Madeleine's legs. Obedient as always, Madeleine obliged.

"You have to decide," she said, looking right into the animal's intelligent little eyes. "On my next day off, shall I go to find him or not? If you agree that I should, lick my face."

Hexi licked her nose.

"You are a highly gifted dog, do you realize?"

Hexi licked her cheek. Had Noah Levi been present, he would have pointed out that Hexi was almost as fond of licking faces as she was of freshly boiled chicken breast, but he was not present.

One hour later, just as Madeleine was entering the Lussacs' house, she heard a scraping of gravel in the courtyard behind her, and then, quite softly, a voice.

"Madeleine."

She turned around. He was there, leaning against the iron gate. He looked exactly the same as the last time, as if he had been out walking ever since her birthday, all in black, except for the olive-green raincoat, the dark, straight hair falling a little over his forehead, a cigarette in the corner of his mouth.

"Hello," she said, and her heart contracted.

"I want to hear you sing," he said simply.

"Now?"

"If it's possible." He paused. "Is it?"

"Of course." And without a second thought, or even a

backward glance, Madeleine went with him, through the gate and up the boulevard. As before, they walked together, still not touching, he with his hands in his pockets, she measuring her steps against his, matching him pace for pace, hardly daring to speak.

They went down into the Métro at Chambre des Députés, and emerged at Saint-Lazare, and Antoine Bonnard said scarcely a few words, just took her arm at street crossings, and ground one last Gauloise under his boot before he led her into a house on the rue de Rome.

"Where are we?" Madeleine asked.

"You will see." He went ahead of her, up the stairs, and on the second floor he opened a door, and they were in a dance studio, with wall mirrors and *barres* all around the room, and an upright piano at one end.

"Give me your coat." He took it from her, then removed his raincoat, folded it over and dropped them both, together, onto the wooden floor. And then he sat down on the piano stool and opened the lid.

"*Chante-moi quelque chose*," he said.

Madeleine stared at him. She wondered if perhaps she was dreaming – perhaps this was just another of the wishful fantasies she had suffered ever since they had first met. And yet she knew that she was entirely awake, that she had never been so awake in her life. That just as she had known that Paris was a part of her destiny, and that the Tuileries would be important to her, this man was *vital* to her. And if he wanted her to sing, then sing she would.

She began with 'J'ai deux amours', and he accompanied her, playing softly, gently, following her lead, then moving forward with her, adapting to her style. She came to the end of the song, and waited.

"Go on," he said.

So she went on. She sang every song she knew, and some she had not even known that she had stored in her memory, songs she had heard on the wireless, and in the cafés, and on the streets. And when she ran out of words, she extemporized or hummed, and her voice, untrained and out of practice, grew tired and huskier, but still Madeleine went on singing, and all the while, the man followed her and, sometimes, led her on the piano, and all the time, his eyes never left her face.

Until, at last, she was out of melodies and out of voice, and Antoine Bonnard played two more soft, completing chords, closed the lid on the piano, and held out his right hand to her.

"*Viens*."

And Madeleine crossed the studio to him, and he rose from the stool, inclined his head, and kissed her, on her throat.

He took her to a night club near the Champs-Elysées, and Madeleine telephoned Madame Lussac to explain that she had been unavoidably detained by a matter more important than she could possibly explain over the phone. And Antoine ordered whisky for himself, and a *vin chaud* for her, to soothe her throat, and then he lit a cigarette and began, finally, to talk.

"I should have liked to have taken you to Fleurette tonight, but it is closed for the evening – and anyway, there is a singer performing here whom I want you to hear and to watch."

Madeleine wanted to watch only him. He seemed different now; he was still relaxed, but there was a greater intensity and alertness about him. She was fascinated by the club, and by the customers slowly filtering in for the evening, but it was hard to tear her eyes away from Antoine.

"All right?" he asked her.

"Wonderful," she replied.

While they had been in the studio, the songs and the act of singing had absorbed Madeleine, lifting her up and out of herself, as they always did. But now that she was back on firmer ground, and sitting so close to Antoine Bonnard, she had the most fervent, overwhelming desire to touch him. He was so *real*, after all those futile fantasies, sitting beside her folded into his chair like some dark, gleaming cat with navy-blue eyes. It was the first time Madeleine had experienced a physical need for a man. She sensed his body heat beneath the thin black wool sweater – she wanted, violently, to curl up in his arms and to press her cheek against the skin of his chest, and to inhale him. . .

"Shall we order some dinner?" he asked.

"Order for me," Madeleine said weakly, and was glad to let him, for she had no appetite for food, did not care what she ate, or whether or not she ate anything at all, though she picked up her knife and fork and made a small pretence of eating, and drank the red wine that was poured into her glass.

"I think that, if you agree, you should take singing lessons," Antoine said softly. "I have a friend – a teacher."

"Would he be willing, do you think?"

"He'll listen to you, and then he'll decide." Having finished his first course, Antoine lit a cigarette and leaned a little closer. "You must assemble a repertoire, Madeleine. If you do that, and if the lessons go well, I would hope that you might sing for the guests at Fleurette." He paused. "Might that interest you, do you think?"

"Very much," she murmured. But for several moments, though she knew that she ought to have felt thrilled beyond measure, Madeleine felt only the bitterest disappointment, for he was still talking about her singing, while she had moved on, and was thinking only about him.

"*Mange un p'tit peu*," he told her. "If you don't eat, you will lose your strength. *Tu es assez fragile*."

"I'm stronger than I look," Madeleine said, and then

she looked deeply, boldly, into his eyes, and Antoine Bonnard returned the look perfectly, eloquently matched. And she realized at that moment that, though he might not be ready, for reasons of his own, to speak of what he felt, he, too, was thinking of much more than Madeleine's singing, and possessed and warmed by that sudden knowledge, she began to glow.

And then the music began.

Madeleine had never been in a *boîte de nuit*, had never sat in the smoky, whisky- and pastis-scented air of a jazz club. She had never seen people sitting so magnetized and still, eyes half-closed, their voices, if they spoke at all, lower than whispers. And all because of the music. Because of the singer.

"Who is she?" She spoke against Antoine's ear.

He turned his head slightly. "Just look," he said. "Just listen."

She was a black American, fifty years old at least and not at all physically beautiful, but she compelled her audience with her presence and her voice and her artistry. She started with 'Stormy Weather', and went on singing mainly in English, and Madeleine understood little, yet comprehended everything. The voice was like nothing she had ever heard, deep and throaty, melodic, yet slipping and sliding deliberately off some notes, then returning to the straight, true note again, often an octave higher or lower. It was emotional, evocative, sensual singing. It caught Madeleine by the throat, by the stomach, by the heart, and tears sprang to her eyes – and when, at one moment, she cast a brief and rapturous glance at Antoine, she found that he was watching her instead of the singer and, in spite of her absorption, an extra thrill of joy shivered through her.

It was after two when they left.

"Shall you be in trouble?" Antoine asked her, as the cold night air struck their warm faces.

"Probably."

"I'm sorry."

"It doesn't matter."

Madeleine realized that she ought to care, but she did not. She felt as if her life as Gabrielle Lussac's *bonne à tout faire* was quite unreal, as if this evening, this night was the only reality. She wanted never to leave Antoine's side – she wanted him to take her to his home, to the small apartment he had told her he lived in above his restaurant. She wanted him to make love to her, and to hell with the consequences.

But instead, he found a taxi and gave the Lussacs' address, and he took her back through the tall iron gate, into the house and up to the front door of the apartment itself.

"It was wonderful," Madeleine whispered, and turned her face up to his.

"I'm glad," he said, and smiled down at her, and the laughter lines around his eyes were deeply etched.

But all her hopes were blighted, for he did not even kiss her, neither her mouth, nor her throat, nor even her hand. He merely touched her left cheek with his fingers, gently, tenderly. And was gone.

Madeleine came closer, the next morning, to being dismissed, than she had ever come before. At ten o'clock, she was due to collect half a dozen spun sugar orchids from the famed Madame Lapierre for the dinner party that her employers were hosting that evening, but on her way back home, Madeleine dropped and shattered them. All her attempts at replacing them in their neatly cellophaned boxes with fresh orchids, even with Madame Blondeau's help, were in vain.

"*Mais qu'est-ce qui s'est passé?!*" Madame Lussac, still awaiting an explanation of Madeleine's absence the previous evening, was horrified by the sight of the already wilting flowers. "What have you done?"

"I dropped the boxes on the pavement, Madame," Madeleine said, her eyes humbly downcast. "I hoped that these would substitute, but –"

"Why didn't you ask Madame Lapierre to replace them?"

"She's always so busy – I assumed it would be too late –"

"I'll telephone her right away." Madame Lussac was distracted, already looking for the number in her address book. She reached for the telephone and began to dial, then glanced up at Madeleine. "And afterwards, I shall want to know what was so impossible for you to explain when you called last night."

"Of course, Madame."

Though against her better judgement, Madeleine was still almost totally incapable of lying. Face to face with her *patronne*, once a satisfactory high-speed order had been arranged with the wonderful Madame Lapierre, she told the absolute, unvarnished truth.

"I was so happy to see him again, Madame – I just went with him."

"Forgetting your obligations."

"I'm afraid so."

"And you are, presumably, very sorry?"

"Of course I am, though –"

"Though?" Madame Lussac's eyebrows were dangerously raised.

Madeleine took a chance. "Though it was so very wonderful, Madame. I'm only sorry that I let you and Monsieur down. You deserve better from me."

"Indeed."

Madeleine waited for the axe to fall, but the same reluctant sense of protectiveness that had kept Gabrielle Lussac from sacking the girl many times before now, held her in check today. However angry she might feel, if she turned Madeleine Gabriel out onto the streets in the idiotic, romantic haze she was in, heaven only knew what fate might befall her.

One week passed without word from Antoine. Madeleine fretted and day-dreamed constantly, one minute expecting him to materialize miraculously in the apartment or in the street or in the food market on the rue de Seine, the next minute feeling desolate and wretched, certain that she would never see him again.

The concierge of the apartment house, a red-haired woman with a sour lemon expression, handed Madeleine the note on the eighth morning after she had last seen him.

Your first lesson with Monsieur Gaston Strasser has been arranged at the studio in rue de Rome at two o'clock in the afternoon next Monday.

A.B.

There was nothing more, no mention of whether or not Antoine intended to be present at the lesson, not an endearment – not even a single personal word. Madeleine, in a momentary fit of pique, frustration and despair, crumpled the note into a ball and threw it away. Only minutes later, she was on her knees, smoothing out the paper, scanning the words for hidden meaning, studying the handwriting – forward slanting, clear and even – for clues to his character.

"I've had a note," she told Andrée, before dinner that evening. The older of the Lussacs' daughters had lately taken to visiting Madeleine in her room, confiding in her the little details of her friendship with her boyfriend Marc that she would not have dared to disclose to her mother, and with which she would not trust her sister.

"From him?" Andrée's dark eyes lit up. "Show me."

"It's just a note."

"Not a love letter?"

"Certainly not. He has organized a singing lesson for me, that's all."

"Really? How romantic!"

"There isn't a hint of romance in it, Andrée," Madeleine assured the sixteen-year-old. "He didn't even sign his name."

"Show me then." She took the piece of notepaper, regarded it for a moment, then raised it to her face, closed her eyes and sniffed it.

"What are you doing?"

"I smell – fragrance –"

"That's his cologne."

"I like it." Andrée still kept her eyes closed. "And I smell – spices, and a touch of fish. He must have written this in the kitchen."

"You're inventing it, Andrée," Madeleine laughed.

"No, I'm not. Wait –" She wrinkled her nose. "Gitanes."

"Now I know you're making it all up." Madeleine took back the note. "Anyway, he smokes Gauloises."

"I like his writing." Andrée was unperturbed. "Honest and artistic, I should say."

"And of course you'd know."

"Why not?"

Madeleine shrugged. "In any case, it doesn't make any difference, since he evidently arranged this lesson to be rid of me."

"If he didn't want you, why should he go to the trouble?"

"Because he said that he would."

"I told you he's honest." Andrée regarded Madeleine curiously. "I'll bet that he turns up at the lesson, but if he doesn't, what will you do then?"

"Nothing. Except sing." Madeleine sighed. "And even that will be a waste of Monsieur Strasser's time, since I can't possibly afford to pay for more than one lesson."

"He'll come," Andrée said confidently. "You're much too gorgeous for him to forget about."

Madeleine laughed.

"Everyone thinks you're much too beautiful to be our maid. I know that Marc fell for you at our party. It was only because you sent him packing, and I threatened to break his arm, that he came back to me."

Madeleine smiled. "Are you sure that you're only sixteen?"

"Sixteen going on twenty, Maman says." Andrée paused. "What are you going to wear for the lesson?"

"I haven't thought."

"You could wear your black dress – "

"In the afternoon, in the rue de Rome?"

"You'll be singing – you should look glamorous."

"Monsieur Strasser is a teacher, not a film producer, Andrée. It won't matter if I wear a sack."

"Wear your blue pullover then – the one that matches your eyes."

"Antoine has already seen that."

"I thought it didn't matter."

Madeleine arrived at the studio the following Monday, wearing a cream wool blouse (borrowed from Estelle) with a turquoise silk scarf (borrowed from Andrée) tied around her neck, and a black wool buttoned-through skirt (her own). She was ten minutes early, and trembling violently.

When Gaston Strasser arrived, the trembling grew even worse.

"Mademoiselle Gabriel?"

"*Bonjour*, Monsieur Strasser." Madeleine put out her hand to shake his. He was, she estimated, in his late forties, and when he removed his hat and coat, she saw that he was as bald as an egg and quite shockingly muscular in build.

"Shall we begin?" He walked over to the piano, opened the lid and sat down on the stool.

"Begin?" Her voice shook.

"I understand from Antoine Bonnard that you want to sing. Did he lie?"

"No, of course not," Madeleine faltered.

"Then sing."

She grew pale. "What shall I sing, Monsieur?"

"What did you sing for Bonnard?" He noticed her trembling hands. "Are you cold, Mademoiselle?"

"Afraid, Monsieur."

"Of me?"

"Yes."

Strasser softened his manner a little. "Stage fright is a common affliction, Mademoiselle Gabriel – it is essential to devise a trick to help oneself to get over it. What do you generally do if you are scared?"

Madeleine smiled. "I sing."

"*Alors?*"

She began, as she had with Antoine, with 'J'ai deux amours', her voice quavering a little in the first bars and the enchantment that usually overtook her when she sang, eluding her just when it mattered, for Gaston Strasser seemed to be glaring at her as he played. Unlike Antoine, who had adapted himself swiftly and apparently contentedly to her individual style, Strasser accompanied her with absolute precision, not permitting Madeleine to linger where she was naturally inclined to, or to use her voice or personal interpretation to deviate from the music as it had been written and published.

"*Continuez*," he commanded her when the first song had ended, and she obeyed, and as she went on singing, some of the time Strasser sat at the piano and played, and sometimes he rose and walked around her, peering at her with his flinty grey eyes.

He stopped her after twenty minutes.

"I have heard enough," he said. "From now on, you are to practise scales, and vocal and breath control exercises, every morning. Have you ever been taught scales?"

"Not really, Monsieur – in the choir at school, we –"

"I shall teach you. But you must promise to practise."

"I don't have anywhere to practise," Madeleine said reluctantly. "My employers would not approve – it would disturb them."

"What time do you rise in the morning?"

"At half past five."

"Then in future, you must rise at least one half-hour earlier, in order that you can go out to practise. Go to a friend's home, or even into the Métro – if the weather is fine, go to a park, but practise."

"*Oui, Monsieur.*"

Strasser glared at her again. "Do you have a laryngitis, Mademoiselle Gabriel?"

"No."

"Have you had a head cold?"

Madeleine shook her head. "I'm very healthy."

"Then why is your voice so husky? Do you smoke?"

"Not at all. It's always been that way."

"A childhood disease, perhaps?"

"Nothing like that, Monsieur."

"It is impossible to have a husky voice for no reason. Has your throat been examined by a specialist?"

"There's never been any need – it was like this even when I was a very small child. It does sound husky, but it's strong."

"I have ears, Mademoiselle."

"Yes, Monsieur," she said meekly.

"If you want to sing, as Bonnard told me you claim you do, then that desire must take precedence over everything else in your life. Your work, your personal life – everything."

For a moment, Madeleine was silent, and then she gathered the courage to ask: "Do you believe I have talent, Monsieur Strasser?"

"Of a sort," he replied, and would be drawn no further.

When Madeleine tried to pay him for the lesson, Strasser refused, telling her that, for the time being, there would be no charge, since he owed Antoine Bonnard a personal debt.

"You are from Switzerland, *n'est-ce pas*?"

"That's right, Monsieur."

"I was born in Vienna," Strasser said. "Both of us foreigners."

"I feel very much at home in Paris, don't you, Monsieur?"

"As much as anywhere."

It was the closest the fearsome, bald-headed teacher came to disclosing to Madeleine anything about himself, and it was clear that the session was at an end.

"And the scales?" Madeleine asked, as Strasser drew on his coat and picked up his hat. "When will you teach them to me, Monsieur?"

"Next time."

"Next week? Here?"

"If you wish."

For the first time since they had met, Madeleine relaxed.

"I wish it very much, Monsieur."

She would have felt happy, perhaps even a little triumphant at having survived the ordeal, but Antoine had not appeared, and as Madeleine made her way back home, alone, she was more perplexed than ever.

He called at the apartment the following day, coming to the front door instead of to the tradesmen's entrance as would have been proper, and carrying a bouquet of one dozen velvety, deep red roses.

Answering the door in her uniform, with Monsieur Lussac hovering in the hall behind her, Madeleine was aware that, as the maid, she ought to feel more embarrassment than anything else, and that as a young woman of breeding, she ought to react with a degree of indifference.

"*Bonjour*, Madeleine," Antoine said softly, and gave her the roses.

Her joy and her profound relief at the sight of him, and of the bouquet – such an open declaration, at last, of reciprocated feeling – were too much for her.

"*Merci*," she said, and flung herself unashamedly into his arms, while Edouard Lussac, in spite of himself, smiled.

Antoine brought Madeleine that evening, with Gabrielle Lussac's permission, to Fleurette. The restaurant stood on a corner of the rue Jacob in the narrow, friendly, charmed heart of Saint-Germain-des-Prés. It was comfortably small, more a *bistrot chic* than a true restaurant, with a simple, unpretentious prettiness, as its name suggested.

"I've passed by so often," Madeleine said excitedly, "and I never knew."

"Nor I, that you were passing." Antoine looked at her. "Do you like it?"

"It's wonderful. Does the owner live in Paris?"

Antoine shook his head. "He owns a second place in Provence, and for now, at least, he chooses to live there and entrust the running of Fleurette to me. It allows me to believe that it is almost mine."

"Why not, since you made it a success?"

He shrugged. "True enough."

Three of the dozen tables were already occupied, and new customers were coming in for dinner, but Antoine made time to introduce Madeleine to his staff of six –

Grégoire Simon, the *chef-de-cuisine*, Patrick Hugo, his assistant, and Suki, their *plongeuse*, in the kitchen, and Georges, Jean-Paul and Sylvie in the dining room itself.

"It was finding Grégoire that made all the difference to Fleurette," Antoine told Madeleine, showing her to a small, discreet table in the back of the room. "He was raised in Honfleur, just a few kilometres from where I used to live. I had wanted to introduce the cuisine of Normandy, since I understood that better than any other, and Grégoire was miraculously available."

"They all seem so happy," Madeleine said.

"I hope they are. Patrick and Jean-Paul live together in the rue de Buci, just a few minutes away."

"Where is Suki from?"

"Born in Singapore, but she's been in Paris since she was five. She paints watercolours when she's not working here, and she has a two-year-old boy – she brings him here sometimes, when his father isn't around to mind him."

Georges, one of the waiters, a fair-haired, round-faced young man, brought Madeleine a menu.

"I'll take her order," Antoine said.

"Surely you're eating too?" Madeleine asked.

"I have to work, but I'll serve you myself." He pointed at the card in her hands. "Shall I recommend for you?"

"Choose for me," she said.

"*Vraiment?*"

"*Absolument*."

"Forgive me for leaving you?"

"Of course."

Madeleine sat back in her chair, utterly happy, watching Antoine in his own surroundings. Fleurette might not belong to him, but it was clear that he had indelibly stamped it with his style and taste. He brought her a *potage cressonnière*, hovered while she tasted it, and poured her a glass of white wine.

"Just a Muscadet, but excellent – do you like the soup?"

"Delicious."

"Do you mind if I leave you again?" He was solicitous.

"Leave me with my soup."

He served her a sole, sautéed with lobster, *morilles*, champagne and cream, and she relished every morsel, watching him all the time. Georges and Jean-Paul, the waiters, cast regular, friendly glances in her direction, though the girl, Sylvie, a pretty, long-haired brunette, eyed her with what Madeleine felt was, at least, suspicion, or perhaps even outright hostility. It didn't matter – nothing could spoil her mood.

"*Ça va?*" Antoine asked, frequently, and Georges offered her a *trou normand* – a small glass of Calvados served between courses to improve the digestion – but she declined.

She had never dreamed that it was possible to find any man so beautiful that she could study him for hours, as if he were a living, breathing work of art. Observing Antoine at his work, Madeleine was entranced by his speed and grace. His hands alone, long fingered and dextrous, were constantly busy: writing orders and reservations, uncorking bottles, smoothing fresh cloths, laying napkins on laps, shaking other hands, picking up the telephone, opening and closing the front door. He was gregarious and charming, yet wonderfully discreet with the customers, inexhaustibly alert with his staff, seeming to know exactly when to galvanize them and when to relax a little, allowing them to have fun with their work, and enjoying himself. Yet all through the evening, at every spare moment, his eyes, those eyes that she already loved – that she had known she loved from the first instant in the Tuileries – skimmed over the room to rest, with pleasure, with concern, with warmth, upon her.

* * *

They were not alone until after one in the morning. Antoine lit his first peaceful Gauloise, poured them both a Calvados and sank into the chair beside her.

"Earlier than usual."

"Really?"

He nodded, and drank a little. "This is how it is. Lunchtime and evening, every day except Monday – and then a few snatched hours of rest before Grégoire and I go to market. Sometimes he goes without me, but I hate to miss it – I love it."

"I can understand that," Madeleine said softly.

"Can you?" He smiled at her. "It's fine for me, but not easy for others to tolerate. It's not easy to have a girlfriend." He stifled a yawn.

"You're tired – I should go home."

"No, no – I'll revive again in a moment or two, I always do."

"But you said you only have a few hours to sleep."

"I can sleep any night." He looked at her intently. "Tonight I need to talk, to explain things to you."

"What is there to explain?"

"The reason I did not come to you before today."

"It doesn't matter," Madeleine said quickly. "You came. That's all that matters." She felt suddenly anxious, almost afraid to hear what he had to tell her, in case it spoiled everything.

"I need to be honest," Antoine said. "It's important."

"All right."

He inhaled deeply from his cigarette, and blew smoke out through his nostrils. "I have been involved, lately, with another girl. I introduced you to her – Sylvie Martin."

The dark-haired waitress with the unfriendly eyes. Madeleine kept silent, waiting, listening.

"We were not in love, but we were lovers." Antoine paused. "I am not a man to play around – I don't like to lie." He gave a little shrug. "It's all over now between us.

Sylvie understands. I knew that I had to end it when I first saw you that afternoon before Christmas. It was instant for me – *le vrai coup de foudre*. It has never happened to me before."

"It was the same for me," Madeleine said quietly.

"I knew."

"You did?" She flushed. "I've never been in love – not just the thunderbolt kind of love. I've never even had a boyfriend –" She faltered over the words, her blush deepening. She sounded so naïve, so young. She wanted to be candid, to be truthful, but she was afraid of seeming foolish. "Are you sure that Sylvie understands?" she asked quickly, changing tack.

"Without doubt." Antoine drank a little more Calvados. "Sylvie is a nice girl, but tough. She isn't like you, Madeleine – she's older, she's had plenty of boyfriends. She told me she has already moved on. Don't worry about Sylvie."

They began to talk frankly, openly, spilling their souls. Madeleine felt as if the space between them was closing up, even though only their hands were touching. She felt as if their minds were linking, entwining, and it was an exquisite sensation. She knew, intuitively, that everything Antoine Bonnard would ever mean to her, he meant already, and that those feelings might develop with time, but would never fundamentally change or be diminished. She found that she wanted to tell him everything now, about her childhood, about her life in Switzerland, about the Gründlis and the Gabriels, about her grandfather and Irina and Alexander, about her mother and Stefan and Rudi. And about her father's exile, and about Zeleyev and about *Eternité*. And she realized, with profound joy, that Antoine wanted to know all about her, just as she did about him.

"Tell me now," she said, when she had finished.

"There's not so much to tell – my life has been dull beside yours."

"Tell me anyway."

"We have a small family," he said. "My father is called Claude, my mother, Françoise, and I have one sister, Jacqueline, two years younger than me."

"I don't know how old you are," Madeleine said.

"I'm twenty-seven. In March I shall be ten years older than you."

"Does that matter?"

"Not to me."

"Nor to me." She smiled. "Go on telling me."

"We have a small *pension* just outside Trouville. Pension Bonnard. One of those clean, dependable places tourists like to return to again and again. The beds are soft and warm, my father is kind and welcoming and my mother makes the most delicious soups you can imagine."

"Surely you miss them?"

"Very much. And I miss Normandy, too, but not enough to think of leaving Paris. Because of my family and our little *pension*, I know that I could escape if I needed to, but I think I never shall."

"I loved the city the instant I arrived," Madeleine said. "Then I grew a little afraid, and then Noah came along and after that everything was all right."

"Paris is everything I want in a city," Antoine told her. "She's brave and bold, a survivor. She reminds me of a beautiful woman, in love with life and with herself."

"A human city."

"*Exactement.*" He lit another cigarette. "Paris has it all – splendour and charm, music and art, food and passion."

He had arrived in 1950, aged twenty, unscarred by the war and raring to go. He had found a job at Fleurette as a waiter within a month, graduating to manager just six months later, and he thrived on the blend of hard work, controlled chaos and the giving of pleasure to his customers.

"Underneath, though, the real Antoine Bonnard is a songwriter."

"Truly?" Madeleine was startled. She ought to have realized, of course, after he had played for her in the studio, ought to have wondered why a *restaurateur* had been so interested in her singing.

"I wrote my first song – both music and lyrics – when I was nine."

He had continued with a rapid succession of *chansonnettes* lampooning the Nazis right through the war, and had managed to have his first song published a year after he had come to Paris.

"It was called 'Les Nuits lumineuses'."

"I want to hear it."

"You will." Antoine smiled. "I carry it with me all the time, the sheet music, tightly folded up in my wallet, like a paper talisman." He paused. "Only one singer has ever performed it until now – Gaston Strasser, when he was singing here at Fleurette for a season." He paused again. "From the moment I heard your voice when you sang for me, Madeleine – when I heard your voice, I knew that it was your song."

She could not speak. Her eyes were full of tears.

"If you're ready," Antoine said softly, "I think I had better take you home."

"This feels like home to me," she whispered.

"Yes," he said.

Madeleine wanted to learn more and more, about him, about his music, every single thing there was to discover, but she knew that there would be time, that they would have infinite time together, whilst now, growing sleepy at last, she was ruefully aware that it was already almost three o'clock, and that she had to rise again before six, and to be a housemaid. Yet as Antoine walked her back, strolling arm in arm along the Boulevard Saint-Germain, one curiosity still pricked at her.

"Tell me about Gaston Strasser," she said, leaning her head against his shoulder. "He seemed so strange."

"Did he try to overawe you?"

"He succeeded."

"Gaston is a pussy cat at heart, but he needs to defend himself."

"Against me?"

"Against any stranger. Against the world."

They walked silently a little way. The city was growing quiet, too. Though it never slept entirely, the music softened, the vitality gentled, the earnest, tireless philosophers and debaters relaxed, the lovers lay at peace. Antoine Bonnard and Madeleine Gabriel, still discovering each other, learned the wonder of strolling close together, arms entwined loosely, leaning and listening.

"How old do you think Gaston is?" Antoine asked her.

"Forty-five, fifty?"

"He's only just forty."

The cold night nipped frostily at Madeleine's ears and neck, but she didn't care, didn't want to put up the hood of her coat. She still loved the feeling of freedom and ease her short hair had given her, and besides, she did not want to hide her face from Antoine.

"Perhaps he looks older because he has no hair," she said.

"He shaves his head, you know."

"Why?"

"It's the image he has chosen, that he needs."

Gaston Strasser, Antoine told her as they walked, had been a successful operatic student when he had fled Vienna and the Nazis in 1938 to come to cousins of his French-born mother in Paris.

"Is he Jewish?"

"Homosexual. Almost as bad in those days."

After the Occupation of Paris, Strasser had found himself no safer than he had been in Austria. At the age of twenty, he had had a full head of soft, blond hair, and a slight, slender figure. A perfect victim. One night in 1942, set upon by a group of Nazi thugs, Gaston had been gang-raped and severely beaten. He had recovered physically, but his psyche had been badly brutalized, and he had become deeply and chronically depressed.

"His cousins threw him out after the *Libération*."

"How could they?" Madeleine was shocked.

"They were bigots themselves, I suppose, and he must have been too much trouble for them. As it happened, they did Gaston a favour."

"How?"

"He was forced to take stock. He looked into the mirror, saw a pathetic creature, ripe for more victimization, and he realized that he needed to change himself."

Strasser had shaved his head and had begun to build himself up, forcing himself to eat the right foods, even when he had no appetite, and befriending the manager of a gymnasium where boxers trained. He had made himself strong and unattractive. No one liked or understood him, but at least no one dared to threaten him. His hopes of a career as a tenor, however, had long since been obliterated, and by now he looked more like a lion tamer in a circus than a serious singer. Accepting his limitations, Gaston had taken a series of jobs at odds with his nature, jobs requiring physical strength: he became, in turn, a security guard, a nightclub bouncer and a night watchman. His sense of achievement had soon melted away and he spiralled down into a new depression that had lasted until he had met Antoine in 1951.

"Where did you meet?" Madeleine asked.

"In the Luxembourg gardens."

"You must have been in a dark mood," Madeleine said, remembering what he had told her in the Tuileries.

"I think I was trying to compose, and nothing was working out." He paused, remembering. "Gaston was sitting on the grass under a tree, watching the little children at the Guignol theatre. Only he was weeping, not laughing. I sat down beside him, and we began to talk."

"And you took him on as a singer at Fleurette?"

Antoine shrugged. "He had – still has a fine voice, and Saint-Germain is accustomed to characters."

Strasser's self-imposed ugliness, however, had worked against him at the restaurant, too, and business had fallen off badly. The Viennese had offered to quit, but Antoine had refused to let him give up. It had been his idea that Gaston should start teaching, but until he could find some fee-paying pupils, he would continue to sing at Fleurette.

"The customers came back gradually – they knew that the food and the service were still just as good. And in fact, as Gaston's confidence grew, he learned to capitalize on his looks. He used them, developed a kind of mock fierceness that became part of his act."

"And that's why he wouldn't take my money," Madeleine said. "He told me that he owed you a debt. I presumed that he meant a financial debt – but it was much more."

"It was nothing, really, just a chance. Gaston had the courage."

"Of course," Madeleine said, but inwardly she rejoiced, feeling an even greater rapture than before at the confirmation that she had fallen in love with a generous, kind human being. If only, she thought, as they neared the Lussacs' house, she didn't have to go inside – if only this night did not have to end –

They stopped walking.

"Tomorrow," he said, looking down at her, "you will

be an even more impossible maid than usual." He took her face in his hands. "I predict that you will break at least one item, and that you will burn their breakfast."

"I don't cook – Madame Blondeau doesn't let me."

"A wise woman."

"I might be a very fine cook."

"It's possible."

Madeleine peered up at him sleepily. "Why are you holding my face?"

His navy-blue eyes were very dark and narrow. "Anticipation."

"Of what?" She felt her body quiver.

"Our first kiss." He paused. "May I?"

She nodded, not trusting herself to speak.

He bent his head. She felt his lips, narrow, cool, soft, firm, meeting her own with such tenderness that her eyes pricked with tears. Oh, it was the best feeling in the world – she closed her eyes and kissed him back, and his lips parted, and his mouth was warm and alive, and for just an instant their tongues touched, lightly, and she grew weak, weak with longing –

And then he drew away.

"All that," she murmured, "in just one kiss."

Antoine smiled, his teeth very white in the dark. "And much more," he said, gently, and releasing her face, he tucked her arm into his, and opened the gate.

Upstairs, outside the front door, he whispered to her: "Tell them that it was my fault you were out so late – tell them that it won't happen again, that we needed the hours to begin to learn about each other."

"But what shall we do?" Madeleine was suddenly anxious. "If sometimes the restaurant doesn't close until after two, when shall we be together?"

"*Ne t'en fais pas, chérie,*" he soothed her. "There will

be time enough, don't worry. This was our first evening, not our last."

"Our first kiss." Madeleine smiled again.

Antoine's expression was intent.

"Our beginning," he said.

11

"Relax."

"I am."

"Like a steel girder – don't be so anxious."

"You make me anxious."

"Let's begin again. Bend over – right over, from the waist. Now let your head flop, let everything flop, like a rag doll. Now come up slowly – very slowly – stretch your back, and the back of your neck. Head up last of all. Now loosen your shoulders, shake them easily so that your breasts shake too – that's right. And now pant like a dog – don't be so self-conscious, just pant."

Madeleine panted.

"Now remember, the support must come from your diaphragm. Keep your throat open, plenty of space for the sound to come out, without effort. And we start again with *la la la* –"

Gaston returned to the piano, and began again the endless, interminable plodding up and down of scales. Madeleine, feeling like a conscript into some insane, aimless army regime, obeyed, hating every minute.

"*La la la laaa la la la.*"

"Now *mee mee mee* –"

It went on.

"It's terrible," she told Andrée and Hélène later. "I just want to sing, but Monsieur Strasser makes me repeat the scales, over and over and over again, till I want to scream."

"But don't all singers have to practise scales?" Hélène asked.

"Yes, of course, but not all the time, and not only scales."

"Doesn't he let you sing anything else at all?" Andrée wanted to know.

"Nothing. He lets me pant, and do breathing exercises. The most fun is when he lights a candle and sticks it in front of my face."

"What for?"

"To make sure that I don't blow it out."

"But what about when you breathe?" Hélène asked.

"It's not even supposed to flicker. Of course with me, it flickers like a wild thing and then goes out, and Monsieur Strasser either shouts at me, or becomes very, very quiet, which is even worse."

"You're not allowed to breathe?"

"Of course, Andrée. But a singer is supposed to take a breath, and then to control it so perfectly with her diaphragm that only a tiny little bit of air is released at a time. Strasser says that you don't really need air to make the sound."

"It sounds very difficult," Hélène said.

"It is, *chérie*, it is."

"Then why don't you stop?" Andrée asked.

"Because I want to sing."

"Gaston hates my voice," she told Antoine one afternoon in the little garden of the church of Saint-Germain-des-Prés.

"Of course he doesn't."

"Yes, he does, and he's right to hate it. For the first time since we began the lessons, he let me sing – really sing. It was one of the Schubert *Lieder* – not at all what I want to sing, but beautiful, of course, and much, much better than exercises and scales."

"And it went badly?"

"Badly isn't the word for it!" Madeleine was distraught. "First of all, I have forgotten almost everything I learned at school about reading music – if only I had paid more attention then –"

"I'm sure it will come back to you."

"But Gaston grew very impatient, and hit the piano with his fist – and then, of course, he was furious with himself for striking a precious musical instrument –"

"And the singing?" Antoine asked gently.

"Disastrous!"

"Surely not."

"You know my voice. Do you think it is suited for *Lieder*?"

"Perhaps not, but –"

"I know, I know, but it's all part of learning," she said frustratedly.

"Precisely."

"So I will try, but Gaston will never be satisfied with me. He's a classical teacher, a classically taught singer. To him, the music as it is written is sacred, not to be tampered with by the singer, and certainly not by a humble, lowly upstart like me."

Antoine chuckled. "I can't imagine that Gaston or anyone could regard you as humble or lowly, *ma chérie* – an upstart, perhaps –"

Madeleine was not in the mood for joking. "You don't understand," she went on heatedly. "Gaston would like me to try to sing like the great, established mezzo-sopranos, and of course I never could, but though I do want to work hard to improve, and practise and practise, what I want is to use what I think I have."

"You have a good ear – natural pitch."

"But I want to feel free when I sing – to use my mind,

my heart, not someone else's idea of what they should be." She paused for breath, beginning to calm down. "Gaston says that I must learn to walk before I can run, that I have to learn emotional control."

"Don't you think he's right?"

"Absolutely right." Madeleine flushed. "And when I listen to myself now, I think how arrogant I must sound to you, and I'm ashamed of myself, because in spite of everything, I love my lessons, and I'm more grateful to Gaston than I can even say, and I do know that he is right, and that I must learn technique and control. But if he would only let me sing one thing – a song of my choice – freely, let me have my head once each lesson, it would make all the difference in the world to me."

"Would you like me to speak to him?" Antoine asked quietly.

"No!" She took her head vehemently. "I want to earn Gaston's respect, not his scorn. If he thinks that you have to fight my battles for me, then he'll hate me even more than my voice."

Antoine held out his hand. "*Viens, ma belle.*" She came to him, and he drew her close. "Gaston respects you already, he told me. He likes it when you challenge him, though he will never admit it to you. And he knows that you want to sing ballads and popular songs and perhaps a little jazz, and that you love emotional, passionate music, and he knows that you will find your way, your direction."

"But I need to be patient," Madeleine said softly. She was watching a mother and her two children, one aged about five, who was running about after a red ball, while his sister, still only able to toddle, was looking at him with clear frustration. "Like that little one – before long, she may run faster than her brother. It's just the waiting that's hard."

Antoine turned her face to his. "I would let you sing at Fleurette now, if you felt you were ready."

"I'm not. Not yet." She smiled at him. "But one day, not too far off, if you'll wait."

"*Pour toujours*," he said.

They saw each other as often as they could, though both their jobs placed inevitable limitations upon the unfolding romance. Antoine took Madeleine up to his apartment, four flights of rickety stairs above the restaurant, and they always talked endlessly and embraced with ever-growing feverish longing, and Madeleine looked yearningly at his bed, but Antoine refused to make love to her.

"I am twenty-eight years old," he told her, on his birthday in the third week of March. "You are eighteen."

"You told me that it didn't matter to you."

"Nor does it. But you have told me I am your first love, that you are a virgin." He kissed her left ear. "And that just makes it more important than ever that when the moment comes, you must be completely sure that it is what you want."

Madeleine knew what she wanted. There was not an atom of doubt in her mind. He filled her every waking thought, and most of her dreams – the only time she was able to concentrate on anything else was during her lessons with Gaston Strasser. Now that she had begun to understand him, her teacher no longer intimidated her, and she knew that, in spite of the differences in their style, he taught well. His unflagging obsession with tedious vocal and breathing exercises still drove her mad with an impatience that she only narrowly managed to keep to herself, but she felt her capacity and performing energy gradually beginning to expand, and her voice, its unique sound growing richer and more fluent, starting to come under control.

On the first Monday afternoon of April, shortly after she had served luncheon to the Lussacs, and just before she was due to change her clothes in order that she could meet Antoine at Les Deux Magots, Madeleine answered the front door bell.

"*Grüezi, Magdalen.*"

Stefan Julius stood outside the door. It was over two years since she had seen him, but he had not altered. His suit was grey, and his tie, and his hair, and his eyes. Madeleine stared at him, wondering whether if she blinked he might disappear as abruptly as he had come.

"Aren't you going to invite me in?"

"Of course." Madeleine stood back, wishing she had been able to change out of her uniform before he had seen her. She felt at a disadvantage in the menial black dress, apron and cap, which, instinctively, her right hand reached up to pat.

"Don't worry," Julius said. "It looks very fetching."

"What are you doing here?" Madeleine felt sick with shock as she closed the door. "How did you find me?"

"A charming greeting," he said coolly. "I thought perhaps you might welcome a visit after so long."

"Madeleine?" Edouard Lussac came into the hall.

"Monsieur Lussac, I presume?" Stefan offered his hand. "Julius is my name."

"This is my stepfather, Monsieur." Madeleine felt a flush on her cheeks. "I'm sorry you were disturbed."

"Not at all." He shook Julius's hand. "*Enchanté, Monsieur.*"

"We should go upstairs to my room," Madeleine said swiftly.

"I wouldn't hear of it, Madeleine." Monsieur Lussac smiled warmly at her. "Why don't you take your stepfather into the *petit salon*? You could talk in peace there."

"*Merci, Monsieur.*"

"As a matter of fact," Stefan Julius said, "I had rather hoped for a few minutes of your time, Monsieur Lussac.

My wife, in particular, has been anxious that I, at least, should meet her daughter's employers."

"But of course. Gabrielle, my wife, will be delighted to meet you. Won't you come into the *salon*?" Lussac glanced back at Madeleine. "Join us please, my dear."

She forced a smile. "*Un instant, Monsieur.*"

The door closed, and quickly Madeleine went to the antique oval mirror on the far side of the hall, and stared at her own reflection. She ungripped the white cap, untied the apron's neat bow, looked again and felt a little better. A pang of shame struck her; the uniform had never caused her embarrassment before today, had never made her feel any less significant or more lowly than anyone else. She was a maid – it was a perfectly decent occupation. It was only Julius who, with that first patronizing remark, had sullied it for her.

Steeling herself, she went into the *salon*. They sat on high-backed armchairs, waiting for her.

"Sit down, Madeleine." Madame Lussac smiled. "Would you like some tea?"

"No, thank you, Madame." She did not want to leave him alone with them a moment longer.

"I'm sure Madame Blondeau wouldn't mind." It was a tacit acknowledgment that Madeleine was now off-duty. "And nothing for you, Monsieur Julius?"

"I don't think so, Madame."

"Something stronger, perhaps?" Edouard Lussac suggested.

"No."

"*Eh bien*," Lussac said pleasantly. "What is it we can do for you then, Monsieur? Except perhaps to tell you how very much we value Madeleine."

Stefan smiled. "We heard that Magdalen had changed her name."

"It's not really changed," Madame Lussac pointed out. "Merely adapted to Madeleine's new surroundings."

"Quite."

The Lussacs sat calmly, waiting.

"It is a pity," Julius said, crossing his legs and letting his hands rest, neatly folded, on one elegantly tailored thigh, "that we had to hear about Magdalen's name, as well as other things, from a stranger, and not from Magdalen herself."

"A pity indeed," Edouard Lussac agreed.

Julius went on. "Magdalen became eighteen last December, Monsieur Lussac, but I wonder if you were aware when you employed her that she had left home as an underage runaway, causing her family intense distress and considerable embarrassment."

"We were aware of some family difficulties," Lussac said, maintaining his calm, courteous manner.

"You might not have been aware that Magdalen's family is a prominent, fine and venerable Zurich family."

"It has never been our custom to pry into our employees' private affairs," Gabrielle Lussac pointed out, pleasantly. "Though since Madeleine is an outgoing, honest young woman, we have come to learn certain facts about her background."

"None of which led you to feel that it might be proper for you to contact myself or her mother?"

"No." Madame Lussac sat forward a little. "Is there something we can tell you, Monsieur Julius, to put your mind at ease about your stepdaughter and her life with us?"

"That might have been most welcome, had your offer been made sooner," Julius replied, "but as it is, I have recently learned more than enough, and I assure you that my mind is certainly not at ease."

For the first time, Madeleine spoke.

"What exactly have you learned?"

"A great deal."

"What, precisely?"

Stefan inclined his head, slightly, and focused his grey eyes upon her face. "I have learned about the type of people you have mixed with since your arrival in Paris. About your first weeks, living with Levi, a man who picked you up on the bank of the Seine –"

"Noah did not pick me up," Madeleine said hotly, "and his title is Reverend Levi."

"And I suppose you felt that your mother and grandmother would be content to know that you were living with a Jewish cantor, an unmarried man? But then again, I imagine that was part of the appeal, the knowledge that you were hurting your family."

"It was Reverend Levi's close friend, Père Beaumarchais," Edouard Lussac interjected, "who introduced us to Madeleine. I assure you that your implication is entirely unfounded."

"Is it indeed? It has become clear to me that Magdalen has done her best to wound us by radically changing herself – her name, her hair – by working at the most menial of jobs, by taking singing lessons from a known pervert, by throwing herself, shamelessly, at a jumped-up waiter."

"How *dare* you?" Madeleine jumped to her feet. "How dare you come here uninvited, to insult my employers, my friends?! You don't know what you're talking about."

"Alas, I do."

Madeleine fought to control herself, for the sake of the Lussacs, aware of their own growing disgust. She had seldom been so shocked. She had thought herself safe from the domination of the Gründlis and Juliuses, had made herself a fresh, new life, never dreaming that she might be spied upon.

"What did you do? Hire a detective?" A flash of bittersweet memory struck home; maybe the characters in her father's beloved novels were coming back to haunt her.

"On the contrary, Magdalen," Julius retorted with satisfaction, "the company you have chosen to keep has betrayed you."

"None of my friends would do such a thing."

Julius shrugged. "Not a friend, certainly. The young woman who wrote, anonymously, to your mother, said that you had stolen her boyfriend, this waiter, Bonnard. She thought it proper that we should know about the shabby life you were leading."

Sylvie Martin. Madeleine was dismayed. Antoine had said that they had not been in love, that Sylvie had accepted the ending of their relationship. She was a nice, tough girl, he'd said, who had moved swiftly on to another man. Madeleine had felt her dislike, but had not given her another thought because she had been so happy.

She sat down again. "Why are you here?" she asked Julius. "Surely you didn't expect, or even want, me to come back with you?"

"Not unless you wanted to."

"Never," she said. "And I won't let you steal my life – my independence. I've worked hard for what I have, and I'm very happy."

"If scrubbing floors and sleeping with waiters makes you happy, my dear Magdalen, then I shouldn't dream of spoiling your pleasure." Julius paused, "I came here because I hoped, naturally, to reassure Emilie and Hildegard that you are safe and well."

"I am both, thank you."

"If that is all," Edouard Lussac said, "then –"

"Not quite." Julius still looked at Madeleine. "I also wish to know if you are aware of your father's whereabouts. Have you had contact with Gabriel, Magdalen?"

"I have not."

"Really? We were all of the impression that you ran away from home chiefly to find him. I recall how furiously you sprang to his defence when last we spoke."

"I did not find him." Madeleine paused. "Why should you care?"

"Simply because I believe him to be in possession of certain valuables that disappeared from your grandfather's house after his death. You remember, I'm sure, Magdalen, that it was you who drew our attention to Amadeus's possessions."

Eternité. She seldom thought about the sculpture, but suddenly she recalled the intensity of Stefan Julius's interrogation the evening before she had left the Gründli Haus, after she had rashly let slip Opi's secret. They had so much, more accumulated wealth than they could ever spend, yet still they needed to punish Amadeus and Alexander for old, unforgiven sins.

"I don't know where my father is," she said again, stiffly.

"And if you knew, I doubt if you would tell me."

Edouard Lussac rose from his armchair. "We have never had grounds to question Madeleine's honesty, Monsieur."

"Perhaps because you never met her grandfather, nor her father. If you had, you would know that her otherwise fine pedigree had been irretrievably tainted."

"Madeleine is not an animal, Monsieur Julius," Gabrielle Lussac pointed out, her voice still quiet but no longer pleasant.

"That must be due to her mother," Julius said, "for both the Gabriel men were little better than rutting bulls."

"I would be pleased if you would not use that kind of language in my home." Edouard had grown pale. "Perhaps it would be best if you were to leave."

Madeleine sat in an agony of fury and embarrassment, not trusting herself to speak. His abuse of her father and Opi was no shock to her, but that these decent, dignified people should be forced because of her to listen to Julius, was too much to bear.

All pretences swept away, Stefan's eyes sparkled with open hostility. "I believe that it is against the law to employ a person who has no legal right to work in France."

"If you have a legal quarrel with us, Monsieur," Lussac said briskly, already moving towards the door, "then I suggest that you instruct a lawyer, but in the meantime –" He opened the door.

"Magdalen was sixteen years old when she ran away from home," Julius said as he, too, stood up. "I am not a hypocrite, so I shall not pretend that I missed her presence in our house. She was always disruptive and unpleasant to me, but her mother and young brother, and her grandmother, an old lady, suffered greatly from their uncertainty and fears of what might have become of the girl –"

"You're a liar," Madeleine burst out, her voice shaking.

Her stepfather ignored her. "You knowingly sheltered her, Monsieur Lussac, and your wife, presumably, was glad to find cheap, strong labour –"

"Please leave now." Edouard's voice was enraged.

"I'm going, but don't imagine that the matter will rest –"

"Get *out*."

Julius passed him. "If I were you, Monsieur, I would throw the girl out before she causes you serious trouble." He raised his voice, directing it back into the drawing room. "*Adieu, Magdalen.*"

As the door shut behind him, Madeleine was already weeping furious tears, unable to wall them back any longer, Gabrielle's arms about her shoulders.

"I'm so sorry," Madeleine sobbed.

"It's not your fault, my dear."

"Of course it's my fault."

"For having such an unpleasant man for your stepfather? Hardly."

"I'm sorry," Madeleine said again, feeling in her pocket for a handkerchief and wiping her eyes. "I should have told him to leave right away – I should not have let him speak to you."

"You couldn't stop him, Madeleine." Gabrielle looked up as Edouard came back into the room. "*Ça va, chéri?*"

"*Oui, oui.*" He sat down, looking strained. "Perhaps I should have held my temper a little longer, but I'm afraid I had such an impulse to strike the man that I thought it best to see the back of him first."

"He's a vile man," Madeleine said. "I'm sorry."

"Stop apologizing, *ma chère*," Gabrielle soothed her. "We should all have some tea, or something stronger, and then try to get back to normal." She glanced up at the clock on the mantelpiece. "Weren't you going out this afternoon, Madeleine?"

"I was, Madame, but –"

"Go and change then."

"But surely –" Madeleine hesitated. "What my step-father said, about throwing me out – I think that you should."

"Nonsense," Edouard said stoutly.

"But he will make difficulties for you – I can't let that happen."

"My husband has a good lawyer," Gabrielle said. "There's no need for you to have a moment's concern."

Antoine had been waiting for more than an hour at Les Deux Magots when she arrived. Seeing her white face and angry eyes, he ordered a cognac and made her drink a few sips before letting her speak.

"Now tell me what's wrong."

"Everything."

"Surely not." He stroked her cheek.

She told him, her distress magnifying again with the telling. "And now I have no choice but to leave my job."

"The Lussacs wouldn't ask you to go."

"Of course not, but I'm convinced that Stefan will do as he threatened if I stay. I couldn't bear to be the cause of difficulties for them – they've been so kind to me."

"*Viens*," Antoine said, tossing money on the table and standing up.

"Where?"

"To the best place for problems."

They went to the Luxembourg gardens and, finding the gazebo unoccupied, sat down in sight of the Medici fountain, surrounded by life, yet wonderfully removed and secluded.

"It's all spoiled anyway," Madeleine said. "Now that they know where I am. Paris was *mine* –" She clasped her hands to her breast. "My life here was entirely separate from them, from the past. They've invaded my privacy."

"Not really," Antoine said. "It may feel like that to you now, but it's not true." He shrugged. "It was your secret, kept from them, and now maybe they know some of the facts – a few details of where you have been and who you have met. But they're bare bones, nothing more. They haven't penetrated your heart or your mind – they can't alter your experiences or your feelings, *chérie*."

"But I feel as if I'm being watched, even now."

"Not if it was Sylvie who sent the letter." Antoine shook his head, his hair falling a little over his forehead. "It's hard for me to think that she could betray us that way."

"Who else could have done it?"

"Who indeed?" His eyes were angry. "I thought we were friends, you know? She worked for me for four years – our affair lasted only three months. I never hinted at any commitment, but neither did she."

Madeleine said, quietly: "Did you talk to her about us?"

"Only a little – but Sylvie has been in the restaurant often when we've been talking, hasn't she? I suppose she must have listened more than we knew." His mouth grew taut. "I was so anxious to remain her friend – I wanted her to know that I valued her as a person, even if I was in love with you."

"What will you do?"

He lit a cigarette. "Sylvie will leave tonight."

"Are you sure?"

"How could you doubt it?"

They left the gazebo and strolled, hand in hand, down to the great octagonal pool where children sailed their toy boats. Madeleine felt calmer now, but still she felt the same dull certainty that she had to move on, that the Lussac family, to whom she owed so much, must not be put at risk, even of the most trivial legal kind.

"The poets and writers always chose this park for inspiration," Antoine told her. "Baudelaire, Hugo, George Sand, and painters too. If I've come here in crisis, I've often left the gardens with a resolution." He smiled. "Or at least with a new song."

"And my crisis?"

"Already solved."

"How?"

Antoine threw down his cigarette, ground it out with his heel and lit another. "Come to me," he said, softly. "Come to Fleurette, to work with me, to sing for me. To live with me."

Madeleine looked up into his face. "You just need a new waitress," she said, only half teasing.

"True."

"You think I'm ready to sing, in public?" she asked.

"We'll see soon enough, when the customers leave or stay."

"And your bed?" she challenged him, gently. "You're ready for me to share that with you at last?" Her cheeks burned with the question.

"My bed," he replied, and his eyes grew dark. "My life – my heart." He paused. "If you wish it."

"I wished it," Madeleine said, "from the instant I first saw you in the Tuileries. I've never changed my mind."

Madeleine moved into the tiny fourth-floor flat over the restaurant at the corner of rue de l'Echaudé and rue Jacob, two weeks later. The Lussacs had, at first, tried to dissuade her, and Andrée had wept with genuine sorrow at the prospect of losing her, but soon enough the family had become aware that whilst Stefan Julius's visit had precipitated the move, it was inevitable that it would, in any event, have happened before long.

"You won't forget us?" Gabrielle Lussac said, when Antoine came to fetch her. "We will certainly never forget you, *ma chère*. You have been the most original maid I have ever known –"

"Unique," Edouard said, smiling broadly.

"She's been much more than a maid," Andrée pointed out.

"She's been our friend," Hélène agreed.

"Do you imagine, *chéries*," Gabrielle assured them, "that we have not been aware of that, every single day?"

"We'd never have put up with her otherwise," Edouard said.

"How true." Madeleine embraced Gabrielle. "May I visit you sometimes, Madame? When it's convenient for you?"

"It will always be convenient," Edouard replied for them all, and turning, took Antoine's hand, clasping it firmly. "I feel almost as if I have a third daughter, and I am granting you permission to take her away from us. Take great care of her, my friend."

"I hope you will come to Fleurette as our guests," Antoine said.

"Very soon," Edouard promised.

Madeleine grew serious. "And please, you must swear to tell me if my stepfather creates any difficulties for you." She paused. "And whatever he says, don't tell him where I am."

"You are of age, *ma chère,*" Gabrielle said. "What you do, where you live, is your concern and no one else's."

On the first evening, Antoine went down alone to the restaurant to give Madeleine time to unpack her belongings and to prepare, gently, for work. But when she came downstairs, at half past seven, jittery at the prospect of waiting at tables for the first time, she found that Fleurette was completely empty.

"No customers?" she asked Antoine, baffled.

"Not one." He pointed to the front door, locked and bolted, and then drew her by the hand to the back of the room. Only one table had been laid – their table, set for two, flickering with candlelight.

"I can't believe it," she murmured.

"Did you really think I would want you to work tonight, *mon amour*?"

"Of course." She let him seat her, lay her napkin on her lap. "It's a business – I'm ready to work, I love the thought of working with you."

"And so you shall, but not tonight."

They dined quietly, on oysters and a soufflé of salmon, too much in love to eat as hungrily as usual, too replete with emotion even to talk as volubly as they ordinarily did, and a little later, Antoine went to the piano on the far side of the bar, and he began to play, while Madeleine sang, just for him, all the songs that Gaston never allowed her to try – the warm, sexy, liberating songs that she had been yearning to sing. . .

"Try this one." Antoine turned the pages of his sheet music and pointed.

"Is it yours?"

"Alas, no, but one of my favourites."

"It's in English."

"Try it anyway. It was written before you were born."

He played the opening bars, and Madeleine, leaning over his shoulder, peered at the notes and began, first to hum, and then to sing 'I'll Be Seeing You', faltering a little at first, then gradually gaining confidence.

Antoine stood up when she was finished, and as he turned around to face her, Madeleine saw that his eyes were moist.

"The customers will not just stay," he told her huskily. "They will come in droves to hear you."

She flushed. "You mean it?"

"That song, *chérie*, was the final proof for me." He wiped his eyes and smiled. "Anyone who sings it as it should be sung, brings tears to my eyes – if it is sung badly, it brings me pain. *Voilà*."

"You're crazy," she smiled.

"Only a little. My instincts in such matters are reliable."

With a huge rush of love, Madeleine flung her arms around his neck. "Thank you, thank you," she whispered against his chest. "For this, for everything, for tonight – for loving me –"

He pressed his lips to her golden hair, smelled its sweetness, felt her fragile form, recognized her strength, and was overwhelmed –

"Come." He could not say more.

"Where?" She drew away, looked up into his face, and felt her cheeks blaze suddenly with hot colour, felt a glow throughout her body, felt her hands, her fingers, even her toes, tingling with glorious, unprecedented excitement. At last, she thought, at long last. . .

She thought, as they both undressed, helped each other to undress, as their naked bodies touched for the first time, as they lay down, together, on the bed she had craved to lie on for so long, that if she had been an artist instead of a singer, she might have felt compelled to leap away again, simply to capture the moment for perpetuity. He was as beautiful, as enthralling, to look at as she had known he would be, and looking down at her own body, she observed changes – in her flesh tone, in the blush of her nipples and their surrounding areolae, in the way the tiny soft hairs on her thighs rose erect as he kissed her shoulder – and they were like a pair of softest Matisse nudes, or Rodin's sculpted lovers, brought to joyous reality, living hearts pumping rich blood through human veins. . .

"Even your feet are enchanting," Antoine said, and suddenly, as his lips brushed her toes and Madeleine felt an almost electrical pulse of lust jolting right through her, she ceased her role as rapturously contented observer, and became a wholehearted participant. If he could do that for her, just by kissing her foot, if he could create such glorious, exquisite high-voltage desire, then she wanted to do as much for him. This was what love meant – this blissful emotional and physical exchange.

"Kiss me," Antoine said, his voice a fierce whisper.

She wriggled down the bed, so that they were both lying across the base, and kissed him, the most completely *giving* kiss that she could bestow, generous and open and thrusting and filled with love and strength and passion, and she felt his response in kind, and he put his arms about her and lifted her up, and lay her down again, her head on the pillow, and he stared at her, devouring her with his eyes.

"*Ma belle*," he said, and kissed her neck, just below her right ear. She shivered, and kissed his neck in return. His right hand stroked her left breast, felt the sweet, small nipple grow erect under his palm, and he heard her moan with pleasure. And then, to his profoundest delight, he felt her begin to touch him, felt her hands moving, roaming over his skin, stroking, touching, fluttering, and Madeleine pushed him gently, so that he rolled over and they were side by side, face to face. And he saw the black pupils in her brilliant turquoise eyes dilating as she drank him in, studied him and, with gentle, firm, intuitive skill, she took his penis in her hand and, discovering its own, independent life force, began stroking it into inflamed, wild urgency –

"Stop," he beseeched her, and she obeyed instantly, groaning with joy as his fingers journeyed over her abdomen and began to probe her tangle of pubic hair, seeking and finding the soft, hidden moistness, starting to play on her body, showing her that he, too, could taunt and provoke and bring her to astonishing, bewildering, violent desire.

"Please," she urged, her voice low and quivering, "make love to me now – I want to feel you inside me."

"Not yet." Antoine's left hand caressed her tight, silken buttocks, so that she arched her hips towards him.

"Please," Madeleine implored, and she put her arms around him and, repeating his own movement, ran her hands over him and felt his strong muscles clenching, heard his low, swift, responding exhalation. "Now," she whispered, and then, again: "*Now!*"

Antoine took her arms and pushed her, gently, over onto her back, kissing her again and again, her mouth, her throat, her breasts, and his left hand held her right hand tightly, while with his other hand he reached down and parted her thighs, so that she gasped with anticipation, and eagerly spread her legs wider, willingly, blatantly, so that Antoine looked down at her, so welcoming, so avid. And he gave a groan of sheer happiness before he entered her, penetrated her glorious tightness, her sweet wetness – and at last, he began to move inside her, and Madeleine moved with him, all her natural instincts leading her towards their mutual pleasure.

He pushed further, felt a resistance, realized it was her virginal hymen, still intact and holding him back –

"Don't stop, *chéri*," Madeleine said urgently.

"I can't bear to hurt you."

"You won't –"

And he pushed on, and Madeleine lifted herself, raising her pelvis to help him, and he felt her fingers dig suddenly into his back, heard her brief, startled gasp of pain, and he began to draw away again. But she wouldn't let him, she drew him back, rocking her hips a little, then circling them, one moment staring up into his face, searchingly, the next closing her eyes, letting herself feel, pure, all-enveloping sensations, giving herself up to it, to him – until the blazing heat in their loins surged to a final, unbearably exquisite peak, and they came together, crying out, clinging on, holding fast, not wanting, ever, to let go. . .

Later, lying close under the covers, warm and safe and unutterably content, Antoine said, softly:

"I meant to stop, but I couldn't."

"Why should you?"

"For safety."

"In case you gave me a child?" Madeleine smiled in the darkness. "I would love, more than anything, to have your child."

"There's plenty of time for that, *mon amour*." He kissed her hair. "I'll be more careful next time."

She pulled away a little, so that she could see his face. "I couldn't bear you to stop, to pull out before. It was almost the best part, feeling you pour yourself into me."

"There are other ways."

"Of course," she said, and hearing him chuckle, asked: "Why are you laughing?"

"At the worldly wisdom of a nice Swiss virgin."

Madeleine nibbled his ear. "A nice Swiss virgin living in Paris," she said. "One cannot live in Paris, without learning about sex. It seeps out of the walls, it's in the air." She paused. "It was wonderful, wasn't it? I thought it was wonderful."

"Except when I hurt you," Antoine said.

"Even that was wonderful," she said. "A beautiful pain. But just think, *chéri*, I will never feel that again – how sad." She thought for a moment. "The next beautiful pain I experience will probably be when I have our child. Imagine."

"I'd sooner not."

Madeleine half sat up. "You don't want us to have a child, not ever?"

"Of course I do. But I hate to imagine you in pain of any kind."

His navy eyes had grown grave at the thought, and Madeleine observed a vulnerability about him that produced a pang of tremendous love and care in her.

"We're going to have the best life together, aren't we?" she said. "Fleurette will become the greatest success in Saint-Germain, and your *patron* will make you his partner, and then after a time, we will buy the restaurant from him, and we'll live here forever."

"Won't it be a little small when there are six of us?" The gravity had vanished, and now Antoine's eyes were dancing.

"Six?"

"At least."

"I agree. Why stop there?"

She slept so deeply, so blissfully, that she was oblivious of Antoine getting up, dressing and going out, unconscious of him returning until he kissed her gently on the cheek and woke her.

"*Bonjour*, sleepy-head."

"Hello." Madeleine smiled at him and stretched luxuriously. "Why aren't you in here with me?"

"Someone had to fetch breakfast."

She sat up abruptly, the sheet tumbling away from her. "You didn't go to market without me?"

Antoine smiled. "Not today – Grégoire went alone."

Madeleine stared past him. "The flowers." She had not noticed, till now, that the little bedroom was filled with vases of roses, wonderful, richly blooming tea roses of varying shades of pink, pale yellow and white. She leapt out of bed and flung herself at him. "I was dreaming of scent, beautiful perfumes, like that marvellous blend that wafts over you in that department in Galeries Lafayette – and all the time, it was you and your roses." She began to unbutton his shirt, covering his chest with kisses. "You are the most beautiful man in the world –"

"And the most fortunate," he mumbled though their kisses, pulling away just to point out the wooden breakfast tray at the foot of the bed. "I thought you might be hungry."

She looked at the tray, saw the white china bowl of strawberries, the delicate saucer of sugar, the rose petals strewn on the white cloth, and said, softly, "It's like the painting, the one I love." One of the paintings downstairs in the restaurant was an Hippolyte Lucas print titled *Strawberry Tea*, which she had commented upon and which Antoine had told her reminded him of summer afternoons in Normandy.

"But we have coffee, and warm croissants as well." Antoine took a napkin off a basket. "*Voilà, Mademoiselle*."

"We'll make crumbs in bed."

"I'll make crumbs all over you, and lick them off."

With a quick, graceful movement, Madeleine was back in bed. She patted the sheet beside her. "Too much talk," she said. "Come back to bed, and let's eat."

Antoine unbuckled his belt. "Hungry?"

"Ravenous."

* * *

They began to live together, setting up an easy, joyful home that was as much hers as his. Antoine continued to run Fleurette much as before, but now that Madeleine was working by his side, he was able to spend a little more time on his songs, which became even more lyrical and romantic than ever.

Madeleine adored her new life; she could not imagine wanting, or needing more. Twice each night, six days a week, she shed her apron and sang for the customers, and they responded wonderfully well, enjoyed hearing her and watching her, for she seemed to become more beautiful with every passing month. Life was honeyed and rich, her relationship with Antoine was honest and natural, their lovemaking grew more wondrous and fulfilling as time went on. They lived every single day and night to the hilt, often hardly sleeping at all, going out into the vibrant Paris night after closing Fleurette, to unwind for a while at La Coupole or to listen to jazz at the Mars Club, or the Blue Note or at Le Bilboquet, before going on to Les Halles at around four in the morning. There they bought fresh produce for the day ahead, gossiped with acquaintances over a bowl of onion soup, watched the grocery store owners pushing their two-wheeled *diables* laden with fresh vegetables, fruits, meats and cheeses; and then, sometimes, if they had an ounce of energy to spare, danced cheek to cheek at Au Chien Qui Fume. They shared each other's friends; they shared everything it was possible to share. They were young, very much in love, and blissfully content.

Happiness making her generous and reflective, Madeleine celebrated the first anniversary of her move to rue Jacob by writing a letter to her younger brother.

"I doubt that he'll answer," she told Antoine, "but I think it's time I set the record straight, with Rudi at least. All that poison, spread by Stefan and our mother, and then Sylvie." She paused. "He's nearly fifteen now. I can't help wondering what he's like."

"He's your brother." Antoine smiled. "It's not surprising."

"You think I'm right to do it?"

"Without a doubt." He took her hand. "And it makes me feel that it's time we went to Normandy for a visit. My family are almost crazed with their curiosity about you."

"How can we leave the restaurant?"

"Gaston knows well enough how to manage Fleurette – he could come for a few days."

Madeleine's eyes sparkled. "When do we leave?"

They borrowed Noah and Estelle's Peugeot, and drove to Normandy the following Sunday, arriving at Pension Bonnard, a charming, ivy-clad house with a thatched roof, in time for lunch. Madeleine observed the uninhibited warmth of the family reunion until she, too, was swept up in a flurry of cheek kissing, embracing and unabashed scrutiny. Antoine's mother, Françoise, was a petite, vivacious forty-eight year old, with naturally curling dark hair, scattered with silver, blue eyes a shade or two lighter than her son's, and a ready smile; Claude Bonnard, his father, was tall and strong, balding but handsome with a blond moustache and eyes of remarkable violet-blue. Jacqueline, Antoine's sister, younger by two years, was so like her brother that Madeleine felt she might have known her in the street.

"We knew," Jacqueline told her, as Madame Bonnard served an appetizing chicken casserole and Claude poured Beaujolais into their glasses, "that you were very special. We were never in any doubt, since my brother could not give his heart so completely unless he was absolutely certain."

"I was certain, too," Madeleine said, softly, "from the first second I saw him –"

"In the Tuileries," Claude said, startling Madeleine. He smiled broadly, showing gold fillings in his lower teeth. "Antoine wrote to us that same day, you know – told us he had experienced a *coup de foudre*, but that you were much better than a thunderbolt, since you were made of flesh and blood."

"*Tais-toi*, Claude," Françoise scolded. "You'll embarrass Madeleine."

"*Pouf*," he dismissed. "She doesn't mind, do you, my dear?"

Madeleine laughed. "How could I?"

The house stood beside a substantial apple orchard, not far from a tangled, picturesque wood just a short walk from a superb view of the Côte Fleurie, and over the next four days, Madeleine and Antoine divided their time between helping out in the *pension*, chattering endlessly *en famille*, strolling in the woods, and driving around the region, drinking in the idyllic landscape, pausing to enjoy the half-timbered farmhouses and the placid cattle that contributed to the famous local cream and cheeses.

"Don't you miss this life?" Madeleine asked Antoine, curiously.

"Terribly, sometimes." He shrugged. "But I would miss Paris even more." He looked down and stroked her cheek, and she laid her hand over his. "Perhaps one day, far into the future, when we're older, when we've had our fill of the city, we might yearn for Normandy – maybe when my mother and father are tired and in need of help."

"They work very hard," Madeleine said. "Jacqueline, too."

Antoine nodded. "When Jacqueline marries and has children, it may be difficult for my parents to manage. They'll have to bring in a stranger, and we've always tried to avoid that."

"You speak of your sister and marriage. Don't your parents disapprove, even a little, of our life?"

There was no hint of awkwardness in Madeleine's question. They had spoken, briefly, of their certainty that they would, eventually, marry, but they were so entirely happy, so filled with the sheer enjoyment that each successive day brought them, that they knew that they would simply go on as they were until they had a need, or were ripe, for more.

"Certainly they disapprove, in the religious sense," Antoine said. "But they are realists, for whom love and feeling come before everything else. My mother always feared for me, a little, living in such a bohemian environment. She's very grateful to you, *chérie*, for saving me from unknown dangers."

Madeleine laughed. "I'm hardly a model of prudence."

"But you have good sense and intuition – Maman knows that because you love me."

They returned to Paris to find a reply from Rudi. It was clear from the speed with which he had answered that he had been glad to hear from his sister. The tone of his letter was strained, yet markedly fair, considering that Madeleine had left home without a backward glance or more than a passing thought for her brother. Rudi said little about Emilie or Stefan, or about their grandmother, yet reading between the lines, Madeleine felt that her brother was far progressed from the unquestioning, compliant boy she had left behind in the Gründli Haus. She realized, more from the omissions in his letter than what he had written, that she had by now been thoroughly disowned by the rest of the family. Now living in sin in what they would certainly regard as the decadence of Saint-Germain-des-Prés, and working with her lover as a waitress and underpaid *chanteuse*, Madeleine had more than fulfilled every dark prophecy that Stefan Julius had ever made. She was the third-generation *schwarzes Schaf* – the third Gabriel black sheep.

"He misses you," Antoine said, after reading Rudi's letter.

"Surely not. We were never really close, and I was never nice to him," she said honestly, feeling a pang of guilt. "I would deserve his hatred – if it were the other way around, I think I might hate him."

Antoine shook his head. "I doubt that you would. You talk of hatred, but I think the only one you truly hate is Julius."

"I hate my mother."

"You feel passionately, *chérie* – it's not necessarily the same thing."

"I hate her for what she did to my father."

"Even though you know now what he did?" Antoine asked gently.

Madeleine looked intently into his eyes. "Do you imagine that I could stop loving you if you did something bad, if you made a terrible mistake?" She paused. "I could not stop."

"Then why do you suppose Rudi should have stopped loving you?"

"I don't know," Madeleine replied softly. "Maybe because I never understood that he loved me in the first place."

She wrote again to Rudi, telling him about their trip to Normandy and about Antoine's family, and before long, brother and sister had embarked on a regular correspondence, both increasingly grateful for the new communication between them. Of Alexander there was no further news, and every now and then, when Madeleine received letters from Konstantin Zeleyev in New York, that single lingering flaw in her happiness was brought home to her afresh, for the Russian, too, had no news for her of her father. But though it still mattered terribly, it mattered less than it had, for Madeleine was no longer alone. She had family. Not the structured family she had been born into, but the one she had built up around herself, the one she wanted. Her love, her contact with Rudi; her dear friends, Noah, Estelle and Gaston Strasser, the Lussacs. But Antoine was the core, the heart of her life. He understood her better than anyone ever had, and the songs he wrote for her pierced her with their sweet, poignant melodies and their sensitive lyrics.

Yet his first song remained her constant favourite. When Madeleine sang 'Les Nuits lumineuses' at Fleurette, she felt that she became an integral part of the song, made incandescent by his words, by his love. Their nights, those few private hours in their tiny home above the restaurant, were luminous, and their days, too, and when Antoine heard and watched her singing his song, he knew that he had written it with premonitory inspiration.

On the tenth of June, 1961, after they learned that Madeleine was expecting a child, she and Antoine were married in the tranquil medieval beauty of the church of Saint-Séverin in the Latin Quarter. It was a quiet, joyous wedding, to which Antoine's parents and sister came from Normandy, and Rudi came from Zurich.

"I can't believe you're really here." Madeleine shook her head in wonder, as they sipped champagne before the luncheon that Grégoire Simon had prepared for them at Fleurette. "Stefan must have been furious, surely?"

"Less than pleased," Rudi admitted wryly, "though neither Mami nor Omi raised too many objections. I think they knew it would be a waste of effort, and besides, though she wouldn't admit it in front of Stefan, I felt that Mami was glad that one of us could be here."

"Isn't that just what you'd like to believe?"

"Possibly."

It was hard for Madeleine to glimpse more than a mere vestige of the inadequate boy of her memories, in the eighteen-year-old young man who had taken her, without hesitation, into his arms, when they had first been reunited that morning, and who had shaken Antoine fervently by the hand; and now, even in the midst of her glowing happiness, Madeleine felt suddenly gripped by fierce self-doubt. She had always been so sure of herself, so convinced of the rightness of her emotions, of her instincts, yet surely it could not be that Rudi had altered so completely. People did not, after all, fundamentally change, so was it, therefore, her perception of her brother that had been at fault?

"You're so alike," Antoine said, joining them, his face wreathed in smiles. "You could almost be twins."

"I always thought we were as different as day from night," Madeleine said softly, and squeezed Rudi's hand. "It seems I was wrong."

"You were young," Rudi said lightly, "and I was even younger." He paused. "And unlike you, I was a cowardly child."

"I don't think so." Madeleine looked into the face that was so like her own, painfully aware that she knew so little about what went on behind the handsome, regular features, knowing only that her brother had shown both generosity and determination by coming to Paris. "You had different feelings, different ideas. I was convinced that you should have shared mine."

"And now," Antoine said, "you have a second chance."

"Thank God," Rudi said.

"Yes." Madeleine leaned against her husband. "I didn't believe that anything could make me even happier, but you have, Rudi."

"I wonder –" Rudi hesitated. "I wonder if some day you might come back, for a visit."

"Never," she said, quietly but resolutely. "I shall never go back."

"Never is a long time, *chérie*," Antoine said.

"And life is short," Madeleine said gently. "But all the clichés in the world cannot alter what I feel about them.

You were only four years old when Papi left home, Rudi – you couldn't understand. But I shall never forgive them." Her expression lightened. "And now I want to forget all about them, and concentrate on you, and on my wedding day. You've met the Levis, haven't you, Rudi, but what about the Lussacs?"

Madeleine's pains began on the fourteenth day of February, 1962, Saint Valentine's Day, while she and Antoine were strolling together in the Jardin des Tuileries. It was snowing lightly, Antoine had brought a bag of fresh-baked brioches so that he might feed his birds, and Madeleine was, as usual, watching him with pleasure, when the first contraction took her sharply by surprise.

"*Qu'est-ce que tu as?*" Antoine asked instantly, his eyes seldom leaving her these days. "Pain?"

"I think so."

"Shall we go?"

"Not yet." She smiled at him. "Let the birds finish."

The next one came fifteen minutes later, so forceful that she gave a small gasp of shock. Antoine threw the remaining brioches onto the ground and was at her side, gripping her arm.

"We'll go straight to the hospital," he said, his face taut with concern.

"I want to go home to fetch my bag," Madeleine said. "There's plenty of time, I'm sure."

"I'll fetch your bag later." Antoine was not to be argued with. "Can you walk, *chérie*, or shall I carry you?"

"Of course I can walk." She looked up at him, and her eyes were brilliant with excitement. "He's ready, Antoine – he's coming!"

"My daughter, you mean." They'd played the same eternal game throughout her pregnancy, neither caring in the least which sex the baby was, so long as it was healthy and strong.

The labour continued, in the hospital of Saint-Vincent-de-Paul, for more than nine hours, and for much of that time, against the wishes of both the delivering obstetrician and the nursing staff, Antoine remained at Madeleine's side, letting her dig her fingernails into his arms, wiping her forehead with cool cloths and murmuring encouragement into her ear. At the moment of birth, however, he was absent, having left to find a men's room and returning to find himself barred from re-entering until the last-minute flurry of urgent activity was past.

"A son," the doctor told him, smiling, twenty minutes later. "A fine, healthy boy."

"And my wife? Is she all right?"

A positive beam of approval spread over the obstetrician's face. "Madame Bonnard is an exemplary patient, Monsieur. Brave and strong. After a little rest she will be more than a match for motherhood." He gave a small bow. "I wish you all a wonderful life, and I look forward to the next."

"*Merci, Docteur.*" Antoine embraced the man. "Thank you with all my heart."

Madeleine lay back against clean white pillows, the baby in the crook of her left arm. Her short hair was still gleaming dark gold with moisture, her eyes were shadowed with fatigue, but her smile was radiant.

"I'm sorry, *mon amour*," Antoine said, stooping to kiss her.

"For what?"

"They wouldn't let me back in – I was frantic."

"To be honest," Madeleine said, "I'm not sure I would have noticed."

"Was it terrible?"

"Terrible, and wonderful – the last few moments I thought he would tear me apart, but I wanted it, I needed the pain. I told you, *chéri*, that it would be a beautiful pain." She looked curiously up at him. "Don't you want to hold our son?"

"You first – now, our son."

Having satisfied himself that Madeleine was well, Antoine focused his attention intently on the baby. Staring at the little bundle sleeping peacefully against his wife's breast, he observed the little face, crumpled, with rosy blotches on his cheeks and forehead, eyes squeezed shut, lashes dark like the sparse, damp hairs on his head, tiny nose snuffling slightly, exquisite lips puckering a little –

He held out his arms, wordlessly, and Madeleine, with the anxious caution of the first-time mother, passed the baby to him. "Support his head, *chéri*."

For several moments, Antoine still said nothing. Holding their child felt, instantly, like the most natural, the most right, the most important thing he had ever done in his life. The infant was so light, swaddled in his shawl, that his father felt a need, carefully, to unwrap the material so that he could, for a moment, touch his body, flesh to flesh, make contact with his skin, feel his body warmth, feel his unchallengeably human heartbeat. And love poured through him, almost sweeping him away, and Antoine covered his son again, wrapped him in the shawl, and the baby opened his eyes, blue, dark blue like his own, and began, suddenly, lustily, to cry.

"*Bon Dieu*," Antoine whispered, and found that he, too, was weeping.

"Do you think he's hungry?" Madeleine asked.

"Already?"

"He's had a long journey." She smiled, and Antoine laid the infant back in her arms, where he ceased wailing almost immediately.

"A wise boy," Antoine said, and then, remembering, added: "His name, *chérie*. He must have a name."

They had spoken, lightly, during the pregnancy, of possible names, but in the last months, stricken by sudden mutual superstition, they had dropped the subject, deciding to wait for inspiration at the right moment.

"I have an idea," Madeleine said, "if you agree."

"Tell me."

"Valentin," she said softly. "Partly for the day, for Saint-Valentin, for love. And partly for my grandfather's sake – for his *grand amour*, Irina Valentinovna." She paused. "What do you think?"

"It's wonderful."

"Valentin Claude Alexandre Bonnard." Madeleine looked at Antoine. "Is that all right?"

"Perfect," Antoine said.

12

One year and one day later, during the evening following Valentin's first birthday celebration, Antoine was opening a bottle of Pommard at a customer's table, when he dropped the bottle onto the floor. He clasped his right hand to his head, looked around in momentary confusion and fleeting fear, searching for Madeleine, and then collapsed, unconscious.

Gaston Strasser, who had been playing the piano, was instantly at his side, feeling for his pulse. "Telephone for an ambulance," he commanded Jean-Paul. "Where's Madeleine?"

The restaurant was hushed. Jean-Paul stared, too aghast to move.

"Don't just stand there, *crétin*!" Gaston, struggling not to panic, turned Antoine gently onto his side, brushing the splinters from the smashed bottle out of the way. Jean-Paul came to life, snatching up the telephone, and the customers began to shift uncomfortably in their chairs.

"Madeleine!" Gaston called, tenderly stroking Antoine's hair.

"She's upstairs, with the baby," Georges said in a low, frightened voice.

Gaston raised his bald head, and the veins in his temples bulged.

"*Madeleine!*" he bellowed.

* * *

They told her that Antoine had suffered a stroke. If he survived the first three weeks, he would recover to some extent. The stroke having occurred on the left-hand side of his brain, it had, initially at least, affected the right-hand side of his body. It would also, they said, probably have affected his speech, and his ability to understand what was said to him.

When she first saw him in the hospital bed, unconscious and utterly still, Madeleine thought he must, whatever the doctors and nurses said, have died. A man lay in that bed, but it was not her Antoine, who was always mobile, always active, always vibrantly alive. This person seemed as much a part of the hospital room as the sparse furniture and walls themselves, his face and body blending into the white linen.

"He is dead," she said to the sister at her side, and Madeleine felt as if she, too, had died.

"No, Madame."

"He's so still. So absent."

The sister touched her arm gently. "Feel his cheek, Madame. Take his hand. Don't be afraid."

Yet it was after Antoine had returned to consciousness, two days later, that the complete horror of what had happened manifested itself. It was no single thing; neither the hemi-paralysis which made his whole right side weak and floppy; nor the distressing slurring of his speech, nor his lack of comprehension when he was spoken to. It was the fear, the panic, the sheer terror that they both shared. For the time being, the only remaining thing that they could share.

Madeleine was in the dark, isolated and engulfed by the unrelenting nightmare that had obliterated their lives, destroyed their joy. They tried to explain to her.

"A stroke," they told her simply, "occurs when the blood supply to the brain is cut off. And in Monsieur

Bonnard's case, we believe that this was caused by a haemorrhage."

"I don't understand," Madeleine said, no less bewildered than before.

"We believe, Madame, that your husband had a congenital weakness in the wall of an artery supplying his brain, and that this burst, damaging that side of the brain."

They told her more, much more, but she could hardly absorb their words. To begin with, she wanted to know only one thing, whether Antoine would survive. And once that seemed likely, she felt a kind of greed enveloping her, pushing everything else aside. She wanted him well again. She wanted him as he had been.

"He's too young for this, surely," she said, repeatedly, in anguish. "He's only thirty-three – he's always been strong and healthy."

"Sometimes it happens, Madame."

"Yes," she said, but still her mind rejected the truth.

"You must accept it," the doctor told her one afternoon, firmly. "It's hard, I know, but it's important now that both you and Monsieur Bonnard cease to try to believe that it is just a bad dream which will go away."

"I cannot accept it." Madeleine looked at him with angry, bitter eyes. "My husband will get well again. We have to fight. Surely you don't expect us to give up?"

"Of course not, Madame. Just to accept the facts."

At Antoine's bedside, Madeleine began to speak to him almost incessantly. Whereas in the first few days after he had returned to consciousness, she had told him only that she loved him, adored him, that he would get well, that all he had lost would return to him, now she spoke of everything that came into her mind. Valentin missed him terribly, she said, for hadn't his Papa done so much more than most for his baby boy, changing him, feeding him as soon as he was weaned, bathing him and playing with him endlessly every chance he had? All was well at Fleurette – they were managing without him, but it was not the same, nothing was the same without him – he was needed, desperately needed by many people –

"Sleep," Antoine lisped in his new, drunken voice.

"Soon, *chéri*," Madeleine would say, and went on regardless.

"Go 'way," he said, and she saw the raw woundedness in his eyes, knew that he thought her quite savage in her relentless encouragement, that he wanted her to stop, but all her instincts forced her on. He had so swiftly built a wall of sickness around himself, covering up his fear, exchanging it for a defeatism which terrified Madeleine more than anything.

She asked if she might bring Valentin to see his father, but they told her that children were not permitted, and when she told Antoine, secretively, that she intended to smuggle the baby in despite them, his face filled with horror and he became so distraught that it took some time to calm him again. But still, she continued to listen to her own private counsel, and one morning, when the hospital was at its busiest, she put on Antoine's big old duffle coat, tucked Valentin, who thought it was a wonderful game, inside it, on her left hip, walked into his ward, demanded that screens be put around, and deposited the plump one-year-old on her husband's bed.

"No," Antoine said. *"No."*

He looked away from the baby, his expression anguished.

"He insisted on coming," Madeleine said softly. "He needs to see you."

Antoine forced his eyes back, filled with tears. "Hate you," he said, with great clarity.

"I know."

Valentin sat very still, staring with huge, puzzled eyes,

and for a moment Madeleine thought he would start to cry.

"Here's your Papa," she said, gently, and took Antoine's unresponsive hand in hers. And Valentin, too, reached out his pudgy arm, and touched his father's poor right arm.

"Papa," he said, and beamed. "Papa," he said again.

The tears began to roll down Antoine's cheeks, and Madeleine, choking back her own for the child's sake, took her husband's left hand and laid it on his son's cheek.

"There's nothing wrong with that hand," she said quietly. "Use it to love him. Use it, and the rest will come."

Antoine improved markedly for the next two weeks, and then, after they were told that it was quite safe for him to go home, after he and Madeleine and Gaston and Grégoire had tried to laugh off the nightmare effort of dragging his stretcher up the four flights of stairs to their flat, he continued to improve for one more week. And then his recovery seemed to stop.

Madeleine had felt elated after the early victories, had been ecstatic when she had learned that he could come back to rue Jacob, but now her spirits plummeted again. The doctors explained to them both that the fastest improvements always took place in the first three weeks, when any temporarily damaged cells outside the main area of impairment healed spontaneously. After that, things inevitably slowed down, though that did not mean they could not hope for further improvements. It was just that now they would have to work harder to achieve them.

"You are both lucky, Madame," the doctor who came to call told Madeleine. "Your husband's disabilities are relatively minor. With encouragement, with your help and a strong will, which I believe he does possess, he should be able, in time, to get out of bed by himself, and to walk again, with crutches."

Mercifully, the slurring to Antoine's speech was already minimal, and although the most commonplace words would suddenly, frustratingly elude him, they were able to communicate almost normally again, and Antoine seemed to have left his temporary aggression towards Madeleine in the hospital. They had love on their side, and hope, and with the strength of youth, the doctors all told them, they should be able to achieve a substantial recovery.

Madeleine knew that she was strong, emotionally as well as physically, and that there was not an ounce of her that, even secretly, wanted to shrink away from caring for Antoine. Yet every passing week lacerated her anguished heart further, and took its toll on her aching, exhausted body. When Claude and Françoise Bonnard, distressed by their latest visit to the small, cluttered flat, pressed her to talk Antoine into coming home to Normandy, Madeleine was sorely tempted, but she knew that it would mean giving up Fleurette. The restaurant and Paris were Antoine's world, the life he loved; if he surrendered now, all hope might be lost.

Their friends rallied round magnificently. Estelle Levi came most mornings to take Valentin to Boulevard Haussmann to play with her two little girls, and Noah came at least once a day, except during the Sabbath, to talk to Antoine and to help him with his exercises. But it was Gaston Strasser who saved them, by going to Les Halles before dawn when Grégoire Simon could not manage it, and by coming in, morning and evening, to manage Fleurette for no more reward than his expenses and one good daily meal, so that Madeleine had little more to do in the restaurant than to maintain the book-keeping and to sing every night.

They *were* lucky, she acknowledged wryly. Valentin was so easy-going and quite uncannily sensitive for such a young child. He was filled with natural energy, yet he appeared to recognize that when Madeleine placed him in his father's good arm he had to be patient and good-natured. But Antoine's frustrations and unhappiness broke her heart. He seldom complained now, but the restrictions of his new life drove him almost mad. The ordeal of getting downstairs, sliding from one step to the next on his bottom, and then having to be wheeled outside into the fresh air, was painful and humiliating, and often the pitying eyes of strangers drove them back upstairs again, where Antoine would collapse onto the bed, eyes closed, so drained from effort and misery that Madeleine would watch him, hawk-like, for at least an hour, terrified that he might be on the verge of another stroke.

For the first time in the seven years since she had left Zurich, Madeleine missed the security she had abandoned. She tried to persuade Antoine at least to discuss the possibility that they might, after all, go to Trouville to stay with his family, but Antoine would not hear of it. The *pension* was too small to accommodate them for any length of time without destroying the Bonnards' livelihood.

"But your parents would love to have us there, *chéri*," Madeleine said.

Antoine shook his head. "I always said that perhaps, one day, we might think of going there to help them. That would be natural, that would be right."

"Isn't it right to allow them to help you?"

"No." His face was set obdurately. "Not for them, not for me." He tried to soften his tone a little. "Things will improve in time, *mon amour*. Try not to worry so."

But every day was a struggle, and Madeleine had no choice but to watch it eating away at Antoine. He had been advised to give up smoking and to eat wisely, but his addiction to Gauloises was far too ingrained to tackle, and whereas in the past he had smoked mostly because he had enjoyed it, now his cigarettes, together with the cheap *pastis* and wine he drank too much of, became as vital to him as the crutches he had begun to use.

At the end of August, Konstantin Zeleyev came to Paris again to visit Madeleine, and to give her, in person, a letter sent to his accommodation address from Alexander.

"Thank God," she said, almost snatching it from him. "Is he well? What does he say?"

"Not very much. Best read it."

In the letter, postmarked Amsterdam in June, her father sounded lonely and guilty, clearly longing to know that his Maggy was well and happy, but apparently still unable to risk giving his address.

"Why doesn't he tell you where he is?" Madeleine asked wearily. "He knows he can trust you – he must know you would tell only me, that neither of us would ever betray him."

"He sounds very troubled," Zeleyev said. "We don't know what he's doing, *ma chère*, or how he survives, or the people he's involved with."

"Do you think he's so afraid?"

"Perhaps."

Madeleine shook her head. "If things were different, perhaps I'd go to Amsterdam, search for him, not give up until I found him, but it's impossible, isn't it."

Zeleyev's green eyes were full of compassion. "I'm so sorry, *ma petite*. I can hardly express what I feel for you. You sounded so happy, so fulfilled. I could not be sure if your Antoine was the perfect man for you, but your letters convinced me that you felt he was."

"He still is, Konstantin."

"Of course."

Zeleyev was more shocked than he admitted by Madeleine's exhaustion and by her young husband's pitiful condition. He remembered all too clearly those old days in the Dischmatal when he had planted dreams of Paris in the golden head of this well-loved girl, and responsibility weighed heavily on him. He heard her sing in the restaurant, observed the moistness in the eyes of the customers as her personal sorrows welled up in her voice, enriching it. He watched her hurrying wearily upstairs to check on her husband and on their little son, and he saw, bitterly, what a far cry this was from the life he had envisaged for her.

Since learning about Bonnard's illness, Zeleyev had made enquiries in New York, and he had discovered that a specialized treatment was available there, using hyperbaric oxygen chambers, said to be having a profoundly beneficial effect upon stroke patients.

"They might help Antoine too," he suggested to Madeleine.

"If we were there, perhaps."

"Why not?"

"Why not a trip to the moon?" she said wryly.

"Is it really so absurd, *ma chère*? I fly back and forth, don't I? If it's just the money, I could help you."

"I wouldn't let you."

"Why not?"

"And it isn't the money. Antoine wouldn't even consider going to his family in Normandy. He would hardly contemplate leaving France – leaving Europe."

Zeleyev did not give up so easily. Just as he had painted those glowing and evocative word images of Paris, now he did the same, almost unwittingly, for New York. It was truly a wondrous city, he told Madeleine, a city of the most astonishing contrasts, of remarkable beauty, entirely man-made and therefore perhaps all the more admirable, and of fascinating ugliness to balance the beauty. There was nothing that could not be found in Manhattan, and no type of person; there were people of great culture, and there were philistines, there were God-fearing men and women and there were unutterable heathens; there were millionaires and there were paupers.

"They call them 'bums', but they're no different to the *clochards* in Paris." Zeleyev looked at Madeleine. "There is a great park right in the heart of all the concrete buildings – hundreds of acres of meadows and trees and lakes and playgrounds. I read somewhere that there are more than one thousand parks in the city, though I must admit I visit only two – but it is a human place, Madeleine, and the most exciting city in the whole world."

Zeleyev had been away from Russia for more than forty years, yet he had lost none of his native capacity for lyricism and fervour. His forceful enthusiasm had stirred Madeleine as a young girl, and it did not fail to arouse her now, a fact that Zeleyev swiftly noticed and capitalized on.

"You should think of coming, *ma chère* – not for ever, but for Antoine's health, for your future. I could see to it that you had a comfortable, more practical place to stay while he received treatment, and afterwards you could come back to Paris if you wanted to." He paused. "Though perhaps you might not want to leave, because Manhattan is a city of music. You have experience now as a singer – in New York I think they would adore you, and when they fête you, Madeleine, it is like nowhere else –"

"Stop, Konstantin, it's impossible."

"Nothing is impossible, *ma petite*." His eyes glittered. "And if you felt free in Paris, you would feel a thousand times more free in America."

She smiled, wistfully. "It sounds wonderful."

"Say the word, and I will investigate further."

"I can't."

"At least think about it."

Madeleine shrugged. "Thought is cheap."

The temptation was intense, for she had begun to realize that the best times in Paris were already past, and that they might never return. And yet she still feared that taking Antoine away from his familiar surroundings, from what he knew so well and loved, might prove detrimental. So long as their friends stood by them, so long as they could keep the restaurant going and survive the worst months, she still had to believe that there was room left for optimism.

And then, in November, without warning, Fleurette's owner, Jean-Michel Barbie, came to Paris from Provence, and absolute disaster struck. No one had informed him of Antoine's condition, nor that Gaston was acting, without his approval, as manager. Barbie took an instant, violent dislike to Strasser and, though expressing a degree of sympathy for the Bonnards' plight, he felt that he had no alternative but to give them notice to quit the apartment within a month, so that he could install a new manager. Madeleine pleaded with him, Noah Levi came to appeal to his better nature. Gaston Strasser, filled with contempt, first implored him and then punched him on the nose. If Barbie had been determined before, now he was immovable.

It was Estelle Levi who contacted Rudi Gabriel, begging him to come to Paris without delay, and who met him at the Gare de Lyon to bring him to rue Jacob so that Rudi could see at first hand his sister's predicament.

"I'm surprised, to be honest," Estelle said, on the way from the station, "that you have not been before."

"If I'd known how bad things were," Rudi said quietly, "I would have come long ago."

"Madeleine didn't tell you about Antoine?"

"She's written very little, but from her letters one might have believed Antoine had little more than a bad bout of influenza." He shook his head. "In case I told our mother or stepfather, I imagine."

"She's very proud," Estelle said.

"And stubborn."

Rudi wasted no time. One thing was clear, he told his sister, collaring her down in Fleurette, away from the sick-room: she must come back to Zurich with him for whatever funds she needed, whether she used the money to take Antoine to America, or to stay in France.

"It's out of the question," Madeleine said. "You know I will never ask them for help."

Rudi looked at Estelle. "Can you stay here to look after things while I take my sister to lunch?"

"We can lunch here."

"We're going out," he said. "There are some things we need to discuss."

"They won't make any difference," Madeleine said.

"Lunch won't kill you, surely?" Estelle commented.

He took her away from Saint-Germain, away from the Left Bank, to the Café de la Paix, and Rudi ordered calf's liver sautéed with onions for them both, assuring Madeleine when she raised an eyebrow that she needed all the strength she could get.

"You look like a stick," he told her.

"Thank you."

"A lovely stick, with a face so strained that it scares me."

"Don't be scared for me," she said, touched. "It's been a bad time, but we're coming through."

"But you have to admit you'd come through a little more easily if money were not so short."

She sighed. "Obviously that's true, but it makes no difference. Please don't make me argue with you, Rudi – I will not touch Gründli money, and I will certainly never take so much as a piece of bread from Stefan Julius."

"I'm not asking you to."

"What then?" She softened. "Are you trying to lend me money?"

"No," Rudi said. "Since my savings are also, fundamentally, from that untouchable source, I shan't even try to persuade you."

The wine waiter poured a little Fleurie into Rudi's glass, which he tasted and approved. "It's delicious," he told Madeleine. "Drink some."

"In a minute."

"Now."

"You have changed," she said dryly.

"I have something to tell you, about our grandfather."

"About Opi? What?"

Rudi broke off a piece of bread and chewed it for a moment. "Two weeks ago, I overheard a conversation between Mami and Omi. They were in Omi's sitting room, with the door ajar. They didn't realize that I was in the house."

"Go on."

"They were discussing a letter, left by Amadeus, in which he bequeathed all his possessions to you. The house, all his belongings – and the sculpture you talked about, the night you left home, *Eternité*." Rudi paused. "The most important thing I heard, however –" he leaned forward across the table, confidentially "– is that our stepfather destroyed the letter."

"Could he do that? Surely the lawyer, Herr Walther –? He must have organized the clearing of the house."

"If it was a letter, and not a properly executed will," Rudi said, "he might have handed it over unopened. With Stefan paying his fees, it's not likely that the lawyer could have intervened in a private family matter."

Madeleine thought. "So Opi's belongings would pass to our father – except that they made Papi give up his rights to our grandfather's estate." She hesitated. "Does that mean it goes to our mother, or does it come down to the two of us anyway?"

Rudi shrugged. "I've no real idea – but that's not the point. The sale of the house should have given you immediate funds, Maggy, and as for that mysterious sculpture –"

"That's gone," Madeleine said quietly.

"But where is it?"

Madeleine looked into her brother's face, and felt a swift rush of relief as she realized that she could, after all, trust him, that he was, truly, her brother.

"Our father took it," she said. "There were only three people aside from Opi who knew where it was hidden: Papi and I, and Konstantin."

"The Russian."

"Opi could never have made it without him. They lived together, on and off, for five years. They put everything into it, Rudi, all for Irina, because they had both loved her so much."

"And those jewels – you think they were real?"

"According to Konstantin, the sculpture is priceless." She spoke softly. "The gems alone were worth a fortune, and if you consider that the whole thing was sculpted in solid gold, white gold, and that Konstantin learned his skills from his father, who worked for Fabergé in Russia –" She shook her head. "It was exquisite, yet I know that our grandfather never thought of it in terms of value."

"But he wanted you to have it."

"I'm sure that Papi will keep it safely for me."

"Are you?" Rudi asked gently.

"Who should I trust?" Madeleine challenged him. "A man who loved me, without reservation, or a man so despicable that he would ignore the last wishes of my grandfather?" She paused. "Not to mention my mother, who allowed him to do it."

"She's guilty about it, and Omi sounded unhappy. They didn't say much, but it was obvious they had not approved."

"But they didn't stop Stefan."

"No." Rudi looked directly at her. "And that's precisely why I'm telling you to come back with me to Zurich."

"I wouldn't lower myself."

"Not to accuse them, I know you wouldn't do that now. But Stefan has stolen from you, Maggy, and you have much more than just a moral right to demand financial help."

Rudi asked her, as they ate their lunch, about Antoine's condition, about the extent of his disabilities, about the treatment of which Zeleyev had told her, about the options open to her now that their livelihood was to be ripped away from them.

"I have no real choice, do I?" she said wearily as they walked back out into the Place de l'Opéra. "The very idea makes me ill, but if I don't take what's mine, if I don't use it to help my family –"

"I'll be with you." Rudi took her arm, squeezed her hand. "How much time do you need to prepare?"

"No time. We'll go tomorrow. If I wait, I won't be able to go through with it." It had begun to rain, and all the taxis normally lined up outside the Grand Hôtel had disappeared, but she was oblivious to the weather. "I'll take Valentin, but I won't stay in the house, we'll go to a hotel."

"Of course."

"Nowhere special, just somewhere near the station, and just for one night. Oh, God –" She felt panic rising inside her, and clutched at her brother's arm. "I swore I'd never go back."

"You're not going back, Maggy, darling."

"I'm going back to grovel – I can't bear it."

"Don't use such a word." Rudi's voice was sharp. "You're incapable of grovelling, and don't even think that way. This is a business transaction, nothing more, nothing less. They owe you, Maggy. They owe you a great deal, and they know it and we know it. You'll just be taking a fraction of what's rightfully yours."

Throughout the journey, gliding smoothly past the lovely scenery, moving back through the old, familiar landscapes, Madeleine tried to relax but failed, gnawing at her nails, her stomach churning, her head aching. She was awash with doubts, about leaving Antoine even for a day, about being perceived to use Valentin as emotional ammunition, but, most of all, worst of all, about having to ask Stefan Julius for anything.

Rudi took them directly to the Central Hotel, near the Hauptbahnhof, acquiescing to her refusal to stay in the five-star hotel that he would have chosen for her.

"We're expected at three o'clock," he told her. "Shall I leave you in peace for a while? You could rest, have something to eat in your room – shall I organize a sitter for Valentin?"

"No." Madeleine held her son so tightly that he gave a small squeal of protest. He had been so wonderfully good on the journey, had bounced on her knee and on his uncle's, staring with fascination out of the window, and then at the other people in the carriage, and for the last hour he'd slept soundly. "I'm taking him along."

"Are you sure?" Rudi had expected her to balk at letting her son enter the Gründli Haus, as if it might somehow contaminate his innocence.

"I'm thinking of this as you suggested I should. It's a meeting, a business transaction. On my own, I'm still the ungrateful runaway, the disloyal child – with Valentin, I'm the mother of their grandson, of Omi's great-grandson."

Her eyes glinted. "Let them see what they can't ever have."

It was strained, unpleasant, and a little sad. Though Madeleine thought that she detected a glimmer of pleasure in Hildegard's eyes as they lit upon Valentin for the first time, and though she felt Emilie's cool hands trembling slightly when they touched, briefly, her stepfather's attitude sliced icily through those fragile, connecting threads.

"According to Rudi, you are here because you want something from us. What is it you want, Magdalen?"

Madeleine summoned all her maturity, rejected forcibly the painful old memories conjured up by the house in case they weakened her.

"Money," she said clearly. "I need money."

She spoke simply, directly and candidly, outlining what had befallen her husband, and expressing her growing belief in the treatment she had been told about in America.

"As things stand, we cannot afford to go to New York. I can't let anything stand in the way of Antoine's recovery, and that is why we are here."

Rudi came to her side. "I told Maggy that I knew you would see to it that she has everything she needs."

"What made you so certain?" Julius asked.

"Her rights," Rudi answered.

"Surely your sister gave up such rights when she left home?"

Rudi looked directly into his stepfather's eyes. "We're not referring to your money," he said quietly, "or to the Gründli fortune. We're thinking of her own rights."

"Has she any?"

"I think you know what I mean."

A flicker of comprehension passed between the older and younger man, followed rapidly by a look of acute antipathy from Julius. Madeleine was aware that she was observing a silent severing of a relationship that must have begun, seriously, to crumble away when Rudi had attended her wedding more than two years before.

"Stefan." Hildegard spoke for the first time. "I would like to make a suggestion."

"Of course." Julius turned stiffly away.

Hildegard had not greatly altered. She had seemed an old woman for as long as Madeleine could remember, old but handsome, her formidable façade seldom softening, though when she permitted it to show through, she had been capable of real warmth.

"Have you considered, Magdalen, bringing your husband and son home?"

"Home?"

"To your own country. To Zurich."

"To this house, you mean?" Madeleine's tone was cool.

"Naturally." Hildegard paused. "I understand that until now you have all lived in a tiny apartment, several floors up, without a lift. New York City, I believe, is a much harder place in which to live comfortably than Paris."

"It's out of the question," Madeleine said, quite gently.

"In this house," she went on, "your husband could have a bedroom created for him, for his special needs. It could be on the ground floor, with access to the garden."

Emilie, silent and pale till now, added: "He could see the finest doctors, Maggy. Wouldn't it be wise at least to come for a while, to consult with them before travelling thousands of kilometres to a so-called cure that may be nothing more than wishful thinking?"

"It might be wise," Madeleine answered, and something unexpectedly like gratitude pricked sharply, surprisingly, at her heart. She raised her face and met her mother's eyes. "But it isn't possible. You must realize that."

Valentin, on the settee beside her, grew fidgety, and quickly Rudi picked him up and began to croon softly against his ear, so that the baby, always responsive to affection, giggled a little and, reaching up, tugged at his uncle's blond hair.

"Wouldn't you like to think it over, Magdalen?" Hildegard said.

"There's nothing to think about, Omi."

"Are you sure, Maggy?" Emilie asked, averting her eyes from Stefan's face. "Isn't it madness to choose hardship when you could have security and comfort?" She paused. "And don't you owe it to your husband at least to consult him?"

The room was silent.

"I will speak to Antoine," Madeleine said, then steeled herself again. "But today, I'm here to ask you for money."

"How much?" Stefan's voice, hard and shrewd, drove away the touch of mildness that had, for a few moments, softened the atmosphere. "What is your bill for this latest irresponsibility?"

With Julius's cheque for fifty thousand Swiss francs in the hotel safe, Madeleine had dinner that evening with Rudi at a fine little restaurant in Zinnen-Gasse. She had been unwilling to leave Valentin with a sitter, so Rudi had brought them both to a place run by two young men who were friends of his, where the baby would not be frowned upon.

"How do you feel?" Rudi asked, once a high chair had been found for Valentin and they had ordered.

"Tired out," Madeleine said.

"But glad you came?"

"Yes." She looked at him intently. "You know it would never have happened without you, don't you?"

"Perhaps not."

"No perhaps about it." She paused. "You've done much more for me than I deserve."

"Nonsense. I'm your brother."

"And have I been any kind of a sister to you?"

"Circumstances," Rudi dismissed. "And I know now that if it were the other way around, you would do the same for me." He stroked Valentin's plump knee. "Shall you ask Antoine?"

Madeleine nodded. "Of course."

"But you don't believe he will choose to come to Zurich." He was wistful. "I can't help wishing, selfishly, that he would. I'd love to have you back at home again."

"It never really was home for me, Rudi."

"I know that."

"If we were to agree –" Madeleine paused, the very thought sickening her "– then yes, Antoine would have every care, every comfort. Yes, he could sit in the garden, and know that his wife wouldn't have to work almost every hour of every day. But the price of all that would be too high. Antoine and I would lose our individuality and our liberty – worse still, our child would be taken over by them, swallowed up into their world." She smiled wearily at him. "That cheque will make all the difference, Rudi, whatever happens. In spite of everything, I'm grateful to them for that."

"They owed it to you, Maggy."

"It's more than I wanted to take."

"But it's yours, by right."

"They didn't admit that."

"Because we didn't force their hand," Rudi pointed out.

"If we had, Stefan would never have forgiven you, and I wouldn't want to be the cause of that. As it is, you're clearly already quite a disappointment to him." She paused. "Do you think he will forgive you?"

"To be honest," Rudi said, "I don't really care."

The encounter with her family had worn Madeleine out, but the good food and pleasant atmosphere of the restaurant, together with the warmth of her brother's company, provoked an appetite that surprised her, and by the time she collapsed into the comfortable bed at her hotel, she knew what folly it would have been not to have come.

She had predicted Antoine's response accurately. If he had been unwilling to burden his own, loving family, the idea of receiving daily help from the people his wife had escaped from as a teenager, was repugnant to him. He knew how comfortable, how easy it might be in the Gründli Haus, he was aware that the medical care and treatments available in Switzerland were likely to be every bit as advanced as in New York, no matter what Zeleyev believed, but he knew that Madeleine would be deeply unhappy in that bitter house, and that her misery would be more painful to him than anything.

"If we've lost Fleurette," he told her, "if we've lost our Paris, then we should take our chances and move forward. America will be an adventure, at least," he said, with the first spark of optimism he'd shown for months. "Better that than even the most luxurious prison."

Konstantin Zeleyev had been right, Madeleine thought, when he had prophesied that she would find happiness in Paris. The Russian had been a wonderful friend to her grandfather, and he was still the only person on earth with a link to Alexander. He had been her ally, too, since she had been fourteen years old, and however rarely she saw him, she trusted Zeleyev implicitly.

Even with her husband's life.

They flew to New York in the third week of February, 1964, just after Valentin's second birthday, having spent two months staying with the Levis and Hexi in the apartment on Boulevard Haussmann where Madeleine had begun her eight-year life in Paris.

They left on the noon flight from Orly, but it proved a

gruelling seven hours. The Boeing 707 was fully loaded, and it was only after take-off that they discovered that the passenger immediately behind them was allergic to cigarette smoke. The deprivation, combined with the restrictions of his aircraft seat, drove Antoine almost mad, and his distress transmitted itself to Valentin who, uncharacteristically, screamed shrilly for much of the journey. Madeleine comforted the little boy and tried her best to soothe her husband, all the while watching him like a protective lioness, almost imagining that her hair was turning prematurely white as they sailed through the bumpy skies towards the unknown.

Zeleyev was at JFK International Airport, with a wheelchair and a long, spacious black limousine, and Madeleine, at least, found relief and comfort in his bear hug. But that soon turned back to silent dismay, and swiftly to acute depression as they skimmed the Long Island Expressway towards the city. It was all so ugly, Madeleine thought, the road itself, and the odd little houses that looked as if they'd been thrown up with hammers and nails with no more *raison d'être* than to give their occupants basic shelter. And even when, about twenty minutes into the ride, the limousine swept up onto a small bridge and suddenly the famous Manhattan skyline exploded right before their eyes, and Madeleine felt a real lurch of excitement and turned to look at Antoine, she saw such a woeful bleakness on his thin face that it took all her will not to beg the driver to spin the car around and drive them back to the airport.

Zeleyev had made reservations for them at the Essex House, a forty-storey hotel on Central Park South where they were shown to their room, spacious and overlooking the park, with a huge bed, a fine crib for Valentin and a kitchenette.

"We don't need this," Madeleine said, looking at the

occupancy rates posted on the door. "I thought we were going to an apartment."

"This is my gift to you," Zeleyev told her quietly. "After all you've been through, you deserve a little comfort."

"It's out of the question," Antoine said stiffly. "You're very kind, but we can't accept."

"You can't refuse, without deeply offending me." He stroked his moustache, still red-gold and beautifully maintained. "Just three nights, *mon ami*." He paused. "If you don't want it for yourself, remember how hard your wife has worked."

"I don't know." Antoine was flushed with embarrassment.

"Take a rest," Zeleyev suggested. "And think about it later."

"Isn't it wonderful?" Madeleine said, after he had gone. She bounced on the bed, and watched Valentin crawling eagerly over the soft carpet, his little face alight with curiosity. "And the view!"

"It's quite a room," Antoine said dourly. "Where are my crutches?"

Madeleine got quickly off the bed and gave them to him. "Where do you want to go? Can I help, *chéri*?"

"I'm going to piss – is that all right?" He heaved himself out of his chair, and limped towards the bathroom. "If your friend had considered me at all, he'd have realized that now I'll have to get used to two new places instead of one."

The door slammed behind him, and hot tears flooded into Madeleine's eyes, and simultaneously Valentin began to howl. She picked him up and held him close, feeling his small chest expanding fiercely before each wail, and wishing that she, too, could release her emotions so uninhibitedly.

The door opened again, and Antoine stood, the bathroom light behind him, watching them. "Forgive me," he said.

"Nothing to forgive." Madeleine wiped first her own cheeks, then the baby's. "I know how hard it must be." She paused. "Maybe I don't really know, not completely – but I feel as if I share your pain."

"I know you do. It might be better for you if you did not." Antoine levered himself to the bed and sank down, relieved. "A little hard," he said, feeling the mattress. "But not too bad."

"And big."

He nodded. "It's a fine bed."

Madeleine, with Valentin still in her arms, sat down beside Antoine. "Would you prefer to leave, *chéri*?"

"Of course not." He smiled wryly. "I was rude. I'm a monster, these days. Your friend means only well – I'll apologize later."

"He understands, I'm sure."

"Nevertheless."

Zeleyev telephoned from the lobby two hours later.

"I thought a gentle walk, before sunset. If you rest too long now, the time difference will have you awake all night."

"I'm not sure," Madeleine said.

Zeleyev understood. "The sooner Antoine comes down into the city, the better for him. No point exchanging one prison for another, *ma chère*."

"You're right."

"Am I not always?"

Antoine complained a little, but then, giving in, he allowed Madeleine to wheel him into the elevator, for he was too tired to use his crutches. And after that it was so effortless in comparison to what he had been accustomed to, so comfortable, with Valentin sitting on his lap in the chair, grinning up at him, and the doorman doffing his cap and bidding them a good afternoon, and the weather still brilliantly clear, in spite of the chill. And although they knew that they were in the New World, in an alien place, there was a quality about Central Park South that reminded them a little of Paris, for the pavement on the side of the park was quite broad, and in the road itself the drivers hooted impatiently and swore behind their steering wheels, while the pedestrians seemed oblivious to the traffic, some striding with great purpose and speed, others with detached serenity.

"Look at the horses," Antoine told Valentin, pointing at the hansom cabs lined up at the kerb, waiting stoically for the February tourists that were unlikely to materialize. "Perhaps we'll take you in one of those one day, *chéri*."

Zeleyev looked at Madeleine. "Remember our sleigh ride in Davos, a lifetime ago?"

"Just ten years," she said.

They progressed slowly, peaceably, into the park, passed beneath the tall, mostly bare-branched trees, saw clusters of pigeons, pecking around in the dirt, a pair of squirrels bounding just ahead of them.

"There is a charming pond not far away," Zeleyev said. "I suggest we pause there a while – Valentin will enjoy the ducks and swans – and then you can see a tiny piece of Fifth Avenue before we return. *Ça va*, Antoine?"

Antoine nodded. "*Ça va bien*."

"They ride horses in this park," the Russian told them, "and bicycles on special paths. There's a large playground not far from here, though our little one is too young for that. There is a zoo, though, that might excite him – and if it snows hard in the next week or two, you may even see youngsters sledding, even skiing."

They emerged from the park onto Fifth Avenue, crossed over Fifty-ninth Street at the Plaza Hotel, and returned to the Essex House passing the St Moritz Hotel, where Madeleine smiled at the striped awnings outside the hotel's restaurant, called the Café de la Paix, and Zeleyev advised them that lunch or tea at Rumpelmayer's could be an amusing pastime.

"The elegant women here are always dieting," he said, "yet they are confronted by gargantuan slices of cheese-cake, and even if they remember to be virtuous, their salads could feed a family."

Moving through the steady stream of New Yorkers, some going home from work, some simply tourists out for a stroll, some walking briskly towards their cocktail-hour martinis, though Madeleine understood little more than an occasional word of English, floating to her ears from scores of animated conversations, she was aware that this foreignness, this strangeness, whilst doubtless presenting difficulties of its own, was nonetheless a blessing; and she felt a wave of gratitude to Konstantin for plucking them out of the misery and pain that had lately become their whole lives and from which, had they remained in Paris, they might never have been able to escape.

Back in their room, even Antoine succumbed willingly to the luxury. To room service, with huge steaks that melted in their mouths, to long, languid baths foaming with bubbles, to the incomprehensible yet amusing babble of the television set. To what both adults realized was merely a period of limbo, a few days of near-fantasy, before they would have to face the new stresses of moving into their rented apartment; before Antoine would have to endure his assessment at the Mount Sinai Medical Center in less than a week's time. For just these few days they did not have to care, even to think. They could relax, without responsibilities, without remembering the past, without worrying about the future; they could recapture the sense of what it was to be properly alive again. The stroke had attacked them like a rampant thunderbolt only one year before, yet it might have been an eternity since Antoine and Madeleine had felt so carefree.

They made love that night, and that in itself was almost a miracle. For the first time since the stroke, the silent wretchedness Antoine had felt about the limp, unresponsive right side of his body ceased, quite magically, to matter. It was still possible, he realized now, gazing at Madeleine's sparkling eyes and glowing skin, for him to excite his wife, even to satisfy her.

"It's as if," he tried to explain to her, later, as they lay close together in the big American bed, "our home had become a jail, and so long as we were still there, it kept reminding me of all the things I couldn't do any more."

Madeleine said nothing, just lay still, grateful that he was, at last, able to talk to her.

"I knew – because they kept telling me – that I was lucky, that it could have been far, far worse. But instead of focusing on all the parts of my body that still worked properly, that were unaffected – most of me, I suppose – I let the bad parts, the useless parts, take over."

"Not useless," Madeleine said softly, and propping herself up on one elbow, she allowed her eyes to roam over him as she had not dared to for more than a year. "You're still as beautiful, still as perfect to me as you were on the night I moved into Fleurette." She paused. "And I don't believe that you're not going to get better and stronger."

"Don't hope for too much, *chérie*," Antoine said.

"But it doesn't matter to me, don't you see that?" she told him. "I care because of the way it makes *you* feel – about yourself, about life – about the way you look at Valentin." She took his right hand and kissed each fingertip in turn. "I don't need more than I have right now, other than for you to feel happy again, to love your life again." She paused. "We never said it aloud, but we were both afraid of this, weren't we?"

"Of making love?" Antoine's eyes darkened. "In the past, I was so seldom frightened. I was a lucky boy, then a fortunate man. Suddenly, out of nowhere I became a coward."

"Don't say that," Madeleine protested. "I've been just as scared as you. No matter what the doctors told us, no matter how often they said that there was likely to be more benefit than risk, I only heard those two words – 'likely', 'risk'."

"A spin of the roulette wheel."

She snuggled closer. "And we won."

They had left it all behind, Madeleine thought contentedly. She felt almost reckless, unfettered, younger again. They had gambled, they had left the city in which they had known joy and had lost it, and now they were strangers in a strange land. A healing place, where miracles might happen.

"Konstantin, you are a genius – Madeleine is right."

"Of course."

"And as modest as ever," Madeleine laughed.

"Modesty is for hypocrites, *ma chère*." Zeleyev surveyed them. "So you think you will be comfortable here?"

"It's perfect."

"Good." Zeleyev paused. "In truth, it was pure good fortune that made it possible. I told my landlady – a fine woman from Moscow – about your predicament, that comfort and a pleasant environment were vital adjuncts to Antoine's treatment. She knew, through her contacts, that one of these houses, which are almost never available, was free for a short lease." He smiled, with satisfaction. "*Et voilà*."

They were renting a picturesque little brick house in Henderson Place, a small cul-de-sac off Eighty-sixth Street, near East End Avenue and Carl Schurz Park, a pretty park which was home to Gracie Mansion, the Mayor of New York's house. With the East River on the far side of the park, and with the added benediction of some of the most gracious apartment buildings in the vicinity, the air surrounding Henderson Place was fresh, clean and blissfully peaceful.

"It was built in the English Queen Anne style," Zeleyev had told them. "There were originally twenty-four connected houses – now only a few remain. I'm sure it could do with a little renovation, and alas there are some steps down from the front door to the street –"

"Only five steps," Antoine said. "After four flights, it's nothing – and besides, it's fine exercise for me."

The Russian's green eyes danced. "If it's exercise you want, *mon ami*, you will have to come to the gymnasium with me one day."

"You go to a gymnasium?" Madeleine asked.

"How else should I keep my physique?" Zeleyev shrugged. "All my life I have liked to maintain myself well, to keep trim and strong. This is no time to stop."

Antoine smiled. "I think it may be a little while before I'm ready to join you, Konstantin."

"No time at all, *mon ami*."

"How old is he?" Antoine asked Madeleine after the Russian had left them alone.

"I'm not certain." Madeleine paused. "I've never considered age when I think of Konstantin. He's an ageless man, timeless."

"He adores you," Antoine said. "Worships you."

"He's fond of me, I know."

"More than fond."

"You think so?"

They had the use of the ground floor, with just one bedroom, a small living room, a tiny kitchen and even tinier bathroom, and room service was already a bygone dream, but it was flamboyantly luxurious in comparison to what they had been used to in rue Jacob. On their first afternoon, Madeleine left Antoine relaxing with a novel, and took Valentin to York Avenue, and then to the shops on First Avenue, hunting for what seemed suddenly to have become a priority: a gramophone and some records. By nightfall, they felt almost at home. The small refrigerator was filled with food, Valentin was sound asleep in a crib in the bedroom; there was a comfortable aroma in the living room of roasted chicken with tarragon and ratatouille, blended with Gauloises, and Madeleine was singing along with Hoagy Carmichael.

Antoine's first appointment was to take place at ten o'clock the next morning. They were both apprehensive, but still buoyed up with the apparent rightness of it all, much as Madeleine remembered feeling when she had first arrived in Paris. The New Yorkers with whom they had thus far come into contact had all been very kind, much more patient with their ignorance of the language than most Parisians were with foreigners. The unspoken anxiety that both Antoine and Madeleine had shared about the inhumanity of the famous concrete jungle, was melting away. They had new faith in the instincts which had brought them to New York. The initial dismay with which they had viewed that first limousine ride into the city had almost been forgotten. If determination and a positive attitude were going to make any difference to the success of Antoine's therapy, then there was little doubt that they would achieve great things.

Valentin woke up crying at midnight, and Madeleine was swiftly out of bed and plucking him out of his crib to comfort him. Nuzzling against her for a few minutes, the two-year-old was swiftly pacified, and in a short while he was sleeping peacefully again.

"He's such an easy little boy," Madeleine said, as she climbed back into bed. "We're so lucky."

"My mother tells me that I was an even-tempered child." Antoine drew her back to the centre of the bed, so that he could feel her against him, all the way down his good left side.

"He's so extraordinarily like you, in every way." Madeleine smiled.

"*Pauvre petit*," Antoine sympathized.

"Lucky boy," she said.

"And man, I hope."

They began to make love again, and it was the sweetest, purest lovemaking they had known, and they smiled, in the dark, into each other's eyes, and felt the most perfect tranquillity, and hope, and joy. And afterwards they fell asleep, their bodies still touching, warm and snug.

Madeleine's first awareness, when she awoke a little before seven in the morning, before the jangle of their alarm clock, before even Valentin, was of the coolness of her husband's skin against her own. And for several moments she lay motionless, hardly breathing. Listening. Feeling. Waiting.

And she knew.

She turned, very gently, to face him, and except that the morning sun now stroked his dark, tumbling hair, he looked just as he had before she had closed her eyes that night. Infinitely calm and peaceful.

Madeleine looked over to where Valentin still slept, unaware, and, finding the strength, somehow, to stifle her almost overpowering need to scream out her grief and anguish, she remained totally silent. And it came to her, a thought like a small, lightly bobbing cloud, that she might simply put a pillow over their little son's face, and allow him to sleep forever in perfect innocence, before she took Antoine's sleeping tablets, and ended her own life.

But then Valentin, too, awoke. He sat up in his crib, very straight, and looked directly at her, smiling his morning smile. And she raised the index finger of her right hand to her lips to hush him, and the child settled back to wait patiently, accustomed to not disturbing his father.

Madeleine lay down again, in the last bed she would share with Antoine, and pressed herself against him, imprinting the feel of him, the shape and the scent and the taste of him, on her memory. And then, very slowly, she got out of bed, put on her robe, picked up Valentin from his crib, and went out into the hall to telephone Konstantin.

Part Three

MADDY:

NEW YORK

13

In the aftermath, grief consumed her, devoured her. The strange land that she and Antoine had briefly believed might be a place of miracles, was instead a hell, a wilderness. Madeleine knew only two people in the United States of America, one of them a two-year-old boy. She understood no one, and no one understood her. And she did not care.

Once Antoine's body had been taken, in a black bag, like so much laundry, from the house in Henderson Place, Madeleine had retreated from reality, from life. Nothing mattered, not even Valentin, certainly not herself. She seldom spoke, did not eat, survived on sips of sweetened tea forced upon her several times a day by Konstantin.

"We must talk," he told her gently.

Madeleine did not answer.

"There are arrangements to be made, *ma chère*."

Not a word, only a dull, small nod of her head.

"The funeral. Where is it to be? Here, or at home?" It pained Zeleyev to see her frozen face, the lovely eyes from which all spark had disappeared, the cheekbones which seemed to grow more prominent each day as the weight dropped from her.

On the other side of the sitting room, Valentin sat on the floor, playing with a soft toy dog, its left ear well chewed. From time to time, he toddled over to his mother, tugged at her skirt and, ignored, retreated.

"Antoine's parents, I feel, would like it if he went home

to Normandy, to them. But it must be your decision, *ma chère*. They will abide by your wishes." He paused. "If you deem it that he should be buried here, in the United States –"

"Here?" He thought she shuddered a little. "No."

Zeleyev took her hand, cold and limp. "To France, then."

He took over all the arrangements. He dealt with the coroner's office and with the airline; he wrote letters and made telephone calls, and packed up their belongings and closed up the house. And eight days after Antoine's death, he drove with Madeleine and Valentin, in another limousine, to the airport.

It was only after allowing their bags to be checked, after permitting herself to be steered through the formalities, that Madeleine came suddenly and shockingly back to life. Seeing the aeroplane, she came apart.

"Not without Antoine."

"It's all right, *ma petite*," Zeleyev tried to soothe her. "We're with you –"

"*No!*" With a sudden surge of strength, she pushed him away and their hand luggage clattered to the ground. "You can't make me!" Valentin began to cry, but she paid him no heed. "Where *is* he?"

Observing their difficulties, two airport employees came hurrying over to help, but Madeleine shook off their hands. She was weeping now, for the first time, yet she hardly knew why she wept. The child with dark hair and navy blue eyes was shrieking, and the red-haired man was trying to hold her, but she would not let him touch her – she wanted only *him* –

"Antoine –"

A ground steward stepped forward and spoke to Zeleyev. "We can't let her board the aircraft in this condition, sir."

"Perhaps a doctor could help." Zeleyev was acutely distressed. "A sedative – she needs a sedative."

But Madeleine was beyond help. The walls were closing in, strangers, milling around and staring, staring into her face – they were like ugly fish at feeding time, goggling at her, mouths gaping. And she did not realize that she was screaming now, dementedly, hysterically, and even that one image she had clung to in her mind, of him, of her Antoine, was slipping away from her, floating out of reach, and the air terminal building and the world became a sick, dizzying blur, and still she screamed.

"Someone call an ambulance," a man said.

"I can manage," Zeleyev protested.

"I don't think so, sir," the ground steward said.

And so Antoine's coffin arrived unaccompanied at the end of its journey, and while the funeral took place in the churchyard near Trouville where three generations of Bonnards lay at rest, his young widow, her nerves finally shattered, lay silent and still in a bed at Jamaica Hospital in the New York City borough of Queens.

Zeleyev brought her back, a few days later, to his one-bedroomed apartment on Riverside Drive, where he had, during her hospitalization, been looking after Valentin. His own physician came to check Madeleine over, prescribed mild tranquillizers and time, and she was too enfeebled to protest when Zeleyev insisted that she and her son would sleep in his bedroom, while he camped out on the ample brocade sofa.

The apartment, on the fourth floor of a handsome grey stone house three doors from Riverside Drive's junction with Seventy-sixth Street, was not large, but the bay window of the living room overlooked the boulevard and Riverside Park, and beyond the park the Hudson River and New Jersey Palisades, giving the room a sense of spaciousness. Zeleyev had created a striking, private world of his own, and after nightfall, when the heavy curtains were drawn, the living room became a warm, cluttered enclave, his precious salvaged pieces of old Russia lending it an exotic quality.

Though Madeleine could not recall her old friend ever discussing his religious faith, a handsome oil-painted icon hung on one red-painted wall, close to three exquisitely framed photographs. Two were of Zeleyev's parents, his father austere and darkly moustached, his mother quiet-faced and elegant, and the third was of the two Malinskaya sisters, Irina and Sofia, young and laughing and very beautiful, wrapped in sables, the dark hair that later had concealed the family jewels on their flight from Russia, piled high on their heads. There was some evidence, too, of the glorious Fabergé days: on a polished walnut table, an ornate and splendid silver samovar, on a second table, a curved dagger with a nephrite and gilt handle and a red guilloche enamel cigar box.

"These belongings have travelled far and wide with me," Zeleyev told Madeleine on the third evening, after she had come out of the bedroom for a while, to sit in her dressing gown and to sip more tea. "They came with me when I lived in Paris, and Geneva, and even during the months I stayed with your grandfather, they graced his house."

The apartment was exactly what Madeleine needed at that moment. She had emerged from her state of almost catatonic shock, and now she sank into her grief, wrapping the warmth and comfort that Konstantin and his home offered, around herself and her child. As the weeks progressed, she seldom ventured out of the apartment. The isolated foreignness indoors empathized with her sorrow, whereas the wintry outdoor landscape which had, during her first few days in America, seemed so attractive, now frightened her.

* * *

Spring came to New York, and Zeleyev brought news of a city pulsing with excitement as the World's Fair opened under the slogan of 'Peace through Understanding', and hundreds of thousands of visitors began pouring towards its six hundred or so acres in Queens. In the apartment on Riverside Drive, Madeleine knew neither peace nor understanding, yet the first softening touches of spring brought a change of mood in her. She became overwhelmed by guilt. She had failed Antoine, betrayed him. If only she had been stronger, shrewder, he would not have lost Fleurette and Paris. If she had been less proud, less inflexible, he might have been safe in Zurich. She had encouraged him, coaxed and, perhaps, even browbeaten him into coming to America. She had allowed her weak, self-indulgent, physical desires to override his instinctive fears on that last night, had robbed him of life itself. And then, finally, she had allowed him to be put into the ground, all alone, without his wife, or his son, to stand vigil or to lay flowers on his grave. She had abandoned him, and her remorse was terrible and unbearable.

The apartment became claustrophobic, and Madeleine took to going out, to wandering the streets, sometimes wheeling Valentin in his pushchair, more often by herself. For a short time, the weather grew warm, and Riverside Park, with its lavish cherry blossoms, became a calming place to sit and contemplate her guilt, and then the temperatures plunged again. Madeleine walked to the marina at Seventy-ninth Street and stood staring at the river and boats, gazed, hardly seeing, towards the big passenger liners docked at the piers further down the Hudson, shivering but not registering that she was cold.

There is wickedness in me, she thought.

It was the first time she had recognized a flaw of such magnitude within herself. Her family had, after all, been right. She was no better than the two Gabriel men she had glorified, but who had been, she saw now, failures and traitors. Hildegard had been justified in her condemnation of Amadeus, and God alone knew that Alexander had betrayed even his daughter. The Gabriels knew how to love, but they were not to be trusted, nor depended upon.

Madeleine experienced a sudden, desperate pity for Valentin, and began, frantically, to care for his every need, became suffocating in her determination not to fail him as she had failed her husband. Thinking that she might expunge some of her guilt over Antoine by trying every possible way to feel close to him again, she went to five smoke shops in search of Gauloises and, having found a source on Amsterdam Avenue, she began to smoke incessantly, not because she liked it, but so that she could surround herself with his old, familiar, aromatic smoke. She had always hated *pastis*, but because Antoine had liked it, she walked regularly to a liquor store on Broadway and, back in Zeleyev's apartment, gulped it down, detesting it, getting drunk. She dressed in black, as he had done, wore one of Antoine's pullovers, never even washing it in case she lost forever the scent of him.

One afternoon, in early May, while she was sitting on a wooden bench in Riverside Park, smoking, a middle-aged, auburn-haired woman, smelling of body odour and Joy perfume, sat down beside her.

"You are mourning," she said.

"*Pardon?*" Madeleine said, startled at being spoken to.

"*Vous êtes en deuil.*" It was not a question.

She was from Montreal, and inquisitive, and by dint of gentle, persuasive questioning, she extracted Madeleine's story from her, and offered her solace. A group of her acquaintance held seances once each month. They would be meeting the following weekend. Perhaps if Madeleine achieved contact with her husband, it might help her to move on into the future. Madeleine went to the seance the next Sunday afternoon. It was held in an apartment in the garment district, on the corner of Thirty-sixth Street and Eighth Avenue, the area in which during the week manufacturers' employees hurried to and fro, arms full of fabric samples, and racks of dresses and suits were pushed up and down the sidewalks, everyone rushing, calling names, getting ulcers. On a Sunday afternoon, however, it was unnaturally quiet, and the apartment was eerie and smelled of incense. Madeleine paid a man at the front door fifteen dollars and sat at a round table holding hands with an old German woman and a girl from Brooklyn who had lost both her parents, and the spiritualist in charge of the session tried, without any evidence of success, to make contact with the departed; and afterwards Madeleine took a bus back to Riverside Drive and, not even remembering to feed Valentin, drank *pastis* until she fell into oblivion.

At the end of the month, summoned by Konstantin, Rudi Gabriel came to New York. Appalled by Madeleine's frailty and the wild, haunted expression in her eyes, Rudi tossed her liquor into the kitchen sink, made coffee and began to sober her up.

"May I leave Valentin with you?" he asked Zeleyev.

"Anything." The Russian spread his hands in despair. "I can do nothing with her – I'm becoming afraid for her sanity."

"I'm going to take her to my hotel, if she'll come. Perhaps the change may help to boost her, bring her back to herself."

"She'll come," Zeleyev said. "There's no fight in her these days, she just gives in, like a lamb half dead." He lowered his voice. "She is filled with self-hatred, *mon ami*, that's the worst of it."

Rudi put Madeleine into a yellow cab and brought her to the Plaza, led her up the carpeted steps of the entrance facing the Fountain of Abundance and the beds of bright, waving spring flowers, and took her up to his high-ceilinged and magnificently furnished suite, where he undressed her as if she were his baby sister, put her into a warm bath and ordered cream of chicken soup with crackers and mineral water from room service.

"I can't eat," she said, weakly.

"I'll feed you."

"No."

"Do you want to die, too?"

"Yes," she said.

"You want Valentin to be an orphan?" Rudi paused. "They'll take him back to the Gründli Haus, you realize, and Stefan will bring him up. He won't remember you or Antoine, he'll probably be adopted and named Julius, and he'll grow up to sell rifles and rocket launchers."

"I'm still not hungry."

"And if you lose your mind, and have to be committed, much the same will happen. Is that what you want, Maggy?"

"Don't call me that," she said. "I haven't been Maggy for years." Her voice wavered. "I invented Madeleine on my second day in Paris – reinventing myself, I suppose. I don't feel like her any more either."

She began to cry, the tears coming slowly at first, and then, as her brother held her in his arms, cradled her and murmured soothing words to her, the warmth of his closeness and the piercingly poignant memories of her few, precious days with Antoine at the Essex House, undammed her grief completely. She had mourned in a series of different ways, yet until now, though she had shed tears, they had not been the beneficial tears of letting go. Now, in the arms of her brother, Madeleine's keening sobs shook her body, racking her until she was completely drained. Rudi let her cry, then spoon-fed her a little soup, then let her weep again, until she slept, more peacefully than she had for months. And in the morning, after a breakfast served to her in bed, which she ate almost without argument, he asked her, gently, what she intended to do.

"What can I do?" she said dully.

"Any number of things," Rudi said. "You could come home with me. You'd have comfort, and a fine, secure upbringing for Valentin. I would be there, don't forget, I'd be with you."

"You know I won't do that."

"You could go back to Paris. At least you have good friends there who would care for you, help you to begin again." Rudi paused. "Or you could make a fresh start here."

"Here?" Madeleine's hands shook, and she put her coffee cup down on the breakfast tray. "Where I lost him?"

"Terrible things happen everywhere. Wonderful things too." Rudi's voice was very quiet. "Antoine might have died in Paris, Maggy – or if he'd gone to Normandy, or Zurich, it might just as easily have happened there."

"But it happened here."

"Then go back to Paris."

"Without Antoine?" She shook her head. "I don't know if I can ever go back, Rudi. We lived that city so much to the full, you know? As if we were draining it to the last drop, almost as if we knew."

Rudi picked up the tray and put it down on the white-clothed table the waiter had wheeled in. "If you were to decide – when you're ready to make that kind of decision –" He stopped.

"Yes?"

He turned to her. "If you stay in New York, I'll join you."

"What do you mean?"

"The bank has a branch here, remember?" He shrugged. "I daresay if I were determined to be transferred, it could be arranged." He watched her face. "You're staring."

"You'd do that for me?" Madeleine's voice was unsteady. "After the way I treated you?"

"I thought we had agreed that was all in the past." Rudi nodded. "Yes, I would do it for you. And for myself."

"I thought you were happy in Zurich."

"I love the city. I love Switzerland." He paused. "But people are more important, don't you think?"

"You know I do. So what about our mother, and Omi?"

"They matter, of course." Rudi's face became stiffer. "But if they had to choose, Maggy, they would side with him."

"With Stefan, you mean?"

"Of course." He forced a smile. "This conversation is premature, Maggy." He made a small grimace. "I can't stop calling you that – it's how I still think of you."

"It doesn't matter," she said softly. "Do you want to tell me about it, Rudi? About what's happened at home?"

"Not yet." He sat on the edge of the bed. "I only wanted you to know that if you stayed here, you wouldn't be so much alone. It's much too soon for you to make big decisions. First, you need to rest."

"But Valentin –"

"In good hands."

"Konstantin?" Madeleine lay back against the plump hotel pillows. "Poor, dear Konstantin. I can't imagine what it's been like for him. He's done everything for me, everything, and I've been –" Her mouth trembled.

"Sleep again, Maggy." Rudi held her hand. "And when you wake, you can eat a little more, and then you can rest again. And if you want to weep, then you should. Don't bottle it up, it's much worse for you. Let it out, just let it go."

"And you?" she asked.

"I'll be here."

* * *

After two days, they collected Valentin from Riverside Drive to give Zeleyev some respite, and to allow him to return to his workroom in the Jewelers Exchange on Forty-seventh Street where, he had told Madeleine, he worked any hours that suited him, as befitted a man of his experience and years. Zeleyev was extraordinary, both Madeleine and Rudi agreed. He was over seventy, she calculated, yet he looked no more than sixty, with the body of a fifty-year-old, thanks to his regular work-out at his gymnasium.

"He was the first man who made me conscious that I was a woman," Madeleine told Rudi as they sat in the back of a cab, Valentin on her lap. "He never treated me like a child, not for a minute – and then, later, when he came to Paris, he was so furious with me for working as a housemaid, he was so convinced I was going to be a singer, a star."

"He loves you very much, you know."

"That's what Antoine said." She gave a small, wistful smile. "I think he tries to make up for Papi not being around. I've often felt that he blamed himself, in a way, for the night Papi left home."

"Perhaps."

"What do you mean?"

"Nothing." Rudi shrugged. "Only that I don't think that he looks at you in a fatherly way."

Madeleine kissed the top of Valentin's dark head. "How does he look at me then?"

"The way a man looks at a beautiful woman."

She smiled. "That's just Konstantin," she said.

A block away from the Plaza was F.A.O. Schwarz, the greatest toy shop Madeleine had ever seen, and the hour and a half spent watching Valentin's astonished delight as he was allowed to roam around, emerging finally with a sweet-faced stuffed squirrel, did his mother's wounded soul more good than anything had for months. They bought hot dogs with sauerkraut, and Rudi insisted that it was time his nephew tasted his first Coca-Cola, and they strolled into Central Park to have their lunch, and Valentin spat out his drink and smeared ketchup and mustard all over his clothes, and had a fine time.

"Are you ready to talk yet?" Madeleine asked her brother.

Rudi nodded. "But not here." He looked around appreciatively, enjoying the loveliness of the early summer's afternoon, the fresh, scented air that would not outlast the month, the rich green grass and foliage that would grow brown and grimy by August. "This is too pleasant. I don't want to spoil it."

It was not until after nightfall, after Valentin had gone to sleep in the cot provided by the hotel, that he began.

"When I was still very young," he told Madeleine, "I believe I was the apple of our mother's eye. I'm not sure if I remember that, but she told me often enough. And when she married Stefan, I was aware that I was his favourite child, mostly, I suppose, because you disliked him so obviously."

"I loathed him."

"But I didn't. He was good to me, and he made Mami happy and he bought me presents all the time. He spoiled me, so I liked him."

"No crime in that," Madeleine said softly.

"After you left home, for quite a long time I continued as a kind of golden boy. Not because I was anything special, it was just the contrast between the two of us, I think. I always liked a peaceful life, I hated the arguments that I believed you provoked."

"I did provoke them."

"I knew that you blamed me for not sharing your dislike of our stepfather, nor your faith in our real father. I also realized that you never knew how much I adored you."

Rudi paused. "The night you left our house, I saw you go, you know. I watched from my window, saw you creep away with Hexi and your suitcase, and I remember that I was crying, and hoping you would look up and see me."

"But I didn't turn around." Madeleine rose from her armchair and came to sit beside him on the chintz-covered sofa. "I'm so sorry, Rudi. If I'd realized –" She hesitated.

"You'd still have gone. The only difference might have been that you'd have felt guilty over me. That wouldn't have helped either of us."

Rudi had come through school respectably, but far from brilliantly, and it had been then that he had come up against Stefan for the first time, when it had been presumed that Rudi would go to work for Julius Industrie. Stefan had been looking forward to having a young man he could trust in his business, someone he could mould, make his own man, but he had reckoned without Rudi's pacifist nature. In boyhood, Rudi had avoided playing with the toy guns and model soldiers that his stepfather had frequently bought for him, but that soft streak had not overly concerned Julius, mostly because the boy was so much easier to control than his older sister. Military service would stamp out any weakness, Stefan had believed, and after the age of nineteen, once Rudi was compelled by law to keep and maintain his army rifle at home, he would overcome his antipathy to weapons. Rudi had known long before his military training that nothing would change him, and so, with a rare display of obstinacy he had applied to join the Gründli Bank instead.

"I knew there must have been some kind of confrontation between you," Madeleine said. "It was pretty obvious when I came with you to Zurich that Stefan was disenchanted with you. I just assumed it stemmed from your correspondence with me – that, and the fact that you'd come to Paris for the wedding."

"He would have got over that, and even, I think, over my rejection of Julius Industrie. If those had been the only ways in which I'd disappointed him." His tone was wry.

"What else?" Madeleine asked.

Rudi looked directly into her face. "I'm gay," he said. "I'm homosexual, Maggy."

She was silent.

"That clinched things, naturally. When I knew I had to tell them. That was the final straw for Stefan."

The slowly dawning comprehension of his own sexuality had cost Rudi pain, and the revelation had taken courage. He had hoped for their understanding and support, but he had been swiftly disillusioned. Julius had made no attempt to conceal his disgust and contempt, and from that day on had invariably treated Rudi with the utmost scorn.

"What about Mami?" Madeleine asked. "Surely she stood by you? No matter what I feel about our mother, I can't believe she could stop loving you for any reason."

"She didn't stop. She lets me know, discreetly, every now and then, that she'll always love me, no matter what I do." His voice had grown bitter and sad. "It's a crime to her, too, you see, or a sin, at least." His mouth twisted a little. "And she still loves Stefan, loves being married to him. She would never openly stand against him."

"No," Madeleine said.

"And you, Maggy?" he asked her. "How do you feel about me, now that you know?"

"How can you even ask?"

"I have no choice."

"All right." Madeleine paused. "It comes in two parts, I suppose, doesn't it? How I feel about you, my brother – that's easy enough. I let the first eighteen years of your life pass without knowing how much I cared about you. From the moment I set eyes on you again on our wedding day in Paris, I knew I might never be able to express the way you made me feel." She took his hand and held it firmly in her own. "You haven't ceased to amaze me since that day, Rudi. I had no idea how brave you were, how kind, how generous."

"And now I've amazed you again."

"It doesn't make any *difference* to me – why should it? You are who you are – you're Rudi Gabriel, and you're all the things I just said you were, only now I know that you're also gay."

"That's the second part, is it?"

Madeleine nodded. "If you ask me how I feel about homosexuality, that's a little harder to answer, mostly because I've never thought much about it. In Paris, I knew several gay men, and women too. Patrick, the assistant to our chef, lived with Jean-Paul, one of the waiters. That was just the way it was, I never gave it a moment's thought." She frowned. "For Gaston, of course – you remember Gaston Strasser?"

"Your singing teacher."

"It was terrible for Gaston, because he lived through the Nazi years. I know that he suffered horribly, but then that was different. Those people were monsters." She paused. "Have you been in love?"

Rudi smiled at the suddenness of her question. "Just once," he replied. "His name was Jürg, and we met just after my nineteenth birthday. It's over now, but it lasted for two years."

The love affair had ended, he told Madeleine, when out of the blue, the other man had become engaged to a girl approved of by his family. Rudi had felt more wounded by Jürg's dishonesty than by the betrayal itself, though his anger had helped him to get over the collapse of the relationship. But it had made Rudi wary. It seemed to him that some people were able to flit quite happily from one affair to the next, whilst he, who had seldom dated, had fallen painfully in love.

"I think that's just the way I am," he said ruefully. "The people I love are just so important to me."

"Which makes it even harder when they let you down."

The breakdown of his relationship with Stefan was, Rudi admitted, one of the major motivations behind his desire to move to New York. In some ways, he felt that he would be making Emilie's life easier by leaving her alone with her husband, and if Madeleine did contemplate remaining in America, his transfer to the Manhattan branch of the bank would mean that they could, at last, be close again.

"I don't even know what you do at the bank," Madeleine said.

"I work on the personal investments side – I'm still quite lowly, of course. It takes decades rather than years to attain trust in an institution like ours." He stood up. "I'll never be a high-flier, and I'll never be as strong as you, Maggy –"

"Of course you are," she protested. "And courageous."

"Only when I'm pushed to the limit." He gave a small, rueful smile. "But I'm a hard worker and, on the whole, I think the people I work with have come to respect me. I'm no threat to anyone, you see, so if I request this transfer, I doubt that I'll be refused."

Madeleine, too, stood up and walked over to the windows. A purplish dusk covered the park, the early evening traffic on Central Park South was moving quite freely, and the skimming cars with their lights switched on gave an illusory sense of serenity to the city view.

"It's lovely here," she said softly. "Easy to sink into luxury."

"You can have it."

"Hardly."

"Claim your birthright, Maggy."

"I did that when I came with you to Zurich. Our grandfather had nothing of real value, except *Eternité*, of course, and even if I had it I would never sell it."

Rudi looked at his sister. "You say that I'm strong, but I'm not. If I escape from the Gründli Haus, it will be to a luxury apartment. I like having the comforts I've grown up with. I need them."

"There's nothing wrong with that, Rudi."

"I have to go back soon," he told her. "Will you be all right?"

Madeleine nodded, slowly. "I think so. Thanks to you."

They went, together, to look at Valentin. The little boy lay on his back, both arms flung out, lips slightly parted. Madeleine bent and stroked his hair gently.

"Here is what I need," she said, very quietly. "I need his father, too, but I know I can never have him back again." A familiar, harsh lump wedged itself in her throat, heralding fresh tears, but she swallowed them down. "I would love it, Rudi, more than I can say, if we could be together."

"Have you decided then? Will you stay here?"

"I'm going to try."

"It won't be easy." Rudi's voice, too, was low. "You need security, for the little one, if not for yourself."

"I can work hard. I'm used to that now." She smiled into his eyes. "I know that you want to help me – I can feel it, even when you don't say it. But you have to let me do it my own way, Rudi."

"So long as you let me love you," he said. "Both of you."

"Always."

Rudi returned to Zurich to pave the way for his move to New York, and gradually, painfully, Madeleine came back to life. It was inconceivable that she would ever know happiness again, or that it would ever really matter, but she felt as if she had woken from a deathly, hueless sleep.

The agony of her loss – of existing without Antoine – still stabbed at her every single day, but other people mattered to her again now, Valentin most of all.

Zeleyev was her rock, practical as well as emotional and caring. He took her to Columbia University, forty or so blocks further uptown on the West Side, and helped her to enrol in an English language programme where she could attend classes three times a week. Conscious of her pride, he gave way to her insistence that he take back his bedroom and, though it was unrealistic for her even to contemplate finding her own place to live, he encouraged her in her pursuit to find a way to earn their keep.

"I can look after Valentin while you look for work."

"But what about your own work?"

"I've told you, I can work any time, even at night if necessary."

"There has to be a limit to how much I ask of you, Konstantin."

"Why, because I'm old?"

"Age is immaterial," Madeleine said.

"You believe that?"

"All through my childhood, I felt I was discriminated against for being young. People put too much emphasis on age."

"So you don't regard me as an old man?" Zeleyev asked, and his eyes twinkled.

"Never."

"Neither do I." He returned to the subject of her search for work. "What about your career? What about your singing?" He still believed in her talent, and he was determined that in New York that talent should be unleashed, discovered and, at last, rewarded.

"That's not important now," she said.

"Why? Because Antoine is gone?" Zeleyev paused briefly. "You've been cheated enough in your young life, Madeleine. Don't cheat yourself as well."

"I don't feel that I've been cheated."

"Oh yes. I know." For a moment, bitterness coloured his voice. "I know how it feels."

"Tell me," she said.

He shook his head, shaking away the fleeting darkness. "It's not so important, *ma chère*."

"You never complain, Konstantin. You must have been through so much in your life, but you hardly talk about the bad things."

"Because I deal with them in my own way. I exercise my body, I pamper myself – and I drink vodka."

"And women?" Madeleine asked, smiling. "I know you love women, and I know they must love you."

Zeleyev blushed, suddenly, though his green eyes, upon her face, did not waver. "Of course," he said, and then added: "I am an optimist, *ma belle*. That is my secret."

That September, a letter from Alexander Gabriel was forwarded to Zeleyev from the accommodation address that he still kept in Paris. Madeleine was out when Zeleyev opened the letter. Gabriel wrote that he was in Paris, and in great trouble. For the first time, he gave an address. He begged his old friend to help him.

Saying nothing to Madeleine about her father's letter, Zeleyev flew to France two days later, telling her only that he was going away on business. Arriving at Orly after ten in the evening, he checked into the Crillon, his favourite hotel, and went straight out again, taking a taxi directly to rue Clauzel, not far from Pigalle.

Seeing the house, Zeleyev's mouth made a small *moue* of disgust. The building itself was very old and in great disrepair, the stairs were crumbling in several places, the handrail was rusting orange and the air smelled of damp and decay.

On the top floor, he knocked on the door. No one answered. He rapped more sharply.

"Gabriel, *c'est moi*, Zeleyev."

For another moment, there was no sound, and then he heard a shuffling on the far side of the door.

"I'm alone, Alexei – open up."

A key turned in the lock, and the door opened.

"Hello, Konstantin."

"I thought you were going to leave me out on this bloody landing."

"Come in, come in – though it's no better inside." Alexander closed the door and quickly turned the key again. "Thank you," he said.

Zeleyev stared, unable to make any pretence at not being shocked. The man who stood before him was not quite fifty, yet he looked ten years older than the Russian. His fair hair was greying and receding badly, his blue eyes were sunken and ringed with dark shadow, the flesh around his mouth was prematurely wrinkled, the lips themselves were chewed and cracked and he was unshaven.

"Not a pretty sight."

"No," Zeleyev agreed.

"Thank you for coming," Alexander said again, his voice hoarse. He took a grubby handkerchief from his trouser pocket and wiped his nose, roughly, like a boy determined not to cry.

"Of course I came," Zeleyev said. "But why now? Why not years ago? Why did you wait so long?" He thought of Madeleine, and all she had been through, and was thankful that he had not told her.

"I need help."

"I can see that."

Gabriel sat down heavily on the bed. There was only the bed, a rickety table and one chair in the room; no rug or any covering on the wooden plank floor, a stained, cracked basin on the far wall.

"How's Maggy?"

"Beautiful, brave. Older."

"Is she married? Does she have children?"

"She has a son. They live in New York, with me."

Alexander looked up, fully alert for the first time. "I thought you were here, in Paris – I assumed she was still in Zurich –"

"You assume a lot."

"Tell me."

"Do you care?"

"Of course I care – my God, I think about her all the time."

"She used to think of you, too," Zeleyev said, with deliberate cruelty. "I expect she still does, sometimes. Perhaps if you had written to her, or told her where you were –"

"I couldn't."

"Why not? Fear?"

"You can't imagine," Alexander said.

"You were always a coward. Afraid of your wife, of your mother – afraid of disobeying their rules, in case they gave you up, in case you were sent to prison." Zeleyev paused. "If Madeleine were my daughter, I would sooner have faced jail than lose her."

"Madeleine?"

"You know nothing about her."

"Tell me," Alexander said again. "Please."

"If only I'd known," he said later.

"What difference would it have made?" Zeleyev asked. "Would you have gone back to Switzerland, or come here?"

"I might."

"We'll never know, will we?"

The sordid room was very quiet.

"What are you on?"

"Morphine," Gabriel replied. "Will you help me,

Konstantin?" He looked down at his hands, saw their trembling, saw the dirt caked under the fingernails, and looked up at the other man. "I won't blame you if you refuse."

"What kind of help do you need? What have you done?"

"Crazy things." He paused. "A few weeks ago, in Amsterdam, I was desperate for money. My usual source had dried up, and so I went to a lender. A loan shark." He licked his lips. "And I did just what I swore I would never do. I put up *Eternité* as collateral." His eyes flicked nervously at Zeleyev, then away again.

"Go on."

Later that same night, Gabriel told Zeleyev, filled with remorse and reckless from the morphine he had been able to buy, he had gone back to the moneylender's office, broken in and stolen back the sculpture. Next day, realizing the enormity of his folly, he had fled Amsterdam for Paris, hoping that Zeleyev – the only man alive who could understand his need to hold on to *Eternité* –was living in the city where he kept his accommodation address. In the week and a half since mailing his letter, Alexander had lived in constant dread, hardly daring to leave the rented room. He no longer knew what to do, where to run or hide. He had known so much shame in the course of his life, had destroyed every chance that had come his way since his mother and Emilie had thrown him out – but having come so close to losing the sculpture that he knew, by rights, Amadeus had meant for his daughter, Alexander felt more consumed by guilt than ever.

"All right," Zeleyev said.

"You'll help me?"

"Where is the sculpture?"

"Here." Gabriel began to move, but Zeleyev stopped him.

"Not yet."

"Don't you want to see it?"

"Of course. But not yet."

A great jolt of excitement had pounded him at the prospect of looking at *Eternité* again, at his masterpiece. But a decade had passed since he had last seen it. A lifetime. He was a man of style. The moment had to be right.

"First," he told Gabriel, "we are going to put some food into your stomach, to strengthen you so that we can talk and make plans."

"I have nothing here."

"Obviously." Zeleyev went to the door, his head beginning to ache with fatigue. "I'll find us something to eat – you lock up after me." He looked back. "Are you to be trusted, Alexei? If you start putting more of that shit into yourself, that's an end to my sympathy."

"I'm not to be trusted," Gabriel answered wearily. "But I have nothing left to take, and I have no cash, so provided you're not too long, you'll find me much as you leave me."

Wasting no time, Zeleyev returned with a warm roasted chicken, a loaf of bread, some ripe Reblochon cheese and a bottle of vodka, chiefly to stave off his own exhaustion from the long journey. The younger man appeared violently hungry, tearing hunks of bread from the loaf and greedily attacking the chicken, yet frequently during the meal he began to choke and was forced to pause, while Zeleyev gave him sparing sips of his vodka, mindful of the morphine still in his system.

"All right," Zeleyev said at last. "I'm ready now." He felt fit now, emotionally as well as physically, to see what he realized, deep in his heart, he had come to Paris for. It had, of course, been mostly for Madeleine – but if a craftsman created only one true *chef-d'oeuvre* in his lifetime, then this had been his.

Gabriel got to his knees and dragged a bundle from beneath the bed, and seeing that he had wrapped the sculpture in a pair of disgusting, dirty pyjamas, Zeleyev felt a stabbing of real pain. He knew its worth, understood its beauty and the source of that beauty as no one else ever had, or ever would. Its place was on a plinth, behind protective glass. Not in this hideous room. Not in the quivering hands of this pathetic, unworthy man.

And then tenderly, with more care than Zeleyev would have imagined him capable of, Alexander placed it on the table.

"Dear Lord," Zeleyev breathed, staring, "it's perfect."

With almost cat-like stealth, he approached the table. He saw it first as a whole, recognized it as a parent might know a child, a decade later, as an adult. He saw the textured gold mountain, Amadeus's filigree cascade, the glorious Malinskaya jewels and his *plique-à-jour* and his *cloisonné*, and he saw that it was, indeed, the masterpiece of his memory, that time, at least, had not cheated him.

"It's unharmed," he said, softening.

"Did you think I would harm it?" Alexander asked. "Knowing what it meant to my father, as well as you."

Zeleyev picked up the vodka bottle. "To Amadeus," he said, and drank deeply. "To Irina." He drank again.

"May I?" the other man asked, humbly, like a boy.

"Just a little."

Zeleyev sat on the chair, crossed his legs, and surveyed his work at great length. Every now and then he leaned forward and touched it with infinite gentleness, raised the hinged jewels, checked his own mark beneath the sapphire, let the tip of his right index finger rest reverentially on Irina's initials beneath the yellow diamond sun.

"It is beautiful," Alexander said, sitting heavily on the bed.

Zeleyev ignored him. He held the vodka bottle in his left hand, tipping liquor into his mouth at regular intervals, and it seemed to him as if the loathsome surroundings in which they sat melted gradually away as he drank, as he stared, as if the grace and loveliness emanating from the sculpture could wipe the sordidness away.

"It took more than five years," he said.

"I know."

"You know nothing."

His innate Russian expansiveness emerged, as if it had slept for years, rising to the surface of his mind and heart like juicy sap overflowing. He felt suddenly poetic, almost rhapsodic, so deeply moved by *Eternité* and the wealth of memories it brought back to him that he needed to speak, to remember out loud the period in which he and Amadeus had created the sculpture.

"I gave up so much," he said softly. "All that time, the life I had built up after leaving Russia, my livelihood. Amadeus gave up nothing, for without Irina, he was nothing."

"But you cared for him."

"Why not? He touched me – his vision touched me. But he never knew, just as you still don't understand, how much I did for him." Zeleyev drank again from the bottle. "Your father was a fool, in many ways – I told him as much, often, made him smile, for he knew what he was. But he knew, at least, how to love, unlike you, my poor Alexei." With a sudden rush of sympathy, he handed Gabriel the bottle, let him gulp twice, then took it back again. "Loving is a talent in itself, *mon ami.*"

"I never had much talent," Alexander said, "for anything."

"Madeleine has it," Zeleyev went on. "Like Irina – she knew how to love, unstintingly, generously, instinctively. She made mistakes, she chose carelessly – she would have learned, if she had had time. Madeleine is much the same, passion over judgment, but she will learn." He swayed a little. "I will help her."

"I want to see her." Gabriel moistened his chapped lips with the tip of his tongue. "God, I'm dry, give me the bottle."

Zeleyev held onto it.

"I need a drink."

"Do you want to see your daughter, or do you want to drink?"

"You weren't always so heartless."

"More's the pity." Zeleyev's eyes hardened. "What do you expect me to do for you, Alexei? Pay off those men in Amsterdam?"

"I don't know."

"Don't you realize that even if I could pay off your debts, they've seen *Eternité*, they must have recognized its value." He leaned towards the table again and lovingly caressed the waterfall. "They would take my money, and then they would take back the sculpture too –"

"Perhaps not," Alexander said hopefully.

"Are you willing to take that chance?" Zeleyev grew still harsher. "Hasn't Madeleine lost enough? Didn't you absorb what I told you about her life?"

"Yes, of course!" Alexander's sunken eyes filled with tears. "All my doing, all my fault, I know, I *know*."

"Then the most important thing for us to do is to safeguard this for her." The Russian spoke softly again. "In the morning, before anything else, I shall place it into a bank vault, until you are ready to bring it to Madeleine in person."

"How can I face her?"

"I will fetch you a doctor, Alexei." Zeleyev raised the bottle again and peered at the other man through the clear glass. "But you know that you have to want to leave this world behind, *mon ami*. You have to be prepared to face your past and future, as well as your daughter." He saw Gabriel's trembling hands. "You are an addict," he said simply. "It will not be easy for you to stop."

"But I want to."

"But you need morphine now, *n'est-ce pas*?"

"You know I do."

"With me it is this vodka, but only the vodka, and quite

seldom nowadays. It still makes me horny as hell – you remember that, Alexei? It always poured life into my cock, gave me extra fire, do you remember?"

"Of course I remember," Alexander replied dully.

"That night," Zeleyev persisted, goaded by liquor. "You remember that too? No, you don't – better that way, much better."

"Don't mention it then." Alexander twisted his face away, though he remained sitting on the bed, his body making a U-shaped indentation in the ancient and damp mattress.

"Just reminding you of the difficulties, my friend. They will have to be faced if you want to go to Madeleine. To your grandson."

"Tell me about Valentin," Gabriel said, grasping thirstily at a change of topic. "Is he golden, like Maggy?"

"Dark-haired, like his father, with dark blue eyes, almost indigo in some lights." Zeleyev paused only momentarily. "If you surface, you must realize there's a good chance Emilie and Stefan will seize the moment. Now that even your son, of whom his stepfather was inordinately fond, has gone the way of all Gabriels, their disappointment may enhance their malice."

"Stop it." Alexander buried his face in his hands.

"Your son is queer, you know, Alexei."

The hands fell away from the white face. "What do you mean?"

"Rudi, your son, is homosexual. A nice, good young man, but gay. His stepfather is, I gather, appalled."

"Poor little Rudi."

"He's twenty-two years old, *mon ami*. Tall and handsome, very like his sister, whom he adores. I like him very much. He reminds me of you a long time ago, but he's stronger."

"You're very cruel tonight, Konstantin."

Zeleyev shrugged. "Flying more than three and a half

thousand miles to have dinner in a piss-hole like this makes me unkind, perhaps. Or is it merely truthful?"

Alexander said nothing.

"Why did you take *Eternité*, Alexei?"

"To keep it safe, of course, you know that."

"Then tomorrow, at last, you will have a chance to achieve your aim."

"If the banks were open, I'd do it this instant."

"Good." Zeleyev yawned widely. "You'd better get some rest."

"Aren't you going to your hotel?" Alexander asked.

"I shan't leave you tonight."

"Then take my bed."

"You're more accustomed to sleeping with lice than I am, *mon ami*. I'll just sit here and drown my discomfort a little more."

In less than half an hour, Zeleyev, having finished the bottle of vodka, was fast asleep, slumped over the table, his head resting on his arms. It was after three in the morning. Still wide awake, Alexander watched the Russian for a while. Konstantin's callousness had wounded him, yet he was honest enough to know that every word was justified. Besides, not many men would have dropped everything and crossed the Atlantic Ocean to come to the aid of a degenerate loser such as himself.

"Who am I kidding?" he said softly. "No one else would have come. Except Maggy."

This man had protected his child when her own father could not. This man had saved him from jail nearly twenty years ago, and had kept faith with him. This man was his only link with Maggy and his grandson.

Very gently, careful not to waken him from his drunken sleep, Gabriel eased Zeleyev off the chair, supported him around his waist and moved him over to the bed. Konstantin groaned. Alexander removed his impeccably polished shoes and covered him with his own well cut, expensive jacket. In spite of the nausea that gripped his stomach, Alexander smiled. This was a man who never altered, never lowered his standards. He touched the Russian's pure silk shirt, unbuttoned at the neck, and reminded himself that Zeleyev was far from unflawed, was himself capable of periods of some debauchery. Yet here he was, still a gentleman, still immaculate and still, despite everything, his friend.

Zeleyev began to snore.

"Sleep well," Alexander said, and sat on the chair. Wiping the palms of his hands against his own sweat-soaked shirt, he was aware again that he was trembling badly and that the familiar cramping in his stomach had begun. He needed morphine desperately, and he had lied when he had told Zeleyev that his supply was exhausted. He was an addict, and addicts always told lies.

He had to stop, he knew that just as clearly as he knew that it would be the hardest thing he had ever done in his life. He knew his own weakness, too, and that he might not survive. But he would try.

After tomorrow. He looked at his cheap wristwatch, a reminder that of the beautiful things he had owned in the distant past, not a single item had not been surrendered to feed his sickness. It was not far off four o'clock. If he took his one remaining dose now, its beneficial effects would be diminished in a few hours, and so he would wait, would sit it out for as long as he could bear it. For tomorrow morning, he would need to function, would need the courage to leave this room and conduct himself as other men did out there in the streets. Normal, healthy men. Decent men.

Another dull pain gripped his abdomen, and he stifled a groan. He stretched out a hand and laid it protectively on the sculpture that had come to represent so much. His father's most cherished possession. Now, more than ever before, he knew that it belonged with Maggy. If he could just do that one thing, if he could place *Eternité* in her hands, if he could see her brightness again and know that he had done one decent thing for her, it would be worth any amount of suffering.

He looked over at Zeleyev, out cold on the bed he had disdained. His eyelashes fluttered a little, his red-gold moustache puffed gently up and down with his breathing.

Alexander wiped his forehead with his sleeve and focused his attention fully on the Russian.

"I am on guard, old friend," he whispered to the sleeping man. "Not a single louse will suck your blood while I'm here."

And his vigil continued.

When Zeleyev awoke, leaden-headed, just after ten o'clock, Alexander was not in the room. He sat up, too quickly, felt the blood crashing in his temples, steadied himself before opening the door to check whether the other man was in the bathroom outside.

"*Merde.*"

Gabriel's sparse belongings were still strewn around, where they had been the night before, but Zeleyev's jacket had gone, and the shabby suitcase he had seen propped against the wall. And the sculpture.

Rage coursed through him like a torrent, fury at himself for his folly, his mindlessness. He went to the dingy basin, ran cold water and splashed his face, took his own handkerchief from his pocket and patted himself dry. His wallet had been in the inside pocket of his jacket – enough cash for a week's supply of morphine, enough to buy him a ticket to God alone knew where.

Zeleyev shook himself, suddenly, like a dog, the pain in his head a fitting punishment. Christ, he hadn't had a hangover like this for years, and just when he needed to think, to summon his resources –

The door opened.

"Where the hell have you been?"

"It's done."

"Where is it?"

"Safe."

"For Christ's sake, what have you done with my sculpture?"

Alexander was trembling again, partly from emotion and exhaustion, partly from the exertion of climbing the staircase, but his eyes were almost bright with achievement. He put down the suitcase, and sat heavily on the bed.

"I'm sorry about your jacket," he said, removing it carefully. "My own was too disreputable. In yours, I looked almost respectable."

"To hell with my jacket," Zeleyev snarled. "Where is *Eternité?*" He picked up the suitcase, realized from its lightness that it was empty, threw it back on the floor. "Alexander, you bloody fool, tell me what you've done."

"What you told me to do." Gabriel was suddenly immensely weary. He had taken the last of his morphine at seven, for otherwise he could never have carried out his task, but he had come close to the edge, had seen over into the abyss of withdrawal, and it had terrified him, as it always did. "It's in the bank – the Banque Nationale, in Boulevard de Rochechouart. In a box in their vault."

Zeleyev sat down on the chair. "Why didn't you wake me?"

"There was no need." He was still breathless. "Besides, it was important to me to do it alone."

The Russian was silent.

"It was what you wanted," Alexander said. "For Maggy."

"Yes."

Alexander looked at him. "I alarmed you. I'm sorry."

"No matter."

"And now?" The question was tentative, humble. "I

need that doctor, Konstantin." He paused. "If I don't get help soon, I'm finished."

Zeleyev, recovering himself a little, reached over and plucked his jacket from the bed, dusting it off and shaking it. "Let's go to the Crillon – I need a bath, and later on we can telephone Madeleine."

"No."

"Why not?"

"I can't go to a good hotel in this state. Look at me – you think I don't realize how I look?" He scrubbed a hand across his eyes. "Besides, in a few more hours, unless I get something, I won't be capable of having any kind of a coherent conversation." He looked up, and his mouth quivered with emotion. "I want to speak to her, more than anything, but it had better be now, or it may be too late."

"It's not even five o'clock in New York."

"Do you think she'll mind?" The dark-circled eyes were beseeching.

"Of course not," Zeleyev relented. "Are you ready to talk to her?"

"I'm not sure I'll ever be ready."

Three and a half thousand miles away from the post office on Boulevard de Clichy, in Zeleyev's apartment on Riverside Drive, Madeleine heard the ringing of the telephone, and stumbled from her bed, cloudy with sleep.

"Madeleine?"

"Konstantin?" The sitting room was still dark. "Is something wrong?"

"Far from wrong." Zeleyev paused. "I have someone with me who wishes to speak to you."

"Who is it?" She rubbed her eyes. "Is it Noah?"

"It's your father."

Madeleine felt herself swaying, and grasped at the wall. "Papi?"

"He's right here, *ma petite*. I'll put him on."

She could hardly breathe.

"Maggy?"

Hot tears flooded into her eyes. "Papi?" She held tightly to the receiver. "Is that really you?"

"Really me." Alexander's throat was taut. "How are you, Maggy?"

"Well, Papi –" Her voice choked. "And you?"

"I'm not so bad, *Schätzli*."

"Oh, God," she said.

"I know."

It was so strange and awkward, a bizarre and frustrating verbal reunion between two people who had clung to the past for years, both of them loving a memory, almost a myth. Alexander had remained, to Madeleine, her elusive, embraceable father, tarnished and tragic, yet always greatly loved, and he in turn had held fast to his Maggy, his wild-haired, sweet-scented, generous and impulsive little girl.

"You have a grandson," she told him eagerly. "Do you know?"

"Konstantin told me," Alexander said. "And about your husband." He hesitated. "I'm so sorry, Maggy."

"How did he find you, Papi? Or did you find him? Are you coming back with him?" The words tumbled from her.

"Not quite yet, Maggy, but soon."

She heard the quaver in his voice. "Why not, Papi?"

"It's not possible."

"Then we'll come to you."

"No, Maggy."

"For pity's sake, don't let's waste any more time," she pleaded. "I love you, Papi, I love you so much. It doesn't matter – not any of it!" Madeleine was crying, and her voice was breaking, but she plunged on, seizing every instant. "I know what happened that night in Zurich, and

I don't care, and I want you to come here to me, to come home. I want to give you Valentin to hold in your arms, Papi – he's so wonderful, the most beautiful child in the world –"

"Forgive me, Maggy."

"There's nothing to forgive."

"I know what I've done, *Schätzli*. And there's no way I can ever make it up to you –"

"Papi, it's all –"

"No, wait, please. Just know how much I love you, Maggy. Know how sorry I am for everything, sorrier than you can ever imagine – and know that I'm going to fight now, I'm really going to try."

"I hear you, Papi," Madeleine said, hardly able to speak, but forcing herself on. "We'll be here waiting for you – and Rudi will be here too, soon. Did Konstantin tell you about Rudi? He's grown up so wonderfully – I never dreamed we would be together –"

The line crackled, beginning to break up.

"Maggy, are you still there?"

"I'm still here, Papi."

"God bless you, *Schätzli*."

"And you, too, Papi."

The link was broken, the line dead. And in the dark sitting room, in the silent apartment on Riverside Drive, Madeleine stood motionless, the receiver still in her hand, and tears of joy and loss running down her cheeks.

Zeleyev took Alexander back to the terrible room on rue Clauzel, and then he went out again, and brought him back two baguettes with ham and cheese and a bottle of Evian.

"I bought some aspirin, too," he told Gabriel. "To help tide you over if it gets too bad, and here –" He tossed a paperback book onto the table. "I remember you were always crazy about Chandler."

Alexander picked it up. "Thank you." His hands were trembling again, and quickly he put it down. "Will you be gone long?"

Zeleyev shook his head. "I must have a bath, and a short rest."

"I'll lock the door."

The Russian smiled gently. "Don't be so afraid, Alexei. If no one came out of the shadows this morning, when you went to the bank, I doubt if they know where you are." He paused. "Do you want me to take the key to the vault, for safety?"

"No. Thank you, I'll be fine." Alexander took off his grubby jacket. He was beginning to perspire. The telephone call had drained him, and he hoped that he might sleep. "It was wonderful hearing her, Konstantin. I'll never be able to repay you."

"Just stay here, *mon ami*. Don't disappear again. That's all I ask." Zeleyev went to the door. "When I've rested a little, I will make enquiries about a good doctor. And I'll return later."

"I can't keep thanking you. For coming in the first place, and now – it's far more than I deserve."

Zeleyev took his hand. "Just don't let Madeleine down again, Alexei. Think of her, and of your grandson."

The luxuries of Zeleyev's room at the Crillon were balm to his hangover and general fatigue, and he soaked in his deep bath until the water cooled, and then he fell asleep between the soothing sheets of the big, clean bed, and all his dreams were beautiful: of Madeleine, wearing Irina's yellow diamond around her neck, and of *Eternité*, displayed on a velvet cushion, gazed upon by an admiring audience. . .

He slept until six o'clock, woke ravenously hungry and ate an excellent dinner of casseroled baby pigeon, drank a single cognac in the bar and then, feeling restored, braced himself to return to rue Clauzel.

His nose wrinkled in fresh distaste as he climbed the stairs and rapped on the door. As had happened the first time, there was no response, so he knocked harder.

"Alexei," he called, loudly, and then, hearing nothing from within, he rapped once more and called again, urgently.

Crouching, he put his eye to the keyhole. The key was still in the lock. There was no alternative but to break down the door. Standing back a little way, glad of his physical fitness, Zeleyev charged with his right shoulder and the door gave way with a splintering crash.

Gabriel lay prone on the bed. Zeleyev turned him over, felt for the pulse in his neck, knew that he was dead, and observed that the aspirin bottle on the floor beside the bed was empty. There were two folded sheets of paper on the table. Picking them up, Zeleyev saw that they were the two front pages of the Chandler paperback, torn out in the absence of writing paper. He scanned the notes quickly. Alexander's handwriting was erratic, but his wishes were clear. He did not want to be left alone in Paris, nor to be returned to Switzerland. He asked Konstantin to oblige him with one last favour, to arrange for his remains to be taken to America, to his daughter.

His note to Madeleine was very brief, but poignant.

I would only have failed you again. Forgive me, if you can.

The police came, once the ambulance had removed the body. They took both notes, giving Zeleyev a receipt for them, and promised that they would be returned as soon as possible.

"We will assist you, if you wish," one officer said, "with

the formalities. Provided there are no unexpected complications."

"Do you foresee any?" Zeleyev enquired.

"Are these all Monsieur Gabriel's belongings?" a second officer asked.

"So far as I am aware."

"The deceased had no home, you say."

"He was a drug addict," Zeleyev said. "His life was transient."

"And you believe that he died of an aspirin overdose?"

"The bottle was full when I left him before noon." Zeleyev paused. "I think that he took morphine early this morning, but he told me that he had no more on him."

"Only the aspirin."

Zeleyev looked the policeman in the eye. "I gave him the aspirin."

"Why did you do that, Monsieur?"

"Because I knew he would need something before long. And I thought it preferable that he swallow a few aspirin than that he might go out in search of other drugs."

"Did you have reason to think he might wish to end his life?"

"On the contrary," Zeleyev answered. "When I left Alexander, he was –" He corrected himself. "He seemed hopeful, and determined to seek help with overcoming his addiction."

"What had made Monsieur Gabriel hopeful?"

"I had accompanied him to the post office so that he could telephone his daughter. They had not spoken in many years, and the conversation was of great solace to him. She wanted him to come to America to join her and his grandson."

"Why do you think then that he took an overdose?"

"Fear of failure," Zeleyev answered calmly. "I am afraid that I must have underestimated the gravity of his condition. He clearly was in no state to have been left alone." He paused again. "Though he had, of course, been alone for the most part for many years."

"So you were not to know, Monsieur."

"No."

The autopsy having borne out Zeleyev's account of Alexander's death, arrangements were made for him to accompany Alexander's coffin to New York a week later. Zeleyev could not bear to break the news to Madeleine over the telephone, and he was afraid for her sanity if she had to face their arrival at the airport.

The formalities organized and the necessary papers signed and sealed, he was free to leave Paris, but Zeleyev had one last call to make. He had known since the moment he had found Alexander's corpse that he would do this, that it was the right and proper thing for him to do.

He had taken the key out of Gabriel's trouser pocket before he had called the ambulance. If they had found it, there would have been endless questions and no guarantee that the sculpture would find its way to Madeleine. He had the key, and if necessary, he would produce both the *acte de décès* and the documents that gave him charge of the arrangements for the conveyance of his friend's remains to the United States.

He arrived at the bank in Boulevard de Rochechouart shortly after ten o'clock on his last day in the city. He left, one hour later, empty-handed. Alexander Gabriel's penultimate act had been – whether deliberately or not Zeleyev would never be certain – a betrayal of his friendship. His instructions to the bank were precise, and inviolable. No one but Gabriel himself, or his daughter, Madeleine Bonnard, née Magdalen Gabriel, attending in person, was to have access to the belongings he had placed in the vault.

"But Madame Bonnard is living in New York," Zeleyev told the manager repeatedly.

"I'm sure she will wish, in due course, to come to Paris."

"It would be very hard for her to come."

"Then I am sorry to say, Monsieur, that until she does, the deposit box will remain locked."

Zeleyev knew that now, more than ever, Madeleine would not want to return to Paris, and that even if she did, since she had recently begun working in New York without official papers, she might face immigration difficulties when she tried to return to the United States. He cursed the oscillating clarity and confusion of Gabriel's drug-ruled mind that had led him first to give these directions to the Banque Nationale, and then to make it unnecessary for Madeleine to attend his funeral in France. If he had only known, Zeleyev would have destroyed that latter note, would never have allowed the police to have read it.

It was hard for him to believe, hard to swallow the bitterness that lodged like a hard ball in his throat when he thought about it. *Eternité* had been in his hands for such a little while. Now it was locked away, out of sight. He would have to return to New York, to Madeleine, with nothing. Except a coffin.

Standing in the warm rain beside her father's open grave two weeks later, her brother close on her left side, Konstantin on her right, Madeleine tried not to listen to the empty words of the minister struggling to eulogize a man about whom he knew nothing at all.

Alexander Leopold Gabriel
Beloved father of Madeleine and Rudolf
1915–1964

This new desolation was entirely different to the all-consuming anguish she had endured over Antoine. This bereavement, Madeleine realized, even now, was more in the nature of losing, finally, the dream she had nurtured for the greater part of her life. Since the age of seven, Alexander had never been more than the most fleeting of presences. Somehow, though, that single telephone conversation, when they had both, at least, found it possible to express their indestructible love, had made it a little easier to bear the news that Zeleyev had brought from Paris – made even these moments a little less agonizing. Had Alexander come to live in New York – had she been able, at last, to see him day after day – Madeleine knew that she might have been forced to recognize his failings. As it was, her father would remain, forever, an abstract force in her life, in some ways almost a figment of her imagination.

No one had truly known Alexander Gabriel. There were aspects of his life of which Madeleine was aware she knew nothing at all, but none of that mattered to her now. What tore at her heart, as she threw the cool, American earth down onto his coffin, was the knowledge that he had been burdened for so many years by pain and guilt and sorrow, and that, in the end, she had been unable to help him.

He had been her father, and she had loved him.

Nothing else mattered.

14

"What can I get for you today, Monsieur?"
"How's the white fish?"
"Excellent, Monsieur."
"I'll take two pounds. Or how about the sturgeon?"
"*Magnifique*, as always. How much would you like?"
"Don't rush me. Which should I have, sturgeon or white fish?"
"Why not both, Monsieur?"
"The chopped herring smells to die for."
"It's Sunday, Monsieur – you have time to eat all three."
"Herring gives me heartburn."
"Then it's just the sturgeon and white fish?"
"You're pushy, you know that?"
"I'm sorry, Monsieur."
"No, it's okay – if you want to get real pushy, I'll take a pound of lox too."
"Scottish, Monsieur?"
"Who do you think I am, Rockefeller?"

As 1965 got under way, Madeleine was working harder than she'd ever worked before, harder even than during her last year in Paris, but she didn't mind. She had found two jobs, both in walking distance of Zeleyev's apartment, one at Zabar's & Co., a renowned delicatessen-cum-gourmet store on Broadway famous for over thirty years for its Jewish specialities, but these days selling more than forty varieties of bread, fresh-roasted coffees and zillions of cheeses as well as its old-faithful and ever popular smoked fish and chopped liver. On Mondays and Tuesdays, Madeleine worked at Zabar's from two in the afternoon until half-past-midnight, giving her the mornings with Valentin; Wednesdays to Saturdays, she worked the morning shift and spent the afternoons with her son, before she went to her second job at a restaurant near Times Square, where she waited on tables from six until closing time, and donned a tuxedo to sing popular show tunes with the other waiters and waitresses. On Sundays, the easiest day for Konstantin to give over to Valentin, she worked all the way through from nine in the morning till midnight at Zabar's. Murray Klein, the proprietor, scolded her for working too hard, but Madeleine thrived on keeping as busy as possible. While she was working, the sorrows were wedged into the back of her mind – and besides, the longer the hours she worked, the more money she was able to put by.

Her sole aim now was to create a secure life for Valentin. One day, she hoped to repay Konstantin for at least a fraction of his generosity – one day, she hoped to repay her debt to her family, which still rankled, no matter what Rudi repeatedly said. But all that was a long way into a future of which the only certainty was its uncertainty. In the meantime, the only demand Zeleyev had made of her was that she start singing again, whether she felt like it or not. And once she had taken the initial, agonizing plunge, even her nights had become full. There were numerous nightclubs all over the city where newcomers were encouraged – if they passed muster – to sing a number or two at the microphone, and as the months progressed, there were many nights when either the Russian or her brother sat amongst the guests at Bon Soir, the Cafe Au Go Go or the No. 1 Bar, all in Greenwich Village, or, on two occasions, in midtown at Jackie Kannon's Rat Fink Room, where customers drank partly to be skilfully insulted by Kannon and where they were not known for their gentleness with unknowns who failed to please. On those nights, Madeleine wore black, teased her short hair so that it shimmered white-gold in the spotlights, and called herself Maddy Gabriel because it was easier to pronounce. And she pleased.

Rudi had successfully made his move to Manhattan just before Christmas of 1964. He had found an apartment on the twentieth floor of a distinguished building on Fifth Avenue, at its source close to Washington Square. Every day, much earlier than he had ever risen in Zurich, Rudi went to work at the bank on Broad Street in the heart of the Wall Street district, worked doggedly at the art and science of personal investments and found that he was enjoying himself as he had never done before.

"Once in a while," he told Madeleine with satisfaction, "I realize that I've made a truly positive difference to a client, and that it's my contribution that's done it, not just my department's. Before, I always checked every move I made fifteen different ways. I never really believed in myself, but lately I'm learning to trust my own instincts – I never knew I *had* instincts before."

Rudi loved the Village life, too, being the perfect contrast to his daytime collar-and-tie existence. Almost every evening he strolled out for dinner at any one of the myriad informal restaurants and Italian cafés on Bleecker Street, sometimes straying a little farther afield into Little Italy itself, or on into the colourful triangle of Chinatown. After eating, he would go home to snatch a couple of hours' rest and then, refreshed, he would go out again to support his sister wherever she had found a singing spot, or sometimes to babysit Valentin so that Zeleyev could come and applaud. Rudi made friends easily; the New Yorkers he met liked his open, eager approach, and he felt both liberated and secure. The move had released him, was undoubtedly the wisest step he had ever taken. His only regret was that, thus far, Madeleine had steadfastly refused to allow him to help her financially.

"Buying gifts for Valentin is one thing," she insisted gently. "But I won't let you pay my rent, and we won't come and live in your apartment. For one thing, you don't have the space."

"I have as much space as Konstantin."

"But no more, and even if you did –"

"You wouldn't come because the bank pays the rent."

"Don't be hurt, Rudi, please don't be hurt."

"I'm not, but don't you understand how much I want to help?"

"Very well, but you have to understand me, too."

"I know, I know." He'd heard it all before. "But why can't I just lend you some cash to start you off in your own place? I'd let you pay me back – we could draw up papers, if you like."

"I don't like. I owe more than enough already that I may never be able to repay." Madeleine stroked her brother's cheek tenderly. "If I'm ever in real trouble, you'll be the first person I come to."

"Swear it."

"Rudi, stop."

Her brother's well-intentioned arguing went on and on, month in and month out, but Madeleine was not to be swayed. That Rudi was now his own man was not in question, but the money he earned was nevertheless still Gründli money. She would not have wanted him to leave the bank for the world; she had no desire to impose her own rigidity upon him. But though she knew that the money she had been forced to accept from her family during Antoine's illness had been hers by right, it had still cut her to take it. She would never take from them again.

* * *

There were dozens of regular customers at Zabar's. There were those who left the store several times each week laden with overflowing shopping bags; there were some who came in every single day for just one preferred delicacy; there were customers who telephoned gargantuan orders for delivery and who hardly ever came into the store in person; and there were others who spent up to an hour at a time just standing around salivating and ogling before they finally departed with a plain bagel, bought out of embarrassment, coming back next morning to start the self-torture all over again.

Madeleine knew all the regulars by sight, and most of them by name, but she had one favourite. He was a big, bear-like man with warm brown eyes, curling chestnut hair and a friendly, craggy smile, and he was a man who cared passionately about food. He called into Zabar's at varying times each day, but somehow he always came while Madeleine was on duty, and though she knew it was the produce that drew him, she was also aware that he liked her to be the one to serve him. His name was Gideon Tyler, he lived down in the Village on Bleecker Street, he had an office not too far from the store, and he sometimes came in carrying a weathered old saxophone. That was all she knew about him, and all she needed to know.

She did not know that Gideon Tyler had been in Zabar's the day she had come for her job interview, and that having overheard her conversation with Murray Klein, Tyler had afterwards taken Klein to one side to give him, whether he wanted it or not, his own point of view. For what it was worth, he had told the discerning, Russian-born proprietor, any girl who could make a slab of Roquefort cheese sound about as seductive as sex on a rug by a log fire in December, was much too valuable a prospective salesgirl to turn down.

"You telling me my job?" Klein had enquired.

"I'm just saying that I'd be likely to spend more time and money here if you took her on."

"You're one of my best customers already," Klein pointed out.

"Well, at least you wouldn't lose me to Manganaro's."

"No chance," Klein said confidently. "Anyway, what do you think I am, stupid? I hired her already."

There weren't too many licensed private investigators in Manhattan with a name like Gideon Baruch Joshua Tyler. The surname was an incongruity thrust upon Gideon's grandfather on Ellis Island in 1898. The Russian family name had been too difficult for the immigration officials to trouble with, and the young man's attempts to explain, in halting English, that he was a tailor by occupation, had been misunderstood, transforming him for ever into Baruch Moshe Tyler.

Twenty-year-old Baruch and Marochka, his wife, moved in with their cousins, who lived in a cold-water walk-up apartment on Rivington Street on the Lower East Side, staying there right through the births of their three children, including Gideon's father, Ephraim, in 1900, until they were able to move up in the world into an apartment of their own in a brownstone on East One Hundredth Street in Harlem. Gideon had been born there in 1920, and had lived in the cramped, three-roomed apartment with his parents, his two sisters and their grandmother (Baruch having passed away in 1919) until 1933, when they had all moved together, lock, stock and lovingly-polished Sabbath candlesticks, over the Hudson River to the Jersey City suburb of Greenville.

Gideon, aged thirteen, had missed the big city and all its inherent, enthralling dangers. Had Miriam, his mother, known that her son frequently took a trolley car to Journal Square and then caught a Hudson tube into Greenwich Village, she would probably have fainted. Once in a while,

Miriam ventured into the area with a friend, mostly to make a rare purchase at John Wanamaker's, on Broadway, and if they were feeling courageous, they might take a stroll through Washington Square, sitting for a while on a bench in the shade of an American elm tree near the great Washington Arch, gazing at the students from New York University, the mothers and small children from the Italian district, and the local artists, feeling as if they were observing an exotic circus. Miriam Tyler was always glad to escape back to Greenville, their safe, Jewish neighbourhood.

Gideon, however, liked blending into a crowd and thrived on an element of risk. His parents' narrow outlook hemmed him in; he made friends easily – Jewish, Protestant, Catholic, black, Italian, oriental. To Gideon, people were just people; you either got on with them or you didn't. There were ice cream parlors in Jersey City where he could have had a 'frosted' or a '2 cents plain', or a grand egg cream made properly with Fox's u-bet chocolate syrup, but Gideon liked the added frisson of spending his money in the Village; and then again, at thirteen, he had developed tastes that would have choked his kosher parents, like chewing on an egg roll on a Chinatown street or buying *cannoli* from Ferrara's in Little Italy. Ephraim Tyler's idea of an exciting evening out was to pile the family into his used Nash sedan and to drive to a kosher restaurant in Newark. Their two-family house in Greenville was very comfortable, with an airy, pretty backyard; Gideon even had a bedroom all of his own, with a handbasin and a mirror. But it was all so dull. So *safe*.

Gideon liked feeling his pulse race when he confronted a street fight between angry Italian kids or a blazing argument amongst some of the typical Village eccentrics, but he also had a strong instinct for restoring order, though until after his fifteenth birthday, when he began growing like ragweed, he knew better than to poke his nose in where it might get broken. There were real dangers on the big city streets, real crimes, some of them wicked and meriting the full force of the law, some of them trifling and brought about by poverty and desperation. The things that mattered most in life, Gideon decided as he strode through his teenage years, were equality, law and order. He thought it would be good to play a part in the dispensation of justice. He thought it would be fine to become a policeman.

Joining the New York Police Department was no easy feat. To begin with, an applicant to the force had to have been a resident of New York City for one year before he could be considered. In the second place, times being hard, with talk of war and America still gripped by the Depression, thousands of able-bodied New Yorkers were out of work, and the competition for good jobs was intense. The Department could have their pick of the crop, so a successful recruit had to weigh no less than a hundred and forty pounds and to be physically 'perfect', with a high standard of intelligence and practical all-round ability.

Gideon left home on his eighteenth birthday, moving to Sullivan Street in Greenwich Village, sharing a fourth-floor walk-up apartment with two rookie police officers he had befriended. At nineteen, he passed his Civil Service written examinations, his psychological evaluation and his physical, took the Pledge of Honor and was sent to training school, where he not only survived but excelled, ready to begin his tour of duty ninety days after his twentieth birthday. His parents were distraught. Ephraim, a tailor like his father and grandfather before him, with his able eye on a second small retail store in Jersey City which he had hoped his son would wish to manage, was a stern, kind, orthodox man who studied the Talmud every spare moment, while Miriam read gentle love stories and poetry when she wasn't cooking or baking, or sewing or cleaning her beloved house. They were both cautious people, with an inherited mistrust of any police force, stemming from the Cossack horror stories that had been imported along with Baruch and all the other Jewish immigrants fresh from the pogroms of Eastern Europe.

"You love justice, you should have been a lawyer," Miriam told him every Friday night when he came to dinner. The times were still to come when Gideon would have to tell his parents he had to work on the Sabbath just as all the other rookies did.

"I never had the brains to be a lawyer, Mom."

"It's not too late – you could go to college, you'd be a fine lawyer."

"He could have been a tailor," Ephraim said starkly. "And if he loves the law so much, he could at least read the Talmud like a decent Jew."

"I can be a decent man, Pop," Gideon answered steadily. "And being a policeman doesn't stop me from being Jewish."

"You'll be shot." Miriam, ladling chicken soup, began to weep for the hundredth time. "My only son will be shot in an alley!"

"He won't be shot, Mom," Abigail, Gideon's younger sister, reassured their mother. Marianne, the oldest, had married two years before, and was now presiding over her own dinner table in Brooklyn.

"I won't be shot," Gideon reiterated gently. "I direct traffic and write parking tickets. I'd stand more chance of cutting myself with pinking shears or sticking a needle through my thumb if I'd been a tailor."

Miriam changed tack a little. "And what do you eat all week? You tell me you can cook, but when you lived at home you burned even water." Her tears ran afresh. "If they don't shoot him, he'll starve to death."

And so it went on, week after week, draining him a little, for whilst Gideon was a big, tall man, a veritable giant beside his mother, he was fundamentally kind and loving, and it went against his nature to cause his parents distress. Yet it was not Miriam and Ephraim's disapproval that led to his leaving the force within two years of joining.

He met, fell in love with and married Susan Klein, a nice, pretty girl from Brooklyn, all in the space of the first three months of 1941. Both his parents approved of Susan, and the bride thought it exciting and glamorous, to begin with, to have a handsome policeman for a husband. All her friends had married such ordinary men – one a doctor, one a kosher butcher, one a bank teller, another a druggist. Being the wife of an officer of the law had sex appeal, and what she realized that Gideon might lack in ambition, Susan had in great quantities. She foresaw an auspicious future on their horizon; sergeant in a year or two, lieutenant after that, then captain – and ultimately, why not even a Jewish commissioner?

Gideon, however, had other ideas. He loved almost everything about his life. He loved Susan and his family, he liked many aspects of his work and most of his colleagues. He appreciated that the new apartment that he had found for them on the north side of Bleecker Street between Sullivan and MacDougal Streets, was far more to his taste than his wife's, and that she had compromised out of love for him. He knew that Susan didn't really understand what made him tick, could not quite see how a man as gentle as Gideon, a man with passions for music, flowers, sex and good food, also possessed the body and will of a street scrapper. Gideon ate hungrily and appreciatively, made love to Susan with great tenderness and bought her small gifts whenever he could, then worked out vigorously every day to maintain the fitness necessary for his job. He was tall and broad, handsome and impressive to look at in his blue uniform. But more and more, he was uneasy about wearing it.

Gideon was not a political man, but he had swiftly come to learn that the NYPD, in common with many police forces, was crammed with opponents manoeuvring for power. The truth had startled him, for the rules that had applied to his entry to the force had been abundantly fair; only the best qualified had made it. Once inside, however, it had soon been made plain to him that all too often it was not only what you did or the way in which you performed that assisted your advancement; it was who you got along with and how ambitious you were. Increasingly, the knowledge made Gideon uncomfortable and argumentative. He was accused of making too much noise, too much trouble, of not fitting in. Disillusioned, he considered throwing in the towel.

And then the Japanese bombed Pearl Harbor, America was in the war, and in the spring of 1942, Gideon Tyler was drafted as a combat infantryman. He served for three years in the European Theater of Operations, saw bloody action, terror, gallantry, heroism and tragedy, and then came back home, received an honourable discharge, and was faced with the choice of returning to the job that had been kept open for him, or of becoming a civilian again. He tendered his resignation.

For a year, he struggled to fit into a normal way of life, but he was ill-equipped for anything but the most mediocre of jobs, and even if he had wanted to, he had not inherited a grain of his father's talent with the needle or cutting shears. Susan, all her ambitions tossed away, tried for a while to be supportive, but found it increasingly hard to cope with her maddening husband. She had done all the right things, found a job in a defence factory, welcomed him home with open arms, but she had expected and needed enough stability to bring the children they both wanted into the world. When, in 1947, Gideon struck on what he saw as the perfect way to fulfil all his needs – by applying for a licence to practise as a private investigator – Susan exploded. Six months later, the marriage was over.

Gideon had stayed in the Bleecker Street apartment, using it as his office at first, before finding a more suitable room for his business over on the West Side, on Broadway near Ninety-first Street. He was saddened by the divorce, guilty over his inadequacy as a husband and over the pain he had caused Susan. Yet as time progressed, he realized that his greatest sin had been in marrying too young, too impulsively, and when he learned that Susan had become engaged to a Gramercy Park dentist, he felt able, at last, to shed some of his guilt and to start enjoying life again. Many of his days and nights, when he had work, were spent spying on people, and Gideon was not by nature a snoop. His clients generally wanted him either to help them find someone or to get rid of someone, most usually by divorce, and a percentage of his clients were not particularly likeable people; but experience and maturity had taught Gideon that neither every case, nor every day, could be worthwhile or fulfilling, and it was up to him to enrich his spare time. Searching for evidence on a waste site, he came across a battered tenor saxophone, which he took home and worked on lovingly and patiently until it was fit for him to learn to play. He met a sax player at the Village Vanguard who gave him lessons in exchange for six months' rent-free accommodation on Gideon's couch, and as Gideon improved, the saxophone accompanied him wherever he went; so long as he had access to music and food, he was a happy man, and once in a while he would stumble onto a case that made him feel like a really useful human being, and then Gideon would set to work with the same gusto that he still brought to the dinner table.

It was food that had led him to Maddy.

Since great food was, to Gideon, one of the fundamental necessities of his life, and since his days and nights as a private investigator were punctuated by 'pit stops', when he paused to refuel himself with junk food and coffee, the importance of finding at least fifteen minutes every day to call in at his favourite store had long since been paramount. From the day that Madeleine had begun working there, however, Gideon had been forced to admit to himself that lox, chopped liver and Swiss cheese, however sublime, had taken a back seat.

This girl was an *angel*, the loveliest creature he'd ever laid eyes on. Tyler was six feet three inches tall in his bare feet, broad and solid, but every time he caught his first glimpse of the day of Madeleine Bonnard, his breath caught in his throat and his legs turned to jelly, and whenever he heard her voice, so warm with its gentle huskiness and wonderful, soft accent, he got real chills. For over six months, the sight of her wedding ring kept him almost silent, but one afternoon, concerned by her absence from work, he asked after her, heard that her son had a bad cold and learned, in the course of the same conversation, that his angel was a widow.

"How long?"

"Don't know. She doesn't say much."

"Is she seeing anyone?"

"She's never mentioned it."

Madeleine was oblivious of Tyler's feelings. She liked the way he spoke to her with courtesy and friendliness, the way he asked about her health as if he really wanted to know how she felt, and she appreciated the fact that he never made any attempt to flirt with her. She envisaged him with a wife or steady girlfriend and at least two young children, but she never enquired, just as she never overstepped the mark with any of the customers. They always chatted for a few moments while he made his selections; their conversations revolved around the way his pesto sauce had turned out the evening before, whether he was in the mood to buy halvah or ice cream or both, and about the weather, and that was all.

Until one Thursday in the middle of May, 1966, when Tyler came into the store, made his purchases with hardly a word, went straight out, and then, abruptly, came back inside and over to where Madeleine stood behind the cheese counter.

"I have two tickets for a Mendelssohn concert tonight at the Philharmonic Hall – would you like to come?"

Madeleine was so startled at the suddenness of the invitation, had, in her heart and mind, so completely ruled men, in a dating sense, out of her life, that she dropped the sharp knife with which she had been cutting a piece out of a whole Brie –

"Oh, God," Tyler said, appalled. "Did you cut yourself?"

"No, it's all right –" She bent down to retrieve the knife and knocked three Camembert cheeses onto the floor. "*Merde*," she said, and promptly blushed scarlet. "I'm sorry."

"No, I'm sorry – are you okay?"

"Fine, thank you."

"The tickets." Tyler, flustered, began again. "Are you free, by any chance?"

"No."

"Oh."

"No, I mean –"

"That's okay."

Looking as if he'd been scalded, Tyler stuck the tickets back into his jacket pocket, apologized, and stalked out of the store, leaving Madeleine as embarrassed as she had been in a long time. Lord knew she hadn't meant to sound so offhand. He was such a nice man, and such a great customer. Quickly, she dived down to pick up the cheeses, glad that the boss had not been around to see her clumsiness.

Next morning when he came in, Madeleine was ready for him.

"Mr Tyler, could I have a word?"

"Sure, but if it's about yesterday –"

"It is."

"Look, I'm sorry – I shouldn't have asked."

"Why not?" Madeleine glanced around, made sure that no one else was in earshot, and took a deep breath. "Mr Tyler, I wish you'd let me explain to you –"

"There's nothing to explain."

"Yes, there is," she insisted.

"Okay." Tyler shifted awkwardly.

"I would have been glad to come to the concert, but I work every night." She paused. "And also, I feel I should tell you that I don't date –"

"I see."

"But I do need friends."

He relaxed a little. "So maybe another time?"

"So long as you understand."

"Of course." Gideon looked into her eyes, felt the familiar weakness in his legs and prayed it didn't show. "Where do you work nights?"

"Here, some evenings, and at a restaurant near Times Square the rest of the time."

"Busy lady."

He found out the name of the restaurant, and went the next evening. It was a Saturday night, and hectic. He watched Madeleine carrying trays, noting down orders, pouring drinks and then, divine in her tuxedo, singing numbers from *Oklahoma*, *West Side Story* and *Oliver* with her colleagues. When she paused for a few moments at his table after pouring his coffee, Gideon was cautiously friendly, determined not to pressure her however irresistible he found her. When she brought him his check, he agonized over the tip. One couldn't leave money for the woman one had fallen in love with; on the other hand, he didn't want her to know that; then again, if he tipped generously, she might feel she was being patronized, but if he tipped lightly, she'd think that he was a cheapskate. . .

They became true friends two weeks later, in perfectly natural, unforced circumstances. Being a lover of jazz, Tyler frequented many of the Village night spots, sometimes just to listen, sometimes taking along his saxophone in case a sympathetic manager might give him five minutes to pour the pent-up frustrations of a grinding day into some would-be Charlie Parker-style blues. Gideon knew he was an average player with the merest smack of talent, but his enthusiasm often transmitted itself to the audience, making them more generous than they might otherwise have been.

He was sitting in the Cafe Au Go Go cellar late one night, nursing a cup of black coffee that had gone cold, when he heard the introduction.

"You loved her the last time, so we invited her back again. And here she is – a little touch of Paris in the night – Maddy Gabriel."

As she walked into a single pool of light centre stage, Gideon sat bolt upright, hardly believing his eyes. She looked so tiny, so fragile, so goddamned beautiful that he thought he might burst with adoration. The band began its few introductory bars of glorious, haunting Jobim, and Madeleine started to sing 'The Girl from Ipanema'.

Gideon's right hand gripped his coffee cup so tightly that it cracked. The cool liquid spilled out over the table and onto his jeans, a splinter of china stuck itself into the palm of his hand, but he took no notice. She wore black stretch ski pants and an unadorned black halter-necked top that hugged her breasts and accentuated her slenderness, and her shoulders and perfect young arms gleamed silken white in the spotlight. Her voice astonished him, delighted him beyond belief – it was strong yet marvellously controlled, it slid effortlessly on its *bossa nova* way through Norman Gimbel's lyrics, gliding to its wistful end and moving directly on into 'Stormy Weather', one of his own favourite thirties' songs. His cup was replaced, his table was wiped over, but Tyler was quite oblivious of everything but Madeleine. He felt as if he had tripped up into heaven and he had no desire ever to come down again, and it was hard to be sure, when she had finished, whether the wildest applause came from him or from another table where two men, one old, one young and very like Madeleine, sat cheering.

She noticed him then, observed his genuine pleasure and smiled back, a warm smile of welcome. Ten minutes later, he met two of the three most important males in Madeleine Bonnard's life: Konstantin Zeleyev and her brother, Rudi. The third, young Valentin, was sound asleep backstage on a makeshift bed. The instant Gideon saw the four-year-old, rosy cheeked, long-lashed and utterly beautiful, every lingering, feeble trace of resistance melted away. And as Madeleine watched Gideon and noted the rapt expression on his face as he stared at her son, she knew, without doubt, that she had found another special friend.

New York was beginning to weave its own particular brand of magic around Madeleine. Though most of her time was spent at work of one kind or another, there were still several hours most weeks when she had a chance to explore the city that she was starting to accept, gradually, as her new home. She selected one neighbourhood at a time and, generally with Valentin for company, tried to get to know it, to understand its character, spirit and shape, and to relate it to the rest of Manhattan. Often she felt like a tourist, a stranger, enjoying her stay but still a little remote; she remembered her first days in Paris, the instantaneous sense of belonging that had enveloped her there, and knew that her relationship with New York was a different kind of creature. Konstantin had described it accurately, for all his lyricism; all the great cities were made up of contrasts, but surely none so glaring, so blatant as this one. If she were to follow Broadway all the way from its beginning down in the Battery, right through Manhattan up to the point where it crossed the Harlem River, she realized that she would inevitably find every flavour of city street and every known kind of human being. And to all of them, she supposed, she would be a foreigner, and yet it seemed that this categorization, above all, might qualify her as a New Yorker, since this was a place apparently made up mostly of aliens.

She and Gideon began to meet frequently. He sometimes came into Zabar's twice a day instead of once, anxious, though trying not to show his feelings too conspicuously, that she was not taking sufficient care of herself.

"You don't eat enough."

"I eat like a horse," she told him, laughing.

"I never see you eat."

"You sound like Konstantin. He worries about me too."

"He should – you work much too hard."

"I'm used to it." She shrugged. "I like it."

"But you hardly get any sleep."

"I don't need much sleep."

Gideon called her Maddy, as everyone except Konstantin and Rudi, who still called her Maggy, did. He loved the sound of her French name when she spoke it, but hated the way it sounded when he did. The only foreign language Gideon spoke with any fluency was Spanish, which he needed on an almost daily basis in his working life. He remembered how much he had enjoyed the varying cadences, timbres and accents that had overwhelmed him during his three years' service in Europe in the forties, but he'd never had much aptitude for foreign languages and if he'd learned any French at that time, or at school, he had long since forgotten it.

"I wish I spoke French."

"You always forget that I'm Swiss, not French." She laughed. "You try listening when Rudi and I get going in *Schwyzertütsch* – even Germans have trouble understanding a word of that."

"Still, it seems unfair you having to make all the effort."

"I love speaking English. All those classes at Columbia, yet I think one week at Zabar's taught me almost more. So many interesting people and all with one common language."

"What's that?"

"Food."

Madeleine felt comfortable with Gideon. She knew that he understood that she did not want a lover, that she could only contemplate friendship, and so she was able to open up to him, to share her past and to let him into her present. She told him almost everything: about her family in Zurich, about Amadeus and Irina, about her father and the pleasure Alexander would have experienced over meeting a real-life private investigator in Manhattan, a fantasy come true for him. She even shared Antoine with him – though only the good times, the joy, for no one in the world could, or should have to comprehend what the bad times had meant to her.

Gideon grew increasingly fascinated. At the outset of their friendship, he had been tempted to treat her much as Miriam, his mother, had treated the tiny Steuben ornaments that her husband had given her on major anniversaries. But gradually, he was learning how much stronger Maddy was than she looked. She was a woman built on and around emotions. Her heart and soul ruled her every action, even now, when she had tightly shut down the part of herself that she had given to Antoine Bonnard. And yet Gideon sometimes fancied that beneath her soft skin and flesh, Maddy was made of fine, malleable steel.

Both his parents were dead, but Gideon still had his two sisters, though Marianne, the oldest, had moved with her family to Chicago and Abigail had settled in Philadelphia. He had a yearning, which he knew he had to quell, to introduce them to Maddy, to tell them that here was the woman he loved, the girl he'd waited for for so many years, but as it was, he had to make do with taking Madeleine and Valentin to the house of his uncle and aunt who still lived in Greenville, over in New Jersey.

They went for tea one Sunday, Madeleine having taken the afternoon off work. Gideon observed his Uncle's Mort's faded eyes twinkling with delight as he caught his first glimpse of Maddy, and he saw his Aunt Ruth's initial, ill-concealed alarm, and knew that it was because after decades of not being shown a single girlfriend, he had brought them a slip of a girl with a child, a foreign woman and a *shikse* to boot.

"Gideon has told me so much about you," Madeleine said, when they first sat down, awkwardly, in the sitting room.

"That's more than he told us about you." Ruth Tyler's mouth pursed a little in spite of her wish to be polite.

"But of course," Madeleine said easily. "I am just a friend – you are family."

"Just good friends, huh?" Mort Tyler enquired, and winked.

"Very much so, Monsieur."

"Please call me Mort, won't you?"

"With pleasure."

"How old is your little boy?" Ruth asked.

"I am four," Valentin answered for himself. He was

growing up to be effortlessly bilingual, and though once he began to spend more time away from the constant influence of his mother and Zeleyev, Valentin's English would inevitably become more relaxed and American, as yet it reflected the slightly stilted and accented English that Madeleine spoke.

Ruth Tyler served tea, poured too much milk into Madeleine's cup, but Madeleine drank it as if it were nectar and accepted a second cup.

"Oh my goodness," she said, suddenly.

"What's wrong?" Ruth asked.

"Your cheesecake."

"What's the matter with it?"

"Nothing at all – *au contraire*." Madeleine laid her fork beside the huge slab of cake on her plate. "Gideon told me that you made the finest in the world, but I confess I didn't believe him, until now."

"It's an old Jewish recipe," Ruth said. "Do you bake, Maddy?"

"I'm afraid not."

"Gideon tells us that you sing," Mort said.

"A little," Madeleine said modestly.

"She was taught by a cantor," Gideon added mischievously, aware that her teacher had been Gaston Strasser, but enjoying teasing his aunt.

"You're not serious?" Ruth looked disbelieving.

"Sure I am, Aunt Ruth. The Levis were Maddy's best friends in Paris, and Noah Levi was a great influence on her."

"Really." Ruth Tyler's eyes brightened, and she turned to Madeleine with new interest. "Tell me, my dear, your late husband – God rest his soul – was he Jewish by any chance?"

"No, Madame, he was not." Madeleine felt almost apologetic.

"But this Levi was really a cantor?"

"Most definitely."

"That's something at least." Ruth lifted her two-tiered cake dish. "More cheesecake, my dear?"

Valentin had warmed to the big American right away. Gideon knew how to play with the child for hours on end, never growing bored, never tiring of the games. Rudi Gabriel liked Tyler, too. So far as he was concerned, any decent man who cared so transparently for his sister could not be anything other than good news. Only Zeleyev had reservations.

"Do you have to spend so much time with this man?"

"With Gideon?"

"Who else do you see in what little spare time you have? Of course I mean Gideon."

"What's wrong with him?" Madeleine asked mildly.

"You have nothing in common with him, for one thing."

"What else?"

"He's a detective. He leads a sordid life."

"Nonsense."

"You think it's glamorous to be a private detective, *ma chère*?"

"About as glamorous as standing behind a counter all day long and coming home smelling of smoked fish. Gideon certainly doesn't think it's glamorous, and neither do I."

"You're being deliberately obtuse," Zeleyev complained. "I can accept, against my will, that there are things one sometimes has to do to survive in this world –"

"Unsuitable things?" Madeleine suggested. "Like being a housemaid, or waiting on tables or serving in a shop?"

"But this man is much older – how old is Tyler, by the way?"

"Forty-six."

"*Voilà*. A middle-aged man who did not have to run away from home at the age of sixteen, without qualifications. He must have had opportunities to do something useful with his life."

"He was a policeman, Konstantin." She saw him grimace. "And if he hadn't joined the police force, he would probably have become a tailor, like his father. Would that have impressed you more? I doubt it."

"You reinforce my point, Madeleine. Gideon Tyler is an unimpressive man – certainly not a man for you."

"He's a friend, not my lover."

Madeleine was trying to remain patient, though it was sometimes difficult with Konstantin. She'd come up against his deeply ingrained snobbery many times before, and usually she was able to laugh it off, but occasionally he went too far.

"I know you're too obstinate to accept help from your brother," Zeleyev continued. "But you could at least mix with his friends. A sensible, wealthy Wall Street broker, perhaps – now that might be suitable. Not ideal, but practical."

"Now there's a type I would have nothing in common with."

"You get along with Rudi."

"He's my brother, Konstantin."

Zeleyev bit down his retort, knowing it would be unwise to continue at this time. Madeleine had begun, lately, to speak of finding her own apartment. All her hard work, and paying the unrealistically low rent that was all he would accept from her, meant that she would have no problems in signing a lease. The prospect haunted him. His beautiful, headstrong girl, fending for herself in some mediocre little place, probably not much better than the pitiful home she'd shared with her husband. And without him to guide her. The thought made him shudder.

"Gideon is an interesting, intelligent, kind man," Madeleine was saying. "And he understands me very well."

"How can he possibly understand a woman of your class?"

"Konstantin, are you trying to make me angry?" she enquired.

"Perish the thought, *ma chère*," he said, and fell silent, at the same time planning to refuse to babysit the next time she wanted to see Tyler. It was bad enough that she saw him every day at work, but Zeleyev was certainly not going to encourage her to spend any more time than necessary with a failed Jewish policeman whose great-grandparents had probably lived in some isolated Russian *shtetl*.

On Wednesday afternoon, a few weeks later, when Madeleine left Zabar's at the end of her morning shift, Gideon was waiting for her outside, leaning against the open door of his car.

"Jump right in."

Madeleine laughed. "I hardly need a ride home – this walk is almost the only exercise I get."

"I'm not taking you home," Gideon said.

"But I have to go."

"You have a half-hour, don't you?" Gideon saw her round to the passenger side, then got in and started the engine. "Please, Maddy – I wouldn't ask if it wasn't important."

"Okay," she said. "Where are we going?"

"It's a surprise."

He stopped the car on Central Park West, outside one of the impressive old buildings that overlooked the park. "This is it."

"This is what?"

"Come on."

"Where?"

"To see the surprise."

* * *

Madeleine watched, bemused, as Gideon spoke for a few moments to the smartly uniformed doorman, before taking her hand and whisking her into one of three elevators and up to the twelfth floor.

"This is it," he said, outside apartment 12C.

"That's what you said outside."

Gideon unlocked the door. "This really is it."

He drew her through into a dark, cool hallway.

"Whose apartment is this?" Madeleine asked.

"Mine," Gideon said.

"Yours?"

"Apparently."

"Could you elaborate a little?" she asked mildly.

Gideon closed the door. "It seems I've been left an apartment."

"This apartment."

"You've got it."

"How do you mean 'left'?" She looked concerned. "Has somebody died?"

"A client." He watched her face in the dim light. "I know. I felt the same way – it's pretty hard to take in, isn't it?" He opened a set of double doors. "Come and take a look around. I need to know what you think."

They were in a large living room, huge by Manhattan standards, dark as the entrance hall because of the shutters blocking out the light, and musty smelling from lack of use, but as Gideon threw open the shutters and the afternoon sun streamed through the windows, Madeleine stared around, seeing a fine parquet floor, splendid cornices, an extraordinarily handsome marble fireplace and, looking up, an exquisite chandelier.

"*Dieu*," she said, softly.

"That's what I thought." Gideon smiled. "It's all like this – stylish as hell. Except for the mothballs."

"Mothballs?"

"In every closet and tucked in little bags in all the

drapes. My mother used to keep them in all our drawers – it wasn't until I left home that I realized all sweaters didn't have to smell of camphor or whatever they're made of."

"So who was this client?" Madeleine was intrigued.

"An old lady named Lilian Becker. I took on a case for her a long time – ten, maybe eleven years ago."

"What did you do for her?"

"I traced her daughter." Gideon shrugged. "It was nothing special, Maddy, not even really a missing persons case. More of a simple estrangement. They'd fallen out over something a few years earlier, and the old lady wanted to see her daughter again."

"And you found her?"

"In Florida." He remembered the details. "In Miami Beach. She wasn't too keen on the idea, either of my tracking her down, or of seeing her mother again. I guess I talked her into it."

"Was that part of the job?"

"Maybe not, but it wasn't all that hard. And it wasn't as if Mrs Becker hadn't paid me. The going rate plus expenses. She was happy, I was happy." Gideon paused. "Now it seems that the reunion with her daughter transformed her life. I thought maybe she was sick at the time, wanting to make her peace before she died. But she lived until a month ago, though her lawyer told me she was in the hospital for a long time before that."

"It's wonderful that she left you something," Madeleine said, "but a whole apartment? Especially one as grand as this." She thought. "What about the daughter? Isn't she angry that her mother didn't leave it to her?"

"According to the lawyer the daughter gets a house someplace up in Massachusetts, and a villa in southern France. Apparently, she doesn't mind about me – she knows the way her mother felt, she doesn't like New York and she wouldn't want the hassles of holding the lease."

"If it's a rental," Madeleine asked, "how could Mrs Becker leave it to you?"

"Hardly anyone owns their apartment in this city, Maddy. Lilian Becker left me a five-year lease with an option to renew, but because she knew I'd never be able to afford the rent, she even set up a trust fund to pay for it. The lawyer said it's uncommon for a landlord to honour that kind of bequest, but in this case she was on good terms with whoever does own this building, and it's all kosher." He paused. "It's pretty fantastic, I know."

"I think it's wonderful. When will you move in?"

"I won't."

"Why not?"

"Can you see me here? All alone, with Village habits – with my sax?"

"The walls look solid."

Gideon took a moment before speaking.

"I thought that, if you liked it –" He hesitated. "I thought you and Valentin might feel like moving in."

Startled, Madeleine felt her cheeks grow hot. "I couldn't afford this kind of rent."

"Rent free. The trust, remember?"

The silence seemed to go on forever.

"You still don't know me very well, Gideon, do you?"

"Oh Christ," he said, dismayed. "I've offended you."

"No." She shook her head. "I'm touched, not at all offended." She paused. "But I wouldn't dream of accepting, even if I could. Which I can't."

"How come?"

She was still pink with embarrassment. "I would have called you this evening to tell you, only you turned up and –"

"Tell me what?"

"I found an apartment. I went to see it early this morning – I'm due to sign the lease later on today. We shook hands."

"Where is it?" Gideon sounded deflated.

"West Seventy-fourth near Amsterdam. Two bedrooms. I'm sorry."

"Why should you be?"

Madeleine chose her words carefully. "I don't want to have things given to me on a plate for ever, Gideon. I've been so dependent on Konstantin, in so many ways since we came to America. I don't know if I would have survived without his help, but I've been ready for a place of my own for a long while – I just dragged my feet because I knew he'd be upset. But it's time."

"I understand, Maddy. It's just that when this came up –"

"You wanted to help." She paused again. "You're a wonderful friend, and I love you for thinking of us. But I need my independence – not that you wouldn't want me to be independent if we were to accept, but I would feel that I was –" She faltered, finding it hard to express herself.

"Freeloading?"

"*Exactement.*"

"In that case," Gideon said a little wryly, "I'll just have to sublet and become a landlord." He shook his head. "I've never really approved of easy money, but I guess I could get used to it."

"At least it'll be easier for you to visit us whenever you want," Madeleine said, knowing that Gideon was fully aware that Konstantin did not encourage his visits.

"How soon can I see your place?"

Madeleine smiled up at him. "I do have to go home to get Valentin – but would you like to come with us when I sign the lease? I'd value your advice."

"I'd be honoured."

Madeleine and Valentin moved into their new home in the first week of 1967. Their apartment was on the third floor of an attractive brownstone house on West Seventy-fourth Street opposite the Calhoun School. Amsterdam Avenue was just a few buildings away and Zeleyev lived only three blocks or so west, but the proximity of her new home had not prevented the Russian from complaining vociferously in his attempts to talk Madeleine out of it.

"You should have looked for something in one of those buildings on West End," he told her. "They have class, they are solid, they have doormen."

"They cost more."

"But the street is broad, much lighter, much safer."

"I get the sun all afternoon," Madeleine said. "And both Gideon and Rudi have checked it out at night, and they think it's as safe as anywhere."

"Not as safe as Riverside Drive."

"I couldn't stay with you for ever, Konstantin," she reminded him gently. "Valentin is growing, he needs space. So do I, and so do you."

"I need you."

"But you're not losing me. You never could."

"I'm not so sure," Zeleyev said morosely.

Valentin loved the apartment. He was a normal, lively and energetic child, but ever since he could remember, he had never had any space in which he could play. Of course, Maman took him out to different parks and let him loose in playgrounds, but in Konstantin's apartment he had always had to be careful in case he broke something. Now he had a room of his own, and Maman let him play everywhere, unless she had company or unless it was time for him to go to bed. That was almost the only time they argued.

"But I'm not tired, Maman," he said on the nights when she was home to tuck him in. He wasn't telling an untruth, for it seemed to him that he had even more of what Gideon called 'zip' after it got dark.

"Just the same," Madeleine told him, "it's late and you need your sleep."

"But I won't sleep. I'll just lie here and fidget."

"Then I'll read to you a while."

Valentin settled back against the cotton pillow case and sheets he'd helped his mother pick out in Macy's. "Konstantin says that I'm a night owl, like you, Maman."

"Even night owls have to sleep."

"And when Uncle Rudi's here, he lets me stay up till just before you get home." He beamed up at her.

"Does he now?"

"He says that when you were a little girl, you were always in trouble for not going to bed at night."

"I always went to bed," Madeleine said. "I had no choice. My mother was very strict with me. Even if I wasn't at all sleepy, I had to lie still and do as I was told."

"But you weren't sleepy, Maman, were you?"

"Not always, no."

"Then you know how I feel."

Madeleine ruffled his hair. "Yes, *chéri*, I know."

"Maman?"

"Yes, sweetheart."

"Could we have some flowers in the apartment, please? I mean, ones in pots, like a pretend garden?"

"Of course, *chéri*, that's a lovely idea."

"Maman?"

"Yes."

"Could we have a TV set, please?"

"No, my darling. Not for a while."

"Why not?"

"Too expensive."

"Maman?"

Madeleine raised an admonishing finger. "Last question."

"Would you let Gideon take us to Coney Island? He said it's great, but I have to ask you. Can we go?"

"Yes, of course, *chéri*, but I don't know when. I'm working so much of the time."

"Couldn't we go next Sunday? Gideon says there's a whole park just for children."

"Sundays are difficult. I work at Zabar's all day, you know that."

Valentin's face fell again. "I get bored when you're at work, Maman."

"I know."

Driven by guilt, Madeleine took the next Sunday off so that Gideon could take them, as he'd told Valentin he would, to Coney Island. They went on the Sea Beach train to Stillwell Avenue – the 'right way' to go, Gideon insisted – all the way to the south-west tip of Brooklyn. A good few hours were spent at Ward's Kiddyland Park so that Valentin could take all the miniature rides his heart desired, after which they strolled along the great boardwalk, the wind lashing their cheeks, Valentin whooping with excitement as he ran from side to side, gazing at the soaring seagulls over the ocean and at the huge, noisy carnival on the land side. They went to the beach, took off their shoes, and kicked around in the sand and still-freezing surf, Madeleine clutching Valentin's left hand and Gideon his right, in case his exuberance lured him further into the dangerous waters.

"He needs friends his own age," Gideon said to Madeleine, later, as they sat on a bench and watched Valentin, hands and feet still sticky from cotton candy, playing happily in a sandpit. "He's such a plucky little kid." He chuckled. "I think he'd have gone on a roller-coaster if you'd let him, and if he'd thought it would give us a good time."

"But he spends all his time with grown-ups," Madeleine said, and her glowing eyes clouded over.

"He's five now, Maddy – he has to go to school."

"I know it – I think about it all the time. But how?"

She had deliberately put off thinking about the dangerous instability of her legal status in the United States. She had entered originally as a visitor, and had been working for more than two years without telling her employers that she was not entitled to work. Lately, it had troubled her more and more, but she was at a loss to know what to do about it.

"You have to do something soon, Maddy," Gideon went on. "Or one of these days, someone will report that there's a little boy living here who never goes out to school."

Madeleine knew that he was right. Rudi had told her repeatedly, Konstantin had nagged at her, the daily sight of her bright, active little boy who needed the stimulus of education and his contemporaries, had torn at her. Yet afraid of change, frightened that if she made any kind of official application she might stir up a hornet's nest, she had buried her head in the sand, hoping that the problem would magically resolve itself.

"I have a solution," Gideon said suddenly.

"What kind of solution?"

"Let's look at all the alternatives first, okay? Even if you were willing to work for your family's bank, which you're not, there isn't really a single banking job for which you could convincingly pretend to be qualified. So to make that work, you would have to appeal to your mother to set something up for you."

"Not unless Valentin's life depended on it," Madeleine said stiffly.

"The second choice is for you to throw yourself on the mercy of the Department of Immigration. They could be sympathetic, or they could just be ticked off because you deliberately waited so long."

"Do you think they might deport us?" she asked quietly.

"I doubt it." Gideon suppressed a shudder. "But I for one am not prepared to take that risk."

"What other alternatives are there?"

"Only one that comes with a guarantee."

"For heaven's sake, what is it?" Madeleine was avid. "Tell me."

"Marriage," Gideon said. "To an American citizen." He wanted to sound calm and relaxed, but some of the tension he felt had crept into his tone in spite of himself. "A marriage of convenience."

"Are you joking?"

"I'm willing and able." He felt himself reddening. "Obviously, we'd live apart – it would simply be an arrangement between friends." He waited for her to speak, and when she said nothing, he floundered on. "Maddy, I just care too damned much about you and Valentin to see you forced to rip up the roots you've worked so hard to put down."

Madeleine was too stunned to speak. She forgot where they were, forgot for a few moments even to keep an eye out for Valentin. She knew that such marriages had been commonplace in wartime, but now? It was so – dishonest. And she was still Antoine's wife, in her heart and soul. She hadn't been tempted even to look at another man –

"It would only be a piece of paper," Gideon said, guessing her thoughts. "It has nothing to do with a real marriage."

Madeleine steadied herself. "What about you?" she asked. "How could it be fair to you, Gideon? You might fall in love, you might want to marry again – no girlfriend on earth would understand."

"It's unlikely to happen, but if it did, then – well, we'd get a divorce."

"It's insane."

"I don't think so."

She looked up into his face, such a good, strong face.

"Many people have done kind things for me, Gideon, but this is the kindest, the most unselfish thing anyone has ever been willing to do, and I love you dearly for it."

"Well then?"

A seagull swooped overhead, and Valentin laughed.

"But it's crazy."

"Only a little crazy."

"And impossible."

They were married at City Hall on the seventh day of April. Rudi and his friend, Michael Campbell, a twenty-six-year-old Wall Street broker with whom Rudi had shared his apartment for nine months, were witnesses, while Konstantin, who had expressed outrage at what he had called their 'charade', nonetheless prepared a luncheon at his apartment to celebrate, he emphasized, Madeleine's new legitimacy, not her marriage.

Her name, on all official documents, became Mrs Gideon Tyler. In the clubs where she continued to sing, gaining increasing popularity and longer spots, she remained Maddy Gabriel. In her heart, she was still Madeleine Bonnard.

Now that he was attending a public school, known uninspiringly as PS 87, in walking distance of home, Valentin – known by his new friends as Val – was thriving, but the marriage of convenience seemed to have driven a wedge between Gideon and Madeleine. She felt it wise to call upon her friend less often, to make sure that he never felt crowded or hemmed in by her or by her son. She couldn't bear to think of ruining his social life. The moment he met someone he really liked, she told Gideon repeatedly, he must promise to tell her, and they would keep well out of his way – and if it became serious, if he wanted a *real* marriage, she would grant him a divorce without a moment's hesitation.

There were times when Gideon felt that he couldn't stand it. He knew that he was, perhaps, too old for Maddy, knew that she had never considered him as anything other than a friend, yet every time she even mentioned the word 'divorce', he felt as if he'd been dealt a blow to his solar plexus. He, too, gave her more space than before, signed official forms as her husband, went with her to Valentin's school when necessary, but never, otherwise, made reference to their marriage in case it upset her. He flung himself into work, took on a heavier case load than he had for years, tracked scores of faithless husbands and wives, took some cases from a criminal attorney, becoming a bodyguard for witnesses needing extra protection, and hunted high and low in and out of New York State for missing persons. He lost his appetite and lost weight, worked out at Gleason's Gym in the Bronx like a man possessed and forced himself not to bring Valentin gifts more than once a month.

Rudi Gabriel knew that Gideon was in love with his sister, and so did Konstantin Zeleyev. But Gideon made Rudi swear on a Bible that he would not tell Maddy, and Zeleyev would not have told her if Tyler had held a gun to his head and begged him to.

15

In September, Madeleine's career took a sharp upturn when a manager named Joey T. Cutter heard her singing her regular spot at Lila's, a supper club on Second Avenue where for the past four months she had been singing three nights a week. She sang a half-dozen songs twice nightly, and during one of them she left the microphone and the little stage and strolled from table to table singing for every guest as if they were her sole reason for being there.

Cutter, impressed by the husky sincerity of her voice and by her beauty, left his card with a note summoning her to his office in the Brill Building.

"You wanna be a star, or you just wanna sing?" he asked as soon as she'd sat down, nervously, facing him across his desk.

"Truthfully?"

"Absolutely."

Madeleine looked at him and liked him. "Truthfully, it never entered my head to be a star. I've been told that's wrong, and perhaps it is, but all I ever wanted was to sing." She smiled at him. "And if it was possible to sing to make my living, then to me that was almost a miracle."

"You're married?"

"Yes."

"Your husband likes you singing?"

"Very much."

"You got any kids?"

"I have one son."

"You got any problems with travelling?"

"That would depend on where I was going, and for how long."

"Would your husband look after the kid for a week at a time, maybe?"

Madeleine looked at him steadily. "It would depend on the circumstances, Mr Cutter."

The manager picked up a small cigar and chewed on the end. "How about if I could get you a booking or three in cabaret, Miss Gabriel? In places like Boston, or Miami – even Las Vegas, maybe?" He paused. "How would those circumstances grab you?"

"It sounds very exciting." Her stomach was leaping.

"I'm only talking about support acts, you understand?"

"Of course, Mr Cutter."

"But then you wouldn't care about that, would you," he said ironically, "since you don't especially want to be a star?"

"Not at all," she agreed readily.

"You're French, right?"

"I'm from Switzerland."

"Swiss, huh?" He thought. "We'd bill you as French, anyway – it goes better with your style." Cutter paused. "Have you ever cut a disc?"

"A disc?"

"A record, you know. Have you ever made a recording?"

"Not yet," she said. "Do you think I could?"

"Sure, why not?" Cutter chewed on his cigar. "We're talking demo discs, Miss Gabriel. I don't just manage singers, I look after songwriters too, and what could happen is you record a demonstration tape of a particular writer's material and that's what the record companies hear." He shrugged. "Sometimes what happens is that an artist cuts the actual disc that's going to be marketed, and someone remembers that the singer on the demo sounded better.

Then, if we're lucky, you get a contract." He paused again. "But don't hold your breath."

Madeleine, never having had either an agent or manager, was delighted when her earnings increased, even in a few of the clubs she'd worked for two years or more. Though none of the cabaret spots Joey Cutter had mentioned had yet materialized, she had already cut several demonstration discs, and Cutter, who loved her style, was encouraging her to work on it, developing her natural flair, teaching her to target an audience and to tailor her appearance and her act accordingly.

"Can't I just be me?" she asked him once.

"Sure you can be you, just more so."

When Madeleine and Gideon had been legally bound for just over a year, Konstantin Zeleyev, visiting her one evening in her tiny dressing room at Lila's, suggested that it might be about time for her to go to Paris to collect *Eternité*.

"You are legally free to come and go as you please now, *ma chère*, and frankly it pains me to think of our beautiful treasure gathering dust in a vault."

Madeleine wavered. She had loved it, too, and wanted to see it again, yet the world in which she had last glimpsed it seemed a million years distant, part of the past that she had put behind her.

"I don't know," she said. "It's safe there."

"It could be just as safe in a vault in New York," Zeleyev pointed out. "But at least we could see it from time to time."

The matter of the sculpture's great value troubled Madeleine in another way, too. She had never seen her grandfather's creation as anything other than a superb expression of his love for Irina, but once it was in her possession, the pressure on her to consider selling it was bound to increase, for how else would she ever be able to repay her debts, and how else would she be able to give Valentin all that she longed to?

"I'm not sure," she said.

"I don't understand."

She tried to explain. "What I really want to do with *Eternité*," she said, "is what Opi might have wanted me to do."

"Amadeus never thought that far ahead," Zeleyev said gently. "It was always enough for him to know that he had played his part in its creation. He told me once, I remember, that he didn't care what happened to it after he was gone."

"But he thought of it as a memorial."

"To Irina, of course. As did I."

"And surely to the life they shared together, in Switzerland." Madeleine hesitated, hating to hurt Konstantin. "I can't see the point of bringing it to America, not yet at least."

Zeleyev's expression darkened. "I've never known you to be dishonest," he said.

She was surprised. "I don't think I'm being dishonest now."

"Certainly you are." He looked grim. "What you really feel, *ma chère*, is fear. You cannot bear to go back to Paris, even for a short visit. Paris is the city in which you were at your happiest, and the city which caused you terrible pain." He paused. "You are simply afraid."

Madeleine could not argue with him.

"Is Konstantin quite well?" Gideon asked her a few days later, dropping by at Zabar's where Madeleine still worked six mornings each week.

"I think so. Why do you ask?"

"I don't mean in a physical sense."

"What then?" She looked concerned. "I didn't know you had even seen him."

"He's been coming to the gym. To Gleason's."

Madeleine shrugged. "He's always been concerned with keeping himself in good shape. All the time we were living with him, I never knew him to miss a day's exercise." She smiled. "If it was decent weather he often went to the park, and if it rained or snowed he skipped inside the apartment or did those terrible sit-ups."

"Would you say he was fanatical?"

"On the verge."

"Well, he's over the verge now," Gideon said dryly. "The man is over seventy, but I could swear he's trying to compete with me, Maddy. No, I know it sounds unlikely, but if you saw him, you'd understand. Gleason's is mainly a fighter's gym – I need to know I can take care of myself, but it's totally nuts for him to even be there."

"Is it dangerous for him?"

"God knows he's super fit for an old guy, but he's certainly pushing his luck. Jump ropes, okay, but if I use the punchbag, Konstantin uses it right after me – if I move on to the speedbag, so does he. If I pull weights, I've seen him checking to make sure he's pulling the same as me." Gideon shook his head. "The really weird part is that he can do it all, and Maddy, I'm in pretty good shape myself."

Madeleine noticed Murray Klein looking over in their direction. "I need to get back to work," she said. "I don't really know what to say."

"I've always known Konstantin didn't like me. And it's been worse since we did the marriage thing." He scratched his head. "Maybe I should cool it at the gym myself, take it easier."

"Let him think he's worn you out, you mean?"

"He's important to you, Maddy, I know that. I don't want to see him get hurt, and I certainly don't want to feel responsible for giving him a heart attack."

"I'd say that I would talk to him," Madeleine said,

"only I know there wouldn't be any point. When Konstantin is set upon something, nothing and no one can sway him."

Just over a week later, Zeleyev invited Madeleine to dinner.

"At my place, on Tuesday – you don't work Tuesday nights, do you?"

"Do you want me early with Valentin, or later by myself?"

"Later, *ma chère*. Definitely later."

When Madeleine arrived, the red-walled, exotic sitting room was ablaze with candlelight, there was Krug champagne and caviar on ice, and a silver tureen of cold borscht on the table.

"*Mais comme c'est beau!*" she exclaimed in delight. "What are we celebrating, Konstantin? Have I forgotten something?"

"Not at all," Zeleyev assured her. "I want you simply to relax and to enjoy yourself, two arts that I fear you may be in danger of losing." He opened the bottle. "A little champagne?"

He was in an oddly elated, keyed-up mood. He poured champagne for her, while he drank shots of ice-cold vodka, refusing absolutely to explain his reason for what still undoubtedly seemed, to Madeleine, to be a festivity of some sort.

"Valentin sends you a big kiss," she said. "He was a little put out not to be invited, but then he became very grown-up and said that I deserved a night off." She sniffed at the air. "What's cooking? It smells wonderful."

"A salmon Kulebiaka – I hope you're hungry, *ma belle*."

"Ravenous."

"Then let us begin."

They ate the caviar first – Beluga served with minced

egg and onion, lemon and black bread – and then Zeleyev ladled the borscht into soup plates, his manner flourishing and posed, serving Madeleine almost like a character actor playing the role of maître d'hôtel.

"Is it good?" he asked, sitting opposite her.

"Marvellous."

He ate little, continuing to drink his iced vodka and watching Madeleine like an alert, intent, green-eyed fox. She found herself glancing at his immaculate hair and moustache, as neatly combed as ever, and wondering for the first time whether Konstantin dyed his hair, for surely it would have gone white long ago otherwise. She had a sudden vision of him, before the bathroom mirror, the tint thick on his scalp, carefully brushing it over his top lip –

"You're smiling, *ma chère*," Zeleyev said. "That's good."

Madeleine blushed a little. "You're hardly drinking any borscht."

"I'm saving myself. We have Vareniki for dessert, with cherry sauce."

"You're not usually so intensely Russian," Madeleine said.

"This is not a usual evening."

"But why not?" she asked again, but Zeleyev only raised his index finger to his lips in a gesture of secrecy and still gave nothing away. He poured more champagne for her, swallowed down still more vodka himself, and brought the main course from the kitchen.

Madeleine could not recall ever having been uneasy in Konstantin's company, but as the evening progressed, a strange sense of disquietude grew inside her. All her attempts at ordinary conversation faltered, her appetite, already diminished by the richness of the caviar and soup, falling away altogether as she watched the vodka flush heighten on her old friend's cheeks and felt the tension increasing in him, too.

"I'm not sure if I can manage the Vareniki," she said lightly. "It was all so good."

"No matter."

"Are you unwell, Konstantin?" she asked, gently. "You've eaten almost nothing."

"Never better."

He rose, to clear the table.

"Let me help you," Madeleine said, standing up.

"No," Zeleyev said. "You sit."

She sat.

When he returned from the kitchen, he took a small, black velvet box from his pocket, and placed it on the table before her. His hands, speckled with liver spots, were trembling.

"Instead of dessert."

Madeleine looked at him. "My birthday is in December," she said.

"I know that very well," he answered. "I know everything about you, Magdalena Alexandrovna."

"What is it?" She tried to keep her voice light-hearted, but she heard its quiver betray her. "This evening has been great enough, Konstantin. There's no need for presents, as well." Her stomach had tautened with a curious dread. "Besides, I have nothing for you."

Zeleyev, standing beside her, leaned over and opened the box. A gold ring lay on a satin cushion within, set with a large, rich green emerald.

"The stone was left to me by Irina Valentinovna," he said quietly. "It is very fine, a Colombian emerald."

Madeleine stared down at the ring, her cheeks blazing hot. She could not speak, did not know what to say. With a sudden, fiercely impulsive movement, Zeleyev grasped both her hands and went down on his knees at her side.

She felt a monstrous desire to burst into laughter, but forced it back down.

"Marry me, *ma chère,*" he said, his voice strangled.

Her mind was playing tricks. It was not possible for Konstantin to have said what she thought she had heard. She remembered Gideon's concern over his behaviour, his anxiety that the old man had been competing with him in some bizarre way, and she realized now that he had been right. But how could that be? This was her lifelong friend, Opi's friend, her father's trusted confidant –

"I want you to be my wife, Madeleine," he said, and looking at his face, she knew that he was completely, intensely serious.

"Please," she murmured, still dazed. "Get up, Konstantin."

"Not until you answer me."

His feelings erupted in a torrent of words. "I loved you from the instant I first saw you – that exquisite small girl at the top of the stairs in Zurich – then later, when you were half-grown. Don't you remember, Madeleine, how it was between us, from the very beginning? How you trusted me, instinctively. And they were sound instincts, wiser by far than any that came later to confuse you –"

"Konstantin, please –"

"Of course my love for you then was for a child. You were purity and innocence personified, my little Maggy, but I knew, as no one else would have guessed, that you were destined for great things. I waited for you to grow up into womanhood, I thirsted to see what would become of you – and when I saw you again in Paris, when you were seventeen and just the loveliest, most enchanting creature, that was when I fell *in* love with you."

He still held her hands in his own. Madeleine, aghast, tried to pull them away, but his grip was tight.

"I don't want to hear this, Konstantin," she begged him.

"But you must – it's time for you to hear it." He was unstoppable. "I knew that you were much too young, of course, that if I had spoken then you would have been shocked, and I couldn't bear to risk our friendship. And then the next time we met, you had already married Antoine."

"You were jealous of Antoine?" Madeleine's whisper was incredulous, the betrayal she felt was nauseating.

"Don't be so outraged, *ma belle*. I accepted that I had lost you forever – when he fell ill, I wept for you. I wanted him well again, for your sake – that was why I urged you to come to America, so that he might be cured and you would be happy again." He paused for breath. "And after he died, I understood your grief as no one else could have done, and I knew that you needed time to recover."

Madeleine's horror magnified. All those months, when she had lived with her child in his home, in his apartment, sleeping in his bed for weeks, grieving for Antoine, and Konstantin had wanted her, had *lusted* after her –

"I knew that I was already old," he went on, "that I was wasting precious time, but I had always understood the meaning of *qualité*. A single year of joy and fulfilment with you would be worth twenty without you."

For an instant she felt dizzy. He still held her hands, and she looked down into his face. She had never considered his age, had never regarded him as an old man, but now she saw every one of his seventy-six years – every wrinkle of loose, pale old skin, the sparseness of the meticulously kempt, incongruously still-red hair – and she knew that all the rigorous hours at the gymnasium had not just been in competition with Gideon, the younger man. They had been for her.

She made herself speak, her voice shaking badly. "You forget that I'm married again, Konstantin." She wanted to stop him without hurting him more than was necessary. "I'm Gideon's wife."

He dismissed the fact, tossed it aside. "Divorce is an everyday event in America, and this was not a true marriage."

"It's kept us here, made us Americans."

"And if you wish to stay here, divorce won't change that." He clasped her hands even more fervently. "But if you marry me, we could go anywhere. I would give you everything I possess. I could show you wondrous things, Madeleine. We could go to Paris together – I would be there to protect you against the past. We could collect *Eternité*, together, as we were meant to –"

She pulled her hands free at last, but Zeleyev, swift as lightning, reached up and held her face, drew it down to his and kissed her. Taken off guard, Madeleine tried to escape, but his hands were clamped over her cheeks and his soft, old, damp mouth sought her lips greedily, hungrily –

Violently, she wrenched away, jumped up from her chair, knocking it over. She was panting, the revulsion she felt naked on her face and in her tear-filled eyes.

"Madeleine, I'm sorry –" He saw what he had done.

"Don't touch me."

"Forgive me –" He struggled to his feet. "I didn't mean to – I didn't want to frighten you –"

She was searching for her bag, found it on an armchair, seized it. She could not bear to look back at him.

"Madeleine, don't go, please. I beg you –"

But she had already opened the front door and was running down the stairs, away from the apartment, away from Zeleyev, out into Riverside Drive, still running towards Seventy-second Street, towards people and traffic, towards her own home and her child, and sanity.

* * *

She seldom saw him after that night, avoided him as much as possible. With the rising sun the next morning had come a certain comprehension, a small sympathy and inevitable pity. She searched inside herself for guilt, wondering if she had ever, inadvertently, encouraged him, led him on, but she knew that she had never, not even for a second, regarded him as anyone other than her old and constant friend.

She hated to be cruel, felt her unkindness keenly, began, after a month had passed, to telephone him weekly to ascertain that he was well, but on the rare occasions that she did see him, she ensured that they were never alone. She permitted him to see Valentin periodically, in the park, or inside restaurants or cafés, but when she needed a sitter, she asked Gideon or Rudi or used girls from a reputable agency. She told no one what had happened that evening, not even her brother, for she had no wish to humiliate the old friend whose many years of true generosity could not, must not be wiped away by one night of folly.

In the autumn, Joey Cutter came through with the long-hoped-for series of cabaret bookings, taking her right through October and into November, finding her engagements at hotels in Boston, Lake Tahoe, Washington DC and Miami Beach, and in the second week of November in Las Vegas, singing on the same bill as Tony Bennett. Gideon and Rudi took turns at looking after Valentin when she travelled, so that one or other of them could fly out with Madeleine, coax her through her stage fright and cheer her on. The audiences enjoyed Maddy Gabriel, warmed to her sincerity, and by the time she got back to New York, desperate to see Valentin, Joey Cutter had signed her for another string of bookings in the New Year.

"And we'll have some more material for you to record before then," he told her. "Are you happy, honey?"

"Very happy," she said, meaning it. "But glad to be home."

"You look like a million dollars, you know."

"Thank you, Joey," she said, and kissed his cheek. "May I ask you a question?"

"Any time."

"Do you ever smoke those cigars?"

Cutter chuckled. "Once. Just once. Someone told me when I was getting started that I needed a cigar for a prop, like window dressing, you know what I mean? Only I don't like to smoke."

Madeleine laughed. "So now you just chew."

She cooked her first real Thanksgiving dinner on the twenty-eighth of that month, inviting everyone in New York who had been a good friend to her and Valentin: Murray Klein, of course, Lila Novak, who had held her spot open while Madeleine sang around the country, Joey Cutter and Betty, his wife. And, of course, Konstantin. Valentin had his best friend, Howie Blaustein, to sleep over, Rudi came with Michael, and Gideon arrived with a newcomer – a short-haired dachshund bitch named Dusty, his Thanksgiving gift for Maddy and Valentin.

"She's absolutely beautiful," Madeleine exclaimed with delight. Noah had written the previous autumn of Hexi's death from old age, and she had thought, more than a few times, how wonderful it would be to have another dachsie.

"She's the victim of a broken home," Gideon explained. "She belonged to a client of mine who hired me to prove his wife's infidelity. I'm afraid I proved it – the decree nisi was made absolute a few days ago."

"That means they got divorced," Rudi told Valentin.

"I know what it means, Uncle Rudi," the child said loftily.

"But neither of them wanted to keep Dusty?" Madeleine asked.

"The husband isn't capable of looking after a dog, and the wife wants to travel. No room in her bags for a dachshund."

"And since you don't work for me any more," Murray Klein said, "the dog struck lucky."

Dusty knew a good home when she saw one. Her previous mistress had been on a permanent diet, and no self-respecting dachshund would look twice at cottage cheese. Madeleine's apartment had a cosy, lived-in feel, and tonight it smelled of roast turkey and all the trimmings. As the evening wore on, the little dog's greatest problems were deciding which lap was the most comfortable, whose caress was the most tender and which dinner guest dropped the most white meat.

After dinner, Madeleine sang a little, and wept a little, which she had a tendency to do when she felt really content, and Gideon helped her with the washing up, and then clipped on Dusty's leash to take her out for a walk.

Madeleine went to the front door with them.

"You always know, don't you," she said softly, "what's going to make me happy?"

"I hope I do." Gideon looked down at her, and his longing for her, which had magnified instead of diminishing, threatened to engulf him. She was still his angel, and still just as unattainable, and there were moments, such as this one, when he could hardly bear it.

"Thank you," she said, "for everything."

"You're more than welcome," he answered, and felt his throat tighten.

"No hug?" she asked.

"Sure," he managed lightly.

And then she was in his arms, snug against his chest, and suddenly, what had begun, for her, as gratitude and affection turned, without warning, into something quite different. They both knew it, experienced the stir of stronger emotion and, to Madeleine at least, wholly unanticipated desire. Gideon held on, gently, understanding her fragility, terrified of frightening her away, wanting never to let her go, and Madeleine, too, just stayed where she was, motionless, until Dusty, grown impatient, gave a small, sharp bark, and they drew apart with utmost reluctance.

"You'd better take her," Madeleine murmured.

"Yes," Gideon agreed, not moving.

She smiled. "Go on."

And he went, and for another moment, Madeleine stood quite still, trying to absorb what had just occurred. A feeling of surprise, and of definite pleasure was passing through her. She searched herself, briefly, for any sense of dismay, but found none. She wondered how long he had felt that way about her, and the answer came clearly and immediately, and she realized that, for the second time, she had been unpardonably blind.

Remembering her guests, she turned around. And saw that Konstantin was standing in the doorway to the sitting room. And she realized that he had been watching them.

And though it was quickly gone, melted away swiftly and completely to be replaced by a smile, the look that she had seen on his face when she had first turned around, chilled her to the bone.

16

Eleven days after Thanksgiving – confused, painful days during which Gideon, filled with self-doubt, had stayed away from Madeleine – Valentin and the agency sitter he liked the most, a girl from Queens named Jennifer Malkevitch, were walking near the Hecksher Playground in Central Park after school, when Dusty disappeared.

The little dog had been let off the leash several times before without problems; she was content with her new life and had displayed no signs of wanting to run away, especially since Madeleine gave six-year-old Valentin small chunks of chopped liver to carry in his anorak pocket as bait, just in case. But this time, after Dusty had scampered off into some shrubbery, she had not returned, and no amount of calling or coaxing or searching could locate her. Valentin was distraught, Jennifer was guilt-ridden, and Madeleine walked the area with Rudi for more than two hours that night, and posted reward notices on every tree and lamppost for miles around, but in the long days and nights that followed, no one came forward.

Madeleine collected Valentin herself from school every afternoon for the next week, and each day, whatever the weather, they trudged though the park, and it almost broke her heart to see her son's ever hopeful face as he called the dog's name over and over again before they gave up and went home, paying a visit to the local police station on the way. Gideon, on the telephone, asked Madeleine if he should try to find a puppy before

Christmas, but Madeleine knew too much about grief. Valentin had not known Dusty long, but it had been love at first sight, and it would be a while before he was ready to give up on her.

On Tuesday afternoon, eight days before Christmas, Rudi telephoned Madeleine's apartment.

"We have a visitor," he said.

"Who?"

"Our stepfather."

A pang of dismay jolted her. "Is he alone? What does he want?"

"He's alone, and he wants to see you." Rudi paused. "He's been here for about a half-hour. He called me at the bank, and Michael and I came home. We've given him tea."

"How are they getting on?"

"Swimmingly, as you can imagine."

"God," she said. "Do I have to come?"

"Unless you want him at your place."

She was down in the Village within forty minutes, having told herself all the way downtown in the back of her cab that Stefan Julius could no longer touch her, could do her no harm. Her confidence waned the instant she saw him, sitting calmly, legs crossed elegantly, in one of Rudi and Michael's soft armchairs.

"Magdalen," he said, and rose.

"Stefan."

He looked older, but otherwise unchanged.

"It's Mrs Tyler these days, I believe."

"That's right."

"Your American period, and an American husband to match." He looked past her. "What a pity, I had hoped to meet him."

"He couldn't make it."

"Not to worry." He sat down again. "Your mother sends her love to you and to your son. Is Valentin in good health?"

"He's wonderful, thank you. How are Mother and Omi?"

"Your grandmother is growing older, as we all are. Emilie is very well." He paused. "Rudi tells me that you're quite a success. I don't think there's ever been a cabaret singer in our family before." He looked over at Michael, who was sitting beside Rudi on the sofa. "But then, there is a first time for everything."

"Sit down, Maddy," Michael said, patting the space on his other side. She sat, grateful for their presence, loathing Julius as much as ever.

"So it's Maddy, is it?" Stefan smiled. "How cosy."

"Why are you in New York?" Madeleine enquired.

"A little business. And to see you both, of course." Julius paused. "And to visit a grave."

No one spoke.

"Since we learned that your father was, rather mysteriously we felt, buried in a cemetery in Westchester County, I thought it fitting that one of us, at least, should pay our respects."

"He wants to make sure Papi is dead," Madeleine said to Rudi, white-faced but outwardly calm. "And there's really no mystery," she added to Stefan. "Our father wanted to be laid to rest near those who loved him."

"Surely none of you could have any objections?" Rudi asked.

"Neither to his death, nor to his burial," Julius answered. "To be candid, they came as almost a relief in comparison to his life."

Madeleine stood up. "Was there something else?" The anger pumping through her veins seemed to reach every nerve ending, so that she tingled with it, felt stronger because of it.

"Just one question." It came casually. "Where is the sculpture? I would enjoy seeing it after all these years."

"I don't have it," Madeleine said. "And if I did, I doubt I would allow you anywhere near it."

"Did you sell it?"

"I would never sell it."

"Do you mind telling me where it is?"

"Not at all. It's in a bank vault."

"In New York?"

"No," Rudi said, coming to stand beside his sister. "Why do you care about it?"

"Have you seen it, Rudi?"

"No."

Julius smiled. "Perhaps it doesn't exist after all."

"Why do you care, Stefan?" Madeleine repeated her brother's question. "Of course it's beautiful and perhaps even priceless – but you don't need it. With all the Gründli money, all your own blood money, why have you always been so interested in *Eternité*?"

"Curiosity," he replied. "And I have never liked to be cheated."

"No one has cheated you," Rudi said coldly.

"I like it no better when my wife is cheated."

"The only person to have been cheated is Maggy," Rudi said. "As you are well aware."

"Ah, Maggy." Julius smiled again. "The woman of ever-changing names, one year Swiss, the next French, and now American." He rose, and directed his attention back to Madeleine. "I believe that marriages of convenience are abhorred by the authorities in this country, are they not?"

"I don't know what you mean," she said coldly.

"Really?"

"I think maybe you should leave now," Rudi said.

"And you, have you paid the taxes due for avoiding your annual military duties?"

"Why don't you go back to Zurich and find out?"

"Oh, Rudi." Julius put out his right hand and stroked his stepson's blond hair. Rudi, ashen, did not flinch. "You have been a great disappointment to me, and to your mother." He looked over at Michael, still seated, and then, looking down at his own hand with distaste, he took out a handkerchief and wiped the palm.

"Get out," Rudi said.

"With pleasure."

"What a charming man," Michael said, after he had gone.

"Maggy?" Rudi looked at his sister. "Are you okay?"

"No."

"No," he agreed. "Nor am I."

Madeleine sat down, weak-kneed now that her stepfather had gone. "It's extraordinary, this effect he has on me. It's only the third time I've seen him since I left home, and he still has the power to unnerve me."

"From everything Rudi's told me about him," Michael said slowly, "Julius is used to getting everything he wants, to being dominant. The two of you have eluded him, and it drives him crazy that there's nothing he can do about it."

"I didn't like the threats over your marriage," Rudi said. "Do you think he'll make trouble?"

"Who can say?" Madeleine shook her head. "He made threats in Paris, too, but never carried them out. On the other hand, they were against the Lussacs, not against me directly."

"Maybe Gideon should move into your place for a while," Michael suggested, "in case he does start something. And if it comes to it," he added, "there'll be more than enough people to swear blind that you're the happiest married couple in town."

"I haven't even seen Gideon for two weeks," Madeleine pointed out. "How do we know Stefan hasn't been having us watched?" She smiled wryly. "Maybe one private detective spying on another."

"Let's not give him the satisfaction of making us paranoid," Rudi said stoutly. "I'd guess he came to town on business, and we were just a little sideshow."

Madeleine was silent, remembering how, in Paris, her stepfather had made her feel as if she were being spied upon. He had forced her out of the Lussacs' home, could so easily have succeeded in ruining her life then, would have done if it hadn't been for Antoine. Stefan had not succeeded then, and she would not allow him to do so now. Valentin was happily settled, and no one was going to taint that. She permitted herself, for just an instant, to think about Gideon and the moments they'd shared at Thanksgiving. She had almost begun to wonder if she might have imagined that sudden, startling intimacy; yet she knew, if she was honest with herself, that it had happened and that, given time and patience, it would again.

Unless Stefan Julius did something to destroy it.

"Maggy, you're shivering." Rudi, concerned, took her hand.

"It's so strange," she said. "When Stefan came to Paris, he only succeeded in driving me straight into Antoine's arms. In a bizarre way, he pushed me into the greatest happiness I've ever known. And yet –"

"What, darling?"

"I feel as if he's a harbinger of bad luck."

"That's bull," Michael said quickly.

"Is it?"

The next evening, Wednesday evening, at a quarter past eight, shortly after Madeleine had left home to go to Lila's, Jennifer Malkevitch was reading Valentin one last bedtime story in the vain hope that the child, who existed without any apparent ill-effects on much less sleep than the average six-year-old, might doze off.

The street door buzzer sounded.

Jennifer stood up and put down the book. "Are we expecting anyone, Val?'

"If it's Santa, he's early."

"I'd better go tell him to come back next Wednesday." At the bedroom door, she looked back. "You stay put, young man."

"Sure, Jen." Valentin picked up his book. "Can I finish this?"

The buzzer sounded again.

"Keep your shirt on."

Jennifer Malkevitch picked up the receiver from the wall-mounted intercom in the hall.

"Who is it?"

She listened for a moment, pushed the release button and then opened the front door.

There were still seven days to go before Christmas, but the caller was carrying two giftwrapped packages, one large, the other small. Valentin, in pyjamas, came out of his room, gave a squeal of pleasure and ran to bestow a hug.

"Is that for me?" he asked, round-eyed.

"The big one is." The caller smiled at Jennifer. "Would you mind very much making me a cup of coffee? It's very cold out."

"No problem."

She went into the kitchen and turned on the faucet. It always took a few seconds until the water ran properly cold. Valentin fell onto his parcel in front of the television that his mother had bought after her cabaret tour, and began ripping off the bright paper.

The visitor followed Jennifer into the kitchen, and closed the door behind him.

Gideon, in the neighbourhood, aware that Madeleine was singing tonight, and feeling an impulse to check on

Valentin, buzzed the apartment a little after ten o'clock. Getting no reply, he started to turn away, but then he remembered that Rudi and Michael had a Wall Street dinner that evening, so that Valentin couldn't possibly be at their place, and Maddy never asked Konstantin to sit these days. Using the emergency key that Madeleine had given him months ago, he let himself in and went upstairs.

At first glance, everything looked normal. The lights on the Christmas tree were glowing, the television set was turned on, Bing Crosby singing 'White Christmas', a big, empty box lay on the floor, torn up giftwrap paper strewn casually around. But there was no sign of Valentin, either there or in his bedroom or in his mother's.

His stomach already clenched hard with fear, Gideon saw that the kitchen door was shut. He had never seen it shut before. He opened it.

He knew that the girl was dead without checking the pulse in her neck. He saw the kettle in her hand, her long brown hair matted with blood at the back of her head where she had been struck, saw no weapon. He felt a flash of fierce anger and pity, experienced an urge to lift her, to move her away from the sink, to straighten the ugly slump of her body before rigor mortis set in. But knowing better, he suppressed the urge and touched nothing, controlled himself and went back into the sitting room.

He saw the second package then, on the dining table. A little white box, tied with blue satin ribbon and needing to be opened. Gideon opened it, found the blood-stained piece of Dusty's ear. And read the note.

The boy's life, for Eternité.

It had been typewritten on a manual machine, the typeface not dissimilar to that on the old Remington he used for his reports.

Gideon had never seen *Eternité*, Maddy's hidden treasure, but he had heard enough about its beauty and of its great value, and he remembered Konstantin Zeleyev one evening, tanked up on vodka, saying that there were people in Europe, unscrupulous people, who would kill for it.

People who didn't realize that Maddy didn't have it, had not even laid eyes on it for over a decade.

Gideon wondered how many other people Zeleyev might have bragged to about his creation. When the Russian drank too much, his tongue loosened and he lost all common sense. . .

He looked down at the note again, and for the first time realized that he was trembling. The thought of Valentin in the hands of whoever had murdered Jennifer – for whether she had died instantly from the blow to her head, or had bled slowly to death, made no difference to the callousness of the attack. That gorgeous, smart, plucky little boy who had, for a long time, been Maddy's only reason for living –

Gideon went to the telephone, picked up the receiver, then changed his mind and put it down again. If he called the police now, if he started that machine rolling, they'd hold him for questioning and would send a car to Lila's to fetch Maddy. Only one thing was clear to him right now. He had to get to her first, break it to her himself, no matter how hard it would be to get the words out.

Madeleine was singing 'Yesterday' when she saw Gideon come into the club. The expression on his face, a grimness she had never seen before, told her that something was badly wrong. Forcing herself to finish the last bars of the song, she spoke quietly to the trio who were backing her, and came directly to him.

"Is it Valentin?"

He nodded tersely.

"An accident?"

"Nothing like that – I'll tell you in the car."

All the way back to the apartment, after he had told her all he knew, right though three different traffic jams, she didn't speak, didn't shed a tear, but Gideon, glancing at her from time to time, saw her hands, clenched into bunched fists in her lap, and when he helped her out of the car at the end of the endless ride, he saw that her fingernails had left tiny streaks of blood on her palms.

"Don't go in there," he said upstairs, looking at the closed kitchen door. "I'll call it in, and then I'm going to have to leave you for a while." He hated abandoning her, but there were things he could be doing while the police got on with what they ought to be doing instead of wasting time questioning him, as they would if he stayed.

"What are you going to do?" It was the first time she had spoken, and her voice was tight, half-strangled with shock and fear.

He found a bottle of cognac in a cupboard and poured her a drink. "I'm going to ask around, see if anyone's heard any rumours."

"Stefan," she said, suddenly.

"What?"

"My stepfather." Madeleine was chalky white. "He's here, in the city. At least he was yesterday, over at Rudi's." She stared at Gideon. "He was making threats."

"What kind of threats?"

"About us – our marriage."

Gideon sat her down on the sofa and gave her the cognac. "Your stepfather wouldn't do this. Would he?"

"He was asking about *Eternité*," Madeleine said. She tried to raise the glass to her lips, but her fingers were shaking so violently that she couldn't even take a sip. "No, of course he wouldn't – it's crazy."

"A coincidence, though." Gideon went to the telephone. "Tell the police when they get here – tell them everything you can think of, it doesn't matter how crazy or unlikely."

She came to the front door with him after he had made the call.

"Will you be okay?" he asked, knowing she would not be.

"Go," she said. "I'll be all right."

"I doubt that Rudi and Michael will be home yet, but try them every fifteen minutes and tell Rudi to get over here. Apart from that, keep the line free in case –"

"In case they call."

"Maybe I shouldn't go," Gideon said, faltering.

"If anyone can find Valentin, you can." Madeleine opened the door, quickly moved into his open arms, allowed herself to be held, tightly, for an instant, then stepped back again. "Go on," she said.

"Lock up after me."

"A little late for that," she said, and for the first time her voice was choked with tears.

"Oh, Maddy –"

"*Go*."

Two uniformed officers arrived first. Calming, kind and efficient, they took down what little Madeleine could tell them, took a swift look inside the kitchen and the rest of the apartment and then called in to the 20th Precinct to notify the detective unit.

"What happens now?" Madeleine asked.

"The duty captain and the patrol sergeant will take over from us, ma'am. The building's going to be sealed off, and all kinds of people are going to be swarming over the apartment and the whole street."

"What can I do?"

"Just sit down and try to be calm, ma'am. They're going to be taking pictures and dusting for prints and interviewing all your neighbours in case anyone saw anything

– you'd be surprised how much people see without knowing it's important."

"But my son? Who's looking for my *son*?"

"Missing Persons will be here any minute. They'll need everything you can give them – photographs, complete description, clothing. Do you know what your son was wearing, ma'am?"

"Pyjamas," she said, and her voice trembled. "Cotton pyjamas, with an elephant on the jacket pocket. He was ready for bed before I left."

"And you say that your husband came back first, that he found the body and the note."

"And the dog's ear."

"Yes, ma'am." The young officer paused. "I'm not sure I understand why he left you here alone, Mrs Tyler. You said he went to look for your son, is that right?"

"And to talk to people."

"What kind of people?"

"I don't know. I told you he's a private investigator – he has friends, contacts –" Madeleine looked at him. "He was a police officer himself, many years ago."

"Why did he leave the force?"

"The war – he was called up."

"And afterward, he didn't go back?"

"No." Madeleine saw how right Gideon had been to leave before they had arrived. He'd said they would waste time on him. "When are they going to start looking for my son?" she asked.

"They'll be here any second, ma'am, and just as soon as they have what they need from you, they'll start searching. They'll put Valentin's description out on the air to the whole borough, and every officer in Manhattan will be looking out for him. Meantime, there'll be officers looking in this vicinity – they'll go to every apartment, every building on this block, and then they'll move out over the next block and –"

The detectives arrived, and the young officer disappeared, swallowed up in fresh, ceaseless activity. They seemed, Madeleine acknowledged, to have their priorities straight, all the immediate urgency focusing upon Valentin and the need to find him as swiftly as possible; but once she had given them the fullest of descriptions and a few of the photographs taken of him at Thanksgiving, the investigators who remained in the apartment began to concentrate with minute precision on Jennifer.

"When will they take her away?" Madeleine asked one officer wearily, for the guilt and horror that pounded her each time she thought of poor Jennifer's body in the kitchen was becoming intolerable.

"Not for quite a while, ma'am. They won't rush it in case they miss anything, and I mean anything. You'd be surprised what tiny little fragments turn out to be hard evidence."

They took her fingerprints, dusted every surface in the apartment, took photographs from every conceivable angle and questioned her at length. They were clearly aggrieved over the delay in summoning them, and far from pleased that the first person on the scene had left without talking to them, and once Madeleine had told them that she and Gideon lived apart, she could see the suspicion written on their faces.

"What about my stepfather?" she asked. "I mean, I can't imagine that he could do such a thing, but he has money and power – he could have employed someone to –"

"To kidnap your son? To kill?" The detective questioning her looked intently at her. "With what motive? This statue?"

"Sculpture," she corrected, and then sagged. "No motive – it's bizarre even to suggest it. It's only that he was here, and Gideon told me that I should mention every possible idea to you."

"Well, he was right about that, at least," the policeman said drily.

They left just before dawn, at a quarter past seven, after the Medical Examiner had agreed that Jennifer Malkevitch could be removed. They had been with Madeleine for more than eight hours, and she felt that she was hanging onto her sanity by a thread, knew that if the mob of strangers didn't leave her alone for just a while, she would fall apart. She had to stay sane, for Valentin's sake, though God alone knew how she would manage that if Gideon didn't bring him back soon. Madeleine remembered this feeling of sheer helplessness; she had experienced it on the night that Antoine had had his stroke, had prayed never to feel that way again.

"Gideon will find him," she said aloud, to the walls.

Her husband, who was not a husband at all, but who had become her closest friend. *Their* best friend – she knew how much he loved Valentin, and how much her son adored him.

Gideon would find Valentin.

She went into the kitchen, unthinkingly, to make coffee, saw the remains of the blood in the sink and escaped hurriedly, heart pounding, feeling nauseated and faint. She tried calling Rudi again, but there was still no answer. She tried to remember where the dinner had been held the previous evening – her brother and Michael adored hotels and had, in the past, turned these Wall Street feasts into all-night affairs. If that was the case, Rudi might go straight to the bank, and it was too early to try him there.

She wandered around the apartment, seeing Valentin's face everywhere she looked. She closed her eyes and tried to send him messages of strength, willing him to be brave, praying for him to be safe. Nothing mattered, *nothing* on earth mattered to her more than he did –

Dusty's leash still hung on a hook near the front door.

She had screwed that hook into the wall just three short weeks before, low enough for Valentin to reach it without standing on tiptoe. Madeleine thought about the dachshund, about the white box stained pink with her innocent blood, and the most intense, wild, sickening rage she had ever felt surged violently up inside her chest, but deliberately, with all her might, she jammed it down again.

This is not the time to think about it.

If she thought about Dusty, she would begin to imagine what had happened to Jennifer, what might be happening to Valentin now. If she imagined that, she would surely lose her mind.

When the buzzer sounded just before eight o'clock, Madeleine ran to snatch up the intercom.

"Gideon?"

"It's Konstantin, *ma chère*."

"Did Gideon ask you to come?"

"That's right."

She pressed the release button and burst into tears of relief. She must have been mad to think she wanted to be alone – she desperately needed someone with her, someone who cared.

"Madeleine?" He stood in the doorway, elegant as ever in a dark grey cashmere overcoat, a matching fedora in his hand.

"Thank God –" She ran into his arms, grateful to be held, then drew away again, remembering in spite of herself the last time. "I'm so glad you're here," she said, to cover her abrupt awkwardness and the accompanying guilt that had swamped her.

"The police have gone?" he asked.

"Not so long ago," she answered, "though I feel I've been alone for ever."

"I'm here now."

"Come and sit down. What did Gideon tell you? Has he found anything out yet?"

"I want you to pack a bag, a small one, just enough for one night."

"Why? I can't go anywhere."

"You must come with me, *ma chère*," Zeleyev insisted.

"I don't understand." Madeleine was confused. "Did Gideon say that I was to leave? What if the kidnapper calls?"

"He won't call."

"He might." She grew firm. "It's kind of you, Konstantin, really, but this is no time for me to stay with you. The police expect me to be here, in any case, and if –"

"Pack your bag."

Madeleine looked up in surprise at the sharpness in his voice. "I don't think you understand, Konstantin. I'm staying here. There may be news, or I may be needed to do something." Her eyes pricked with tears. "Or Valentin may come home."

"It's you who have not understood," Zeleyev said, and suddenly his tone was harsh. "You will do exactly as I tell you. And if you waste even one more minute, you will never see Valentin again."

He put his right hand into the deep pocket of his overcoat, and Madeleine stared as he withdrew a knife. The curved Fabergé dagger from his sitting room. He held it out in front of him, the gleaming blade pointed down to the floor, the nephrite and gilt handle snug in his grasp.

"Dear God," she said, and the words seemed to hang in the air, to reverberate with the intensity of her shock. "Not you."

Zeleyev looked towards the kitchen. "I hit the girl with the blunt end. See?" He touched the handle with two fingers of his left hand. "Regrettable, of course, but –" He made a shrugging gesture with both hands.

Madeleine felt violently ill. Just a month ago, this man

had stunned her with his marriage proposal. And now this. She struggled against her faintness, fought to hold onto reality.

"Where is Valentin?"

"He's safe, for now."

"Where *is* he?"

"There's no need for you to know that, *ma chère*. All you have to do is to pack your bag and give me your passport."

"For pity's sake, what for?"

"We are making a journey." He looked at his watch. "And we have little time to spare, so do it now." His eyes were sharp and keen. "And I want the key."

"What key?"

"The key I gave you when I brought your father back from Paris. The key to the vault."

Madeleine sagged. "Is that the reason for this? *Etern-ité?*" She could not believe it. It was impossible. "You killed a girl for a sculpture?" She stared into the face she had known, had thought she had known, for so many, many years. "You would kill my son just for that?"

"I am seventy-seven years old," Zeleyev said. "As fit as a man twenty years younger, perhaps, but nevertheless time is running out for me. I am not prepared to wait any longer, Madeleine."

"I'll get it for you," she said hastily, eagerly, her voice shaking. "If you let Valentin come home, I'll go to Paris right away and I'll bring it to you." She reached out and touched his left arm, but he shook her off. "I'll never tell a living soul about Jennifer, I swear it."

"I don't trust you any more," he said quietly.

"But you must know that I'd do anything for Valentin."

"Which is why you will do as I tell you now."

"I can't."

"It's entirely your decision, *ma belle*." Zeleyev smiled. "You can come with me to Paris now, this morning, and you can give *Eternité* to me, and your beautiful Valentin will be unharmed."

"Or?" Her heart pumped steadily.

"Or he will die."

Although it was a regular weekday morning, the traffic was unusually light, and they caught the TWA flight with several minutes to spare. The sense that she was trapped in the most grotesque of nightmares seemed almost to buoy Madeleine up, to carry her through the necessary motions of passport checks and boarding. And now she was sitting in the window seat of the twentieth row of an aeroplane, accepting a cool drink from a smiling stewardess and listening to, but not really hearing, the voice of the captain over the loudspeakers. She was on her way to Europe for the first time in more than four years, travelling with a man who had been her friend for over half her life.

A murderer.

He began, after a while, to talk.

"I did not wish to kill the girl," he said, softly. "I intended to put her to sleep for an hour or so, to allow me to leave with Valentin and to frighten you, to continue to punish you with fear. So that you would believe the note."

"And Dusty? Did you kill her?"

"She was living when I left her."

Madeleine looked at his profile. "I find it hard," she said, and shook her head. "No, much more than hard – I find it *impossible* to believe that you are doing this to us, Konstantin." She paused. "Are you ill? What has happened to affect you this way? You're my oldest friend – you've done everything to help me, always –"

"Must I explain it?"

"If you can."

"It's not difficult to understand, if you listen."

"I'll listen."

He looked at her. "I love you. I told you that not so long ago, that I have been in love with you since you first left childhood. I always wanted you, Magdalena Alexandrovna." He looked away, fastened his eyes straight ahead at the back of the seat in front of him. "Just as I always wanted *Eternité*."

"Why did you never tell me? That you wanted it for yourself."

"Until three years ago, you didn't even know where it was. And since then, since it has languished in its box in Paris, you have been too afraid to go back to claim it." Zeleyev paused. "And I did not want it for myself, *ma chère*, I wanted to share it with you."

It should have been his by right, he said. The Malinskaya jewels should have been left to him, not to Amadeus, that simple mountain man. Back home, before she left, before her sorrows overtook her, Irina had loved Zeleyev, and she had been his first love in that lost world, in those glorious St Petersburg days when she had still had her health and strength and a *joie de vivre* that Amadeus Gabriel had never seen.

"I came to Davos looking for Irina, and I found only your grandfather. But I could see that he, too, had deeply loved her, and so for Irina's sake, for her memory, I helped him recreate her waterfall."

He had grown truly fond of Amadeus, had given himself willingly, all his creativity and skill and artistry, but those first wounds had never entirely healed. Irina had left him one single emerald, and the simple jeweller had given him a ruby, and later, when they had finished, three more stones, and had believed that it was enough.

The crossing became turbulent, around them passengers shifted with mild unease, the crew smiled reassurances and checked their seat belts, but Zeleyev, now that he had begun, continued on and on. He spoke in intermittent bursts of monologue, the words spilling from him like bitter bile, suppressed for too many decades.

"I never told you about the injustices I suffered through the years – I wanted you to believe the stories I had told your grandfather and Alexander, about the glittering life I had led in the great cities of Europe."

"They weren't true?" Hardly an instant passed without Madeleine thinking about Valentin, remembering that she was here for him, for his safety, yet still she struggled to speak rationally, almost gently. "None of those stories?"

"I was comfortable enough." Zeleyev smiled, a sour smile. "I always had work, which was more than many émigrés could boast, but no one appreciated me. Those who did understand, those who did respect me, said that they could not afford a craftsman of my talent and experience, but many of them scoffed at the old days. They reminded me, as if I didn't know, of the magnitude of the Master's empire – more than five hundred people had worked for Fabergé at the height of his renown, they said, and I, Konstantin Ivanovich Zeleyev, was merely the son of an outworker."

"But they were just ignorant."

"And I despised them for it, I hated them for their disrespect. I knew my own worth, and I knew that if any of these peasants had ever laid eyes on my finest creation, they would have been forced to grovel at my feet."

"Opi told me once," Madeleine said, tentatively, "that you took *Eternité* away to show to an expert, but that you were secretive when you returned."

"Because I saw no one." His lips tightened. "There was a famous Swiss collector named Maurice Sandoz, who was known to have collected many of the Master's most magnificent creations. I learned that he was in Geneva, so I went to see him. He was not there."

"So you took it back to Davos, as you promised."

"I was an honourable man, Madeleine. I would never have betrayed your grandfather as he did me."

"You felt betrayed because he left *Eternité* to me?"

"Naturally. He always admitted that it would not have existed but for me. I understood that he clung to it for Irina's sake in his lifetime, but after his death I assumed that it would have been mine, by right." Zeleyev paused. "Had it come to you, as he intended, I would have swallowed my resentment, for at least I would have known it had gone to tender, loving hands. And I knew that you would have seen reason and permitted it, at last, to be shown, as it deserved."

"But my father took it."

"Alexei was a fool all his life, possessed and destroyed by his drugs and his fears and inadequacies."

If Zeleyev had not gone to Paris in response to Alexander's appeal, the sculpture might have fallen into the hands of philistine thieves, the gold melted down, the precious enamelwork smashed, only the gems themselves surviving.

"Alexander Gabriel was not worthy either of his father or his daughter," he told Madeleine after the stewardess had removed their untouched luncheon trays. "And even in death, even after I had come thousands of miles to help him, he betrayed and insulted me. If he had not made it impossible, *ma chère*, I would have brought the sculpture to you in 1964, and both our lives, I believe, might have unfolded very differently."

They landed at Orly at a quarter past ten in the evening, and Zeleyev brought her to the Crillon, held her arm while they were shown up to a large and beautiful room overlooking the Place de la Concorde, a room with just one bed. Madeleine thought that if he raped her she might die, and yet she knew that she would endure even that if she had to, for Valentin's sake. But Zeleyev did not touch her, only watched her, all through the remaining hours until she fell asleep, and even then, whenever she awoke from her fitful, unhappy dozing, his eyes were always open, still watching her, although he hardly spoke a word now, as if the monologue on the journey had drained him of the power of speech.

In the morning, at nine o'clock, they went by taxi to the Banque Nationale in Boulevard de Rochechouart, and were admitted to the vault without delay. Madeleine showed her passport as identification, signed their book and told them that she was giving up the deposit box, and there were no queries and no complications. Zeleyev did not look at the sculpture, still wrapped in Alexander Gabriel's repellent pyjamas. He just felt its shape, knew that, at last, he held it in his hands, and then placed it into the leather bag he had brought with him.

At the Crillon, they went directly to the room. Zeleyev locked the door, opened the bag and placed the sculpture on the ornate mahogany table close to the window so that the sunlight struck it and made it gleam.

"*Enfin.*" he said. "At last, a suitable setting." He threw the old pyjamas in her direction. "Your father's – perhaps you wish to keep them." He went into the bathroom and Madeleine heard him washing his hands. He returned still wiping them, with fastidious thoroughness, on a Turkish towel. "Do you know, *ma chère*, that the columns at the hotel entrance were built by a namesake of yours, Jacques-Ange Gabriel? It has always been my favourite hotel in Paris, and so close to Maxim's."

"Konstantin?"

"*Oui, ma chère?*"

"You have it at last."

"Indeed."

"What happens now?"

He took the towel back to the bathroom, came back

and stood before her. His sparse, still bright red hair shone in the light from the window, and his face was in shadow.

"You have one last choice," he said.

"And what is that?" she asked quietly.

"Divorce Tyler. Marry me." He paused, and his voice quivered. "I will give you everything. I will love and cherish you for the rest of my life."

Her answer came swiftly and starkly, without consideration.

"I would sooner die," she said.

He turned his head, sharply, as if she had slapped his cheek, and the sun struck his face, illuminating it. And as Madeleine witnessed the last vestiges of his love for her disintegrating, evolving into a mask of hatred, she knew, with absolute certainty, that he was going to kill her.

17

After leaving Madeleine shortly before eleven the previous night, Gideon had driven through most of Manhattan tracking down contacts he had hoped might have heard something, anything that might be useful. Even the cheapest low-lives tended to be helpful where crimes against children were concerned, but this time no one had even a grain of information. Gideon began calling in favours, trying to ascertain whether a six-year-old boy with navy blue eyes had been seen at JFK or La Guardia or at any of the three major heliports; or boarding a train at Grand Central or Pennsylvania Stations, or perhaps being hustled onto a bus at the Port Authority terminal. Wanting to cover all outside possibilities, he even went in person to the tiny Consolidated Terminal on Forty-first Street and then drove at high speed uptown to the George Washington Bridge terminal, before changing tack and starting to check out all the city's finest hotels to try to locate Madeleine's stepfather. It took less than an hour to learn that Julius had left the Pierre to catch an evening flight a few hours after he'd seen Maddy and Rudi. That removed him from the enquiry, unless he'd hired help, in which case anything on God's earth might have happened.

It had occurred to Gideon that Konstantin Zeleyev was, perhaps, the man most likely to hazard a guess at who might know about the sculpture, or better yet, as he had himself said when he was juiced up, who might want it badly enough to commit murder and kidnapping to get it.

He had tried calling him off and on through the night, getting no answer, and just after eight in the morning, he had gone to the Riverside Drive building and, having rung his doorbell several times, had learned from a neighbour that Zeleyev had only recently gone out.

"Are you sure? Only I've been calling him –"

"Sure I'm sure – do I look blind?"

"No, sir." Gideon paused. "Was he alone?"

"All alone."

"Could I use your phone, sir?"

"Does this look like the post office?"

"This is a real emergency, sir."

"So use a pay phone."

The door had closed in his face, and from somewhere in the house a dog had barked. Gideon had driven around the corner, looking for a telephone booth, when the first warning prickle had raised the short hairs at the back of his neck.

He found a phone and called Maddy. When she failed to answer, he had grown suddenly, intensely afraid. He tried Rudi's apartment, got no reply, scrabbled through the directory, found the Gründli Bank of Zurich and dialled the number. Rudi had just arrived at his desk.

"What's up?"

"Get over to Maddy's right away."

"What's happened?"

Gideon told him.

"Christ," Rudi said tensely. "I'm leaving now."

"And tell the cops too."

Gideon hadn't picked a lock for years, but it was a skill once learned, never forgotten. The first thing he saw was the Remington typewriter on the Russian's opened fold-down desk.

"Valentin!" he called out. "Are you in here?"

The voice was small and frightened.

"Gideon?"

"Where are you?"

"In the bathroom."

The door was locked and the key was missing.

"Get clear of the door and cover your face," Gideon shouted. "I'm going to break it down."

"Great."

Gideon allowed himself a tiny smile, and smashed into the door. Valentin huddled in the corner, below the wash-basin, cradling Dusty in his arms.

"He cut off half her ear," Valentin said, close to tears.

"Is she okay? Let me have her." Gideon took the dachshund into his left arm and raised the boy from the floor with his right. Valentin pressed hard against him.

"Did he hurt you?"

Valentin shook his head.

"Are you sure? Let me see." Gideon held him at arm's length. "Okay, that's great. Now can you tell me what happened?"

"Can we go home, please?"

"Soon, Val – just tell me first."

The child's face was pinched and tired, but his eyes were full of relief. "I was at home in bed last night, and Konstantin came. He gave me a stuffed tiger – I left it out there, on the rug – and then he and Jen went to make a cup of coffee –"

"And then?"

"Then he came out of the kitchen and told me that he'd found Dusty, and that he'd called Maman at Lila's, and she'd said it was okay for me to go with him. So I went."

"Sure you did."

Gideon led him out of the bathroom, sat him down and set the still quivering dachshund on his lap. "What did he say about Dusty?"

"He said he found her in the park, near where we lost her, but I reckon he was lying. I asked him about her ear, and he said she must have been in a fight with another dog, but when I came in, Dusty was really happy to see me, but she growled like crazy whenever Konstantin came near her. And Dusty never growls, does she?" He hugged the animal close.

"When did he lock you in the bathroom?"

"After I asked if we could go home. He told me we had to stay the night, but I said I wanted to show Dusty's ear to Maman, and when he got mean, I cried. And that's when he pushed us both in and locked the door."

"So you were shut in all night?" Gideon's rage was mounting.

"He didn't even give us anything to eat," Valentin said. "He was acting really weird." He paused. "I don't like Konstantin any more."

"No," Gideon said. "Nor do I."

Gideon telephoned Madeleine's apartment again, but Rudi had not yet arrived and there was still no answer. Giving Valentin and Dusty a drink of water, he began a rapid search, but with no real idea of what he was looking for, he came up with nothing.

He tried calling Maddy's again, and this time Rudi picked up instantly.

"The police pulled up just as I did," Rudi told him. "But there's no sign of Maggy. Where are you, Gideon?"

Before Gideon could answer, a detective came on the line.

"Listen up, Tyler. If you don't get straight over here, and I mean right now, you can kiss your licence goodbye and that's a promise."

"I've found the boy," Gideon said tersely. "But my wife –"

"Is the boy okay?"

"He's not hurt. But I think –"

"I don't care what you think, Tyler. I want you here *now*."

In the car, on the short drive back to Seventy-fourth Street, Gideon did his best to soften what the child was, inevitably, about to be exposed to. Jennifer had met with an accident, he told Valentin, and Madeleine had had to go out for a while. The police were there because of what Konstantin had done to Dusty and to him, and if they asked him a lot of questions, he was not to be scared and to answer everything as truthfully as he could.

"Where did Maman go?"

Gideon glanced at the boy's grave face, and decided that a partial truth was wiser than a pack of white lies that might come tumbling down in the space of the next few hours.

"I don't know, Val."

"Is she okay?" The child's voice was suddenly small and fearful.

"Sure she is." Gideon paused. "And soon as the police have finished with me, I'm going to find her and fetch her back."

"Do you swear it?"

"Cross my heart and hope to die."

Their questioning of Valentin was gentle and swiftly over, but when it was Gideon's turn, the interrogation became belligerent, endless and frustrating beyond belief. Gideon could see that at least one of the homicide detectives liked the idea that an estranged husband – a man who'd abandoned the NYPD as a young man – might be implicated, far better than he liked Gideon's cock-and-bull claim that an invisible Russian and his fabled gold sculpture, locked in the vault of a bank in Paris, held the answer to a Manhattan homicide and kidnapping.

"Look at it from our point of view, Tyler. Last night

we had one body, a missing child and a frantic mother. This morning you miraculously come up with the child, and now the mother – the wife you don't live with – has done a disappearing act."

Gideon struggled to hold onto his temper. "You've talked to Valentin – he's told you that Zeleyev came here, that he went into the kitchen with the girl. He's told you that the Russian took him away and locked him up."

"But we don't have this Russian here and now – we have you."

"Are you at least looking for Zeleyev?"

"What do you take us for, a bunch of amateurs?"

"God forbid."

"Nobody likes a smartmouth, Tyler."

They were escorted back to Riverside Drive so that Valentin could show the detectives where he had been held, and once Rudi had been given the okay to take the boy and dog to the veterinarian, and then to go back to Rudi's apartment, Gideon was taken to the 20th Precinct station for further questioning. It was after four in the afternoon before he, too, was free to leave, and then it was with a strict warning not to withhold even the tiniest morsel of evidence unless he wanted to find himself behind bars.

Gideon went directly back to Zeleyev's apartment and began a second search. This time, he found what he needed within minutes. An airline timetable, inside a night table drawer. It was softbacked and it was easy to see where it had been folded open for a while. Stuffing it into his jacket pocket, he ran downstairs, jumped into the car and drove like a madman back to Maddy's.

"Her passport," he said on the telephone to Rudi. "Do you know where she keeps it?"

"I don't know for sure, but she keeps some important papers in the bottom of her lingerie drawer in her bedroom."

Gideon found their marriage certificate, a stiff-backed envelope containing Antoine's death certificate and their *acte de mariage*, Valentin's birth certificate, some photographs and her father's suicide note. No passport.

He called Rudi back.

"They've gone to Paris."

"Are you sure?"

"I can't be sure of anything, but it's got to be odds-on."

"Have you told the police?"

"Not yet." Gideon looked at his watch. "It's too late for them to get someone to stop them at Orly. There were two flights out of JFK this morning. Either way, unless there was some big delay, they'll have left the airport by the time Interpol has a chance to get its act together – that's if anyone even believes me."

"What do we do now?"

"I'll call the cops – the more people looking for them over there the better. But I won't call them until I'm about to board the plane."

"You're going?"

"What do you think?"

"I'm coming."

"You've got Val."

"Michael's come home. Besides, since when do you speak French? If you want to find out anything in Paris, you need someone with you who speaks the language."

"I'll call the airport and get back to you."

Ten minutes later, he was talking to Rudi again.

"The Pan Am flight's full, but we have two seats on an El Al flight that leaves at ten and gets us into Orly at eleven in the morning."

"Nothing earlier?"

"Not even a freight plane."

"I'll pack some stuff." Rudi paused. "Will you come by and pick me up? I think you'd better be the one to tell

Valentin what's happening. He seems to think you're Philip Marlowe and Superman rolled into one."

Gideon's smile was grim. "I'll be there around seven." He felt his pulse racing, forced himself to quieten, knowing there was little he could do until they reached Paris. "Will Michael be able to stay with Val until we get back?"

"Every minute. And I think I should call Joey Cutter, let him know so he can tell Lila."

"Maybe Joey and Betty could stop by. Val likes them a lot."

"I'll leave Michael every number in case." Rudi hesitated. "Gideon?"

"Yes?"

"What does Zeleyev want her there for? I mean I know it's because of the damned sculpture, but do you think that's all?"

Gideon felt a tightness in his chest.

"I wish to Christ I knew."

Heading into Paris mid-morning on Friday, Gideon and Rudi, with plenty of time to have talked and planned, knew exactly what they were up against. They had to assume that since Zeleyev and Madeleine would have arrived the night before long after banking hours, they must have spent the night somewhere in the city, but persuading Parisian hoteliers to allow them access to their guest registers was likely to prove almost as difficult a task as trying to discover at which bank Alexander Gabriel had deposited *Eternité*.

"I can't believe she never told you where it was," Gideon said to Rudi.

"She was happy to leave it there. You know she didn't want to come back here, and we just never talked much about it. You know my sister – she's not the most materialistic woman."

Gideon stared out at the city streets. It was as attractive

as he had remembered from his brief wartime sojourn, and at another time he might have been warmed and excited by the prospect of seeing it all again, but as it was, right now, it felt like hell on earth.

The taxi driver said something he didn't understand.

"He wants to know where to drop us." They had told him at Orly to bring them into the city centre.

Gideon opened the address book he'd brought from Madeleine's sitting room. "Tell him 32 *bis* Boulevard Haussmann."

"The Levis?"

"We need all the help we can get," Gideon said. "We need a respectable French citizen."

Noah was out, but Estelle was at home and knew where to reach him. Hearing that Madeleine was in trouble, Noah dropped everything and came directly to the apartment. He had never met Gideon, but Madeleine had written to them about their *mariage de convenance* and of their great friendship. Noah took one look at the big, frantic, brown-eyed American and knew right away that, whether Madeleine was aware of it or not, they were perfect for each other.

"Since you don't know even the name of the bank, let alone its location," Noah pointed out to them, "and since, in any event, Zeleyev will most likely have been in and out of the vault by now, the hotels are certainly our best bet."

"Do you know where he used to stay when he was here?" Gideon asked.

Noah shook his head. "I met him only in the early days, when Madeleine still worked for the Lussacs, and I never knew which hotel he lived in, or even if he stayed in different ones each time." He paused. "But I do recall that he spoke of *grand luxe* with great appreciation. If he has come back to Paris to satisfy an old obsession, it's unlikely that he would choose a lower class of hotel, *n'est-ce pas*?"

"Might the Lussacs remember?" Rudi suggested.

"I doubt it," Noah said.

"I'll telephone them," Estelle volunteered. "But meanwhile, I think you should begin your search."

They began at the Plaza-Athénée in Avenue Montaigne.

18

Zeleyev had hardly spoken to Madeleine since she had made her last, fatal mistake. She realized now that she should have accepted his proposal, should have agreed to anything. She was also aware, looking at his new, changed, granite face, that it was too late to pretend to change her mind now. It had been impossible, until now, even through the discovery that he had killed Jennifer, even through the journey across the ocean, even through the long, eerie night and this morning, at the bank – it had still been impossible for her to comprehend that Konstantin Ivanovich Zeleyev was insane.

He had always been eccentric, faddish, a man of mercurial temperament, a man of tremendous ego, but he had not been mad and he had not, Madeleine still felt certain, been evil. He had been her friend. Or had even that been a grotesque charade? If she thought back over the years, the decades, even back to the night of her father's banishment –

She did not dare to think.

He ordered a light lunch for them both, *oeuf en aspic* for himself, a grilled sole for her, a bottle of Montrachet for her, a bottle of vodka for himself. When the waiter arrived, Zeleyev tipped him at the door and wheeled the table into the room himself, watching Madeleine all the time. And then he locked the door again, and sat down between her and the telephone. And he began to read.

"Victor Hugo again?" Madeleine commented, and her voice was husky with fear.

"A book of endless fascination for me, as you know." He bowed his head again, and she observed that he was not really reading the well-thumbed book, just staring fixedly at one page.

"You should eat," he said, without glancing up.

"I'm not hungry."

"A pity."

At one o'clock, Zeleyev rose and fetched two white linen towels from the bathroom, in which he wrapped the sculpture carefully, his fingers tender, loving.

"Come."

"Where to?"

"To the hotel safe."

"And then?"

"You will see."

"You have *Eternité* now," she said. "Surely there's no reason for me to stay any longer." She paused. "I would like to go home."

"Home?"

"To Valentin."

"And to Tyler."

"To my son."

Zeleyev went to the door. "Remember," he said, and his voice was very calm, "when we are downstairs, that Valentin's life is still in my hands, even though I am here."

Madeleine looked into his hard face. "I never imagined that I could come to hate you, Konstantin," she said.

He nodded. "It is remarkable, is it not, what curious twists life has in store for us all?" He opened the door. "Come along."

They left the hotel at half past one, without packing their bags, leaving everything in the room. Konstantin wore his cashmere coat, his fedora and a black cashmere scarf. Madeleine wore a long-jacketed, wide-bottomed trouser suit that had been on the first hanger that had come to hand when Zeleyev had given her only moments to change the previous night. It was very cold, and she was shivering as Zeleyev asked the doorman for a taxi, but she supposed that she might have shivered even if the temperature had stood at seventy degrees.

Their taxi drew up, Zeleyev tipped the doorman generously, ushered Madeleine into the back of the car, leaned through the front passenger window to give the driver their destination, and got in beside her.

"Where are you taking me?"

"A little surprise," he replied, and said nothing more.

She closed her eyes briefly, and prayed.

The instant she realized that they were approaching Place Denfert-Rochereau, Madeleine knew.

"No!" she said, in horror. "For the love of God, Konstantin, *no*."

"Keep your voice down," Zeleyev said. "Remember Valentin."

"I think you're bluffing about Valentin."

"But are you sure?"

They got out of the taxi and he linked his arm tightly through hers.

"Don't forget the dagger, *ma chère*. I swear to you that if you do the slightest thing to attract attention, I will make your son an orphan without an instant's hesitation."

She looked at him, remembering what lay inside the place to which he was taking her. "I think I thought you were a little mad when you brought me here all those years ago."

"It was in 1957," he said. "The month was April."

"I had bad dreams for weeks afterwards," she recalled, and suddenly, with the onslaught of ugly memories came a new, curious numbness that felt as if someone had injected Novocaine into her mind. "I thought I might never forgive you for it. I wish I hadn't."

As if she had not even spoken, he walked her across the street.

"Good," he said. "The door is open."

Madeleine stared at the pavement, saw the words she had seen eleven years before, engraved in the concrete.

ENTRÉE DES CATACOMBES

"Please," she said. "Don't make me."

"Shut up," he said, and unlinking his arm, he gripped her firmly with one hand and paid the cashier. "And so we go down."

She remembered it all, had never forgotten any of it, the awful, narrow, interminable spiral steps, the dizziness, the sensation of burrowing down deep into the earth. He climbed down behind her, so that she had no choice but to go on, down and down, until at last, coming to the bottom she tripped and swiftly, easily, Zeleyev caught her arm and steadied her.

"Go on," he said, and now, although the tunnels were not wide, he linked arms with her again. "Just to keep both hands free," he explained with bizarre courtesy. "One for the knife, the other for my torch."

He switched on the beam of the little torch he had taken from his right-hand coat pocket.

"You can let go of me," Madeleine whispered. "I shan't run away."

"Be quiet," he said. "Just walk."

She could not seem to think, she felt nothing but the nameless dread that clamped across her chest like a giant's spread-fingered hand, squeezing her heart and her abdomen. The tunnels went on and on, twisted and turned, the wet clay beneath her feet squelched, the dank chill penetrated her nostrils, froze her throat, made it hard to breathe. Filthy, murky water dripped onto her head from the roof, and she wondered whether the sewers were above or below them. The ground was uneven, and she slipped again, dragging at him, and heard him hiss a curse under his breath.

"I'm sorry," she said, and her voice was a gasp.

"Be more careful," he said, and they walked on.

Madeleine remembered that last time there had been people, tourists, young and old, lured by the macabre, ancient attraction, but this time there was no one, for who on earth would want to come down into this nether world a few days before Christmas? No one but an insane man.

"*Bon Dieu*," she prayed out loud, suddenly, hardly realizing that she was praying, and Zeleyev, to punish her, pulled her even closer to him, so that she felt his strength, his muscularity, even through the coat and the pullover he wore beneath. "*Bon Dieu, sauvez-moi –*"

"I told you to be quiet," he said, and his voice sounded like a growl from deep inside his throat, and Madeleine's fear, her numbing, partly suppressed, groping fear, began to mount and to expand, for she knew that they were approaching the core of the catacombs, the heart, and she remembered it, oh God how she remembered it –

And Zeleyev pointed his torch up at the sign over the black and white painted entrance, and she knew that her nightmare was only just beginning.

They were entering the empire of death.

Gideon, Rudi and Noah had discovered that Zeleyev was registered at the Crillon with one other person, a young woman, in his party. The telephone in their room was not being answered, but they had not checked out.

"They may be in the bar," the concierge suggested. "Or perhaps they may still be in the restaurant after lunch."

"We've looked," Gideon said. "They're not."

Rudi leaned forward and spoke quietly. "It is vital that we see Monsieur Zeleyev's room."

"Impossible."

"Ask him if he took a safe," Gideon nudged.

"*C'est une affaire absolument privée, Monsieur.*"

The shutters of discretion slammed relentlessly down, and it took all of Rudi's bank-learned diplomacy and Noah's offer to take full responsibility before they could ascertain that there was a box in their safe in Zeleyev's name, and that it was one of their largest.

It was almost three o'clock before they gained access to the bedroom. Gideon saw Madeleine's bag, the few essentials she had thrown in – and that unassailable proof that he had been right, that she had been forced out of her home by the mad old man and dragged back to the city she had not been ready to return to, filled him with wild, impotent, new rage.

"Where are they?" Noah asked, knowing they could not answer.

"Assuming the sculpture's in the safe, why aren't they *here*?" Rudi was agonized.

"If she knows that he killed the girl –" Noah stopped.

Gideon, saying nothing, beyond words, was scanning the room intently, raking every inch with his eyes, hunting for some small clue, anything that could help them find Maddy before it was too late.

"Look at this," Rudi said. He picked up the open copy of *Les Misérables* from one of the bedside tables. "Something's been marked – it's rubbed out, but –" He grew pale, and passed the book to Noah. "Translate those lines for Gideon, will you?"

"'The sewer,'" Noah read, "'in ancient Paris, is the resting-place of all failure and all effort.'" He looked at Gideon. "Have you read this book?"

"No."

"Hugo wrote at length about the *égouts*, the sewers of Paris, a labyrinth of stinking tunnels beneath the city that clearly fascinated him." The tunnels carried more than sewage, Noah explained. They also housed the clean water pipes, telephone wires and the *pneu*, the pneumatic postal network.

"If all the tunnels were laid end to end," Noah told Gideon and Rudi, "I have heard that they would extend from Paris to Istanbul." He paused, and his voice was strained. "It is a perfect place for a man to hide."

Gideon had seen Jennifer Malkevitch's body, had seen her head smashed in, her life blood drained away.

"It's also," he said, softly, "a perfect place to kill."

They called the police.

Konstantin Zeleyev and Madeleine stood in the heart of a huge, grotesque charnel house that had been created in tunnels infinitely older than the city's sewers. The walls of bones that she had been unable to forget in eleven years, surrounded them, hideously, suffocatingly. The bones of the long dead, and the skulls, flesh long since mouldered, peeled away in the coffins from which they had been dragged more than a century before. Madeleine stared at the skulls, stared as if hypnotized through the empty eyesockets, and an unbidden vision of maggots burrowing, fattening, swept her with such a violent nausea that, for a few moments, she thought she might vomit or faint.

"Almost there," Zeleyev said.

Madeleine could not speak. All the merciful numbness had gone now, and there was nothing left, no lingering layer of shock or disbelief to protect her from her terrors.

"They cleared the cemeteries all over Paris and turned these catacombs into a necropolis," Zeleyev said in a quiet, calm voice. "Did you know, *ma chère*? In the eighteenth and nineteenth centuries, when they needed the space for more corpses in the graveyards." He still walked her on, but now he was slowing a little. "These tunnels stretch for miles under the city, do you realize? You see the chains, the barriers across some?" He pointed with his torch. "They are to keep us out, to keep us from making a terrible mistake, for if we leave this route, if we lose ourselves, we will never be found."

He stopped, abruptly.

"What – ?" Madeleine began, but he jerked at her arm to silence her.

He did not speak. She thought that he was listening, and she, too, strained to catch the least sound of someone coming, anyone to whom she could appeal, for the spectre of the dagger no longer frightened her as much as the unknown, unimaginable dangers Zeleyev planned for her.

And then, suddenly, without any warning, Zeleyev moved. Pulling Madeleine towards the black, gaping mouth of one of the blocked-off tunnels, he put out one hand and wrenched the chain out of the wall with a strong, sharp twist, dragging her through into the darkness. She began to scream, but he clamped a hand over her face, slammed her against a wall and then, swiftly and brutally, he used his fingers to force open her mouth and stuffed a handkerchief inside, pushing it all in, flattening her tongue so that she gagged and choked and fought for breath, hot tears coursing down her cheeks as she struggled.

"Don't fight me," he whispered, close against her ear.

Her mind, for a while, seemed to stop functioning. She felt that she was on the edge of a hysteria from which she might never return, on the brink of death, locked tightly in the embrace of a man she no longer knew. A stranger. A madman. A killer.

"We must wait now," his voice said into her ear, and she felt his warm breath. And abruptly she realized that they were waiting for the *Catacombes* to close, for the time when they would be entirely alone.

She forced herself to breathe through her nose, tried

not to swallow, not to choke. She kept her eyes focused on the dim light in the main tunnel that they had left behind. And silently, in her mind, she prayed.

For a long time, no one passed by. Then, two voices, male and female, young and breathless and giggling. Then silence again. And about fifteen minutes later, two guards strolled through, gruff and bored, checking idly that no one was left inside. Madeleine prayed that they would notice the broken chain. Zeleyev's grip was fiercer than ever. The voices of the men, grumbling, grew fainter and fainter, and disappeared.

The lights went out.

And Zeleyev began to talk.

"I'm going to tell you," he said quietly, slackening his grasp on her arm just a little, "about Alexander Gabriel. It is not fitting for you to die without knowing the truth, about your father's life, or about his death."

Madeleine moaned, and her eyes, blind in the dark, appealed to him, but he did not see and did not care.

"You never believed him capable of what he was accused of, did you, Magdalena Alexandrovna? You were right. It was I who attacked the woman, the whore." He paused briefly. "It was the vodka, the time and the place, the atmosphere. Alexei was so drugged, so beyond reason, he could remember nothing. It was easy to let him believe that he was guilty, for he might so easily have been the one."

Madeleine felt her world tilt, sagged against the wall, the blackness seeming to swell around her face, her eyes, suffocating the life out of her. And suddenly Zeleyev took the gag out of her mouth and, listening to her retching and sucking air, he used the damp handkerchief to wipe her face, knowing, in spite of the darkness, that there were tears on her cheeks.

"I knew that his family, so rich and powerful, would

help him, that he would not see the inside of a prison, whereas if I –"

"You are monstrous." Madeleine hardly recognized her own voice, hoarse and choked from the gag and from the terrible erupting hatred triggered by his mocking confirmation of her suspicion.

"There is more," Zeleyev told her. "Did you really believe that I left that aspirin bottle with your father in innocence? Yes, of course you did, for you were always a naïve child in many ways."

She stared into the dark. "You killed him," she said flatly.

"Not exactly – I merely assisted him, in the event that he wished to die. He said he was going to fight, to make you proud of him, *ma belle* Madeleine, and if he had meant it, or been capable of it, he might still be living today. But I knew his weakness, I left him in that miserable room with the overdose I believed he longed for. I knew he might be dead by nightfall, and of course, he was."

"And now you're going to kill me." It was a statement.

"If only you had accepted my proposal, Madeleine – if only you were able to *lie*. If you had not been so honest and so cruel, I would never have had to tell you these things, and we could have lived together as man and wife until my own death. Just a few, short years with you, sharing *Eternité*, that was all I asked of you. But now there are no more alternatives." He shuddered perceptibly. "I did not come this far to die rotting in prison."

"So what are you going to do?"

"Take what's rightfully mine, and make the most of what time is left to me."

"Why do I have to die?" Madeleine whispered. "Don't you care at all any more? Not for me, but what about Valentin?" She grew rigid with a fresh, new terror. "You wouldn't kill him as well as me?" She could hardly move her right hand, but she clawed at him impotently with her fingers. "You wouldn't do that, Konstantin, for pity's sake, you *couldn't*!"

"No," he said, quite gently. "I would not do that."

"Then take me out of here," she begged softly. "I'll help you – whatever you want. I'll tell them that you didn't mean to kill Jennifer, and you'll keep *Eternité* anyway –"

"I don't believe you."

"I've never lied to you – you said that yourself."

"But you have betrayed me, haven't you? I've suffered betrayals all my life – first Russia, then Irina, then Amadeus and your father, and finally you, too. After all my dreams for you, you proved you were little better than the other Gabriels. You always disappointed me, you chose, time and again, to live beneath yourself –"

"Beneath your expectations, not mine."

"And then, in the end, you spat on me, on my love for you."

"That's not true, Konstantin."

"Even now," Zeleyev said, "in spite of everything, I still want you, do you know that, Madeleine? Here, in the dark, when I can't even see your lovely face, I can still smell your hair, your skin –"

She felt his face close to hers, fought her desire to shrink away. "Then do as I ask, Konstantin, take me out of here –"

He still held her tightly with his strong left hand, while with his right he opened her jacket and felt for her left breast, caressing it through her pullover and squeezing its nipple. Madeleine gasped, feeling nauseous, desperate to escape, wanting to scratch his face, wanting to knee his groin, but his weight against her was too heavy, and she knew that if she fought him now, she would lose and he would kill her without hesitation.

"Kiss me," he said.

She couldn't speak.

"If you want to live, then *kiss* me."

His mouth found hers, his soft, wet, disgusting tongue forced its way between her lips, his teeth grazed hers, and instinctively, Madeleine moaned with revulsion. One of his knees pressed between her legs, his hand left her breast and moved down, past her waist and she felt his hard fingers fumbling between her thighs –

"*No!*" She pushed him away, violently, using her whole body. She heard him grunt, like an animal in pain, and then, almost immediately, he was in control again, pinning her back against the wall.

"You see?" He was panting. "You see how you betray me, what a bitch you are, what a liar! I would have worshipped you, I would have been the finest, the most tender lover you had ever known, but you turned me into this, you brought us to *this*."

Madeleine felt him shift a little, heard small sounds as his free hand moved, getting something from his coat pocket. *The knife,* she thought, and her eyes opened wide, staring into the nothingness.

"You will never be found, Magdalena Alexandrovna."

There was a click, a torch blazed and Zeleyev set it down firmly on the wet clay ground. Madeleine's eyes closed for an instant against the shock of the brightness, and as he held her back again against the wall, she saw for the first time that this wall was made entirely of skulls, of small, some tiny-babies' skulls –

He pinioned her arms behind her, held her fast with his own body weight, freeing both his hands. His breath was hot and sour and Madeleine heard her own whimpering of terror and disgust. Zeleyev reached into an inside pocket and withdrew a small glass bottle, then the big, crumpled handkerchief, and he unscrewed the cap of the bottle and sprinkled its contents onto the grubby white linen.

Madeleine smelled the chloroform.

She took one great breath, gathered all the strength that remained in her body and shoved him hard, using her head, her breasts, her stomach. Zeleyev, taken off balance, staggered and she kicked out with her right foot, striking his leg. Something clattered to the ground – she knew it was the dagger. Sobbing, panting, grunting, she crouched swiftly, scrabbling for it, her fingers clawing dirt, and found it.

"*Bitch,*" he bellowed, and reached for her.

Madeleine sprang up, grasping the knife's handle firmly and drove her arm sideways, plunging it into him. She felt resistance, the cloth of his coat, and then she felt the curved blade sliding home, into his flesh, slicing past bone, into his body –

Zeleyev screamed, harshly, briefly.

"For my father!" she said, gasping.

He fell towards her, his foot kicking over the torch so that the light flashed crazily over the rounded roof, his wounded body even heavier than before – and then Madeleine realized that the chloroformed handkerchief was still in his hand, and she felt him struggling to reach her face, and she twisted her head from side to side, thrashing to escape from his weight, from the last of his power, but he found her, covered her nose and mouth with the wet, stinking fabric –

Madeleine tried to scream – felt herself slipping, falling, sliding. And the dark became darker.

The men had agreed that Noah would remain at the Crillon in case Zeleyev returned, while Rudi and Gideon went to meet the police at the main entrance to the sewers in the Quai d'Orsay.

It was just after five o'clock when the deputy manager came to Zeleyev's room with one of the hotel doormen.

"We have some new information for you, Monsieur Levi."

The doorman had been off duty for a few hours and had recently returned to his post to learn of the drama from a porter. The doorman remembered hailing a taxi for the Russian man and the blonde lady.

"But they did not go to the *égouts*, Monsieur."

"How do you know?"

"Because the gentleman told me before I called the taxi that he wished to go to Place Denfert-Rochereau." The doorman shrugged. "They may, of course, have gone to the Quai d'Orsay afterwards, but it seems a curious coincidence that the entrance to *les Catacombes* is located in that square."

"Maybe it signifies nothing," the deputy manager said, "but I thought it wise to inform you right away, Monsieur Levi."

"You were absolutely right, and I thank you." Noah's mind, which had, for the first time in all his adult years, entirely obliterated all thoughts of the Sabbath and his synagogue, was racing. Attempting to relay a message to the police at the sewers might take longer than driving there directly. "Would it be possible, I wonder, for the hotel to put a car at my disposal?"

"You wish to go now, Monsieur?"

"Right now."

Noah arrived at the Quai d'Orsay entrance to find a hubbub of activity at street level. Questioning four men before receiving an answer, he was told at last that Gideon was down below studying maps with the *égouteurs*, the experts who cleaned and maintained the sewers, and who had volunteered to help in the search.

"For the love of *God*!"

Noah heard Gideon long before he saw him, heard his deep New York voice raised in anger and sheer frustration at the meticulous but agonizingly slow approach of officialdom.

"Gideon!" Noah called, stepping carefully towards him, already, with a pang of selfishness which dismayed him a little, heartily grateful that there would be no call for him to remain down here or to venture further, for he had a dread of encountering even a single rat.

"Noah, thank God! Will you explain to these people that I just want to take one of their boats and get the fuck on with *looking*?"

"Gideon – "

"I know they mean well, and I know they could be anywhere by now, but if we don't ever start – "

"Gideon, for pity's sake will you listen?"

"What?"

"They're not here."

Gideon's head jerked up, his eyes wild with hope. "Did they come back? Are they at the Crillon? Is Maddy okay?"

"No, no, just listen to me."

Drawing the American aside, Noah told him the assumption of the hotel doorman, told him also what he had remembered in the instant that the man had mentioned the catacombs.

"Zeleyev took her down there once before – ten, eleven years ago. He had this fixation about Hugo and the *égouts*, and he thought it would be amusing to explore the catacombs with Madeleine. She told Estelle afterwards, who said she was appalled." Noah's face was contorted with guilt. "I should have remembered when we saw the book, but – "

"Never mind," Gideon interrupted him. "How do I get there?"

"The hotel gave me a car and driver."

"I'll take it." Gideon was already striding back the way Noah had come, Noah almost running to keep up with him.

"You can't go alone, Gideon."

"You bet I can." Gideon spoke rapidly, giving commands. "Find Rudi – he's up there talking to the police. Tell him what you know – tell him to get them moving fast, and you go back to the hotel."

"I'm coming with you."

"You're a cantor," Gideon said, with a brief, grim smile at Levi, who was already breathless. "You'd be a liability, and I need you at the Crillon in case they still get back there."

"Do you have a weapon?" Noah fretted.

"I have a revolver and a flashlight – just don't tell the cops until I've gone, okay?"

"Gideon?" Noah grasped his arm, panting. "Be careful."

Gideon's eyes were very dark. "I'm going to find Maddy," he said. "Whatever it takes."

Madeleine struggled up out of her deathly sleep with the sickening sweetness of the chloroform still thick in her nose and throat. Her head throbbed, she felt nauseous, the ground under her cheek was wet and cold and reeking. She opened her eyes and saw only blackness – raising her head, she put one freezing hand up to her face. She couldn't even see her fingers – she was *blind* –

And then she remembered.

Her heart began to pound. Slowly, cautiously, she sat up, feeling around on the ground, looking for the torch, or for the dagger, for – her right hand touched something cold and furry and she gasped and recoiled, leapt away, struck her shoulder against the wall, remembered the skulls and bones, sprang away again, sobbing fiercely –

"Oh God, oh God –" She fought to calm herself again. For a moment she listened, hearing only the silence, complete, pure silence. She was alone, entirely alone. If Zeleyev was there, with her, he must be dead, finished, unable to hurt her.

"Find him," she muttered.

She crouched again, spread her arms, felt with her hands. The object that had terrified her was his hat, his fedora. *Find him*, she told herself. *Find him and be sure, and then you can get out of here.*

He was not there.

Madeleine knew that she had stabbed him, she had felt the sharp curved steel sliding into him, crunching past his ribs and then slipping easily, lubricated by his blood.

But he had survived, had smothered her with chloroform. And he had vanished.

She tried, desperately, to think rationally, not to give way.

"Matches," she said. She remembered that she had put a matchbook in her jacket pocket, had picked them up off an ashtray in the hotel room, almost idly, without special purpose. Now, urgently, clumsily, she found them, tore a match off the cover and tried to strike it, but it was damp and bent in her fingers and she let it fall. *Calm, calm*, she told herself, and tore off another. It struck, the flame flickered briefly and blew out, leaving her only with the sulphur smell. She tried once more, this time cupping the little flame with one hand – a hundred gaping skulls mocked her, a thousand bones gleamed white for an instant, and her hand shook so violently that she dropped the match and was in the dark again.

She had never known darkness like it. It was blacker than pitch, and it smelled of death and of Konstantin's blood, on her, around her.

She sat down, bent her knees, hugged herself. She wanted to sleep for ever. She wanted to die this very instant, to end the terror. She knew that if she moved, left this spot, she would be lost in the labyrinth, that she would die slowly, embraced by the nightmare until the very last second when her life would ebb away –

She heard a sound.

The blood surged in her head, her heart hammered against her chest as if it, too, sought escape, she felt dizzy, disoriented. Zeleyev was still here, in the dark, somewhere, waiting for her.

And Madeleine knew that she had been very wrong. She did not want to sleep, she did not want to die. She wanted, with all her soul, with all her might, to live.

Gideon, at the silent, deserted entrance in Place Denfert-Rochereau, used his shoulder and the butt of his revolver to smash the locked green door. It splintered easily and he ran through, flashing on the torch he had borrowed from a young officer at the sewers. Vaulting the turnstile, he started down the narrow spiral steps, every muscle, every nerve on alert. Levi was right, this was the place. Maddy was down below, somewhere. He would stake his life on it.

Gideon Tyler had been scared of dark places since early boyhood, though he seldom admitted it to anyone. Night-time stakeouts had never been a problem in the city, where the streets were lit till dawn, but he still disliked the dark, hated being underground, rarely used the subway, and would not have taken a job as a miner if it had been the last job on God's green earth.

Now, biting down those deep-seated fears, he reached the bottom of the steps and plunged into the first tunnel, conscious of the need to tread softly, to hear but not be heard. It was the worst place he had ever been in, but he pushed that knowledge aside and thought only of Maddy and the evil madman who had brought her down into this black, desolate underworld. He heard and felt the ground squelch beneath his feet, the moisture dripping, leaking onto his hair, and imagined the sewers above, the foul river bearing down on the ancient roof over him.

Maddy, he wanted to yell. *I'm coming, don't be scared.*

But he curbed the longing and went on, lengthening his pace but restraining himself from breaking into a sprint in case he missed something. His own breath sounded too loud in the silence, he forced himself to quieten even that. Zeleyev might hear him first, might see the torch, see the revolver in his right hand. The light was dangerous in itself, but without it Gideon would be as much a victim as Maddy and useless to her.

The instant he saw the first skulls, he stopped in his tracks as if he'd been shot, rooted to the spot with shock and revulsion.

"Oh, dear Lord," he said, under his breath. "I can't do this."

He wanted to back up, get the hell out, run back up those damnable steps and out into the fresh, clean air. But then, battling with himself, he dragged out the memory of his first time in the house of horror on Coney Island when he was just a kid and Murray Goldblatt had dared him. He'd thought he was going to die there and then, that he would never make it out of that place, yet he'd ended the day sick as a dog on cotton candy but very much alive. Now he was forty-eight years old, and the woman he loved was trapped with a real monster somewhere in this lair, and Gideon was going to find her. He shone the torch around, forced himself to look at the stacked bones and to outstare the skulls, and he thought of Maddy and he thought of Valentin, back in New York, depending on him, and he went forward into the next tunnel.

He had been underground for about a half-hour when he smelt her perfume. Just a frail, wafting trace of it, so faint that for a moment or two he thought it might be some kind of crazed wish fulfilment. But then he closed his eyes and breathed it in, and he knew, with certainty, that she was not too far away.

And unable to help himself, he called her name.

* * *

Madeleine, on the ground in her private hell, huddled into a ball, hugging her knees, trying to stop the constant shivering, trying not to go out of her mind, thought that she was hallucinating. It was like being in the desert without water for days – you saw what you wanted to see. You heard what you wanted to hear more than anything else in the world.

"*Maddy* –"

She heard it again. It was not possible. Gideon could not be here, thousands of miles from Manhattan, down here in this appalling tomb.

But then she knew that it was, after all, true, that it was his voice, and she raised her head from her knees and felt the blood rushing into her cheeks. And she answered him, as strongly and as clearly as she was able.

"I'm here!"

The relief was indescribable.

"Maddy! I'm coming to find you !" He paused. "Maddy, are you alone?"

"Yes," came the answer. "Alone."

She sounded further away than before, the sound weaker and strangely hollow. It was terribly hard to gauge which direction her voice was coming from as it echoed and bounced off the roof and walls.

"Talk to me, Maddy," he called. "Keep on talking. You have to guide me to you –"

"Gideon, can you *hear* me? I don't know –"

"I hear you." He heard her rising panic. "*Maddy, I hear you!*" he yelled. "Don't move, whatever you do! I'm coming, it'll be all right!"

He smelt the blood a split second before the massive blow, as Konstantin Zeleyev slammed into him from behind with all the relentless, maddened strength of a great wounded bull. Gideon went down, his head striking the ground hard, sending him spinning, the revolver and his flashlight both flying from his grasp. Zeleyev's own torch blazed light into his eyes, then careened in a frenzied zigzag over the ground as the Russian sought the weapon –

When the gun went off, a two-centuries-old wall of bones, the stripped, fleshless heads and arms of scores of long-dead men, women and children, shook and vibrated, then fragmented and collapsed.

And covered the two men on the wet clay floor.

The explosion of the gunshot and the rumble of the wall drove Madeleine into fresh panic, lifted her from her huddled position on the ground and propelled her back, fleeing from the sound, away from Zeleyev, further into the labyrinth. The only sound she heard now was her own sobbing breath. Her arms outstretched, she ran like a blind woman – twice, three times she crashed into walls, keening with rising terror –

And then she halted, suddenly, her senses returning. And she knew that she had committed the greatest folly of all. If Konstantin was still alive, he would not find her. But if Gideon had survived, neither would he. Zeleyev had decreed it hours before. No one would ever find her.

She was utterly, irretrievably lost.

It was a lifetime before the voice came, out of the blackness. It came from a great distance, soft and muffled.

"Madeleine."

She sat motionless, frozen, straining her ears and every nerve to try to tell whose voice called her. The catacombs, ancient and treacherous, took away all natural distinguishing features, blanketing the sound like thick, wet fog.

"Maddy." A pause. *"He's dead, Madeleine – it's all right."*

She heard it again, the syllables of her name pleading with her, the voice of love and care. And then again, cajoling and persuasive, the voice of insanity and death.

A vast weariness swept over her. She could not bear any more, she was beyond tears, beyond fear, nearing the end.

"Maddy, sing to me," the voice called, suddenly. *"Sing to me, so that I can find you. . ."*

All Madeleine's nerve ends stabbed at her like needles, jolting her back, forcing her brain back from the precipice into coherent thought. She knew what to do. It was worth trying – anything was worth trying if it could take her out of this place, whether it was to life or to death.

Her own voice sounded oddly shrill in her ears, reverberating off the rigid skeletons that surrounded her.

"Tell me what to sing!" she called back. "You tell me!"

And again, she waited.

The answer was a long time coming. The man understood, knew what she wanted, needed to hear, but his memory was slack with his own physical and mental exhaustion.

He ransacked his memory and, at last, he had it.

His voice was strong and sure.

"Maddy – sing 'Unforgettable'!"

Madeleine began to tremble even more violently than before. She thought that she might break into pieces, that her body, overloaded with tension, filled with her wildly pounding heart, could not possibly survive to feel his strength.

He had chosen the first song that she had sung at Lila's on the night after their marriage, a number she had never sung before. She remembered that she had wept a little as she had sung, and that she had focused all her attention on Gideon, her dear friend, her husband.

Konstantin had made luncheon for them that day. But he had not come to the wedding. And he had not come to Lila's that night.

Madeleine began to sing.

* * *

Gideon's need to find her quickly was so overpowering that he almost began to run, crazily, towards her voice. But then reason took over again, and he shone his torch around, aware that he needed to leave some kind of a trail so that he could bring her back to the main tunnel.

Bones. It was probably sacrilegious, but right at this minute he didn't give a damn. The bones were the only things to hand. He started collecting them, tibias, femurs, even whole skulls –

"Keep on singing!" he yelled to her. "I'm coming, Maddy – you're going to be fine – just keep singing!"

And Madeleine sang on, her voice hoarse and rasping from cold and damp, from fear and distress and exhaustion, but she did not stop for an instant, hardly drew breath, just sang and sang and sang. . .

He found the broken chain and knew that he was closer, but still the labyrinth and the darkness played tricks on his hearing and on his sense of direction and even on his balance. He took turnings, felt suddenly that he was losing her, became frantic and backtracked quickly, remembering to pick up the bones he had dropped until he felt he was back on course again. He was unaware that he was weeping, was oblivious of his pain or of any physical consideration. He wanted only to find her, to hold her, to take her out, up into the air –

Her voice was almost completely gone when his nostrils caught the whiff of sulphur and his ears snatched at the small, new, scraping sound.

And then he saw her, captured in the beam of his torch.

She was hunched over on the ground, knees jammed up against her chest, singing almost soundlessly and striking matches from a small matchbook, letting one burn right down and then lighting another.

"Maddy?"

She seemed not to see him, just stared blindly into the

light. Her face was grimy, her brilliant, still unseeing eyes were huge, and still she croaked out the words of 'Unforgettable' over and over, not realizing that there was nothing left to hear.

Gideon walked the last few feet to her, his legs shaking, and he crouched down beside her and, with infinite gentleness, he touched her cheek.

And Madeleine stopped singing.

"Can you stand?" he asked, and his own voice was hardly more than a whisper. And she nodded, and as he helped her to her feet, he saw blood on her, and desperately he shone the flashlight over her body, checking to see where she had been hurt –

"Not my blood," she rasped.

"Thank God."

He tried to take her into his arms, but for another moment or two, she held him back, and as her eyes grew accustomed to the light, she peered up into his face and, as she saw that it truly was Gideon beside her, his expression wild with anxiety, she began, at last, very weakly, to cry.

"Maddy, my love." Very carefully, he folded her into his arms, heard her moaning with anguish and relief and joy against his chest. "You're all right now, my love," he crooned softly, holding her, rocking her gently as if she was a tiny, fragile child.

She said something, into his chest.

"What, my darling?"

She raised her face, just a little.

"Valentin –" She clung to him. "Did you find Valentin?"

"Safe and sound." He kissed the top of her head. "Safe and sound."

* * *

He picked her up, marvelling at her lightness, and pointing the torch down onto the ground, he began to follow his grotesque trail back towards the real, safe world.

"*Dieu*," he heard her say, and looking, he saw that they were passing Zeleyev's body, half-buried by the skeletal wall that had fallen on him when the gun had fired, ending the terror.

"Don't look," he murmured against her ear, and felt her relax, for the first time, against him, and he wanted, suddenly, to yell with happiness, to roar his jubilation and gratitude for the world to hear, but instead, he kept silent and walked steadily on, blessing the weight in his arms.

It seemed a long way back to the spiral steps, where he had to put her down, though he hated letting her out of his arms even for a few minutes.

"There's no room to carry you," he said anxiously. "Do you think you can make it?"

"Try and stop me," she croaked.

"I'll be right behind you."

They both started up too fast, forgetting how far they had to go, and Madeleine grew so dizzy that she almost fell back against Gideon, and he made her stop for a little while to catch her breath before they went on, his hand at her back, supporting her, protecting her, until, after an eternity, they both felt the slap of fresh, blessed air, and heard the low noise that was the city on an early Friday evening.

It had seemed to Gideon that he had been below ground for hours, yet it had been little more than ninety minutes in all, and the massed police squad had only recently assembled, some engines still being turned off all around the square, lights flashing, spectators chattering, avidly staring.

"*Maggy!*"

Rudi ran towards them, chalky-faced, drew his sister away from Gideon and into his own arms.

"I'm all right," she whispered, and clung to him.

"Thank Christ." Rudi's shoulders shook with his own weeping for a few moments, holding her tightly, and then he looked up at Gideon, his wet eyes asking the question.

"Zeleyev is dead," Gideon answered starkly. "Finished."

Rudi nodded, satisfied.

A police inspector stepped forward to wrap a blanket over her shoulders. "We have an ambulance for you, Madame."

"Not yet," Madeleine said, hoarsely but decisively, and looked at Gideon. And for another moment, the policeman stepped back understandingly, and her brother, seeing Gideon's expression, gently steered her back into the tall American's open arms.

They had not kissed until then, had never kissed as lovers, as husband and wife. But that first, true kiss, out in the freezing December air, the pure, exquisite night air, represented infinitely more than a touching of lips, a tasting of tongues, a faint, but undeniable stirring of passion.

The kiss held all the joy that they both shared, their relief and their gratitude, the physical, tangible proof of their survival and of life itself; and most of all, the symbol of the love that they had not permitted themselves, until now, and that, for all those interminable, hideous hours, they had feared they might never be able to share.

The horrors were past. The rest was just beginning.

19

Having discharged herself from hospital after less than twenty-four hours, Madeleine joined Gideon at the Hôtel Saint-Simon, a charming and intimate hotel only minutes away from the Boulevard Saint-Germain, the heart and soul of all the memories she had hidden from for more than four years. She was ready now, after all that had happened, to face it, to welcome it all, the sorrow as well as the sweetness, and to share it with Gideon, to share all of herself.

Gideon had spent most of the first day with the police, concerned to protect Madeleine as far as possible from reliving her trauma, and once they had taken her statement, the authorities were content to leave her in peace. Rudi, having made the hotel arrangements, was to fly back to New York on Sunday morning, planning to return with Valentin on Monday evening in order that the family might be together in Paris for Christmas.

After hearing Gideon, on her behalf because of her poor, overstrained larynx, making the two calls she insisted upon before she could rest – the first to her son, the second to the deeply bereaved Malkevitch family in Queens, to give them the news that Jennifer's murder was, at least, avenged – Madeleine had slept away most of Saturday without the slightest aid of sedation. And by the evening, sharing a bedroom for the first time with her husband, she felt so awake, and filled with a vaulting sense of release and gladness so intense and so expansive, that she realized, simultaneously, that it could not possibly last for long.

"They tell you, don't they," she said to Gideon, "that when you've been close to death, your desire to live life to the maximum is enhanced?" She kept her eyes on him, seeing how utterly drained he was by the length of his debriefing by the authorities. "I expect I'll come down to earth soon, with a bang."

"Not if I can help it," Gideon said, pouring himself a glass of whisky, his hand trembling slightly with fatigue.

"A pity," Madeleine said lightly.

"What is?"

"That you're going to miss our first night together in the same bed."

"Who says I'm going to miss it?"

"Your wife."

"What does she know?"

"She knows that you're going to be fast asleep the second your head touches those pillows."

He was too tired to argue.

"I'm sorry," he said.

"What do you have to be sorry about?"

"I hate the idea of wasting even a minute, let alone a whole night."

Madeline began taking off his clothes.

"There will be many, many nights," she said.

He slept deeply for seven hours, and for much of that time, Madeleine, close to him but not touching, lay propped up on one elbow, watching him. She was taking stock, she supposed, of this man she already knew so well in many ways, yet who, she realized, in other ways she hardly knew at all. As Gideon slept, he shifted periodically, stirring and pushing back the covers, and Madeleine took advantage of her wakefulness to study him intently, taking in every line, every hair, every scar, every muscle and sinew, and every visible ounce of flesh, all in unconscious repose.

And in the early morning, when he awoke, refreshed, she was ready for him, and Gideon, who had waited so long, who had yearned for just this very moment, was overwhelmed with gratitude and ecstatic joyfulness. Nothing, not a single fragment of this cherished lovemaking was to be hurried, not an inch of his angel would he overlook in haste, not a thimbleful of her pleasure would he neglect for his own ardour or hunger. . .

For a while, in the beginning, though her body responded, quickened and grew thirsty with desire and passion, Madeleine maintained an almost deliberate mental distance, for she felt a need to do more than simply experience this first sharing. She wanted to memorize every second, to absorb its significance, to comprehend this new, heady and glorious progression in her relationship with this man, this valiant, quietly tenacious, remarkable creature. She had only been intimate with one other man, and she felt not a trace of guilt as her mind celebrated his memory. Antoine had always seemed to her so very beautiful, so silken in his strength and masculinity, so intriguing, her young girl's fantasy come down to earth to bring her joy and life and love – but now she was here, in the same city of romance, with Gideon, her new love, so immeasurably different, rugged and handsome and straightforward as a great, gentle bear, earthy and solid and dependable, and passionate – and so astoundingly skilful that she thought, blissfully, suddenly, she might explode –

And Madeleine allowed her memories to soar away, released Antoine, let him go, aware now that her heart and soul would always retain him, no matter what, but realizing that there was space enough for more loving, more living, that the human heart had an infinite capacity for physical and emotional rapture, of which this reinitiation was merely the beginning. . .

"*Merci, mon amour*," she murmured, feeling him deep within her.

"Thank you, my love," Gideon echoed, and there were tears in his eyes even as they moved together and urgency began to overpower all lingering rational thought –

And Madeleine's eyes shut as her husband, her lover, thrust even further into her, and as her pelvis rose and her back arched and her legs entwined with his to draw him tighter, yet her mind still functioned, on a higher level, still absorbing, still learning, still understanding.

This is life, his and mine, it told her. *Together now, for life*.

During the next few days, once Rudi, Valentin and Michael had arrived, as the Christmas holidays unfolded and then passed, Madeleine took them all on her voyage of rediscovery, brought them to all her favourite places in Paris, those she had shared with Antoine, those she had known before they had met. And she took them to look at Fleurette in rue Jacob, though she refused to enter, would never, until death, forgive Jean-Michel Barbie, the owner, for what he had done to her husband. And on their last evening in the city, Noah and Estelle gave a dinner for them, and Gaston Strasser came, and the Lussacs, and Grégoire Simon and Jean-Paul from the restaurant. And Rudi had gone, that afternoon, to the police, and he had collected *Eternité* from them, and as they all gazed at the sculpture and admired it, Madeleine wept bitterly for a while as she thought of the purity of the forbidden love that had created it, and of the dangerous fascination it had inspired, and of the agony and bitterness it had caused.

They took the train to Zurich, next morning, for Madeleine had determined to see the family as swiftly as possible, to clear her father's name for once and for all, and to be rid of the debt that still, illogically, preyed on her mind.

Rudi had told their mother, on the telephone, about the events of the past two weeks, and Emilie was at the front door of the Gründli Haus to welcome them, and when she put out her arms to her daughter, Madeleine did not entirely reject the tentative embrace, but stood stiffly in the circle of her mother's arms.

"I can't believe all that's happened to you," Emilie said. "It's too terrible to imagine." She put out her icy, nervous hand to Gideon. "Mr Tyler, I know we owe you a great debt."

Gideon accepted the handshake. "I'm glad to meet you, Frau Julius." He put his arm around Madeleine's shoulders as Emilie hugged Rudi, came face-to-face with Michael Campbell and, finally, stooped a little to shake the hand of her shy, discomfited grandson.

"You don't remember me, do you, Valentin?" Emilie asked him gently.

"No," Valentin answered honestly.

"How could he?" Madeleine said. "He only met you once, and he wasn't even two years old."

"Where is Omi?" Rudi asked.

"In the salon, with Stefan." Emilie paused. "She hasn't been well, and the news has upset her."

"Then perhaps we should talk without her," Madeleine said, a shaft of anger piercing her voice, "for what I have to say will only serve to upset her more."

Emilie's glance was filled with apprehension. "No," she said. "I imagine it's something we should all hear."

"Good," Madeleine said, and walked towards the salon.

"Do you want me to stay out here with Val?" Michael asked.

"No, thank you." Madeleine smiled at him. "He's

family, and so are you." She reached out her hand to her son. "All right with you, *chéri*?"

"Sure, Maman."

She gave them the account, as Konstantin had described it to her, of what had occurred in the room off Niederdorf-Strasse on the Saturday night in June of 1947, the night that had led to Alexander Gabriel's exile from his home and country when she had been seven years old and her brother had been only four. Madeleine saw her grandmother blanch with shock, her mother begin to weep and her stepfather sit more straightbacked than before.

"He never denied it," Emilie whispered.

"Because he believed Zeleyev," Rudi said.

"As you did." Madeleine was quite calm.

"Can you really blame her," Stefan interjected, "when you, who knew the man far better and longer than your mother, believed he was your friend until he tried to kill you?"

"I blame her," Madeleine replied, her voice quiet but strong, "as I blame my grandmother, for not believing in my father, as I did. Whether I'm right or wrong, whether I'm justified or not, I shall always blame them for tearing him away from his children, for trying to poison our love for him. And for destroying his life."

"Konstantin Zeleyev did that," Stefan said. "You're an honest woman, you must know that much is true."

"Ultimately, of course I admit that." She paused. "Our father was a weak, flawed man, and I don't doubt he was a poor husband. But he was never capable of violence, and even as a little girl I knew that. And so should his wife and his mother, especially his mother."

Hildegard spoke for the first time, her voice quavering and her blue eyes watery. "I shall have to take that to my grave, Magdalen."

"Yes, Omi," Madeleine said, softly. "I'm sorry."

"What can we do?" Emilie asked.

"Nothing," Madeleine answered. "Except acknowledge the truth."

She smiled at Valentin, planted firmly at the side of her chair, his small face grave, taking everything in, aware that, in spite of the grimness of the conversation, and the shock and sorrow on the faces of the two old ladies, his mother seemed sad but somehow satisfied. Gideon and Michael, the two outsiders, sat perfectly still, hating the encounter for Madeleine's and Rudi's sake, yet knowing that it was entirely necessary, that none of them could hope to move forward, freely, without it.

Madeleine faced Stefan. "You weren't even here in 1947," she said, "and yet, in many ways, I focused much of my hatred on you from the moment you entered our lives." She paused. "I've never liked you, and you always detested me, and I doubt if that will ever change." She looked into his cool grey eyes. "But what happened to our father was not your fault, and I suppose, if I am, as you said, an honest woman, I must acknowledge that what I blamed you for most of all was your loyalty to my mother."

Julius's jaw was tight and unswerving as ever, but there was a hint, just a glimmer, of respect beneath the impassive expression. "Your wife," he said to Gideon, "has always been able, I am afraid, to bring out the worst in me, Mr Tyler."

"That's unfortunate," Gideon said quietly. "She generally seems to bring out the best in most people."

It was when Madeleine took the sculpture from the bag in which Gideon had carried it, and placed it on the coffee table for everyone to see, when she told her mother that this was the only way she was likely to be able to repay the money they had lent her in 1963, that Emilie broke completely.

"No," she said.

"You have to take it," Madeleine said, quite harshly. "It's beautiful, isn't it?" she asked Stefan, seeing the glint of fascination in his eyes as he appraised the gems and the fineness of the workmanship. "Why don't you pick it up? You want to know if the gold is solid, don't you?"

"Don't touch it!" Emilie Julius was distraught. "It's yours, Maggy – you know it's yours."

"I don't know whose it is by right," Madeleine replied, more gently now. "I only know that my grandfather never intended it to cause anyone an instant of unhappiness, and it's done little else. At least it's back in Switzerland now, which he would have liked."

"Maggy –" Emilie tried to interrupt her.

"Do what you want with it – sell it, if you must."

"Maggy, please listen to me." Emilie, even now hating to show disloyalty to her husband, could not look at Stefan. "You owe us nothing, not a single centime. On the contrary, we owe you a great deal." Her fingers twisted a handkerchief in her lap. "Your grandfather left a letter –"

"Mother, it's all right," Madeleine said.

"No, let me tell you, please."

"Go on, Mami," Rudi said quietly.

"He meant you to have *Eternité*, just as he meant you to have his house and all he had. God knows his possessions didn't amount to much, but they might have been precious to you, Maggy, and you should have had them." Emilie began to weep again, soundlessly, pressing the handkerchief to her mouth.

"Don't," Stefan said, and rising, he went to his wife and took her in his arms. "Don't upset yourself so – it wasn't your doing."

"It was spite," Hildegard said abruptly. "Foolish, meaningless revenge, and mostly for my sake, for the pride of a rejected old woman." She faced her granddaughter squarely. "No one ever intended that you should be deprived in the long-term, Magdalen. When the letter was discovered, your running away still seemed, to us, in the nature of a tantrum, a whim from which you would recover, see sense."

"We couldn't foresee what would happen – that you would be so strong, so determined," Emilie said. "That your husband would become so sick and that you would need money so desperately. There was always going to be so much wealth coming to you eventually – the letter was thrown into the fire out of anger, on the spur of the moment, and by the time you came to us to ask for help, it was too late to confess what we'd done."

"What I had done," Stefan said brusquely. "The sculpture is yours, for pity's sake, Magdalen. Take it." He picked it up from the coffee table and placed it into her arms. "It's worth a fortune for the gems alone, though I'm not sure about the workmanship. If I want a sculpture, I'll go to an auction and bid for one, if I want jewellery for my wife, I'll go to Cartier and buy her a necklace."

Conscious that the confession had cost Emilie dearly, the visitors stayed for the night, the first that Madeleine had spent in the house on Aurora Strasse for nearly thirteen years. And late into the evening, after Valentin had been put to bed, while Gideon and Michael sat drinking cognac in the library, Rudi and Madeleine sat by the big log fire in the sitting room talking to Emilie in a more open and relaxed manner than even Rudi could recall ever having spoken to her before.

Madeleine had been sixteen when she had left Zurich, and now she was less than a year away from her thirtieth birthday. In some ways, she felt just the same: still subject to impulse and strong, unquenchable emotion. She would always be honest, often unwise, would always make mistakes because of the headstrong streak in her character. But she had learned many things, mostly about love, and a little about hate. She had been so convinced, all those years ago, that she had truly hated her mother, yet she knew now that what she had felt at the time had been bitter, unbearable disappointment. She would never be able to forgive completely, and certainly not to forget, and she didn't really believe Emilie when she had said, late that night, that she had always loved her. But her mother had also said that she respected her and her brother, and perhaps, Madeleine thought, that was almost as important as love.

Rudi and Michael returned to New York, and Madeleine, Gideon and Valentin went up to Davos, partly for memory's sake, and partly because she had already decided that, if they would accept it, *Eternité* should be offered on a permanent loan to the Heimatmuseum in Davos Dorf, where it would be part of the particular world that had inspired its creation.

A family of strangers were living in the timber house in the Dischmatal, but they were kind people who had heard about Amadeus and Irina, and they made the visitors welcome, invited them to look around and to sit for a while on the sun terrace that Valentin's great-grandfather had built with his own hands for his love.

It was when they walked up to the little walled graveyard where the lovers lay side by side, that Madeleine thought, for the first time, about Konstantin's burial, disturbed suddenly, in spite of all he had done, by the knowledge that the old man had no one to grieve for him. And Gideon took her aside, while Valentin played in the snow, and he told her what he had not wanted her to know while they were still in Paris.

That when the police had gone down into the catacombs after Madeleine and Gideon had emerged, they had found the shattered wall of bones and had found blood. But they had not found Zeleyev's body.

"That's just impossible," Madeleine said, shivering. "I saw him – so did you." She stared up at Gideon. "I stabbed him in his side – I felt the knife go into him."

Gideon put his arms around her, held her tight. "And I know that my bullet struck him in the chest."

The old man could never have climbed the steps, could not have left the ancient necropolis alive. The official assumption of the Paris police and of Interpol, and their own, was that Zeleyev had wandered blindly further into the labyrinth, that he had become hopelessly lost, and had died soon after.

"Buried alive." Madeleine shuddered violently.

"It's what he wanted for you," Gideon said gently.

"I know."

They had one more call to make before they were ready to return to New York, to Antoine's family in Normandy. Claude and Françoise Bonnard had waited long, hard years to see their grandson again, but knowing how grievously Madeleine had mourned Antoine, they were happy to see her looking so contented with the big American, so utterly different from their son.

Madeleine went alone, the first time, to the grave. She took velvety, deep red roses, the variety he had most often given her, and she sat, for a long time, on the grass beside his headstone, and she talked to him, told him all that had happened to her, about her American life, about Valentin, and about Gideon. And as she left the churchyard, gently beautiful even in this bleak winter month, she felt the affirmation of what she had realized on her first night with

Gideon. That her grief for Antoine had not passed, that it never would, even if she lived for a hundred years, but that it did not mean that she could not experience happiness again, could not love again.

20

They flew back to New York, and Gideon moved into her apartment, and four months later, after they learned that Madeleine was pregnant again, they all moved into the handsome apartment on Central Park West that had been left to Gideon by Lilian Becker. And although Joey Cutter had signed Madeleine for a series of bookings in Vegas and Florida, he refused to allow his favourite client to fly anywhere after her fifth month. But she recorded her first album for Columbia in November of 1969 and, wilful as ever, she insisted to Joey that she would only make the recording on condition that 'Les Nuits lumineuses' was included on the disc.

"They'll never go for it, believe me," Joey told her, still chewing on his cigar.

"Then I don't want to make the album."

"Maddy, you're nuts."

"I'm pregnant. Humour me, please."

They humoured her, and Madeleine continued to sing at Lila's most evenings until she went into labour and gave birth, after just five hours, to a daughter they named Alexa.

And when Alexa, who had wild, unruly, curling golden hair and turquoise eyes just like her mother's, was two years old, and Valentin was ten – long after their terrible adventure in Paris, long after Konstantin Zeleyev's home on Riverside Drive had been closed up and his belongings sold at auction – Madeleine and Gideon had a call from the Heimatmuseum in Davos to tell them that the museum had been broken into the previous night. And that, although nothing else had been touched, *Eternité* had been stolen.

Three days later, on a Sunday night in the middle of March of 1972, while Gideon and Madeleine were watching the end of the Channel 2 News, a report came through that an old man, as yet unidentified, had walked into the Museum of Modern Art late that afternoon, had deposited a solid gold, jewel-encrusted sculpture on an exhibit table and had, just moments later, fatally wounded himself with an antique dagger.

Gideon went, the next afternoon, to confirm the identification. The Russian looked old and pathetic, the sparse hair and moustache now white, the obsessively maintained body now wasted.

"There wasn't much doubt," the accompanying detective told them. "He had two scars to match your account, one on his left side, and an old bullet wound in his chest, but we had to be sure."

"It's Zeleyev," Gideon said.

The evening after the funeral, Madeleine asked him:

"Was he always a mad, conniving, wicked man, do you think? Or did we do some of it to him?" Her eyes implored him. "Did we all betray his friendship?"

"I don't think so," Gideon answered, steadily, firmly. "And I honestly don't think it matters much any more."

"Oh yes," Madeleine said. "Yes, it does."

"In that case," Gideon said, "I'll have to do what my parents told me I should never do. Speak ill of the dead."

She was silent.

"Konstantin Zeleyev," Gideon said, "was a gifted man who wanted to possess everything and everyone he loved.

He had some good points, I'll grant you, but I'd hazard a guess that he was always a bastard. He beat up a hooker when you were just a little kid, Maddy, and framed your father for it. He more or less arranged your father's death. He cut off a little dog's ear. He took the life of a lovely, innocent young girl. He kidnapped your son. And he did his insanest, damnedest best to murder you." He took a breath. "And I'm gladder to know that he's really, honest-to-God *buried* than I have been about anything in a long time – and believe me, I've been glad about a lot of things."

"Well," Madeleine said slowly, smiling in spite of herself. "If you put it like that –"

"I do." Gideon paused. "So now what?"

"The children are both asleep, and Dusty's had her walk."

"So?"

She smiled again. "So you're going to pour us both a big drink."

"And then?"

"Then you're going to help me forget."

"Will I succeed?"

"You've never failed me yet."

HILARY NORMAN

CHATEAU ELLA

Two generations of women and their men: two great houses and the legendary grand hotels they became . . . *Chateau Ella* traces the tumultuous history of Krisztina, foundling child brought up by a Hungarian merchant, and her daughter Ella – a child of luxury and privilege who grows up to be a woman torn between love and justice.

Set in Alsace, Budapest and New York State, it is a story of inheritance, of passion and love, of strength and madness, of tears and laughter.

'An excellent saga . . . doom, destruction and deep, dark passion. You will want to know what's going to happen next and to whom . . . a truly entertaining read'

Best

HILARY NORMAN

IN LOVE AND FRIENDSHIP

A passionate story of love and ambition – triumphant against all the odds.

Two young boys are briefly united by a fateful wartime meeting which binds them forever. Many years later an exceptional woman enters their lives . . .

Dan: From a childhood clouded by the Nazi menace, he carves himself a brilliant career as an international gourmet writer – despite his fear of a past which threatens to destroy him.

Andreas: Born to be a champion, Grand Prix motor-racing is his whole life – until fate plays the cruellest trick, and his courage is tested to its limits.

Alexandra: Beautiful, independent and a talented artist, she sacrifices her career for her husband. But still she can't have what she most desires.

From war-torn Germany to a haven in Switzerland, from the glamour and excitement of New York to the French Riviera, it takes four decades of dreams and conflict to understand the value – and cost – of love and friendship.

'Ms Norman, a skilful writer, keeps this book moving at an absorbing clip; she's got the recipe for entertainment right: a dash of Leon Uris, a dollop of Sidney Sheldon and a sprinkle of Judith Krantz'

The New York Times Book Review

HODDER AND STOUGHTON PAPERBACKS

HILARY NORMAN

SHATTERED STARS

One hot Tuscan night of tragedy will rip the young Cesaretti family apart, orphaned by their mother's suicidal act of madness and scattered over the world to carve out their lives alone.

Francesca – Courageous, determined and irresistible, she faces the future alone in America and emerges as a gifted photographer, endlessly searching for the faces she has loved.

Juliet – She survives to become a journalist in London, but her physical and emotional scars will affect her whole life.

Luciano – Though he grows up to be a carefree novelist in the South of France, he is haunted by an inexplicable psychic link with the twin sister he believes dead.

Only by finding each other can they hope to resolve the terrifying trauma of their beginnings.

Powerful, dark and passionate, *Shattered Stars* is the dramatic and mystical story of a family divided – and of the bewitching bonds of blood and love.

'Hilary Norman's *Shattered Stars* is a treat'
She

HODDER AND STOUGHTON PAPERBACKS